Rosa's Story

Rosa's Story

A Woman's Courageous & Inspirational
Struggle for her American Dream

A NOVEL BY

JIM DAMIANO

TATE PUBLISHING & Enterprises

Published by Tate Publishing & Enterprises, LLC
127 E. Trade Center Terrace | Mustang, Oklahoma 73064 USA
1.888.361.9473 | www.tatepublishing.com

Tate Publishing is committed to excellence in the publishing industry. The company reflects the philosophy established by the founders, based on Psalm 68:11,
"The Lord gave the word and great was the company of those who published it."

Book design copyright © 2013 by Tate Publishing, LLC. All rights reserved.
Cover design by Janae Glass
Interior design by Stephanie Woloszyn

Published in the United States of America

ISBN: 978-1-62902-756-2
1. Historical Fiction: Immigrant: Italy   2. Fictionalized Biography
13.09.20

DEDICATION

I often look back fondly to the many wonderful times I had as both a child and an adult visiting with my Grandma Rose. She was always there for me when I needed her, in both good and bad times. I never knew her full past. She kept her pain well hidden. It wasn't until I reached my sixth decade that I learned, through difficult and fading research and tidbits here and there, mostly from my mother, the real story that our Rosa Maria hid so well for all her years.

This is Rosa's story, and it is to her shining example that I dedicate this work to her lasting memory. She has left us for a far better place, yet she will always be with us.

Many thanks need to be given to my wife, Betty, and my sister, Rose Marie, who meticulously edited, coerced, picked me up when down, and encouraged me to continue writing when I wanted to quit. This was, after all, a very difficult subject to write, once I got into it. They too, both loved and cherished this wonderful woman. But mostly I want to thank my mother Jennie, whose life values prepared me for this world and gave me the love of reading and eventually story telling, for she is the true inspiration for this novel. She died on October 31, 2002, at the age of seventy-six.

Like all writers, I feel my tale is one that must be told. I try to avoid Rosa's final days and that is for good reason. I wish for the reader to see the real person, not that gallant soul caught in the web of sickness. Rosa and Mom are gone, both victims of Alzheimer's disease. This infamous malady also victimized my uncle Rocky, who died a victim of this terrible disease on December 23, 2004. It is my wish for the world that science will find a cure, and therefore I am dedicating a portion of any proceeds earned to the Alzheimer's Association.

I was often asked at book signings and talks at many book clubs to share pictures of the characters in Rosa's Story. At first I was reluctant as this is a fictionalization of a true story. But, I eventually started to take photos to my talks and they were well received. Thus, in this our Second Edition, we have included a few pictures to bring the reader closer into this story, which I feel is a tribute to immigrants who have ever come to this Promised Land we call the United States of America.

Last, but by no means least, during the course of my research into the story and my unknown family, I was blessed to meet so many of my mother's kin. While it is a family I never knew, growing up, it has become my family going forward. If there was any reward in writing this story, it was this great opportunity to not just meet up with my past, but to live to see the present and to look forward to a future which includes my now complete family. If there are any regrets, it is in getting to grow up never knowing my many cousins. However, God has a way of correcting things and for this, I am forever grateful.

The following passage from Isaiah 40:31 (NIV) best describes my grandma Rose's devout life and has always been an inspiration to me. It reads:

But they that wait upon the Lord
shall renew their strength;
they shall mount up with wings of eagles;
they shall run and not be weary;
and they shall walk and not faint.

May the blessings revealed in this tale teach us the simple lesson that every child of God has an interesting story. This is Rosa's story and now it is yours to ponder.

Sincerely,
Jim Damiano

ACKNOWLEDGEMENTS

Time is a treasure that we all spend every second that we breathe, whether we like it or not. That is why I take pleasure in acknowledging those folks who have given of their time to make Rosa's Story a special experience for all who may read it.

I couldn't finish if it not for the dedication of my wife, Betty, who has read through every draft and managed to keep me in line. My daughters, Becky and Cheryl, who helped to proofread, and my sisters-in-law, Kathy and Carol, who patiently read the unfinished copy.

I am especially thankful to the team at Tate Publishing for their dedication to a fine quality product for the reading public and all their professionalism throughout the publication process. Their desire to produce books that can be enjoyed by all, inspired me to continue when I wanted to just take a rest from unexpected turbulence in my personal life.

In particular, I also want to give my thanks to Dr. Richard Tate, the founder of Tate Publishing, for having the faith in my work and the conviction to see it in print.

I thank you all from the bottom of my heart. Last but certainly not least, I wish for everyone, including my reading audience, the blessings of our Father's love.

ABOUT THE STORY

This is a true story about my grandmother as told through my mother's eyes. I chose to write the tale as a novel because I feel the reader needs to live the experience through its dialogue to appreciate its impact. It is about Rosa's struggles starting as a fifteen-year-old Italian immigrant coming to a strange, new land of freedom, hope, tragedy, and disappointment.

For Rosa, the American dream came with an expensive price tag. Her struggles were interlaced with tragedy, love, perseverance, and above all, faith. Only some of the story has been changed with personal speculation applied where specific details were unknown or best left forgotten. This is done to help make the story flow naturally. The speculation, though, is based on what I know of the true story and is not intended to subtract or add to its impact on the reader, for Rosa's story is all too real and all too familiar for the many unwary immigrants who came then and now to this country.

THE ROSE

Aspiring beautiful flower,
An Italian Rose,
Full bud, awaiting destiny,
Gentle, strong,
Naive, rich, colorful—
Promising.
Reaching, unafraid, exploring,
Impervious to life's challenge,
Feminine, yet thorny,
Fragrant, enticing,
Hardly adult,
Wishing otherwise,
Independent, resolute,
Stubborn, prickly,
Nothing to prove,
Multicolored life—waiting,
Impatient,
For its time
In the sun.
Adjusting!
Fearless until,
Cut deeply, while still pulsing,
Ripped from all awareness,
Challenged to bloom,
Losing,
All familiarity—all feeling,
Change!

"Growth, in some curious way, I suspect, depends on being always in motion, just a bit, one way or another."

Norman Mailer, b. 1932 American Writer

ONE

My name is Jane. In my youth, Mother called me Jennie. Now the window of my life is closing, though I try desperately to stop it. Slowly it descends, erasing my precious memory, stealing my senses, tempting me to remain forever silent. It seems right and so easy to be still and let these secrets die with me.

But no! I must put aside personal preference and tell someone. Mother's story must be told before these scattering clouds make the telling impossible. These brazen clouds unnerve me. Why must their rumbling presence remind me of when this all started, so very long ago.

It was a day like today, bittersweet cold—mid December. The new snow covered the ground like a silk blanket, all pretty like, yet so very cold. Christmas, my favorite season, was in full swing. It was around 1960. John Kennedy was just elected president and the country was having high hopes about his youthful visions.

Mother and I were working together in our family store. It was a slow day and the lunch trade was still two hours away, a good chance to talk. She looked at me and smiled that wonderful smile that she always had when she wanted to talk. A smile that forever spelled happiness and a certain relief that she could still smile. Yet, the worry lines on her face were never fully erased, even when her life had turned good. Then, I remember that she dropped the simmering saucepan onto the tiled floor, spilling most of her rich tomato sauce, its pungent red splattering everything. When the pan crashed to the floor it sounded like thunder—though not like thunder that goes away once the storm has passed. Upset, Mother began to clean up the mess. I reached to help, but she waved me away.

"Jennie," she said matter of fact like, her voice calm though whispering. "It was a day like today, all cold and snowy, I can't believe it's over thirty years to this day that he almost killed me, and my whole life got worse, if that could have been possible. Such painful memories. Jennie, I need to talk."

"How's that?" I asked, confused, but somehow expecting to learn what I had guessed for so many years.

She began her story and talked like she never had before, wanting me to know all, but not before swearing me to silence. It's a silence that I have kept till now. It was then that all those barriers and defenses that she had so industriously built to defend against all those bad times, tucked away so neatly, came spilling out. It was like fresh boiled spaghetti, all steamy and ready to be consumed, except the sauce was all on the floor.

It was at this moment that the light of understanding flashed for me and all the jagged pieces that I had held for so long began to fit, like when you figure out a good jigsaw puzzle. Suddenly, Mother's story became real, and in a flash she went from being a wonderful mom back to a time when she was a naive young and hurting stranger. It was at this vivid moment that Rosa's story, as I now know it, came to life, and all past speculation was erased.

I'm certain Mother would not want me to reveal all, definitely not her beginning and difficult quest for the American dream, and certainly not the confused ending which for someone of her era was too gruesome and so very embarrassing.

Yet, I must break my silence, though difficult. I owe this to her, to my children, and to theirs too. I must tell her story before I drift slowly away, forever, into those terrible foreboding clouds. I can see them surreal, hovering and waiting for me. Yes, waiting, like messengers of death, dark and beckoning and quickly floating by, passing swiftly, just like time itself.

Rain played a grand tribute to the parched soil, a welcome cleansing that pounded, staccato-like, upon the ancient hillside village, slaking the thirsty land. Rosa, mesmerized, stood marveling in the rain. *Today, I must stay inside,* she thought, *but not now. Now I will collect enough rainwater to wash.* Her red hair was already soaked, glistened from the storm, and the rainwater made it feel silken.

Antoinette stood in the weathered doorway of their ancient home. Hands on hips, chin out, she called, "Rosa, what're you doing, standing out there in the rain? You'll catch your death, and then what?"

"Mama, it feels so good. Come here and stand with me."

"Foolishness! We've too much work to do before Papa returns. It's a long walk from Naples, and knowing him, he'll be hungry as a lion. So come quickly. Help me prepare dinner." *She is so much like her father, a dreamer.* Smiling now, she said, "You know, a little bird told me Papa will have a surprise to share with you."

Rosa stopped, "What surprise—a new dress? Or that wonderful comb I liked?" Water hit the old tiled floor as she followed her mother, dripping wet, into the house.

"Patience. You'll know soon enough." *Soon enough the cat will be out of the bag, and then what?*

"Oh Mama, anything Papa brings will be wonderful. Compared to this old place anything is better. It's so boring here!"

Antoinette's stern impatient voice faltered, and she seemed to separate each word as it was uttered. "And what do you know of boring? You are just a teen. This village has been our family's home for centuries." Making the sign of the cross, she mumbled, "Faa, I swear, today's children will be the death of us."

"Mama, really! It's 1924, not the dark ages! It is different from when you were a bambino. Much change has happened since the war—except in this place."

"Daughter, that war, that terrible war." Strong, painful memories crept into her voice; her face strained, forcing a mournful sound from her throat. "My brother, poor Vincenzo, killed. Your father gone away with the king's army, and for what? I'll tell you—four, long, painful years, forever lost to my love and me."

She hesitated, thinking despairingly, *Now, how many more years must I bear his absence?*

"Rarely did we hear from my Rocco for four years, and me here with two children, fearing all the time that I'd never see him again! Yes, Rosa, things are different now, especially with your papa. Such grand ideas he has. I pray constantly to all the saints to set him right. So, my rose bud, don't tell me about change. You're too young to understand change."

Rosa stood silently, wishing she had thought before she had spoken. *Me and my big mouth.*

With sad watering eyes she said, "Sorry, Mama, I didn't mean to upset you."

"No, you didn't upset me. Don't worry. Come give me a hug."

Rosa happily reached for her mother and together they basked in the warmth of each other's arms.

Antoinette's usual unyielding look turned a complete circle, changing to one that seemed almost pleading, yet perplexed. She brushed back her jet-black hair then tied it into a neat bun, her eyes reflecting a familiar special warmth. "Rosa, at least then, we had each other, now, didn't we?"

Confused, Rosa looked into her mother's saddened face; anxious, both began to cry. She raced across the tiled floor to her mother's arms and embraced her, clinging tightly. Softly she answered, "Mama, please forgive me if I've caused you any pain."

Rosa's trembling moved Antoinette to hold her daughter closer. Rosa's wet clothing was clinging to them both. She took in Rosa's innocent blue-green eyes. *My angel is no longer a child. When did my baby grow into this beautiful young woman?* Antoinette felt warmth and also a little jealousy and longing for her own youth that was now a fading memory, her own swiftly passing years; she had been so roughened by her hard life.

She moved her daughter to arm's length. "Rosa, you are almost fifteen, and it's time we had a serious talk."

"About what?"

"Nothing that can't wait for the right time. But I promise, we will talk, in good time. Now, we have much work to do. So, my wet angel, you get dry, and then let's get going. Tomorrow is Sunday, and I promised Father Mario I'd bake him my special sausage bread. We have only enough ingredients for one loaf, so we'll have to hide it from your papa."

Rosa smiled as she quickly changed into dry clothes and combed her hair back. Grabbing a worn apron, she reached for a pan. Her face puckered up in a smirk as she playfully scolded, "Mama, what are you standing around for, don't we have work to do?"

Antoinette stopped stirring the sauce and gently kissed Rosa's cheek. "Rosa, you have a quick way to everyone's heart, and you are the light of my life. Don't ever change. Now, I wonder where that daydreamer brother of yours is. He was supposed to clean out the chicken coop and bring me some eggs."

"Do you want me to go look for him?"

"No, you've already been soaked once, and you will run out of clothes. He'll be here soon enough, and then he will have some explaining to do."

The incessant rain slowed to a steady mist. Rocco Ameduri trudged deliberately up the muddy road, carefully watching his footing. The three-day trek from Naples seemed endless; each footstep was like an endless expedition. He had fallen clumsily several times, trying to keep his heavy baggage from spilling off his back. The red clay mud of the road covered his well-worn traveling shoes, adding to his load and testing weary spindly legs. It didn't matter. Rocco was excited. His mind was made up, and an adventure lay ahead.

Unafraid, or so he fooled himself, he thought about his plan. It was difficult. What faced him was an adventure, yes, but a change so big was difficult to contemplate. Though he tried to tell himself he wasn't afraid, it was impossible not to feel anxious. He tried valiantly to reason with himself. *After all, I've lived through four years of war. Surely nothing could be worse than that. I cannot let foolish fear get in the way of bettering my family's future.*

Life in Southern Italy had taken a turn for the worse. Years of privation and war had taken its toll. Antiquity and family heritage no longer seemed to matter. Italy's poor and desperate were leaving daily in a great exodus to the Americas for the universal hope for a better life. Many of Rocco's friends and family had already left for greener pastures in faraway places like the United States, Brazil, Mexico, and Argentina. Over one-third of Italians had left its shores in the past thirty years. And now, with Mussolini's reign of fear beginning to overtake the land, millions were taking the necessary steps to leave all that they knew. They put aside centuries of heritage and things long cherished, and willingly exchanged it all for the hope that a new land would bring. After all, the streets in America were said to be lined in gold and there was employment for anyone willing to work. And Rocco was more than willing, for he was tired of the constant struggle. He and Antoinette had spent hours and hours discussing every practical option. His good wife was still a bit anxious but had told him that she would do whatever he decided. And when the letter came from America asking for Rosa's hand in marriage, the doors were suddenly opened to what must be done.

In the dimming light of early evening, he could see faint signs of life as he approached the ancient village. Some people were still out despite the inclement weather, walking amongst the cobbled walkways in between centuries-old rock homes that were glistening, slick with rain, the people appearing ghostlike as they went about their daily lives.

Rocco felt a surge of relief with Missanello in sight. Soggy, tired, and anxious for the warmth of hearth and home, he envisioned familiar comforts and the succulent aroma of sweet Antoinette's cooking.

He was not disappointed. When he was less than a Bocce ball's roll to his home's entrance, the wooden door burst open, swinging precariously on ancient hinges. A slight gangly boy wearing ragged clothes raced out the door. All arms and legs, the excited child rushed like a whirlwind to Rocco who waited with much bravado. Once there, he jumped into his father's rain-drenched, outstretched arms, almost tumbling him into the mud. The boy's coarse homespun shirt, now wet, felt rough though happily familiar to Rocco's stubble cheek. Rocco hugged his son tightly, caressing his matted hair.

"Papa, you're home. I've missed you. And there's a lot I need to tell you." Domenico, small for eleven years old, looked like his mother. His large brown eyes glistened with excitement as he grasped Rocco's muddied hand and joyfully shouted, "Papa, come! Let's get out of the rain before Mama sees me."

Rocco, bent from his load, had seemed even smaller than his already slight stature. But in the presence of Domenico, he stood tall. He whispered in Domenico's ear, "Somehow, I think your mama already knows." Domenico cast a false downward look.

Laughing, he savored his son's enthusiasm. Opening his arms wide, he happily embraced both his children when Rosa ran out to join the wet tangle of his arms.

Rocco cast a roguish wink toward the dim light in the doorway, where his wife stood grinning, wearing a simple peasant dress that she had made years earlier during the war.

"What's all this fuss? I've been gone only a week. Could it be this?" Rocco, curtly smiling, pulled a small bag from his large traveling coat, laughing as he passed it to his son. "Here, Nico, savor the riches of Naples."

With a vengeance, Domenico tore the bag open, tearing at the protective wax paper. He pulled out a peppermint stick, took a lingering taste, smiling broadly. "Papa, oh Papa, thank you."

"And Rosa, I'm sorry. I couldn't find a dress worthy for an Italian princess. But, I did find something." Rocco pulled a tissue-wrapped parcel from his bulging pocket, handing it to his excited daughter.

"Papa, I knew it; I just knew you'd buy it for me."

"Stop talking, Rosa." Rocco said warmly, "Open it."

Rosa folded back the tissue, now wet, to reveal the beautiful ivory comb she had desired months earlier. "It's beautiful, Papa! I love you so much. Mama hinted you'd have a surprise."

Rocco cast an anxious glance at his wife. His mood sobered, but the children did not notice.

Antoinette did not miss her spouse's consternation and broke the silence. She playfully waved a large wooden spoon, slicing it back and forth through the air as if she were carving a piece of pie, or perhaps a slice of her life—a life that was about to begin a new adventure that she would rather forget. She demanded, "What are you all going to do, stay out there all night in the damp cold? Or do you want to eat the supper that Rosa and I slaved over before it gets cold? Now, get in the house before you cause the death of me!"

Catching his wife's playful glare, Rocco winked in her direction and earnestly picked up his travel case, shaking a contrite head. "Ah, yes, *cara mia*," he smirked, "I'm for supper; I could smell the sausage bread from down the road. Such a smell can stir the blood of a happy, though famished, man."

"Sorry dear," she teased, then snickered. "The sausage bread isn't for you. It's for God's servant. Come and see what's for you before I toss it out the window."

Grinning, he turned to the children, "Come, Mama's right, we have amused the neighbors enough. It's time for privacy and, most important, supper."

With water cascading like a waterfall from his soggy fedora, Rocco grasped his load with stout arms. Trailed by his children, they walked together into the familiarity of their warm, though humble, inviting home.

Once inside the doorway, Rocco embraced his Antoinette, giving her a lingering kiss as the children smiled at seeing their love.

After a hearty meal of pasta and vegetables picked fresh from their small garden, Rocco pulled an old wooden pipe from his vest pocket, his only inheritance from his father who had died of one of the many diseases that hit the poor when Rocco was off to war. Packing it expertly with aromatic tobacco and lighting it, he savored its aroma. The small room's soft glow came from one of their two kerosene lamps. It cast protective shadows upon the shelter's rough walls, hiding the night's gloom. The room served as the kitchen and the living area. The large, now cluttered, table was its focal point.

Speaking softly, as was his way, he announced, "Antoinette, it's time we discuss our surprise. Do you agree?"

"Yes, husband. Children, gather around the table. Papa has something important to say."

Rosa sat confused. *Didn't Papa already bring my surprise?*

Domenico, in the middle of a large lick from his peppermint stick, reluctantly pushed his body to the table, contemplating only the next lick on the candy.

Rocco hesitated, looking at his wife for encouragement. None came, for she was as perplexed as he was committed in what they were about to discuss. Taking a deep breath, he stood. His five-foot, seven-inch frame appeared to tower over the rustic, hand-carved table.

"Children, what I tell you will affect your future, probably more than ours. Your mother and I have spent countless hours seeking a way to survive here. Times in Southern Italy are difficult, particularly for our village. It is worse now with Mussolini's *Fascisti* and all the terrible fear they're now spreading with a joy only they can understand. Many friends and even family have left for other parts of the world, seeking greener pastures. In America there is much work, and more important, there is hope. I have been promised a job there. Soon we will leave, hopefully, sometime early next year. There is more." His eyes focused on Rosa.

"Rosa, this concerns you. Do you remember the Lavalia family? They left here when you were very young."

"No Papa, I do remember you talking of them. They seemed nice by your descriptions. Why?"

"They moved to America several years ago, to a city called Utica in a place called New York State. They have an unmarried son. His name is Antonio Rocco. I have agreed to his overtures to an arrangement of marriage between you and him. He is very handsome from his picture. He also served in the American Navy during the Great War. He has a good job. In fact, it has been with him that I corresponded and not his father Nicola, with whom I go back many years, long before you were born."

"Oh, Papa, this Antonio Lavalia, is he old?" Trying to hide her panic, she thought, *No, I don't want to marry. Not yet. Not someone I don't even know! I don't even know what to do!*

"No, Rosa, not everyone who served in the war was ancient like me. He's twenty-three. Is that so old?"

"Papa, you're not that old. Forty-two is not old. Is it?" Rosa's smile lifted her father's somber mood.

Laughing, Rocco continued, "So there you have it. In a few weeks, sometime after Christmas, we'll seriously begin to plan our move. There is one problem, though. Mama must stay here for a while. I'm sorry to say we don't have the funds to take us all. Antonio Lavalia is paying for Rosa's voyage. We only have enough spare money to cover my voyage and a child's passage for Nico. Good friends now living in Utica, from Missanello, have arranged the paperwork necessary. Most important, I have proof of a sponsor required by the American authorities. These friends have also promised a loan, which I'll have to repay once I start work there. Mama will come as soon as we have saved enough money from our earnings. I promise it will not be long."

Involuntary tears filled Rosa's eyes. "But Papa, must we leave Mama?" *And why must I marry someone I don't know?*

Feeling her daughter's consternation, Antoinette reached for Rosa. "Dear one, I'll be fine. In these difficult times, this is not uncommon." Antoinette held Rosa's hands gently in hers, smiling. "And remember, my marriage was arranged too. Look how well it turned out."

"Mama, how will you live with no money?"

"Remember the Ruggeri family? They did the same thing we're doing. My friend, Theresa, left for America to join her family after only two years. We have a little money and what extra we can spare, Papa will leave so I can live. With God's grace, I'll sell off our property at a good price. If we all leave together, people will know our desperation and take advantage. This home has been in my family for generations, and we can't sell it for a pittance. If we do, my ancestors will come back and haunt me." She made the sign of the cross as an afterthought, for Antoinette, like so many Italians, was very superstitious.

Antoinette noticed Domenico, who had almost been forgotten in the discussion. She patted his curly hair and kissed his forehead, wiping an errant tear from his cheek. "Don't cry, Nico," she soothed. "You must be brave. I'll join you in America before you can shake a stick. I have great faith in Papa, and you must too. After all, he is one of the best cobblers in Missanello. And that's a fact!"

"Really, woman, what is this? One of the best!" Beating his chest, chin extended, with mustache quivering, "I am the best, and don't any of you ever forget it."

The children jumped from their chairs to hug Rocco. For the moment, their still-growing determination was firm. Rocco, somewhat relieved, was happy to spare them the details of their pending ordeal. Though he tried to hold back troubled thoughts, he could not shake them from his mind. *Third-class passage from Naples to New York is not known for its luxury, and the journey to Naples will be a long walk for young legs. At least we'll have time to prepare. Maybe I can ask Cousin Angelo to take us in his donkey cart. But after all, this is a problem to be solved tomorrow.*

Looking fondly at his wife and filled with longing, he took a deep breath, then exhaled pipe smoke, slowly, buying time to gather his wits. Right now, today is all I have, and tonight, well tonight, I must make the most of it. He unconsciously touched the broad, jagged scar on his left cheek, his war trophy, an unrelenting memento of what is important. Receiving that wound made him see for the first time how essential it is to appreciate the moment.

Rocco naughtily winked at Antoinette. *I hope to the heavens that she'll be fine. Who am I fooling? After we leave, it may be months before I can hold her in my arms again.* He quickly forced the disturbing thought from his mind. Rocco was usually a positive man, not bent on serving the demands of unhappy thoughts.

Not missing her husband's sudden silence and shifting moods, Antoinette said, "Children, it's time to clean the table and wash the dishes. Be quick, for we need to ready ourselves for tomorrow and church. It is late, so when you're through, it's off to bed."

With Antoinette and the children busy, Rocco grabbed a knife, intent on having a slice of the sausage bread. But before the knife could touch the fragrant loaf, Antoinette hit his hand with her large, seemingly ever-present, wooden spoon. "Rocco, I told you this was for Father Mario."

"*Cara mia*, one little piece will not be missed by the good priest."

The dour look on her face was sufficient to dissuade further argument.

Returning her attention to the children, she noticed them smiling instead of doing chores. Scowling playfully and still waving her large spoon, she forced a stern look. "Now to the chores, and then to bed! The amusement is over!"

Rosa groaned, "Oh Mama, after chores, can I stay up a bit and read some of the papers Papa brought from Naples? I saw something in one of them about America, and I want to read it tonight. Please?"

"Sure, but only for a few minutes. Kerosene is expensive and we need to save it for important things, not silly news. Most of what's in the paper is lies anyway."

Rosa read the article and was unsatisfied. It unnerved her young mind with talk of America and its wealth, along with its speculation on why so many country-men were crossing the ocean to an unknown fate. The disturbing reports stated that many were returning after disappointing experiences, or having difficulty adapting. Others had returned to Italy feeling abused and worse for wear. Even the well educated could not find work other than menial jobs that no one else wanted. *Once I'm there, I'll not return. No, darn it, I'll never give up! How can it be worse than here? Here all we have is our past. There we have new hopes and my future to dream about.*

"Nevertheless, I sure hope Papa knows what he's doing," she murmured softly, not wanting to wake anyone. She folded the paper, put out the light, and retreated to the small closet-like bedroom she shared with her brother. Domenico was sound asleep, a pleasant smile upon his face. She wondered if he was dreaming of voyages and adventure.

Antoinette, holding back sobs, tried not to disturb Rocco's gentle snoring. Tenderly, she touched his reddish-grey hair, caressing, savoring its familiar feel. She stared blankly at the blackened bedroom ceiling, hearing an errant fly beating its wings, desperately trying to find an exit through the open, narrow window. For a fleeting moment, she felt like that frustrated fly, alone, stuck and unsure. It weakened the stoic reserve she usually fostered as her veneer.

She prayed: *Please, Lord Jesus, give me strength. I cannot show Rocco my fear, not when he is so excited. However, at the risk of being impertinent, is this really the right thing? And Lord, is it wrong of me to ask why, especially now? I need Your help to survive this terrible change my Rocco desires. Please, grant me strength. You alone know I'm not as strong as my Rocco thinks. Lord, I mustn't let him down. So please help me to hide my fear.*

Antoinette pushed her head into a feathered pillow already wet with her tears, trying to hide her sobbing.

Rocco, awake, heard Antoinette's weeping, keeping council to himself, unsure. Then reluctantly, he placed his arm around her, holding her tightly and gently kissing her.

Clinging to Rocco and shaking in uncontrollable sobs, she fell asleep.

With his resolve unbent, yet his fears very real, he lay quietly in the warmth and safety of the bed, giving up on any thought of slumber for the night.

"Travel and change of place impart new vigor to the mind."

Seneca, Roman Dramatis, Philosopher, and Statesman

TWO

Road dust took up uninvited residence, plastering its gritty substance into every crevice of Rosa's body. It was the last day of their long three-day walk to the port of Naples. The day was clear and the air sultry hot, unusual for the end of March.

Rosa, Domenico, and Rocco walked near the tightly packed four-by-six-foot wooden cart pulled by Cousin Angelo's mule. Tied securely in the cart's bed lay their meager belongings, consisting of one large travel trunk, four small aging cardboard suitcases, tenting equipment, and food. It was a light load, though still heavy for the old mule. It left no room for the weary travelers.

The narrow country road had been slow with traffic since leaving sleepy Missanello. The path eventually widened into a sizable road as they neared the big city. Rosa thought of the sad goodbyes. *I'll never forget the forlorn look in Mama's eyes. Will I ever see her again? Will she change? Will I?*

Confused, Rosa reached for inner strength, trying not to think, seeking a safe haven from her worry. *I must be strong. Papa says it is only a little farther. Yes, I can smell the sea air.* Briskly she glanced to her left and saw her brother walking, short legs pumping, a happy smile showing bright white teeth. In his youthful vigor, he took in every little change, every twist and turn in the winding road, always searching for the treasured instance of a newfound discovery.

"What are you dreaming about, little brother?" asked Rosa.

"Oh, nothing special, but yes, I am dreaming of America." With liveliness, playfully he kicked at the dust, "Rosa, isn't this a grand adventure?" Domenico's face appeared pixie-like, animated with excitement. "Do you think we will like America?"

Rosa clutched his dirty hand, at the same time wiping grit from his face, sweaty and crusted with road grime. She looked at him lovingly, acting like she figured her mother would have. After all, she reasoned, *I will have to be a mother to Domenico until Mama joins us. And Papa said it might be as long as three years.* Sadly, she thought, *Three whole years—such a long time.*

Collecting herself, she said, "Domenico, we'll like America, I promise. It probably won't be easy at first, but we must try very hard to adjust. Remember what Papa said."

Domenico jumped in, mimicking Rocco, "Yes children, we'll need to learn new customs, and things will be far different from what we know. You are young and must grow to accept this and if you try…la, la, la."

"Nico, you're very smart; sometimes, though, too smart. You'll do just fine." Rosa held him close, against his will, kissing his persistent, grimy forehead as he squirmed away—exercising the universal right of all young boys when hugged by a big sister.

"Papa said it'd take at least three weeks to reach America. Won't it be boring?"

"Nico, how should I know? All I do know is that I'll be happy when it's over. I'm not sure about going on that big ocean—it is kind of scary."

"Ah, Rosa, you are such a girl. I'll be there for you when it gets scary, don't you worry."

"Thank you, Nico. Now here is another hug for my brave brother, and don't you pull away this time," Rosa scolded lovingly.

Just the same, Domenico pulled away from her arms, afraid that someone passing might see the unmanly gesture.

Up ahead, Rocco anxiously shouted, "Angelo, why are we stopping? We're almost there."

"Rocco, I cannot kill my mule. She's family." The mule bellowed in agreement. "My Esmeralda needs rest, food, and water." He lovingly patted the mule's shank. "We'll rest here for a bit. Don't worry, cousin; I'll have you there on time."

Playfully, Rocco chided, "Where did you get such a grand name for such an ugly mule?"

Angelo, ignoring the comment, just smiled and continued patting Esmeralda. Then, as if an afterthought, he smirked, "She is a girl, or I would have called her Rocco!"

Angelo Tedesco was a very patient and quiet man. Nothing ever seemed to disturb him. Patience hadn't always been his strong point. Not until the Great War changed him, on that terrifying day, somewhere long ago or so it seemed, in the deep confines of a muddy trench, where he had pledged to Rocco, "If we live, I'll never worry again."

His vow that terrible day was made in no-man's land at the Austrian front, and it became his credo, and he followed it like a newly converted religious zealot. Rocco, then as now, was silent out of respect. Angelo was more than a first cousin; he was also Rocco's big brother. In Southern Italian families, where respect and tradition is everything, Rocco wasn't about to break custom.

Domenico interrupted, "Papa, are we almost there? My feet hurt." Domenico reached for Rocco's hand, pain showing in his eyes. Until now he had not said a word of complaint.

"Domenico, let me see your shoes. Maybe I can help." Rocco lifted his son to the back of the wagon and pulled off his son's shoes, revealing bloody socks.

"Why didn't you say something sooner?" Rocco signaled to Rosa, who quickly walked to the wagon. She returned Rocco's distressed stare with one of her own.

"I'm sorry, Papa. I didn't want to worry you, especially since you made these fine new shoes just for this trip."

Rocco hugged his son, patting his matted hair and gave him a sincerely sorrowful look. "Son, it's my fault. I should have insisted you break in the shoes. I forgot, what with all the excitement. I'm really sorry."

"What's done is done. Papa, I'll survive."

Domenico's broad smile gladdened his father's heart.

Rocco turned to Rosa, "Princess, please fetch the salve that Mama packed, I need it for your brave brother."

Domenico beamed. *I'm brave.*

Rosa found the ointment in the bottom suitcase and quickly applied it, carefully wrapping the wounds in linen, found in the meager first aid kit that Antoinette had packed.

Angelo, watching, his disturbed whistle went loosely into the air and then he spoke. "Rocco, I'll make room in the cart. You, little man, can't walk, not with those feet. We'll have to carry some of the baggage."

"Thanks, cousin," said Rocco as he pulled a large paper-covered cardboard travel case from the donkey cart. Angelo grabbed two more, placing them on broad shoulders, and Rosa helped her brother back into the cart. Esmeralda, now revived, began slowly pacing forward, each step deliberate and determined. Up ahead, over one last steep hill, awaited the large, ancient Roman portal city of Naples.

When the Ameduri family reached the bustling port of Naples, Rocco immediately inquired as to which pier their ship was anchored. After asking several men, he finally received helpful directions. He gathered everyone, checking tickets and passports. Turning to speak to his cousin, he said, "Angelo, if you could take us another quarter mile, our journey with you will end. But before we reach our destination, I want to thank you for all you've done. I shall never forget you, cousin. I need to express this to you before we have no decent privacy to say honest farewells."

Rocco hugged Angelo. They kissed each other's cheeks, the Italian way, with tears and emotion. Both men did not try to hide feelings, staring blankly until Angelo broke the quiet. Then pulling a wad of money from his pocket, Angelo smiled broadly and handed it to Rocco. "Cousin, I have a gift and I will not allow your pride to stand in the way of my generosity. It's not much, yet perhaps it'll come in handy on your long voyage."

"But Angelo, it's too generous; I can't take this. I know more than anyone how much your family needs it. Times are difficult and not getting better. I'm sorry, cousin; honor requires that I must refuse your generosity."

"Little cousin, if you do not take my small token, I'll be heartbroken two times. First, it is a gift, not charity, and second, I remind you of your proper place in our family. Darn it all, Rocco, I owe my life to you. You know this. It was your bravery that saved me from death by that Austrian bayonet. And anyway, cousin, bayonet or not, I still will give this money to you. I'll miss you and your children, more than I can express. It pains me to see you go, though I know it's best for you."

Rocco shuffled his feet, trying to think of an appropriate response. Nothing came.

Sternly, he said, "Rocco, as an older relative, I insist, no, *I demand*, that you take this gift…" He choked up, "from me, your best friend and brother."

Thoroughly moved, Rocco tightly grasped Angelo's hand. They fixed eyes and then threw arms around each other, clinging, each reluctant to let go.

"Thank you, Angelo, I will never forget you. We have shared the good times and bad, you and me. With reservations, I will take the money, and thank you for your generosity. As far as that enemy's bayonet goes, were the tides reversed, you would have done no less to save me."

Domenico came forward, "Won't Cousin Angelo join us in America someday, Papa?"

Before Rocco could reply, Angelo reached down and lifted Domenico with strong arms, looking boldly into the child's eyes. "Nico, God has willed that I stay in Missanello. My life is here with my family. Someday, maybe one or more of my children will follow your path. If they ever do, I pray you will help them."

"I will Angelo, I promise," Domenico beamed, never doubting his ability to fulfill this newfound responsibility.

"Domenico, you have a big heart, don't ever change." Angelo kissed the boy and then turned to hide his tears.

They reached their destination and unloaded their baggage from the cart. Esmeralda snorted and then brayed, as if saying goodbye. Rosa and Domenico stared in wonder at the great ship before them, blocking the view of the harbor with its red-rusted magnificence and three giant stacks.

Angelo turned and left without saying a word. His goodbyes having been said. When the family turned from viewing the great ship, anxious to say their final goodbyes, he had already melted into the crowded wharf.

The finality of his departure caused a quiet moment, that is until Rosa intentionally broke the deathly silence. "Papa, the boat! It's so big!" she exclaimed. She stared open eyed, excited for the first time since leaving Missanello.

"Princess," he gently scolded. "It's called a ship, not boat, and her name is *The Mayflower*. It was called the *Credic* back when my cousin Mario sailed on her for America. Her new owners recently renamed it, I'm told, after a famous English ship. She's old, but very well built. Come, children," he motioned, "let's see what we must do." Rocco picked up his baggage, a balancing act, and shuffled through the crowded wharf. He did not look back; it would hurt too much if he did.

Angelo looked on from afar, tears flowing.

What my mother Rosa remembered most was that her third-class voyage felt like living in a cattle pen. It was a hellish excuse for transporting human cargo. The crossing left a terrible mark on her memory. She commented once in a rare moment how passengers were briefly allowed on deck, weather permitting. They savored the chance at fresh sea air and the rest from the terrible stink of the hold that was near the bowels of the great ship. Only a small area was allowed to steerage passengers. It was filled with tobacco smoke, mingled with the ship's various smells, which did their best to defeat the healthy purpose of the passengers' very limited time in the open air.

The food was bad. Many were seasick, and some unlucky emigrants, mostly the very young or very old, died. When the seas were rough, all Mother could do was pray in between all too frequent sessions of vomiting.

Worse, smells of human excrement from seeping toilets and soiled clothes, from overcrowded, unwashed bodies, laced with the lice and vermin that were every-where, clung to the poorer third-class passengers like a never ending bad dream.

Most tried their best to make do. Regulations set by the United States government to provide separate washrooms for men and women were ignored. Saltwater made washing difficult and sometimes painful.

British crewmembers generally treated them as lesser beings, occasionally harassing them. Worse, women traveling alone, and even young women like Mother who traveled with family, were targets for rude and lecherous remarks, and the advances made freely by the crew and some of the male passengers. There were several cases of rape that went unreported because it would not have made a difference. Mother's natural beauty, though she was still a naive teenager, became a problem. Some ogled her, often making lewd remarks that she tried to ignore, though with much difficulty. One man, a fellow Italian passenger, particularly became a real problem that would catch the ever-watch-ful eye of my grandfather.

"Hey, you with the face only your mama could love, what are you looking at! *Sei un citrullo!* (You're a jerk!)" Rocco hissed, with a threatening gesture that only a fellow Italian could properly understand. The ship gently rocked on the open sea, like a peaceful cantata, as if purposely trying to avoid controversy. A sharp breeze, a rarity, cleared the deck of smoke, making it almost bearable for steerage passengers.

"Mind your own business, geezer. I do as I want."

"Not if it's insulting my daughter! She is my business and your mistake," said Rocco, a snarl emanating from his gut.

Rocco rolled up his sleeve; loathing darted from his anxious, determined eyes. *This is no more, no worse, than my war. Only then, I killed men I never knew, and only when ordered by superiors. Now I follow my own path and honor. This fool is insulting my Rosa. He leaves me no choice.* Values wrought through generations of tradition would not allow Rocco to let the indignity pass—not if he was to maintain his self-respect. With a war veteran's ease, he acted quickly, grabbing the younger man by his shirt collar and pummeled him to the ship's tarnished teak deck, adding the man's crimson blood to its veneer.

Frightened more so for her father than herself, Rosa screamed, "No, Papa, let it go. I'm fine!"

Rocco, his ears deafened to reason, grabbed the man's bloodied head, readying again to smash it into the deck.

His daughter's continued pleas finally had their effect, bringing back Rocco's temporary loss of sanity. Leaning hard into the man's bruised face, Rocco was repulsed by the sour breath—a mixture of garlic, onions, liquor, and blood. Rocco snarled, "Fool, you are saved by my princess' good heart. If you dishonor my daughter again, I promise, on Santa Lucia and the souls of all my ancestors, that I won't be so generous."

The man, embarrassed more than bruised, after being beaten by a much older man, got up quickly and made a hasty retreat. No one stopped him, and there were a few cheers from onlookers.

Domenico rushed up to his father who was leaning on the ship's rail, both fear and pride in his eyes. "Papa, you're so brave."

"No, son, I was foolish. Worse, I now have the fool's lice. What might have happened if I failed? What would you and Rosa have done?" Rocco shook off his pulsing adrenaline, feeling a sudden awareness of his mortality and a sadness that erased all satisfaction in the minor victory.

"Nevertheless, Papa, this man has been bothering the women from the beginning of this trip. It is good that you put him in his place, no?"

"Perhaps so, but son, fighting is never the best answer. Do you understand?"

Domenico nodded his acknowledgement.

Rocco then motioned, "Sit with me, son, I must speak to you."

"Yes, Papa, what is it?"

"Soon we will reach our destination. Those who are in the know have told me that once there, we must make the changes necessary to make us more American. So, from now on you'll be called Dominick which is your American name."

"What will your name be, Papa?"

"I haven't thought much on it, but I shall try to find out from those who know. I think I have heard my name called Rock or Rocky. Sounds funny to the ear, doesn't it?" Domenico smiled in agreement.

Rosa, watching and listening only a few inches away, feigned a quick smile. Papa had already told her that her name in English would be Rose Mary. But no, she stubbornly refused. She must always be Rosa Maria, for this was who she really was. It was important to her, especially when she was alone and so far away from home. It was the real her. *Yes, I'll do everything I must to fit in, but I shall not change my name even a little.*

Rosa also vowed in that moment to be independent, just like the movie starlets she had occasionally read about. It felt right to her that if she must change everything by moving to America, then by golly, she'd become her own true self once and for all, just like real Americans. She would never be a halfway American like so many on the ship advised. *No, this new land will be a place of a new beginning that allows me an opportunity to shine and to be who I really am.*

Little did she know how advanced her thinking was, even for America.

The voyage's hard hours passed slowly into long hard days, with each day bringing them closer to their destiny. Rocco lay on his slowly swaying cot, now oblivious to the stink, moving with each wave, dreaming a pleasant dream when he was rudely awakened by the loud peel of the *Mayflower's* ship's horn blowing its loud cacophony repeatedly.

Passengers in steerage at first feared the worst. Then in elation, as one, they clamored on deck as word spread throughout the ship. People shouted in excitement, "Come see the special lady in the harbor. Come! We're here. It's New York. See the skyline! It's America." The ship's all too familiar brutal ugliness suddenly seemed far away now for the happy passengers.

Rocco grabbed Domenico's hand, gesturing for Rosa to follow. They raced up the crowded stair to the upper deck, forbidden territory to the third class, steerage passengers. But at the moment, it did not matter. Once there, they realized as one that they were breathing American air, fresh and beautiful. However, Rocco reasoned, that any air was better than what they had become used to on the ship. To Rocco, the New York skyline appeared magnificently modern in comparison to Naples.

Later, when all was quiet, Rocco would recall, perhaps with poetic license, how sweet the air smelled, sweeter even than home. Foremost, he would forever remember the great feeling he had when first seeing the giant lady in the harbor and his first words spoken in America, the land of the free, and home of the brave. "Children, there she is, looming majestically, the great American Statue of Liberty, standing, to greet us. Her arms are opened and welcoming, promising a new life and a new beginning for us." Taking a deep breath and swallowing hard, he thought, *And now, I fear our real journey's about to begin.*

Mother often spoke about her first exciting day in America. It was a day complete with emotions and passions, fear, and resolve. The arrival system for immigrants at Ellis Island was pretty much established by the spring of 1925. Debarkation had its dreadful challenges and no small amount of hidden hoops to jump through.

Many immigrants failed to pass the various physical examinations. Some were quarantined, while others were turned back, forced to return to Italy for the slightest of reasons, increasing the stress and fear of the anxious immigrants.

The American immigration officer tried some trick questions on Grandpa Rocco, but he had been well prepared by friends who had walked this path before. They had diligently prompted him to answer no when asked if he had a job waiting for him. For some unknown reason, it was explained to Grandpa that he and his family had no help in the passage cost, nor did he have a sponsor. Later, I found out that the government wanted to crack down on the outrageous moneylenders that were preying on the unwary newcomers and the job brokers that were turning the immigrants' lives into a feudal system of bondage, and Rocco was one of those that they were trying to protect. It bothered him to lie. It was not his nature to fib. But this was how the system worked, so he would have to play the game if he wanted to reach Utica and the Promised Land.

The excitement was not the same for Mother. She had the doubts and typical fears of a teenager of almost sixteen. She wondered and worried what her future husband, Antonio Lavalia, was like. She had vowed that just because he had paid for her voyage did not mean he owned her. She swore to herself that though she'd try her best to be a good wife, she must always be herself. After all, this was what America was about, or so she thought at the time.

Grandpa had a job set up for him, along with lots of debt waiting to wear him down. It was too soon for him to worry, though; that would come later.

The worst blow came when the immigration officer misspelled Grandpa's surname. Now for the rest of his life, by the indifferent act of one ignorant bureaucrat, his name would forever be Ameduro. This bothered Rocco, a learned man, to his grave. However, on this day he did not dare argue with the authorities for fear of being sent back to Italy.

The newly renamed Ameduro family, having passed their Ellis Island ordeal, was instructed by a smiling and friendly officer to exit out the large doors in the massive hall and enter freely into the United States of America. Rocco, inquiring about sending a telegram, was directed to an Italian speaking interpreter, who aided him in sending it to Utica, announcing their safe arrival to Antonio Lavalia.

With the telegram sent, he looked at the open sky, seeing the beginning of a spring storm. "Children, before we get drenched, we must find transportation to a place called Grand Central Station. There we book tickets with our remaining funds for our new home."

"Papa, how far is it to this Utica?" Rosa's concern wore heavy on her tired arms as she grasped her meager belongings.

"Not far. I'm told it's about a seven-hour train ride, not much compared to what we just did." Rocco wondered to himself if he could hold true to his ambitious words. The streets of New York seemed huge, bustling with excitement and life. More life than he had ever seen, even in Roma, when he was once there during the war. Immediately, he noticed everyone seemed in such a hurry. *Why? Well, soon enough I'll know and understand these strange Americans.*

Rocco hid from his children his discomfort and fearful thoughts about the alien place he must now call his home.

"All significant battles are waged within the self."

THREE

Surprised, Anthony Lavalia read the telegram with extreme dismay. *I never expected her father to come. They're too poor. Not my plan. What went wrong?* He sat quietly, fidgeting with loose papers scattered on the roll top desk in his boss' small unkempt office. Originally he had planned to travel to New York City to meet Rosa at Ellis Island, but he never received a confirmation that she had left, let alone traveled with her family.

Utica, an industrial city in central New York State, boasted about 100,000 citizens. It was first settled in the 1790s at a rare crossing on the Mohawk River, an ancient waterway of the Iroquois Indians. It became the center for progressive growth in the youthful United States when the historic Erie Canal followed the ancient river, and in the 1830s it ran through Utica, now a major port city. Soon thereafter, the nation's first railroad was started, running from Utica to other nearby cities and cutting into the canal's freight revenues. It eventually became the massive New York Central Railroad owned by the tycoon Vanderbilt's. Textiles were its predominant industry in the 1920s, and Italian immigrants, a primary source of cheap labor, were a major factor in its many varied industries.

Rabiso Fruit & Vegetable Company was located in the city's mammoth freight district just south of the massive New York Central train yards that edged up to the Barge Canal. It was lunch break, and Anthony's sandwich almost choked him. It wasn't the almost stale Italian bread surrounded by its tasty ethnic contents of provolone cheese, fried peppers, and Genoa Salami that troubled his digestion. Normally he'd savor every bite of Ma's homemade bread which seemed to taste better with age. It was the one thing he missed most during his stint in the Navy. Its taste and smell, pure and sweet, was pure home. However, once he had decided to leave all that he had known, he never missed home enough to desire returning willingly, despite constant longing for good home cooking.

The windowless room's dim electric light from its lone bulb, dangled from the ceiling on a simple wire. It's flickering glow unintentionally represented his funk and his failure, casting an inescapable gloom upon his faltering attitude. In his pocket was the telegram, dated late yesterday. The sight of it further soured his overworked stomach. The ticking of the antique office clock reminded him that time and his life were moving once again in a direction totally out of his control.

"Tony, what's with the sad mug?" Gino, who had been sitting quietly, eating his own Italian concoction of pepperoni and cheese, playfully poked his boyhood friend and coworker. It was a sociable gesture, nothing more. However, Tony's irate glare gave Gino shivers. Gino Carvetti, though taller and heavier than Tony, didn't want to awaken his friend's monumental temper.

"Gino, ole buddy, it seems life for me never goes as planned. I need time to think. I may have put myself into a box that I can't get out of."

"What are ya' talkin' about? Nuttin's so bad it can't be fixed." Gino's right hand caressed his knife's ivory handle, safely seated in a scabbard held by a wide leather belt. The knife was Gino's talisman. Tony saw his gesture as a bad habit, and it annoyed him. Nevertheless, the knife was a permanent fixture on Gino for as long as anyone had known him. Tony's disgust went unnoticed.

"Gino, you sure are the eternal optimist. I suppose that sometimes this is a good thing. Right now for me, it's not, so lay off. I don't want to hear it. So just shut up, and let me think." He took another nibble from his sandwich and a swig from his warm Coke.

"Then you better do it later, ole buddy, because the big boss-man might object." Gino nodded toward the turning knob on the door, its huge opaque window casting the large shadow of a bald man.

"I better get this over with," Tony hissed.

Mario Rabiso exhaled a large quantity of smoke from the Havana cigar dangling precariously from his puffy lips. Entering the office, he spat out, "Hey, what are you bums doing? Don't ya got some babes you need to peddle? Time's money and don't forget it. Not unless..." he didn't continue, he didn't need to. "Now, move outta here, before I get mad!"

The big man slammed his two hammy fists together, mocking. During the war, he was a drill sergeant. His bilingual and minor sixth grade schooling was what the army needed to help mold the non-English speaking Italian immigrant recruits. He liked giving orders then, too, but now the pay was much better, even though he had several good paying scams in the army.

"Yeah, boss, we're going. Come on, Tony."

"No, Gino, you go, I'll catch up. I need to talk with Mario if he has a minute." Tony looked at the boss who nodded his approval.

Tony waited for Gino to leave. The door slammed shut before he opened his mouth to speak, carefully picking each word, considering his dilemma.

"So kid, what's so blasted important you gotta waste my time? Spit it out, war hero," he mocked, enjoying his ability to make Tony squirm.

Tony blurted, "Mr. Rabiso, I screwed up big time!"

Rabiso's eyes grew wide, staring and waiting. Rabiso was not a very patient man, and definitely not a man you could cross.

Tony continued. "Remember the Ameduri girl, you know, the fifteen-year-old broad that I lured here? Well she's on her way. In fact, should be here tonight."

"So, why the sour mug? This is good news, no?" Rabiso liked Tony, whom he thought of as sort of a protégé, training for higher things. Right now his protégé was starting to try his slim patience. "Tony, spit it out—I'm dying here waiting for youse to get to the point!"

"Sorry, I was just trying to explain."

"Look, I can see through the crap, kid. What gives?"

"Mr. Rabiso, the girl's here, not alone like we planned, like you instructed, but with her papa. The dummy actually expects me to marry her." Tony shuddered, giving an ever-so-slight hint of fear.

"Well that's a problem," Mario snorted, taking another long drag on the stale-smelling cigar. "Why worry? The papa is just a grease ball, a Ginny, who won't make trouble and probably owes someone his life to get here. We'll just persuade this man's benefactor to sell us his note and then we'll see." Mario's smirk sent chills down Tony's back.

Snickering just a little, "They're just fresh over from the old country, they wouldn't dare make waves. And if he did, I'd arrange an accident." Pointing a menacing finger, he yelled, "Take care of it, Tony. It's your pot, empty it."

"It's not that easy!" Tony's discomfort showed as rivulets of sweat formed on the cheek of his handsome face.

"Spill it kid, *mannaggia a te!* You really are beginning to try my patience."

"Mr. Rabiso, it isn't that easy. Her father is Pa's boyhood friend. I sent him the money you gave me to lure her here, never expecting the whole family to come. Worse, my family doesn't know about her. I saw no need. You know firsthand how straight-laced my old man is. When Pa told me they're good people, but dirt poor, I took a chance, never expecting Ameduri to get the money and come with Rosa too." Tony's face deepened into chagrin, penitent.

"Big deal, so the unexpected happens! What's the problem? Doesn't your old man know what you do here?" Rabiso's anger was beginning to wane, though his face remained stoic, his voice was mocking.

Chagrined, but hiding it well, Tony answered, "Nah, you got to be kidding. If he did, he'd break my legs. Pimping isn't what he had in mind for his oldest son. He thinks I work in your fruit business. The late hours fit my cover."

Rabiso put a friendly arm on Tony's shoulder, a rare gesture for him. "You kill me, kid! It is a certainty that someday the old man will find out. Get real."

Tony nodded sheepishly, choosing wisely to remain quiet and listen.

Rabiso dropped a large ash from his cigar as he took another prolonged drag on the stub. "So marry the broad. She's very young, probably not set in her ways and from her picture, mama mia, a real looker. She'll give you some respectability, kid. And it's good for business to make a show of respectability every now and then."

Rabiso made an obscene gesture. Tony, pretending to laugh, let it ride, temporarily relieved and not knowing what else to do except get out of Rabiso's office as quickly as possible.

"Tony, I've got big plans for you. Don't screw 'em up. All youse have to do is play it out. And kid, it's better than a shotgun in the rump, don't cha think? I can only protect ya so much. You above all know of our Dago ways. Respect and tradition are about all the poor have in this land of the free. Except for us, the special few. Need I say more?"

Snickering, Rabiso chomped on his soggy cigar, taking another drag. "I'm certain; this man has friends here who would be more than happy to help him hold up the family honor. Get my drift? I don't want trouble. It's good for our business when you can avoid a problem." Rabiso's unnerving laugh carried into the next room.

Nervously, Tony replied, "I'll pay you back, you know, for her expenses, I promise." Tony sighed, resigned to his fate.

"Anthony, my boy, that is what you'll do, and much more." Rabiso glared, "Now get your sweet butt outta here and go hustle a couple of Johns. Mannaggia, I'm losing money talkin' to youse." He took another drag on his cigar, now a stub.

Frustration deals no vacations from worry. Tony's angst was no exception. Walking, he wrapped his light coat tightly to ward off the chilling early May winds. He found Gino at the corner of Bleecker and John, opposite St. John's Catholic Church. In deep conversation, Gino was talking to one of the girls from their stable. It was a good corner to hustle the higher class Johns.

The trick handed Gino several dollars from her night's work. A frown furrowed the young girl's once pretty but now worn face, her disgust evident at whatever Gino had said. Tony approached, signaling Gino to come to him.

Gino's crooked broken-tooth smile glowed as he said his farewell to the teenage hooker. "Ciao baby, see ya later. And don't forget, I'm expecting an extra trick or two for me tonight, after you're done." Her angry frown sent waves of unveiled hatred. Gino ignored her.

"Gino! Are you through goofing off?"

"Hey, Tony, I see you're still in one piece. Sure took your time to get here, though. Hey, did you get straight with the boss-man?"

"Yeah, sort of, in a manner of speaking." Tony, frowning, pulled out a Lucky Strike cigarette, handing one to Gino and lighting one for himself quickly stuffing the pack into his coat pocket.

"Gino, why the devil do you pick on the girls? You of all people know that most of 'em didn't ask for this life. What if one of them was your sister?"

Confused Gino responded, "You know I got no sister."

Tony, ignoring him, poked him hard on the shoulder.

Almost all of the women in Rabiso's gallery were little more than teenage sex slaves, most from Southern Italy. They were brought over by the lure of America and the better life. Once in Utica, they found instead an American nightmare.

"You know Gino, some days—no; correct that—most days I wish I was back in the Navy. Life was hard, but actually easier somehow."

"Tony, here you go again. Why the heck do ya care about the Navy? Didn't the prissy jerks throw ya out on your ear?"

Tony thought, *Yeah, I memorized the rotten letter that straight-laced Navy ensign reviewing my case showed me.* It had looked to him like one of his little sisters' handwriting; reading convincingly like it came from a poor immigrant or a child, not from the hand of his educated father who probably didn't know of it until after his humiliation. From memory, Toni repeated it in his mind, with all its grammatical errors, all the time ignoring Gino, who was still talking.

Dear Sirs:

My son Antonio Rocco Lavalia, run away from home and he was sixteen of age and he join the Navy without my Consent And he told the Man that was in the Navy Office that he had no mother and no father. I want my son to come home to help me. And I was not working for two months because I was sick. My wife is crying night and day because she wants him home and you have him.

Yours truly,
Nick Lavalia

"Hey Tony, you listenin' to me?"

"Nope, was somewhere else, sorry. What was you sayin'?"

"Nuttin.' How about you tellin' me what really is bothering you? Get it off your chest so we can get to work, before the boss finds us standin' here."

"Okay, sorry. I was thinkin' about the undesirable discharge I got from the Navy, thanks to my pa, or whoever wrote it. I spent almost two years in the Navy, one during the war, even saw combat on the *Kansas, Battle Boat Number 21.*" His face broadened into a happy smile, with the memory of the huge ship and its twelve-inch guns, "It was the best time of my life, a real adventure, with honest pay."

"Aww, give me a break and stop pullin' my chops." Gino took a final drag; tossing the butt, smoke billowing into a cloud above his head.

Tony shuffled his feet. "Gino, shut up about what you don't understand. I was a lousy Ginny, immigrant kid, serving on this beautiful ship. You know, I even made Seaman Second Class. I liked the Navy. It was my home, my one-way ticket outta' here for a better life."

"Stop beating on the past. You got screwed. Lots of us get screwed. Forget it! Don't you know it's the American way for us undesirables? Look dreamer, don't you ever realize the obvious? We're here for the cheap labor, nothing more. You *stunad*! Don't you know we ain't supposed to amount to anything? Why you ever lied about your age to go fighting for this country and a lousy twelve dollars per month is beyond me. Heck, when I was sixteen, I had more important t'ings on my mind than fightin' this country's war, like broads for instance. Furthermore, Tony, your problem is you feel too much."

"That's a bunch of bull. And when did you start thinking, you Ginny buffoon? Does your brain hurt from all that work?" Tony hit Gino playfully on his shoulder. He reached into his coat pocket and took another cigarette from his pack, handing one to Gino, who lit it and then lit one for him.

"So war hero, what did serving your ungrateful Step-Uncle Sam ever do for you? I'll answer you: nuttin, *nada*. Get with the program and back to earth and off the freakin' high seas. If you liked the Navy so much, run off and join the Merchant Marine, they got ships too, don't they?"

"They won't have me."

"And why the blazes not?"

"Because of my bad discharge."

"That seems like a lot of baloney to me. You lied once, why not lie again? You're good at it."

"That's what I like most about you, Gino; you get right to the point."

Ignoring him, Gino said, "Tony, why did your pa really write that blasted letter? Your folks have more money than most of us stuck in East Utica. He didn't need your help."

"I don't know. I'm not sure that he actually knew about it. You know my ma; it might have been her doing. She probably missed the extra money I brought home more than she did me. Then there's the oldest son's responsibility crap. I suppose they found out from one of their many *paisanos*. A lot of their old Dago friends had sons in the military. One might have seen me in San Diego, one day or another when I was on leave there. It was the only American port I ever went into. And you know the rest. It's as much as I do." Tony's face showed a rare pain, removed from his usual stoicism.

"So you lied your age, big freakin' deal. Cripes! You joined when others waited for the draft or dodged it. You fought, had your dumb adventure, and luckily you survived. Now move on. Heck, you risk your backside everyday now for Rabiso. Only from what I see, for a lot more money than your Navy pals paid you. As far as I can see it, you just traded the sea for hard ground. Friend, it's all water under the bridge. Get it! Let it go!" Gino sighed, tiring of the never-ending subject.

"You don't get it, do you? With this bad mark of disgrace I can never do anything but what I'm doing now. I'm doomed because of my stupid father and my Ginny background."

"*Sei un maladrino*, so you're a hood. Live with it. It pays the bills. Faa, if looks could kill."

"Gino, my boy, you can go to blazes! As for me, well…someday, I'm going to California."

Gino rolled his eyes, "Here we go. Tell me again, but somethin' new about why's California so darn special from what ya' got here?"

"For one thing, it's got more class. It's new and exciting. When I first saw it, I felt real hope. There, it's beautiful, and the best thing is that the weather's mild. I see the place as a chance, my chance, to get away from all this wrong living we've become a part of. We foolishly continue to tell ourselves that this is our destiny. If what our parents wanted was this," Tony swung his arms in a wide arc, "well, they should a' stayed in the old country. From where I see it, all we did was exchange the forsaken doomed life of Southern Italy for what's here, more doom. And what have we become? I'll tell you, we've become like cockroaches looking for a meal. After they eat, they're still roaches. Pa says the family had a beautiful farm in Missanello. We didn't have to come to this— selling our souls, just to survive for this dream that we'll never see."

"Tony, whatever is bothering you has screwed up your thinkin.' You seem to be forgetting a lot of the details. Survival in the old country depended upon crops. Crops don't grow well without rain or in poor dilapidated soil. And debts there are the same as here. Only there you are more likely to be beaten senseless if you don't pay back. Now get off your high horse; we gotta go check on the boss-man's stable. I better not find another one beat up."

"Okay, you're right. And yeah, my knuckle still hurts from the beating I gave that iron-jawed John last night. I don't suppose his mayonnaise face will ever be the same again."

"See, your Navy training was good for sometin' after all—don't cha think?"

"Go kiss a donkey, Gino!"

"Not in your lifetime!"

They both walked slowly east into the rising sun, up Bleecker Street, toward little Italy. A horse pulling a milk delivery wagon deposited his daily ration of hay upon the street and whinnied, breaking the silence of the early morning.

Grand Central Station was huge. Its grandeur was beyond anything Rosa had ever seen. "Papa, is all America like this?"

"We shall see. Ah, here is where we must go. Track 20, for Utica, New York, on the New York Central Railroad, limited. Dominick, grab your stuff. Rosa, help me drag our boxes."

With his money almost gone, Rocco purchased two warm loaves of bread from a street vendor. It would have to hold their hunger until they reached Utica. They drank their fill of water from a drinking fountain in the rail station and headed toward their platform.

The Ameduro family boarded the aging steam train; its engine chugged steadily, following the Hudson River north in the early afternoon. The train rode the iron tracks, slowly working its way to the connector in Albany, on a daylong trip that would take it to the Mohawk Valley Region and Utica.

It stopped at every small town, city, and village along the way, none nearing the splendor of New York City, yet each had its own aura. Each station had a strange-sounding name, displayed on the side track as the train approached, that they had difficulty pronouncing. The green expanse of the countryside was alive with early spring. Before them, sprawling, was revealed the area's wealth, teaming with agricultural prosperity. The train passed endless beautiful pastureland, ripe and rich, inviting, its steam and noise, uncaring, disrupting the Hudson Valley's tranquility.

By the time they reached Albany, the rickety ancient seats of the old passenger car began to mold unpleasantly to their tired bodies. The train then turned in a westerly direction, its tracks now following the Mohawk River. In view were the foothills of two mountains that bordered the ancient valley. To the north lay the Adirondacks, to the south the Catskills. The tracks beat a constant path past strange places with names like Schenectady, Rotterdam, Amsterdam, Gloversville, Johnstown, Ilion, Herkimer, and finally Utica.

Their train slowly pulled into Utica's magnificent Union Station, built to its glory in 1914. It was late in the evening and beginning to rain. Exhausted, the family gathered their belongings and began the long trek to the main station, pulling and carrying luggage, going down wide stairs and under a long tunnel carved conveniently under the tracks of the giant train yard. As they entered the terminal, its bright lights illuminated its grandeur, welcoming the Ameduro family to their new home. A good-looking young man in his mid-twenties, standing about five feet, seven inches, held a sign made from an old cardboard box. On it scribbled in grease pen was the name "Ameduri."

"Papa," Rosa whispered shyly. "Is it Antonio? Is he the one I am to marry?"

"Rosa, hush, you must act properly. We shall see soon enough, though it does look like him from the picture."

The young man, seeing their curiosity, came forward; he spoke fluent Italian in a Southern dialect. "May I please inquire, are you the Ameduri family?" The Ameduri's nodded as one. "I'm Antonio Rocco Lavalia. Here in America, I'm called Anthony, but my friends call me Tony."

Rocco extended his tired hand in warm greeting to the young man. "Yes, it's us; however our name is now changed by the Americans to Ameduro." He chuckled, his eyes wide and inviting. "It's a good middle name you have," he smiled warmly, "you know, the name Rocco."

Smiling forcedly, Tony answered, grasping the older man's extended hand. "*Non ti preoccupare!* (Don't worry about it!), this name changing happens all of the time. It's a small price we all must pay to live here." His false smile was infectious.

"No matter! I agree!" said Rocco. "Let me introduce my *familia Americana*. This young man is Dominick and by obvious deduction, this is my Rosa Maria, your betrothed."

"And your wife, Senor Ameduri, is she here?"

"No, not until I earn passage. It was a difficult decision." Rocco's face did not hide his unease.

"Sorry to hear this. May her arrival be soon, safe, and swift and without adventure."

Rocco smiled, happy to hear Tony speak so warmly. He said, "Thank you. I look forward to knowing you more."

"Let's gather your bags, I have transportation. My family lives on Second Avenue, a few blocks from here. You'll stay with us until the wedding." Tony could not miss the demure look from the beautiful redheaded young woman standing before him. He had not imagined her to be so stunning. Her picture did not do her justice. *Maybe this might work out after all. Screw plans. Anyway, I'll be sure to break in this virgin beauty personally and then maybe go to California after I do. I might even take her with me.* His mind, quick and devious, began to work overtime, searching as always for a quick solution.

He had finally built the courage to tell his family, only an hour earlier, about his intended bride. His parents had shown some surprise, mostly from concern and dismay, as to why he had waited to tell them. Questions were tossed at Tony, mostly from his mother. Giovanna's Sicilian heritage made her suspicious of her son. Having heard his explanation, she said little.

The smile Tony flashed to the newly arrived family hid well his impure thoughts for the blue-eyed beauty standing before him.

Rabiso's Army surplus truck was better than walking. The truck, primarily used for a front company called Rabiso Fruit and Vegetables, was not built for passenger comfort. Tonight though, its ancient frame hauled Tony's most recent mistake. Its well-worn canvas cover did little to protect Rosa and Dominick, huddling together on the rough and wet wooden floor, trying to stay warm in the damp, early spring cold.

"Rosa, do you like him? He seems nice," said Dominick.

"Time will tell all, soon enough." Rosa brushed aside the rainwater that had seeped through the canvas. She was too tired to care. Troubled, she thought, *Soon, too soon, I must understand the mysterious divide between being a child and a woman.*

Huddled, Rosa tightly grasped Dominick's hand. Head bowed, she made a quick sign of the Trinity and began praying softly. Respectfully, Dominick bowed his head, listening. Rosa grasped the small cross hanging from her neck, a departing gift from Antoinette, which had also been handed down from her mother, Grandma Stella. "Virgin Mother Mary, please make us strong. Help Papa and me to find work, so that Mama can come here soon. And Lord… please help my brother stay away from mischief." She smiled at Dominick, who was frowning, then smiling. Lightning suddenly lit up the truck bed as the storm raged, pitching its fury on the night. The two children huddled closer, trying to act brave in this new land.

"When you encounter difficulties and contradictions, do not try to break them, but bend them with gentleness and time."

Francis De Sales

FOUR

To say he was surprised was an understatement. Nicola Lavalia had never understood his oldest child, though he tried; he'd been a mystery to him since birth. This very evening, Antonio had sprung his self-arranged marriage to Rocco Ameduri's daughter. *Of course, it is well past the time for the boy to marry. After all, I was married at nineteen; he's almost twenty-five. But, like this? It is just not our way.*

Nick sat alone in the dank basement of his home, enjoying the peaceful quiet before the storm. He could hear the mice scrambling, aware of his presence. *Tomorrow, I'll put out the traps and catch you little vermin, but tonight you're safe. I've got bigger concerns.*

Giovanna, Nick's once beautiful wife, wasn't helping matters. Time, hardship, and nine children had long since erased her inner beauty as well as her patience.

Giovanna had worked diligently over the previous two hours to make Nick's life miserable, blaming him for his lack of control over the situation, taunting him for being too easy with Tony since his birth. Nick, and especially Tony, knew otherwise. He had simply shaken his head in resignation at the incessant bickering and droning; he was too numb to argue, knowing to do so would only make his life more miserable than it already was.

Crisp thunder followed by jagged lightening illuminated the early evening, casting eerie shadows on the faded walls of the crowded second-floor flat. The kitchen's lone, dim ceiling light cast a faint glare. Eight Lavalia children—five sons, three daughters—stood like stair steps in the small room, dutifully quiet, awaiting their eldest brother who was the current cause of their mother's tirade.

"Why, my all-too-forgiving husband, does he always do this to us…not asking?" Giovanna raged at Nick.

"Giovanna, the boy's twenty-four. He doesn't need permission." Nick knew instantly that this was the wrong thing to say before he even finished saying it.

She answered using only her well-honed Sicilian glare. It could scare the will out of the most fearless person.

Unfortunately, my son inherited his mother's glare, Nick fumed. Santa Lucia, my patron saint, forgive me, but sometimes she drives me crazy.

Giovanna spoke in her quick, rustic Sicilian brogue, difficult for the younger children to follow. She seldom used her broken English, never trying to master it like Nicola had. All the children but Antonio had been born in Utica and were American citizens. To Giovanna's disdain, Italian was a foreign tongue to them. But Vincent, her second, and Joseph, her number three, clearly understood everything, though presently they stared blankly, trying to remain safely aloof.

Catching their glare, she attacked. "I see your dumb stares, and worse, you are both standing there like stumps. Don't you two have something better to do?"

Vincent answered to Joseph's relief, "No, but Ma!" he pleaded. "This is pretty interesting. I think I'll stay."

Giovanna cast him her glare, and he and Joseph retreated to the parlor, taking the rest of their siblings with them. They all sat on the couch and floor, straining their ears to catch their parents' disquieting conversation.

Back in the kitchen, Giovanna harped at Nicola. "We must post bans at church. This wedding must be respectable, or I'll not have it!" She picked up a rolling pin from the kitchen table, shaking it with each word, to emphasize her point. "And this Rosa, she's too young. Only fifteen you say? What kind of a wife can someone this young make for my Antonio? He's a full-grown man."

"Giovanna," Nick also spoke in Italian, his dialect from the Basilicata region of Southern Italy, "I agree, but we must be patient and persuade him. You of all people know that he's often sporadic, always prone to jumping into things too quickly. It's better to coax him—take this one day at a time.

"Patience, *cara mia, viena qui.*" He smiled, holding out his arms to his wife, comforting her as she leaned against him. "We'll see this through. You'll see. It's better this way." Nick planted a big, wet kiss on her cheek, largely for the benefit of his eavesdropping children. He then hugged her tightly, hearing the younger children's low snickering and enjoyment. Nick loved Giovanna, but lately they argued incessantly. Sometimes it was good to remind the kids of their deep love. Nick's credo placed family above all else in his life.

The Lavalia kids didn't know they were poorer than most, despite Nick's dependable city job. And right now it didn't matter. They had each other, and tonight they must deal collectively, even if only by placid acceptance, with this new concern of their parents. They instinctively knew it would eventually affect them.

Collectively, the siblings saw all the excitement as an adventure waiting to happen, a moment of excitement in their mundane, humdrum existence. With luck, and as one, the children hoped this latest distraction to their family's peace would eventually serve to focus their mother's attention on happy thoughts of marriage plans and maybe grandchildren. Lately Giovanna's constant bickering, caused in part by a constant and sudden longing for family in Italy, was making life miserable for everyone. The understanding that she would never see many of her loved ones again made her longing for them ripen to an insatiable appetite.

Giovanna returned her attention to the children, calling them back to the kitchen. "Remember, you are to be seen and not heard." She pointed a finger at each child, like a sword, with its continual promise of sharp pain. She stopped when she reached Vincent and Joseph, twenty-two and twenty years old, respectively. "You two—be sure they stay quiet."

Joe winced. Giovanna didn't miss his reaction.

"Joseph! No guff from you, my number three. Come here!" She glared at him, swinging the rolling pin in a menacing arc.

"Ma, I didn't say a thing."

"No, but you thought it, and thinking is the same in my book."

Joe shook his head, mumbling, wondering what book she referred too. *She never read anything, not even the newspaper.* He kept his thoughts to himself, though, knowing that to his anxious mother, all this silliness mattered. *This is Ma no more, no less. Accept her or leave her, love her or not.* Tolerant like his father and the opposite of Antonio, he always took Giovanna in stride.

More important, Joe was curious to see the cause of his Ma's anger. *Tony always has a surefire way of testing Ma. But when he does, everybody but him seems to have to pay the piper. She sure went into mourning when he ran away. Sometimes*

I wish he'd never come back! His foolish acts sure made life miserable, especially for poor Pa. But he is my brother and I love him.

"Where're we gonna put 'em?" asked little Johnny, six. "We haven't any room."

"That's no concern to you," Nick scolded.

Vincent spoke softly, running a calloused hand through John's thick brown hair, "Johnny, they'll sleep in Tony's room over the garage. Tony's going to bunk with us until he marries the girl. So don't worry, you won't lose your place on the bed, not for now," he chuckled.

Several children snickered at Vincent's choice of words. Only baby Marie, fifteen months old, was quiet, sleeping in the arms of her sister Cora, twelve years old.

Michael, eight, looked out the water-streaked window to the street below. The street lamp illuminated the storm, showing rain mixed with hail pounding the cobbled roadside. Seeing the truck's lights, he shouted with animation, "Tony's here! I see Rabiso's big truck, and boy it's rainin' buckets."

Giovanna called, "Boys, hurry, go down and help with the luggage. Put it up in Tony's room. Cora, Angelina, help me set the table and get the coffee cups out. Michael, bring the cookies and don't eat any," she scolded.

Caught, Michael frowned, and replaced the cookie he was about to gobble down.

The old wooden steps creaked under the weight of the weary travelers. Familiar homey scents of garlic and spice wafted down the narrow stair, greeting them. Rosa stared, fixing weary eyes on the worn, badly faded wallpaper lining the stairwell's walls. Each step became an increased burden to the suspense in her heart about what waited at the top.

Sudden fear coupled with stark realization framed her like a prison cell. She looked at Dominick, forcing a smile. He acknowledged her. As always, he appeared happy—on a lark, experiencing, absorbing, and remembering every detail his keen eyes could find.

Brushing aside damp hair, she tried to give order to its tangled mess. Her rustic peasant clothes, wet and dripping, clung to her fully developed body, exposing details she would prefer remained hidden. Her mind raced. *The way I look, meeting them will be an embarrassment. She wanted to run. She turned and looked at her father, eyes pleading, desperate.*

Alert to her concern, Rocco took off his damp coat, placing it around her shoulders. She smiled, and it melted his heart. Not for the first time, nor the last, he thought, *am I doing the right thing? Please, Lord, let this work.*

The cracked oak door to the kitchen swung open, exposing the very large family dutifully awaiting their entrance. Several sets of staring eyes focused on East Utica's newest immigrants. Introductions were quickly made; hugs and formal welcoming kisses in the purest Southern Italian and Sicilian custom were exchanged, along with towels to ease their discomfort.

Rosa involuntarily sobbed, the anxiety, and then the warmth of the moment, catching her by surprise.

"Child, don't cry!" Giovanna pleaded, her indifference melting upon witnessing Rosa's distress. "You're among friends."

"I'm sorry, Senora Lavalia, will you forgive me?"

"No need, child. All's fine. It takes time to adjust. I understand." *She reminds me of me, when I first met my Nicola.* "Right now, you're tired from the long trip. Come, we'll drink some hot tea. There's coffee for the men. Let them get to know each other and also catch up on the years. Domenico, you go with the children; there are cookies and some cold milk. We'll go into my parlor where we can talk, learn about each other."

Giovanna's reassuring smile, creased with experience, eased Rosa. "Thank you, Senora. America is so new and yet because of you, it feels like home. Does everyone here speak Italian?" she asked.

"No, not everyone in this city does, but here in Little Italy, or what we locals call East Utica, it's our way of life. Mostly Italians live on this side of town; it'll help make it easier to adjust." Giovanna offered Rosa a cookie while little Cora offered sugar and cream for the tea. The hot liquid began to work wonders on Rosa's depleted spirit.

"Dear, you must take little steps at first, and then later, take larger ones. Soon all this will seem normal. For now, if you would like, I'll be your mama and teach what you need to know to get by."

Rosa wiped at her tears, smiling ear to ear. She stood, and leaning over Giovanna's chair, bent down to hug her. Tony, sitting at the kitchen table, peered through the doorway on the scene playing out in the parlor, wondering what he'd gotten into, but determined to play out the charade.

"Senora, was it difficult for you to adjust, you know, when you first came here?"

"Yes, at first, that is until a wise old woman told me this and I will tell it to you. It helped me to accept that I was just as good as others despite my ignorance as a new person in this new country. The old woman wisely said, 'When you awake tomorrow morning, do so before the sun comes up so that you may watch it rise to the new day. And when it comes up, remember that its soothing rays will hit the East side and us, its lowly inhabitants, before it shines on the rest of the city, making us equals for that moment to our supposed betters on the other side of town. Do this, and you will no longer allow them to have rule over you.' So remember this when others try to make you feel low and for those days that you feel like a fish out of water."

Rosa nodded her understanding though she was in truth confused. Her renewed gentle sobbing underlined her vulnerability.

Tony watched his mother and Rosa, a sight that perhaps would linger in his thoughts later, but he shook it off as bad karma. He thought prophetically that nothing could further weaken his already poor poker hand in this, his current game of life. Could this beautiful, yet ignorant immigrant redheaded girl be his lifelong partner? *No, never*, he railed silently. *I have better plans than to be tied down by this child. Yeah, she's pretty to look at. What a moneymaker she would have been for Rabiso. It's a good thing the boss didn't see her before I talked to him. Boy, that would've been my misery to pay.*

Mother didn't really talk much about her first day in Utica, back in May 1925. She said it was all a blur of rain, fear, and adrenaline, and meeting what seemed like a hundred potential new in-laws. She once said she had felt like a piece of prime meat being viewed by a gathering of village butchers. Worse was her discovery of the scant quarters she would occupy above the old garage, which once had served as a stable. Her future husband had converted it after his undesirable discharge from the Navy, though at the time she was unaware of his past.

The garage, a few feet behind the main house, was in many ways even more primitive than her home in Missanello, she often laughed when telling me. It had no running water; bathrooms were in the main house. It had an old rickety stove for cooking, standing against the backdrop of hewed wooden walls. She vividly recalled how her father began his campaign to improve things: making new furniture, little repairs, and comfort changes. In his limited spare time, he repaired the Lavalia children's shoes, all done after working six twelve-hour days during each week. It made him feel good, and it was his only way to repay hospitality.

Things initially were very good for the Ameduro family, for they were in America, land of opportunity.

However, Mother's fiancé seemed distant. Content to allow Giovanna to control his destiny; he went along with a proper wait. After all, like Giovanna, he agreed it was not correct for Rosa to marry right away. He was very happy to wait until she reached sixteen.

Her sixteenth birthday arrived in August when the city was hot and humid. It would be Mother's first of many birthdays in her adopted country. Marriage bans were to be set at St. Mary Mt. Carmel Church, but for reasons never really explained, Tony stalled taking this important step, upsetting Giovanna along the way. That in-between time had increased his desire to run.

Mother said that it was a time that should have been spent bettering, not prolonging and straining, relations. Life, though, knows no time but the present. In the present of that time in the world, especially for immigrants, it was difficult to separate the forest from the trees. When one worked up to sixteen-hour days, six days a week, many things were allowed to slide in the interest of sanity and the ever constant human need to rest.

Rosa, like her father, worked. Her first job was at a local cotton mill that was more like a sweatshop. Their combined wages barely paid their meager living expenses, and the loan sharks left nothing to put aside for Antoinette's passage.

Every penny was accounted for. Even Dominick took up shining shoes. He was unable to attend school until he learned English. Foreign kids were allowed to start school only in kindergarten if they had no English skills. There they would be taught English. Unfortunately, Dominick, at twelve, was too old for the luxury of school anyway.

Many children, like Rosa's future husband, learned to speak English first in school and then taught it to their parents. There were not enough bilingual teachers, nor programs or money to accommodate the immigrants like there are now. Immigrants were expected to get by on their own initiative. It was the American way back then to build a solid nation of independent citizens. Times sure have changed.

Grandpa Rocco made Dominick a shoeshine box and taught him to shine shoes so bright that customers could see their reflections. Grandpa Rocco's greatest wish was that he'd someday set up a shoe repair shop. He looked forward to the day when he would teach his trade to Dominick. But a lot of money was needed. So Rocco, a very patient man, would wait. Grandpa Rocco was very good at waiting.

The day was August 21, 1925. Candles glowed brightly on the big, freshly baked vanilla cake spread generously with smooth white icing. Rosa's scarlet hair shimmered in the dimming light of early evening. She blew out the candles, a luxury provided by Tony, with one puff. She made a wish. *Please Lord, may every day be like a birthday party with cake and family and soon Mama.*

I'm sixteen today. Now I'm a woman, but I don't feel different. She looked up to see her fiancé staring, a blank look on his face. *What's he thinking? He never talks.*

"Rosa, tell us what you wished for," little John begged.

"No, Johnny," she replied in broken English. "It would be…a bad luck uhh…to reveal my wish. You wouldn't a want that a now, would you?" She smiled, caressing his chubby face.

"No, Rosa," he giggled as only a little mischievous boy could. "But whisper it to me and I won't tell anyone."

Rosa leaned close to Johnny's ear and whispered in Italian, "Johnny, I wish to be happy like this forever and that you'll always be my little brother." She kissed his forehead and Johnny beamed.

"I promise your secret is safe." Johnny's big eyes filled his small angelic face.

Rosa looked into Tony's large brown eyes, his handsome, stern face, bright and mysterious. *What can be on his mind that is so important?* Playfully, she cast him a large grin, blowing him a kiss. "Now I'll cut the cake and present the first piece to…let's see…" She spun her eyes around the room, seeing expectant faces. Cake was a rare treat, and each child waited in anticipation, hoping to be the first lucky recipient.

She gazed at Tony, standing on the opposite side of the large kitchen table, all too serious. Smiling, she coyly handed over the big slice. He beamed his appreciation. Rosa's unexpected grin, surprisingly beautiful, natural, and captivating, momentarily took away his breath.

Giovanna knowingly took in the scene before her, looking quickly at her son. Without saying a word, she took the cake knife from Rosa, overseeing distribution. And like a good drill sergeant, she lined up her children according to age, snapping out orders before giving each a generous piece of the moist ambrosia.

"Everyone, I have an announcement," said Tony, raising his arm to get attention.

All eyes turned to him.

"I talked to Father Rossellini today." Tony looked directly at his mother, as if to fend off argument. His eyes seemed to be saying, "See, I finally did as you asked."

"The good priest has agreed to marry Rosa and me on Christmas Eve; that is, of course, if you consent, Ma." He looked squarely at his mother.

Giovanna cast a surprised glance at her husband, unsure about the date, not the marriage. "Son, as tradition requires, have you formally asked Senor Ameduro for Rosa's hand?"

"No, Ma." Tony looked sheepishly at his future father-in-law, standing with his fork in midair, with vanilla cake impaled on it. "Really, I kind of thought all that was taken care of long ago; you know, when I sent money for Rosa's passage. I guess I forgot tradition. Sorry, Rocco," he said, feeling like a liar.

Rocco stepped forward, chest expanded, greeting the occasion head-on while momentarily glancing sheepishly at his daughter. "No harm, Senora, your Antonio had my permission."

Rosa took a deep breath, unsure, only certain of her inner conflict. *I barely know this man. He never talks to me when we're alone and now he plans the date of my wedding without consulting me. I want to love him, but I have no feelings for him. He seems cold—impersonal and so remote. Are all men like this? What has Papa done?*

The room came alive with the added excitement. Giovanna's mind raced. With a formal date set, and a wedding now on the horizon, a lot of planning would have to take place. *There is a dress to be made and so much to do.*

Aloud she said, "Yes, this'll be a Christmas to remember. Thankfully, there still is plenty of time left to gather the necessary food for a feast. Nick, you'll have to work extra hard with the boys in the garden. I'll need to can several more jars of vegetables."

The house, warmed to steaming with the heat and humidity of an upstate New York summer, did little to lift Rosa's spirits, less so as the reality of making wedding plans set in. She thought, *Today truly marks the end of my childhood and the beginning of the unknown.*

The climate surrounding the festivities increased in excitement when Tony announced, "Hey, listen everyone, I can get Rabiso's truck for a day. What do you say that tomorrow we beat the heat and go to Sylvan Beach?"

Rosa wondered, *What is Sylvan Beach? Whatever the place, it makes the kids happy and my Tony is the reason. Does he have another side that he's kept so well hidden?*

Nick explained to Rocco, "Sylvan Beach is an amusement park on Oneida Lake. It's about, maybe, twenty or so miles from here—a wonderful beach and a great place to escape the daily drudgery and enjoy a hot day."

The racket ricocheted off the shallow walls as Anthony's ecstatic siblings rejoiced in the rare treat of a day at the lake. The excitement, though, was suddenly dampened when Giovanna yelled, "Quiet!"

"No, Antonio, you go with Rosa. Cora, you can go to keep it proper in the eyes of the world. We'll stay here. You two need to spend time alone. That is, if Senor Ameduro agrees."

"Of course, they have my permission, though Senora, a day at a cool lake sounds wonderful. Forgive me my selfishness, but I would love to see this Sylvan Beach." Chuckling, he said, "Perhaps we can all go and…how you say in English, chaperone."

Nick boldly stepped forward, beaming, taking control while glancing his wife's way. "Rocco, I couldn't agree more. Let's go swimming Sunday, but right now let's celebrate my future daughter-in-law's birthday." Nick winked at Giovanna, who, remaining silent, threw him a wicked glare meant for his eyes only.

Walking to the hall closet, Nick retrieved a very old violin case from its top shelf. The violin once belonged to his grandfather and was passed down to Nick from his pa. He took the shiny instrument from the well-worn case. It was shined to perfection. Without uttering a word, he began to play an aria to everyone's enjoyment.

Tears filled Rosa's eyes as she absorbed a familiar tune. The music's mellow sounds of home made her long for her mother. She looked quickly at Tony, wondering and wishing she could start to understand and maybe like him, even just a little bit. Even with today's change, he still seemed too distant for her to feel otherwise. Yet, she definitely felt deep down that he seemed to be trying.

She was plagued with many questions, with no way to really understand anything about this mystery enveloping her called adulthood. Thinking, *Antonio has never so much as tried to kiss me. Am I ugly? Does he wish he had never sent for me? Is he involved with another? She sighed. Why must this life be so confusing?*

Rosa, though surrounded by her new family, escaped for the moment into her private little world, saying a silent prayer, hoping some saint—any saint— would listen to her plea and set her free again from all this uncertainty and confusion. *I'm not ready for this!* She challenged God defiantly, and then she tried to stifle her angst. Sheepishly she thought, *I'll never attract an honored saint to take up my prayer if I offend them with a lack of faith. Lord Jesus, I need a miracle to stop these fears.*

Embarrassed, she returned her attention to the crowded festivities held in her honor to find her reverie had gone unnoticed. Taking a bite of the delicious cake, she forced a smile. *This is wonderful.* Licking her fork and catching every crumb, she thought, *I must learn how to bake such delicacies.* Excitement, food, and noise momentarily erased her fear, but it hovered at the back of her mind like a dark cloud promising a thunderstorm.

"Our grandest duty undoubtedly is: not to seek for that which lies dimly in the future, but to do that which lies clearly at hand."

Thomas Carlyle

FIVE

The courtship of Rosa and Antonio began slowly. Not because Tony was lazy or not attracted to women. No one who really knew him would ever think that. It was simply his constant fear of being tied down. He secretly had hoped that by procrastinating, his blunder would somehow slip away, forgotten. Unable to figure of a way out of the marriage, he had decided avoiding Rosa was his only current option.

However, deep down, Tony knew beyond a shadow of doubt that his unease was not Rosa's fault. The true cause of his discomfort and his zest for greener pastures was the Navy. His two-year sojourn as a seaman had given him the adventure he always had lusted for, and it was the defining taste of life he craved and needed to continue. He yearned for more excitement, more discoveries, and most of all, freedom. Remaining in the city of Utica meant only more of the mundane and, worse, more of the loathsome uncomfortable tasks tossed at him daily by his boss, a man that he dreaded and feared. Being tied down might be fine for others, but it was not for Tony. He wanted to fly like an eagle, free above it all; even someday perhaps flying in one of those amazing aeroplanes he often stopped to watch at the airport on the edge of town.

However, today he was forced by custom and perhaps sanity to continue the maddening charade and begin the formal courtship of the unfortunate and unsuspecting Rosa Ameduro. Pushed by his mother and then by embarrassment, he had reluctantly consented to start courting properly, in the traditional Italian manner. Dressed in his finest church clothes, his image in the mirror frowned back at him, reflecting his sour mood. What he saw was a frightened young man, and it unnerved him. It was like seeing a ghost of what he was to become if he stayed.

Trying to rationalize he thought, *Yeah, I've known fear. It was real fear. Not so long ago either.* Six years had passed since he served on the *USS Kansas.* During the war, the battleship had scrambled in the North Atlantic, dodging enemy sub patrols while escorting convoys. The convoys had dozens of ships the *Kansas* was trying to protect. Despite the battleship's protective mission, German wolf pack submarines slinked through the convoy's protective barrier and managed to sink several of those merchant ships and it had happened before his very eyes. He, like his fellow sailors, had felt helpless in the face of those tragedies; he felt much the same turmoil today.

Vivid memories of dead men floating, and worse, the pitiful screams from the wounded and dying were carved into his brain—pictures and sounds that often haunted him of men burning to death in the water, like beacons in the cold and unforgotten night. Worse had been the incessant worrying that he'd suffer a similar fate. Thinking, *I made it then by trying not to feel and by accepting fear like my daily rations. But, then I never felt like this, so trapped and confused. And just because of some pretty, innocent, naive peasant girl. But my, she is a beauty.*

He adjusted his new black bow tie. Gathering his wits and taking a last look into the mirror, he tried not to view the prominent jagged scar on his forehead. He touched it, gently rubbing its raised surface. It brought back more ugly memories, renewed fears, and a terrible dread. Only this time his recollections were current and maddening.

The foolish man who had forever marked him no longer had worries, no longer stared at mirrors. Plagued by anger and some remaining conscience, Tony recalled the man's last dying gasp of life—the daunting, unforgettable death rattle and the pleading in his grotesque bulging eyes. Eyes haunting and unforgiving, eyes he now remembered every time he dared look into a mirror. Vindictive eyes that would never grant him peace. The day it happened, Tony, now good at lying, had told Giovanna an errant fruit crate tossed by a tired worker caused the wound.

It's not easy killing someone, he pondered, even in self-defense.

Looking at his silver pocket watch, he came back to reality. Late, he raced out the door, ignoring Vince's crude remark about his monkey suit. He rushed down the narrow, back stair. Alert and himself again, he fumed as he still felt out of control. He focused on his newfound responsibility, at that moment more afraid of defying Giovanna than his fear of the pending uncertain future.

Rosa stretched up on her toes, trying to see clearly into the cracked mirror hung on the crude wooden wall. *I must talk to Papa about lowering this a few inches.* Her father had found the old mirror one evening while rummaging through trash bins on his way home from work. He fixed it in a rush to acceptable condition, hanging it hurriedly without measuring. Rocco was a practical man, always more interested in quantity than quality when it came to repairs outside his given trade.

Alone, she stared into the mirror at her budding image, wondering. *Am I as pretty as people say?* Rosa had sincere doubts.

Humming no particular song, she fleetingly thought of her mother far away in the old country. Guilty, she thought, *Mama would never approve of this dress.* A new, deep blue cotton dress lay waiting on the bed, ready to cover her slight, five-foot, two-inch frame. It had been made at the factory where she worked and was a "reject." She didn't understand why they called it such, nor did she care. All she knew was that it was beautiful and American and she had bought it for half a dollar. It was of the latest fashion for what the Americans called the Roaring Twenties, short, flashy, and definitely not Southern Italian. It fit her well-developed teenage body like a custom-fitted glove, accenting more of her blossoming body than her mother would have ever allowed.

When she had brought it home, she had felt uneasy while still admiring her treasure. Rocco had laughed at her confession, saying he wished that he could have bought it for her. To her surprise he had commented, "Rosa, if we're to become more like Americans, we must shed peasant clothes and make way for our adopted country's attire. You'll surely look beautiful in this dress—more American than even American girls." When she modeled it for him, he remarked, "More beautiful than even I, your papa, thought possible, maybe too beautiful."

Rosa ran the ivory comb, a stark remnant of her childhood, through her silken hair. *Was it only a year ago Papa gave me this beautiful comb?* She quickly put the dress over her frayed slip about the same time she heard the knock on the door and Dominick's excited, "Hello."

"Come in," Rocco called, shaking Tony's hand.

Rosa, hearing the prattle from behind the old privacy sheet Rocco had draped from the ceiling, entered the small room that served as both a kitchen and a living area. Surprised, she took in the unfamiliar yet dapper image of her fiancé. She suddenly saw him in a new light, dressed to the nines as he was.

Tonight he became a handsome prince and, in her naiveté, not the brooding fiancé she had become used to. Before her stood a stranger with slicked-back dark black hair, deep brown eyes, and a gentle face, accented by a frightening scar. This new young man standing before her suddenly unnerved her, shooting an unfamiliar twinge deep in her belly. Her pulse was rapid, and she felt her heart beat with unfamiliar irregularity.

Before her, appearing somewhat sheepish, stood the reason for her coming to America. The man she was to marry. Unexpectedly, he looked very good to her.

Tony smiled, showing good white teeth. He handed her a small bouquet of flowers he had purchased from a street vendor. She beamed at his thoughtfulness, taking the flowers and placing them in an old vase she took from a shelf on the wall.

"Sit, visit for awhile. I'll make some tea," said Rocco.

"Thank you, Rocco, but there's a movie I want to catch. We'll be late if we don't leave now."

Rocco said, "I understand. Someday I'd like to go to a movie house. You kids have a good time, but not too good a time."

Tony stared at Rosa like a devilish five-year-old and looked in awe at the radiant and respectable woman standing in the crude kitchen before him. He offered his hand, reaching for hers, pleased at finding it soft, yet firm and determined. Her eyes seemed to pierce his, yet they were gentle eyes filled with uncertainty. Her face, sweetly rounded, was framed by beautifully combed hair, swept up in the latest fashion.

To Tony, Rosa had transformed from a cocoon into a gorgeous butterfly. She was no longer a peasant rose; no, right at this moment she was a vision, lovelier than any girl he had ever seen, American or Italian. He thought, *She did this in less than five months. And she's mine if I want her. Maybe I should settle down, and please everyone at the same time.* He shook off his positive thought as if it were vermin. *If only I can forget what I really desire.* Tony felt he was being pulled apart by invisible arms. On the one hand, he liked what he saw standing before him. On the other lay a place called California with new adventures and real freedom, a life apart from what he'd become.

Tony caught himself gazing, but not soon enough. He was embarrassed, but he couldn't quite understand why. Though struggling not to show interest, he suddenly was drawn to Rosa, wanting to know everything about her. The movie was a fun romp of madness and mayhem, with Charlie Chaplin. The silent movie had been difficult for Rosa to understand, with her sparse command of the English words flashed in intervals on the picture screen. Anthony patiently translated it all for her. He softly whispered into her ear, breathing rapidly, smelling her cheap lilac perfume—capturing her essence.

"Did you like the movie?" said Rosa, who smiled genuinely at Tony as she pensively looked up at him as they were leaving the theater.

"It was sure funny and nice, and the piano music was really good, don't you think?" he replied. They had just seen the latest movie hit, *The Gold Rush*. Chaplin, the current rage of the movie industry, was at his best.

"Yes, it was," Rosa answered, shyly now, her eyes low. It was small talk, unfamiliar; each of them was feeling gently for the next move, like dancers waltzing to an unknown tune, yet somehow keeping perfect time to the music.

"Rosa, would you like to get some ice cream, maybe a soda or a banana split?"

"Yes," she beamed, "I would really like that. You know, I've never tasted a banana split. What is it?"

"Well then, it's time you did, so let's find out."

Tony gallantly held out his right arm to Rosa. Her left hand softly grasped his unfamiliar offering, nestling into his, molding to him. Slowly, arm in arm, they walked down Genesee Street to the brightly lit Woolworth Store. Once inside they found a small booth and sat opposite each other. Without looking at the menu, Tony ordered two banana splits and coffee, his English perfect.

"You're staring again," she laughed.

Tony liked her laugh, hearing it now for the first time, thinking her voice lyrical in its soft soprano. "I'm sorry, Rosa, forgive me for staring, but tonight you're stunning and *sei bella*. I can't seem to take my eyes from your magnificence."

Shaken by his obvious yet unusual sincerity, Rosa avoided Tony's eyes as she took a quick, delicate nibble from her spoon, sampling the banana split that the waitress, a moment earlier, placed before her. Thick chocolate syrup smothered the vanilla ice cream in a boat-like dish. The unique taste was fabulous and new, yet she barely noticed.

"Antonio."

Tony felt her roll his name off her tongue like primitive music.

"It's okay for you to stare. I was only worried there might be something wrong about me," she said.

"Rosa," he stammered, "we're getting married in a few months, and up until now, I must admit, I have been unsure."

"Are you unsure now, Antonio Rocco Lavalia?" Rosa played with his name, rolling it off her tongue like a dangerous game, singing it sweetly in Italian like a new love song just for him, unsure, yet somehow both knowing the beat and the tune.

"I can't really be totally sure, Rosa, though tonight I feel different. Maybe it's because you're different, suddenly more real, and more alive. I only know this, and it is simply that now I must know more about you. No, let me correct my silliness. I want to learn everything there is to know about you. What you think, what you like, and why? What it was like in Missanello? You know, I was born there too. But I left when I was a bambino." Tony stopped talking and then apologetically, "Forgive me, I am rattling on too much."

"No, Antonio, please continue."

Tongue tied for the moment and not knowing why, he stammered, "Okay, let me continue. I need to know what you really feel and what you think of me. I painfully realize that it's too soon, and I recognize I've been somewhat, no, very distant." Tony hesitated, thinking of the true reason that he had brought her to Utica. Instantly the thought sickened him, and he felt himself choking from the hidden embarrassment. Rosa thankfully had not noticed his sudden change in demeanor.

"Rosa, I've been uncertain. You see, I have been wondering about what I want in life, and, well, I'm beginning to accept that I can't always have what I want." Rosa nodded, understanding fully.

Tony hesitated, and then continued, starting to feel alive for the first time in months. He was beaming, "When I was in the Navy, I saw places so magnificent, so exotic, too difficult to describe, but I just know you'd like them. They were places far, far away. But still, there's a place in this vast country that I fell in love with. It's called California, and though not as unusual nor as beautiful as some of the islands I saw in the Pacific, it's very close to matching their wonder."

Rosa's laugh fell into the silly giggle of a young girl. "Perhaps someday we can visit. Do trains go there? After all, I crossed an ocean, why not visit this California?"

"Yes, trains go there." He smiled, "One place that I particularly liked was a city called San Diego. My ship had its port there. It's really a place too beautiful to describe. There I saw water so blue and clear, palm trees, warm breezes, and no snow. Boy, just wait until you live through one of our winters."

Pensive at the mention of winter, Rosa responded, "Are they really that bad? Carmella at work told me how cold it gets here, and how the snow piles higher than my height. Surely she is exaggerating? Her comments all seem a bit too much." Rosa frowned as she took another bite of the ice cream, letting its exquisite cool smoothness slide gently over her palate.

"Rosa, I'm afraid your friend didn't exaggerate. Our harsh winter is one of the few things I didn't miss when I was in the Navy."

"Papa said I'll need to get a warm coat soon. I don't know where we'll find money for such an extravagance. I'll just use what I have."

Tony shook his head and pursed his lips. "Rosa, I'm doing well working for Mr. Rabiso. I'll buy you the warmest coat in all of Utica. You won't be cold," he said, smiling.

She looked into his large, gloomy, mysterious eyes, feeling suddenly absorbed into their brown sadness. Both alarmed and elated, she reached across the small table, touching his hand.

"Do you think we're right for each other?" she asked.

Another side of Rosa, mysterious and exciting, appeared bright and real before Tony. He saw the depth of her youthful understanding. *She may be barely a child, but somehow she reads my doubts.* It unsettled him; he could not lie, could not put off her honest question. In that precious moment, his better self triumphed and his inescapable interest in the young woman began to take root.

"Rosa, if I said I knew the answer to your question, I would not be fair to you. I don't know. Marriage is such a big, important, and yes, a final step. We must take it seriously and with patience. I do believe though, that in proper time we will know if we're right for each other."

It was not the answer she wanted or expected. Yet it was sincere. She asked, "What if we don't work out, then what? We're living in your house. Your family is becoming my family. Your brothers and sisters have become my brothers and sisters."

"Rosa," he stammered, unsure of the right words, trying to look into her very soul, focusing, fixing, penetrating. "I feel that I've seen you tonight for the first time, not that this is your fault. My heart is overwhelmed and filled with sudden happiness. I am not just interested with your beauty, which, by the way, is more than any man deserves. It's your mind and your soul that has captivated me, like a thunder bolt from the sky, just like it did that first night we met at the station."

"Does this mean you no longer have doubts?"

"No Rosa, it doesn't. But please believe I'll do everything I can to get to know you. And if we go the next step, I will learn to love you, as only a proper husband should. I promise you this. If after our courtship, you feel this is a mistake, just tell me. I'll understand and release you from our marriage agreement." Tony, for the moment at least, was forthright. Yet the thought of freedom, a total independence that would dissolve with marriage, did not escape him. *We will have to see where this takes us. What do I have to lose?* Giving Rosa an out was perhaps the only way he could get out of his predicament.

It was ironic that at this moment of Tony's greatest doubt, Rosa began to fall in love with him, not having any way to know his misgivings. She saw only his outward sincerity, and maybe, she pondered, that is all that she wanted to see. She extended both hands, reaching for him, giddy.

"Tony, I promise to try. We'll see where it takes us. I will look forward to the coming months as an adventure of promise for both our futures, whatever it may bring. But if somehow we do not agree to go through with this marriage, I will pay you back the money you sent to get me here."

Tony smiled; his demeanor was solemn. Then he began to laugh nervously. He caught himself. "In America, the children have a funny way of sealing an agreement. You spit into your hand and then shake. Let's make a deal like the Americans. What do you think?"

In answer, Rosa spit gently into her hand, offering it. He laughed openly and met her halfway with his own slightly wet hand in raw tribute to their contract.

"It's a deal then," he said.

Reaching into his suit jacket pocket, he pulled out a small white, fancy cardboard box, handing it to Rosa.

"What's this?" she asked.

"Just something I wanted to give to you if we ever got this far." He had bought it in the hockshop a few days earlier, intending to give it to one of his girls as a reward for a banner week of tricks. He had fought with himself trying to understand why he didn't do so, and now he knew.

Rosa opened it slowly; her eyes gleamed and then glassed over. A tear trickled down her delicate cheek. "It's beautiful. It's so beautiful! May I wear it?"

"That's what it's for, pearls to go with my beautiful Rose. Wear them; they'll go well with your pretty blue dress."

Rosa placed the large string of pearls around her neck. Suddenly she stood out in the crowd, his crowd, his Rose. Tony instantly felt he had made the right move. Then his ever-present doubt swept in like a tornado, slowing him down.

"It's getting late. We better return or Rocco might come to get us, and I wouldn't blame him one bit."

She stood, and he in politeness joined her in front of their table, unaware of the restaurant's patrons. She stared into his eyes as if searching and then reached for his hands. It was the closest they had ever been since meeting in Union Station. Her warmth stirred him, unnerving; unveiling a tender feeling for her that he didn't try to resist.

She kissed him, tenderly, not waiting for his move. He returned the kiss, tasting her and liking it. They briefly melted into each other's arms, absorbed in the moment, alone in a crowd. Suddenly aware that they were not alone, Tony broke from their embrace.

He whispered, "Rosa Ameduro, we're moving too quickly for my Latin blood. We must go before I act my age." He smiled, taking her hand, proud to be her escort. He shook off thoughts of all the things he was hiding from her. He could never tell her what he did for a living. He pensively hoped it would never matter. Deep down, far in his gut, he knew that he was only fooling himself. The beginnings of guilt ran circles around his newly vulnerable conscience.

Rosa cast a glance at him, wondering what he was so serious about. She grasped his hand and looked into his eyes, saying nothing. Together they walked the dark streets, the occasional street lights guiding them home.

"Regret is an appalling waste of energy. You can't build on it; it is good only for wallowing in."

Katherine Mansfield, New Zealand writer, 1888–1923

SIX

Rocco Ameduro brushed the bright red and orange falling leaves from his coat. His eyes lit as he saw his daughter. She was standing in the small backyard garden next to their garage home. Cheerfully he shouted, "How're you doing, Rosa?"

Startled from her daydreaming, she responded, "Oh, I'm fine, Papa."

"Then why the sad puss?" Rocco approached, gently touching her flushed face, chilly from the early frost. "Your face, it's so cold. You must go inside."

"No, Papa, I'd like to stay here for awhile. I need to be alone to think."

"Now I know there is a problem. You must tell me, and I'll make it better."

"Papa, you can't solve my confusion. You won't understand. Besides, you'll disapprove."

"Oh, now you're a mind reader."

"Papa, it's too complicated."

Rocco, wanted to hold back, knowing his daughter would tell him sooner or later, yet his curiosity got the best of him. So he threw caution to the winds, "Try me, Princess. I can be full of surprises, you know." Rocco forced a serious frown, and then made a funny face, a trick he had used often to get her goat or to unravel her strong persona.

Rosa tried to hold back a smile, but couldn't. "Don't, Papa; I'm a grown woman now, not your little girl. Don't try your fancy tricks," she scolded.

"*Cara mia, vieni qui.*" Rocco opened his arms, beckoning her to him. "Rosa, no matter how old you are, you'll always be my little girl. Now tell me what's troubling you, before you break my heart."

"Papa," she blurted, all resolve for silence broken, "it's just this place, this country. There are too many confusing things. Did you know that here the American women have more freedom to be what they want to be? Not like in the old country. Yes, they have many restraints too, but they don't seem to let them get in the way."

"Why should this bother you? I should think for you this is a very good thing. You think I haven't noticed how hard you try to be independent?" Rocco talked with his right index finger pointed skyward, his hand and finger going a mile a minute, his speech sang out like a fine concerto, his finger seemingly directing his every thought.

"Papa, it bothers me because I want what American women have. I often hear you say, 'When in Roma, do as the Romans do.' But when you're a lowly woman here in Little Italy, it seems all men want is for their women to never change and to be subservient to your every whim, just like the old country." With fire in her eyes, she hissed, "Only you men get to change if you want to, not us women."

Rosa's voice was raised like an indictment. "Papa, I want more of what this country has to offer, and you know what else?" she nodded. "I want it all, not just a piece of the pie. I want the whole pie. Is it so wrong, my wanting this thing that's as natural here as breathing the air?"

Deep down, Rosa hoped, though sometimes with doubt, that she would not be locked forever in her new little world of East Utica. *No,* she cried, hiding the thought from her father, *not if I want to make my mark in this country. Not if my future children and their children are to become somebody important.*

Her words struck their target centering on Rocco's large heart. "Rosa, have I ever said to you that you couldn't have it all?" he pleaded. "Princess, whatever you want is good with me. This is a new beginning for all of us, not just me. But Princess, we must not move too fast. How ah you say in ah English, ah, let ta me ah see ah…" he searched for the right word. Finding it, he continued, "One step…at a time," he struggled and then smiled at his accomplishment. "So Rosa, we, learn ah togeth ah, what ah you say ah, huh?"

Rosa beamed, reverting to Italian, knowing how difficult English was for him. "Papa, I say yes. But Papa, I also must say I've found that I like being me, and I don't care what others think. I like this new thing called liberty and now that I have tasted it, I don't ever want to go back to being the proper little peasant girl. Am I so wrong in my thinking?"

"But Rosa, peasants are what we were and still are. It is good to think otherwise, but I fear it is also impractical. What will your future husband say? This is not our way," Rocco pleaded, though he was struck by her sincerity.

"Papa, I am learning that here in America, people are not stuck with how they were born. Isn't this why we came here, to better our lives? This is the real reason why I'm so confused. If and when I marry Tony, he'll have to get used to me becoming a hundred percent American girl," she said. "I am determined that there must be no halfway for me. You'll see."

"But you are first an Italian and always will be," Rocco scolded politely.

"Oh, Papa, this I know, and I'm truly respectful of my heritage and who we are. This is the one thing you don't have to convince me of."

She frowned, her dainty nose in the air, "No; I shall never forget my roots. However, the direction I walk from this day on must be forward, not fall backwards to the old ways. Once I left Missanello, I vowed never to look back. As long as I'm here, I must, in my heart and soul, become an American in every way. If it is my true destiny to become an American woman, I shall act like one, free and alive, and always aware of my potential and true worth."

Rocco shook his head, stifling a laugh. His Rosa had always been self-sufficient. He had never held her back from thinking for herself in Italy, even at Antoinette's pestering. Thinking, *Oh how I wish she were with me. Then again, if she were, surely the sparks would fly today.* Rocco's mind returned to reason with self-assurance planted by years of pounding tradition. *It does no harm to allow Rosa her moment. Such things will change when she's married to Tony. Surely then all her silly ideas will flutter away like the crimson and yellow and orange leaves falling on this crisp autumn day.* Convinced that now was not the time to push, Rocco chuckled to himself, *This will soon be Tony's problem. Let him deal with it.*

Changing the subject, Rocco said in an almost pleading voice, "Rosa, I'm hungry. It's been a long day."

She laughed, "Come then, your hunger will of necessity have to put my worry away for a while longer. I've got pasta and beans on the stove and some good hard bread for dunking in the red sauce, just the way you like it. What do you say?"

"I say let's eat. By the way, is Dominick home?"

"No, Papa, I thought Dominick was coming home with you. He was all excited this morning when we left for work. He said something about shining shoes at that big Hotel Utica near the corner on Genesee and Elizabeth Streets. He'll probably be home soon."

"That boy, is he becoming an American too with all his ambition? What is a father to do with such rebellious children? Let's go eat. I am too hungry to wait. You be sure to save some for him." He took Rosa's arm and led her up the narrow rickety stair to their apartment's warmth.

The savory smell of Rosa's meager spaghetti supper greeted her as she climbed the stair, but it did little to sway her doubts nor her ambitions.

Dominick had awakened earlier in the day with a plan. He missed his mother desperately and today he had decided it was time he helped his father and sister earn the money needed for her passage. If his plan worked, he could quicken the slow grind his family now experienced trying to save the required funds. He thought, *Then maybe I could spend more time learning English, and then be able to go to school to be with some of my new friends.* Dominick loved to learn new things and yearned for the opportunity to go to school.

Some Italian-American boys he had recently met had told him that the fancy hotel on Lafayette Street was a good place to shine shoes. Better tips and more elegant customers were waiting there for an enterprising bootblack who wanted to work. There was only one problem; he must be on the lookout for the Irish kids. They considered downtown Utica their turf, resenting any new immigrants who invaded it, especially hardworking industrious Wops. He would have to be extra careful to pull out quickly if trouble arrived.

Dominick considered it worth the risk. An extra half dollar a day meant he would see Mama sooner, and he surely missed her cooking. Not to say that Rosa's cooking wasn't improving, but she was no Mama, not yet anyway, and Dominick, a growing boy, loved to eat.

Dominick looked down at his stomach, leaning to tie his shoes. It was small and hard and almost always hungry. He was tall for a twelve-year-old Italian kid, almost five feet, five inches tall, having enjoyed a growth spurt since he had come to America. He picked up his shoe shining kit, wrapping the leather strap around his right shoulder. In his left hand, he carried the reused crumpled bag that contained a lunch of the two pepper and cheese sandwiches Rosa had made. He'd beg some water to wash it down at whichever hotel kitchen he wasn't chased from. It would have been easier, if not safer, to shine shoes in Little Italy's Bleecker Street, but the income was little when compared to the riskier places, and Dominick was not afraid of risk. *After all, he reasoned, I have the blood of ancient Rome's legendary soldiers flowing through my veins.*

Dominick worked near the front entrance of the Hotel Utica for the entire morning. Business was good as the locals and visiting businessmen took advantage of his expert shines. This was his second day here, and for some reason, the Irish had failed to show. *Maybe it's too cold for them*, he thought. It was a cold thirty-five degrees, cold even for an upstate October.

Someone had told him that it was exactly one week from Halloween. He couldn't wait. He heard the rich people on Rutger Street gave treats to kids who dressed up in costumes. *Maybe they won't notice I'm a foreigner if I dress up real good as a hobo. How close to the truth such a costume would be.* He smiled at the irony.

He had practiced over and over the words "Trick or Treat" until he sounded almost American, *With luck, the rich people won't ask me anything else,* he thought as he rubbed hard on the shine cloth as a final touch to the dapper man's black boots. The man tossed him a thin dime, no tip.

It was a little less than six months since they had arrived, enough time to get to know the ropes. Dominic could even say his name now with hardly an accent. Rosa and he had practiced English whenever they could, and little by little were catching on, fitting in. Tony and the younger Lavalia children had been helping them, and it was beginning to show. They could even read a few words.

Finished with the next shine, he caught the dime the stout man tossed him, along with an extra nickel, a tip for a good job. Dominick smiled broadly, saying his thanks.

Famished, Dominick opened the brown paper bag, reaching for a sandwich. Today he splurged a nickel buying a Coke from a street vendor. It was a rare treat, and a small however very real chance to feel American. Sitting on his shoeshine box, he took a lingering sip, enjoying the tingle of the carbonation. He had just chomped a big bite from his sandwich when suddenly a large shadow loomed over him. He looked up into a mean pair of grey-green eyes glaring with unrelenting hatred.

Standing next to the intimidating boy, who was about fourteen years old and about five feet, nine inches tall, stood two others, almost as tall, and about the same age. Loathing fumed a violent hatred spewing from their collective voices. They were saying something in a rapid, stilted, Celtic brogue that Dominick could not understand.

The largest boy leaned down without warning, pushing Dominick off his shine box. Taken by surprise, Dominick dropped his Coke. Its glass shattered and liquid splattered abruptly on the concrete sidewalk. People walking by watched, some amused by the altercation; none did anything to interfere. The shortest of the trio quickly grabbed Dominick's box and began to run east, his cohorts followed close behind. The hooligans raced east on Lafayette then turned north up Genesee Street. In the shine box, in addition to his supplies, were Dominick's coins, over $1.50; it represented all his efforts this morning—more than twice his normal take in a full day's work.

Dominick without hesitation, fearlessly chased after the thieves, pumping his shorter legs for all his worth, racing, determined to regain his property. He passed the aging Bagg's Square Hotel and the train station, hardly noticing its booming activity. Then he passed the New York Central's massive freight yard, filled to its capacity with boxcars, and teeming with activities, waiting for the freight handlers to fill them. Slowly, he was gaining on the Irish kids.

As he chased, now out of breath, he briefly worried if he failed at how he'd explain this to his father. He followed until they abruptly stopped about a half-mile or so from where they had started, waiting casually, or so it seemed, on a large bridge that crossed over some murky water. Dominick remembered being told it was the Barge Canal. They were taunting him; he understood their intent, but not their words.

The bigger boy stopped first, fist balled, shouting, "Come on, Ginny! You think you can horn in on our territory? Come on, hurry up if you can." He snickered, his grin menacing. "We'll show you, you spaghetti-bending son of Satan, who really owns this city."

Dominick could feel the hatred sizzling from the boy's mouth. He reached the bridge just as the smallest of the three threw his shine-box into the water, where it hit the murky surface mercilessly and with a splash. The box sank almost immediately. His heart sank with it as it disappeared. Enraged, he ran pell-mell into the nearest boy, swinging his fists wildly, connecting solidly with a right uppercut, causing the boy's nose to bleed. But he was no match for the older kid. It didn't matter, though, because before Dominick could wink his eye, the three as one, grabbed him and picked him up. Then, without care or thought, they tossed him into the freezing cold water. It was about a thirty-foot drop. Fear hung heavy upon Dominick's heart as he fell, arms waving frantically, and his body splashing unceremoniously like his shoeshine box into the dark, uninviting, dirty water. A waterway that served as both a historical commercial navigation route and the city's sewer.

Dominick screamed pathetically, struggling; his final words, in Italian, were, "I can't swim, please help me!"

The Irish kids looked down at him, cynical, laughing, uncaring and proud at what they had done. They did not have to comprehend Italian to understand Dominick's pleas for help. What did a dead Ginny mean to them anyhow? After all, if he had stayed where he belonged, back on the East side, this would never have happened. It was his big mistake, and now he must pay. They watched gleefully for a moment and then casually walked away from the bridge after seeing him sink into the gloomy water as if nothing of import had happened.

The last thing Dominick ever saw was their mean grins, and he was very hurt. *Why?* He cried out, but no words came from his stunned lips. *Now I'll never see Mama again. Now I can never help her to come here. But maybe,* he thought with his last breath, *Mama's better off in Italy.*

He closed his eyes to eternity; his lungs involuntarily filled as his face fell under the chilly water. This was another side of America that no one had ever talked about to the starry-eyed, handsome, twelve-year-old whose future was now wasted forever.

It was Tony who broke the news to Mother and Grandfather. He had happened by the bridge, becoming curious when he saw the activity, and the police carrying the slight body. He had heard someone say gruffly, "It's only one of those Ginny kids, no big deal."

Someone had seen the fight and the tossing of the victim into the frigid water. But they couldn't say if they could identify those responsible, only that there had been three. Tony talked to the witness too, asking others, trying to get answers.

I'll never know who did this to my Uncle Dominick, but the Lord knows, and I'll find out soon enough when I meet him in the Great Beyond. Yet I have often wondered if my father knew who killed my uncle. He was definitely a man who could be tight-lipped when he wanted. To my knowledge, he never said much about this incident. But I felt he knew something. If he did, it would never sit well for those boys. I guess that I can forgive those boys, for somehow my faith says I must, but I'm still saddened, not just for Dominick, but for those misguided boys too. After all, I have four sons, and one who also died too young. Dominick was an uncle I never knew, but such violence was an all too real component of what immigrants back then had to endure. What happened to my uncle still happens daily here at home in my adopted hometown of Atlanta. The daily newspaper's reek with this violence that never seems to end. I suppose some things just don't ever change.

"Death is but crossing the world, as friends do the seas; they live on in one another still."

William Penn, English Quaker and founder of Pennsylvania, USA

SEVEN

"Rosa, doesn't your brother look handsome, so innocent, in his white suit?" Carmella, a simple girl, was at a loss at what to say. *The poor child's murder is so pointless,* she thought. Unfortunately but not surprisingly, the police department did little to nothing about Dominick's murder other than make a cursory investigation. She thought, *Yeah, I can just hear 'em. "What's one more Dago killed but one less to worry about."*

Rosa, still numb, nodded to Carmella, too hurt to respond. Just a scant few inches before her, in a sterile cheap white wooden casket, lay her precious little brother, not yet thirteen. *No, he doesn't look good lying there in that terrible box, the only one we could afford.* He was not, nor would he ever again be, the little brother she adored. *I must not remember him like this. He must always remain the kind and generous and loving adventurous little man I knew.*

Turning her focus from Dominick, Rosa, polite yet strained, gazed into Carmella's well-intentioned eyes. Reaching, she took her friend's hand, grasping it warmly, as if it were a lifeline. She couldn't speak, though she tried. *Please, Lord, set me free. Take me some place, any place, but here.* Tears streamed in rivulets across the planes of her face. Sitting on her right, her fiancé Tony wiped her tears away gently with his handkerchief. He had tried desperately to console her, but felt helpless, useless, and worse, ineffective. Rage ate away at his soul. *When would the prejudice stop?* He thought, *The kid never hurt anyone, but he was small and weak, a perfect target for bullies. But I'm not weak, and I'm not small, and I'm not afraid to do what's right, but how?* His angry thoughts raced down a well traveled street called vendetta; his persistent character would not rest until he found a way to satisfy his thirst for revenge. Tony grasped Rosa's small, delicate hand, holding it firmly, feeling her trembling, terrible grief.

Standing to Rosa's left, Rocco looked dazed, trying his best to be polite. Though surrounded by loving people, he still felt alone. His restless mind reeled like a runaway train on a track to nowhere. In his brief letter to Antoinette, he had scratched out as much as he could without going into the gory details. Rocco needed to spare his wife; it was the only thing left in his power to do. *It's bad enough she'll read about our son without knowing everything.* The funeral director had taken a surreal photograph of Dominick lying in his coffin, and said he would post the picture with Rocco's letter as soon as it was developed. Sending such a picture was the fashion of the day, but it bothered Rocco that his wife would have to see Dominick that way. He felt wounded and hurt, angry and repentant, guilty and vengeful, all at one time. He felt somehow responsible for his son's death feeling that he had let his son down and though knowing deep within that this thought was foolish, it still haunted him.

Rocco sighed deeply, trying desperately to repress a sob. He feigned a smile at Rosa. Suddenly he felt foolish. *After all, I am her father, and look at me. I've done nothing to console her grief.* He pulled over a chair and sat next to her, gently putting an arm around her, holding her warmth tightly to him. Suddenly he began to shake uncontrollably, sobbing, empty, as he looked at the still figure of his son, dressed in the used suit Giovanna had given him. In it, Dominick looked like a fallen angel. Each Lavalia son had worn the suit for their confirmation—there would never be such a wondrous day for Dominick.

Rage, sorrow, revenge, vendetta—all winged like arrows to penetrate his soul, vying for his attentions, like ants at a picnic. Rocco pushed the hatred reluctantly though genuinely aside, for he was a peaceful man. He reasoned, *What happened is the will of God. But what kind of a God would do this? No... no, I must not blame God.*

Confused, and then sorry for criticizing his God, Rocco forced himself to attempt to take command of the situation. He dutifully took the hand of a man giving his condolence, not noticing who he was. Blinded by uncontrollable emotions no matter how he tried to fight them, he stared blankly, aware, yet numb, still holding Rosa's left hand. Somehow he managed to talk. He felt the words roll out, yet later, though he tried vainly he would not remember any of them. Short sentences, practiced calming words of thanks—all seemed meaningless. No one at the funeral parlor seemed to notice, and if they did, they made allowance for the tragedy.

Rosa gently leaned her head on Rocco's shoulder, whispering, "Papa, it'll be okay. This too shall pass, won't it? It must." She grasped Rocco's hand, gazing at him through tear-laden eyes, and then she broke down. She didn't want to make a scene; she intended to be strong, if not for herself, for her father. She just could not pull it off, the strain was overwhelming. She just wanted to be a child again, free from all this. Looking into Rocco's grief-torn eyes, she realized forcefully that life as she once knew it would never be the same.

"Papa," she sobbed, saying words to comfort her father, though not believing them just yet. "Domenico is with the angels now. He was good and wonderful and we must be happy for him, for he's with our Lord and making a place for us."

Solemn, Rocco reached to comfort her; words would not come as he began to sob.

Looking on the scene playing out, Nick Lavalia, surrounded by his large family, wiped a tear, followed by many more shed in sadness for his old friend's grief. There wasn't a dry eye in the funeral home. Not a dry eye except Antonio's. He sat stoically next to his Rosa, staring at the casket and his once energetic future brother-in-law.

The funeral director walked to the casket, kneeled, making the sign of the Trinity and then rose and turned to the mourners reciting a few calming words and gestured to a young priest who then said a prayer of comfort. He came forward to Rocco and Rosa, offering blessings in Italian, giving further words of reassurance. The casket's lid was slowly closed in preparation for Dominick's final ride to Calvary Cemetery. Rosa sobbed anew at seeing the shadow of the coffin lid descend upon her brother. Tony held her close, quickly wiping away a stray tear as if it were his enemy.

The cemetery was on the southern outskirts of Utica. The drive, only a few short miles from Matt Funeral Home, passed the Corn Hill section of town. There, several farms still prospered, having yet to fall victim to the city's rapid growth. Dominick's gravesite, on a high ridge, was to the left of a large plot purchased years earlier by the Lavalia family when Nick's mother had passed. From here, the dead (or so the living hoped) could see the beautiful Mohawk Valley and its winding river outlining the city below. The few native blue spruce trees in the relatively new cemetery were heavy with the early first snow, bending as if in sorrow. Many small trees had been planted at the newer gravesites by relatives hopeful that someday they would make a beautiful setting for those loved ones at their final rest.

On this day, the remnant of the early October winter storm covered the landscape, making it all appear peaceful. Yet, the starkness of the barren scene before Rosa soured what was to be the first snow she would see in her adopted land.

The Catholic priest said a few quick, comforting words, and then read the 23rd Psalm in Italian. Individual flowers, some roses, but mostly carnations, were placed on the casket's lid, first by Rosa and then by Rocco.

First Rosa, then Rocco, kissed the casket and slowly turned away. Tony followed Rocco to pay his last respects. His family and the balance of the mourners followed him.

Rosa looked away, unable to watch the slow, impersonal and deliberate lowering of the coffin into the cavernous dark earth. She turned away, shaking in grief. Staring blankly, she walked to the waiting funeral director's car. Thoughts small and broken reflected her pain. Desperately she tried to shield her ears to the plopping noise caused by the clods of dirt shoveled unceremoniously on top of the casket. Suddenly, everything felt so final, and so incomplete.

The day's cold had abbreviated the ceremony. With the temperature rising, the early snow had started to melt, giving the landscape a glistening, sleek covering. Everyone at the small gathering eventually reached private transportation, each in his or her own way, saddened, yet perhaps relieved. Relieved, and also somewhat guilty, that while this current tragedy had surely hurt the whole of East Utica; this time it had missed their respective families. Simply put, many felt, but did not say aloud, "But for the grace of God, go I." For this scene was for many, too many to count, the real immigrant's America, playing out its mournful song.

Rosa silently contemplated the question that was on everyone's mind—would Italians ever be accepted in America as Americans? This she reasoned was not the time to brood over things that one could do little, if anything, about. *Dominick is gone. Nothing can bring his happy smile back. No,* she argued to a rude self-conscience she could not seem to suppress, *nothing about this makes any sense. Long-lasting acceptance of my people will have to wait for another day—perhaps even another era.*

When asking some of the non-Italians she worked with—that is, those who would talk to her—she learned how their families had eventually been accepted. All their stories seemed to have one common denominator, whether Irish, German, Polish, or Swede. All had similar stories of grief, pain, and prejudice. Those quizzed universally stated that America could be a very cruel place. However, as one, they had equally said that America was still the best place to be and worth the risk. They truly believed that the early injustices were the price their ancestors had paid for freedom and the chance to become real and accepted Americans. *The Italians*, Rosa reasoned, *are no different and no better. We'll have to bide our time like the brave immigrants before us.* Rosa knew what she had to do. Determined to have patience and bide her time for as long as it would take, at that moment, she slowly moved forward and away from the tragedy.

Soon Cousin Nellie would arrive from Missanello. It would be wonderful for Rosa to see her again. Feeling a pang of guilt, she quickly brushed aside the happy thought as though it were vermin, thinking it wrong to feel even temporary happiness. Sitting like a rock herself, between the two men in her life, the funeral director's slowly moving limousine seemed illusionary. She closed her worried eyes, trying not to think. It did not work. *All our money saved for Mama is gone for Dominick's funeral. I hope she'll understand. How hurt she'll be when Papa's letter arrives. What else could we do? Worse, we had to borrow money from my Tony's family to make up the difference. Now we have more debt on top of what we already had.*

She sobbed, clinging to her father, feeling the same terrible thoughts that were going through his troubled mind. To her right sat her future husband, intent and calm in the storm, looking blankly out the window. Rosa wondered what he was thinking.

She leaned over, close to his cheek, "Antonio, how can I thank you for being with me and for helping us?"

"Rosa, this is where I belong. I'm so very sorry about Dominick. He was such a good kid, a hard worker, always cheerful. I liked him a lot and I loved him like he was my own. I wish I could have done more."

"Being here for Papa and me was enough. It happened, and now we must trust God and go on with our lives."

"Rosa, this may not be the best time, but I'll say it any way. I understand if you would prefer to wait, especially now."

"Tony," Rosa's reddened eyes penetrated into his, trying to reassure him. "I thank you for your concern." Tony nodded, not choosing to utter a word.

She placed her hand in his, "Neither you nor I should stop living. We must move on and put this behind us." Rosa tenderly touched his face. "I shall always deeply miss my brother, but I truly believe he's in a better place. My faith in God tells me this. And we should not postpone our lives. We must continue with our wedding plans. Knowing Dominick as I did, he would never want us to give up what we have."

Rosa couldn't bring herself to tell Tony what she really believed—that life, as she knew it, was over. Painfully, she realized it was necessary to leave Rocco, more so to lessen his burdens than from her own desire. Marrying Tony would settle some of their immediate money problems.

She shook away her hesitation. *Maybe by marrying, I can make life easier for Papa.* Then there was Mama. How were they ever to get her here?

Tony, seeing Rosa's eyes appearing to be far away in another place and apparently in deep thought, fought the urge to speak, trying to decide if he should. Throwing caution to the winds, he whispered softly, "Rosa, what's really on your mind this very moment? I need to know that I may help. Your face looks troubled, beyond even that which should obviously be troubling you. Is it anything I said?"

Rosa saw something new in Tony, now he seemed caring and empathetic. She liked what she saw. "Antonio, it's just this day, it has been too much to bear and certainly nothing that you've said. I really miss my mother and need for her to be here more so now as I pain for the grief she is yet to feel."

Tony touched his forehead in the sting of his discovery. "I'm sorry, how foolish I am. I should have known. Forgive me for being so stupid and, worse, so callous. I should've kept my mouth shut." Tony thought, *I keep forgetting how young and inexperienced she is. Yet despite her age she has it all together.*

Rosa said, "No harm and no need to say more. You were very thoughtful to ask. The faster this day is over, the better I'll feel."

Rocco, hearing the conversation, interrupted. "Princess, it will be over soon. First there is a gathering we must face and food for our guests that must be served. It's tradition and is expected. Rosa, you need only to make a brief appearance, and then you can rest. People will understand."

The limo stopped at the Lavalia home, one step closer to the end of the agonizing day and, unknown to Rosa, the beginning of many more.

Mother never forgot about Dominick. Every change of season found her visiting the cemetery, planting flowers, cleaning the plot, scrubbing the stone marker that she would eventually buy several years later.

Her love for her brother never lessened, and his memory was with her until her death. However, she never cast the blame for Dominick's death on God or the Irish, nor did she ever publicly blame her adopted country. It just was not her way, and it plainly was not a part of her strong Christian faith.

She truly believed that death was only a part of our journey, a temporary step in the long march of time. To her, life on earth was only a cycle of ever-turning events, where you reap and you sow and you live and eventually die. She once said, "Earth is a place where we are here but a moment, so make the most of the time you have. But always remember to include the Lord in all your adventures." Her faith would soon be sorely tested.

"Abiding love surrounds those who trust in the Lord."

Psalm 32:10

EIGHT

The two weeks following Dominick's funeral passed slowly. Rosa faced the humdrum of everyday life trying to fill the void caused by her sorrow. Snow was falling; its white flakes, visible from the street lamp, clung to every surface. She no longer thought it beautiful; it was now old hat and unwelcome. Their home above the Lavalia garage seemed even smaller now, and Rosa's little world seemed more like the hovel it was and had become a suffocating and dreary place.

She had not seen much of her fiancé. Tony had returned to his former self, keeping mostly to himself. Giving Rosa room to mourn was his convenient excuse these days. Occasionally, he'd do little things, like buying her flowers or fancy, fresh, Italian pastry from the bakery on his way home from work. And now, he was sure to always be smiling at her, not scowling like before. To Rosa, his big brown eyes were still wide and exciting, yet not so mysterious. Rosa was beginning to love that smile. In its glow, she tried in earnest to see what she thought to be a window to his soul. Somehow, she wished and then believed his smile to be an offering of a safe haven—natural, and most importantly, genuine.

Tony was trying, and Rosa, in the wake of Dominick's death, realized it was time to taste life again. Yet, she had serious doubts, wondering constantly if this was the real Tony or if he was only a man lost, searching for the impossible. Worse, she worried, *Will he eventually return to the inward person he had been or grow tired of me?* Perhaps, she wondered if what she felt for him was only infatuation. These doubts, though very troubling, were cast aside as chaff is from wheat, in the positive hope that she was wrong. Rosa was a positive person.

She smiled, all aglow, when an improper thought crossed her mind. *Even though the times are modern and it is* 1925, *it still isn't correct for a lady to be forward. But, I do like ice cream and why not? If I don't light a spark under him soon, I may have to wait forever. He might never ask me out again, not with all this proper mourning that our families insist upon. Yes, I'll do it. I'll ask him if we can go out for a date after work next Saturday.*

She licked her lips, thinking of the banana split they had once enjoyed. She even had a new fancy red dress, another reject, just begging to be worn. She had purchased it, this time with her father's permission, a week before Dominick's death. *I hope Papa won't mind if I choose not to wear black, if only for one short evening.*

Rosa disliked wearing black. The color, she had said angrily to her father, was dour and wrong. Naturally, she had felt badly about her outburst, but Rocco seemed to understand, saying little, giving only a stern look as his reply.

With logic well beyond her age, she reasoned. *Didn't those who died, especially if they were good people, go to heaven? If so, wouldn't the dead want the living to be happy and celebrating, wearing bright and beautiful clothes? Would they want us to mourn for so long, especially if they're in heaven?* She firmly believed this, and no matter the argument pro or con, she would never change.

Rosa's musings were interrupted when the thin apartment door suddenly came alive, rattling with the hard sound of knocking. *Who could that be at this hour?* Rosa raced the few short steps to look through the cracked door, and saw Tony's big brown eyes, surrounded by smile lines.

"Hi Rosa! Open the door, it's freezin' out here." As he came in, he handed her a bouquet of carnations that he held in his right hand. Under his left arm, he cradled a large, neatly tied white box. He didn't offer it, leaving Rosa to wonder about its contents.

The carnations' fragrance once thawed, instantly filled the small, warm room. Rosa thought, *He shall always keep my heart filled as long as he brings flowers.*

"Tony, oh thank you! I love flowers so much. But you shouldn't waste your money like this." Her coquettish smile gave her away, though she was practical and determined to stay that way.

"Rosa, hello to you too," he laughed, a soft, happy chuckle. Thinking, *Am I really falling in love or is it an obsession?* Tony did not know which of his varied emotions was pricking at his steely veneer.

Rosa reached for an empty vase from the crowded kitchen shelf. The vase was one she had saved from her brother's funeral. To buy time to think, she put the multi-colored carnations in the vase, adding water from the tin bucket on the floor.

"You know, Antonio," she smiled hesitatingly, getting her bearings, "It's funny, I was thinking about you only a moment earlier." *I like the ring of his name and how it sounds rolling from my lips.* She would unconsciously find herself repeating it often, over and over.

"You were! What about?" he asked, grinning.

Rosa giggled, ogling the large box. "Maybe I was wondering what was in this mysterious box."

Smirking gleefully, "Oh, wouldn't you like to know. Why don't you guess? But you must do it in English."

"Antonio, that is so unfair," she said in Italian. "Maybe I will try, just a little bit."

"Okay, then," Tony said in perfect English, "guess."

Rosa picked up the box, which was tied with a thick string. It felt heavy. "Inglese, hmm," she muttered. "Let ah me ah see ah, mebbee you ah bring ah ta me ah surprise ah, eh how say ah dat, no?" she asked haltingly.

"Yes," he smiled his grin broad and expansive. "It is a surprise, but what is it?"

"Perhaps, my Tony, a leetle hint would be nice."

"Okay, I shall grant you one clue," he said.

"*Mamma mia*, Antonio, no *capice*! What is this word 'clue' mean?"

"Rosa Maria Ameduro, it means a hint to help you guess," he said in Italian.

"Thank you, you are, how you say, a sweet boy, handsome boy, or is it a pretty boy?" Rosa, knowing the difference, toyed with him, intentionally pulling at his heartstring.

Tony could see her mirth and liked her all the more for it. She was so different, so alive and exotic, already so much more American than even the few American girls he had bravely talked to when he had attended elementary school years earlier.

In English, he said "Okay, Rosa, here's your hint. The box contains something that will keep you warm this winter."

"Antonio, is it…"

Tony put his hand gently to Rosa's mouth, stopping her. "Rosa, English, remember."

Rosa frowned, shyly looking at the box. She knew the answer, but was trying to remember the English word they used in the factory. The word suddenly came to her and she screamed it out. "A warm ah overcoat ah, am ah I correcto?"

Tony shook his head in the affirmative, laughing. "Yes Rosa, it is a coat. Open the box and try it on." He handed her his pocketknife to cut the string.

Rosa carefully cut the string, putting it aside to save on the growing ball of string she hoarded and opened the lid, her eyes wide. She slowly lifted the heavy, black woolen overcoat from the box, jumping like a small child at Christmas.

"Tony, it's so beautiful, and right now, the color black is perfect," she said, slipping back into Italian.

"That's what I figured, although if you don't like it, the people at the store said I could return it."

Rosa tried it on. It fit perfectly, reaching to her ankles. "It's wonderful. I shall treasure this moment forever. Thank you, thank you." She rushed over to hug him.

"You're very welcome, Rosa. It does look just right on you and so American. I couldn't have my fiancé cold this winter. Do you remember? I promised you this a few weeks ago. I had to save some money, that's why it took so long."

"Antonio, I never expected you to buy me a coat. You shouldn't have. Now as long as it stays cold, when outside, I can hide my bright clothing and still appear to be in proper mourning."

Tony laughed. *Bravo*, he thought, *she is a maverick, all right, and she's my maverick.* "Well Rosa, what's done is done, and don't fret, I wanted to do this thing. Now tell me what you were really thinking about earlier, before I arrived. You said it was something that concerns me?"

"Oh, Tony it was foolishness; forgive me. I was hoping we could go to a movie, or maybe get some ice cream, maybe sometime soon. You know, a date, like we were starting to do before." She couldn't say Dominick.

"Rosa, I've been wishing for the same, but I felt it best to wait for you to tell me when it was okay. Sometimes our darn heritage requires us to be too blasted proper about so many things. In the Navy, when someone died, we'd bury the poor fellow at sea almost as soon as it happened, and then we'd immediately go back to work like it never happened."

"How sad it must have been, to be buried with the fishes, so far from home."

"I suppose it was. I'll say this, though, I was sure glad to get it over with. After all was said and done, there was little else anyone could do. We were at war, and in war you start to feel numb about things, and you know, it is times like that that make you want to stop thinking. It's sort of a defense mechanism for survival, but it doesn't really work."

Rosa, wanting to change the morbid subject, said with flair, "Would you like some pasta? We have much left. Papa's already eaten and has gone to visit some new friends he has made and some old ones too."

Without waiting, Rosa took a dish and a fork from the wooden shelf Rocco had made and dished a heaping portion. "I made this sauce; it's Mama's special recipe. I hope you like it."

"Well, I will admit that I'm sure hungry, so I won't pass up your offer. And I will say that it smells great." Tony took his fork in his left hand, swirling the pasta like an experienced aficionado. He took a generous bite.

"Do you like?" Rosa stood aside, anxious. She knew her cooking had improved, but was still unsure. "Someday maybe I can cook as good as my mother."

"Rosa, what did you do to the sauce?"

"Is it bad?"

"Heck no, it's the best I've ever had. Thick, tasty, not runny like Ma's, I just want to skip the pasta and get some hard bread to dunk into this wonderful treat and enjoy. Don't tell my ma," he pleaded, "but this is great. And don't you worry, you must be as good a cook as your mom. This simple meal is proof enough." Tony's broad smile and the little touch of thick red sauce flowing from his lips made Rosa laugh.

Rosa filled a small glass with red wine from the gallon crock jug Rocco had received in exchange for a couple of shoe repairs he had done. It was home-made wine, what the locals called Dago Red. It tasted like a close match for Chianti table wine. Tony took a short sip, the smile on his face broadening as the wine's fine nectar hit his palate.

"This is the best. Simple, honest fare is what is for us, the worker bees of our little community. Someday, though, my wonderful Rosa, you'll see, I'll bring home the best fresh meat for the table, and fine French wine, and many delicacies fit for my queen. I promise to make you very happy."

Rosa liked listening to him talk. It was all beginning to feel natural. She had slowly been growing comfortable, at ease, slowly thinking of him as her future husband. This night, it finally was the way she had dreamed that her courtship would be.

Tony, though, was pained by an uneasy conscience. He liked Rosa more and more with each passing moment, and though still a skeptic, he thought he might be feeling real love. What bothered him most was a deep-down, passionate feeling that he was totally unsure of what real love was supposed to be. Never in his life had he intentionally tried to get close to anyone, let alone a lowly female. Yes, he had often sampled Rabiso's fine feminine wares, enjoying every opportunity. Nevertheless that was only lust, pure and simple. What he felt for Rosa was not just lust, but something unfamiliar. He looked fondly at the bright-faced teenage vision standing at the improvised wooden and tin sink, washing dishes in a soapy wooden bucket.

Tony stood and walked to the crowded sink. "Can I help you dry the dishes or something?"

Rosa turned. "Just sit and relax. We can talk while I wash, and anyway, there is not enough room here for two to work." As she took in the sight of him, she scolded in jest, "What a mess you made. Look at your shirt; it is red with sauce stains."

Tony looked down, aware for the first time of his sloppiness. He knew right away the reason wasn't just clumsiness. He felt that he was on unfamiliar ground when around Rosa—giddy, filled with expectation, out of control.

"Take off your shirt, Tony. I'll see if I can get the stain out with this lye soap your mama sent. There's still some hot water left."

Tony did as asked. After he took off his once white shirt, and then she could see the stain had gone through to his undershirt.

"You might as well take that off too," she said. "I'll get a tee shirt of Papa's for you to wear. You can bring it back tomorrow."

Tony handed the undershirt to her. His strong chest rippled with muscles, stirring unfamiliar feelings in Rosa. She reluctantly fought them off, turning to continue her scrubbing. She struggled with ripening emotions, both afraid and embarrassed by her confusing thoughts.

Tony touched her shoulder; she turned and he put his arms around her, kissing her like it was their first time. In a subtle way, it was. They both tingled all over in expectation, reaching for more. Together they hit new horizons in unfamiliar territory, even for Tony. And then it happened, the most natural thing between a man and a woman who believe passionately that they are in love. And it felt good, to be locked in each other's arms. With his experience, and she learning quickly, they reached heights previously unknown to either of them.

"Rosa, why are you crying? It was great. You have nothing to fear, aren't we getting married in seven weeks?"

"It's just that I wanted to wait. Do the right thing. I'm not this kind of woman, and now I feel ashamed."

"If anyone should be ashamed, it's me." Tony put his arm around her, drawing her close. "Rosa, what we just did is special, and it was magnificent. I know it's wrong in the eyes of the church and our parents. But it was good and wonderful. I know this. I'll never be ashamed, and you shouldn't either."

He held her face in his hands, looking into her eyes. "Rosa, I love you. Not only for this moment. I love you for you and for coming into my bleak life and making it bright and beautiful, making me feel alive again, for the first time, well, since…" He hesitated, changed direction, not wanting to talk of his life in the Navy, "Can you forgive me?"

Rosa could see genuine pain in his telltale eyes. Some people could hide things well, even after one knew them for a long time. Tony was not one of those people. His eyes spoke volumes, and she could see and feel his intense sincerity.

"There is no one to blame," Rosa gently scolded. "I know that what we did was special, at least to me, and it took two, didn't it?" She smiled, her newfound love showering radiance, causing him to open his heart even further than he could ever imagine possible.

Rosa said, "I've never thought that this could be so good, so how can I be ashamed and think it bad? You once said that I could walk away from you whenever I wanted. Antonio, you have captured my heart tonight and also have slain my childhood. You must believe me when I say that you have become my soul, and yes, I want you to be my husband. I do love you."

"And I love you, Rosa," he answered, kissing her passionately. She returned his kiss with equal fervor.

"Rosa, I must stop before I do something more that I'll surely regret. While we can't change what's happened, I must now return and be the proper gentleman and await our wedding." He tenderly touched her face, holding it between his hands, kissing her gently and with a reverence that he had never felt before.

"*Cara mia*, I'm yours. I pledge you this. I shall be a good husband. Next Christmas Eve shall be the best day of our lives, for it marks the true beginning of our happy life together. Now, I must go before I lose my willpower and beg you for more."

"Must you, Tony? Stay a while longer."

"I better not. Your papa will be here soon, and I see that my shirt is almost dry."

He reached for the clean, somewhat damp shirt, hanging next to the old pot-bellied stove. "This fire has warmed the room to a boil. It did double duty tonight, don't you think?" He grinned as he put the shirt on.

"Let me iron it for you." Rosa reached to take it from him. "I'd be happy to make it look presentable for my handsome husband to be." Her rapturous look was infectious. It almost worked to change his resolve.

"No, *cara mia*, I must go," he smiled, contentment upon his face. "It's better this way. And what is best, I now know that what I have to look forward to is very special. You, my Rosa, have hooked me like a giant fish, and I love the feel of that wonderful hook."

Sudden fear came to Rosa's eyes, "Tony, do you think we made a baby?"

Thinking, *Whoa girl, a kid is the last thing I want!* He said smoothly, hiding his own fears, "Only if God thinks it necessary. Who are we to judge? Seriously, if we did, it was out of real love, and nothing is better than that I'd say." Pushing aside other thoughts, he continued, "And if we did make a wonderful miracle, I hope it's a girl as beautiful as you. Anyway, aren't we almost married? No one will ever know."

Tony wrapped his arms around her and hugged her tightly, holding her for a long time, not wanting to go. Finally, he summoned the willpower to break from the embrace, and gathered his coat and hat. He quickly grasped the door, lest he lose his determination. He turned to look at Rosa one more time, and with a wink, a smile, and a tip of his hat, he left.

Alone, Rosa sat holding her stomach, suddenly wondering if she had made a terrible mistake. She looked at her regal new coat, hanging on the wooden hook Papa had installed on the wall. Rosa sighed. *Too late,* she chided herself, unwilling to torture her newfound emotions with reason. *I love this man. It is real, and I will make him a beautiful bride and loving wife, just like in the fairy tales. And God knows I desperately need to do this.*

She changed into her heavy cotton nightdress, pulling the telltale sheets from her bed. She better wash them tonight, while she had the energy and the heat to dry them. She tossed more wood into the stove. Once washed she would hang the sheets on the rickety clothes rack her father recently made and then go to bed to dream good dreams about returning to a life she had longed for. She smiled the broad smile of a satisfied woman, happy in her new world, ready and willing to face whatever came.

She had just put the last sheet up to dry when the turning of the doorknob announced her father's arrival. He appeared happy and drunk, staggering some. It was unlike him to drink too much, she thought.

"So, Papa, I see you had a good time."

Rocco grimaced, trying to keep his balance. He said in a tipsy voice, "Daughter, perhaps too good, the wine was mellow, the company inviting, the cards friendly, and the talk lively. What more could a downtrodden and drunken and, yes, sorrowful man ask?"

Teasing, "That's nice, Papa. There's still pasta left, and I could make some coffee. Would you like some? It sure looks like you can use a hot cup."

"No, I ate too much with the boys. Mrs. Rossellini—you know my friend Salvatore's wife—well she is a very good cook. When I told her my Rosa made me a fine dinner already, she insisted that I was too skinny and had me taste some of her lasagna, and boy it did look inviting. It was, how you say in English, 'very belle lasagna.'"

"No, Papa, I think you want to say very *good* lasagna."

"*Scusa*, Princess, I thank ah you!" he said in broken English, smirking. His body was bobbing like he was back on the *Mayflower*, and his breath was filled with the stale pungent fragrance of homemade wine.

Then, talking faster than usual, Rocco said in his native tongue, "I am embarrassed to say that I stuffed my stomach until it hurt. After, it made me think of my Antoinette, and then you know how I get when I'm that way. Yeah, I got mellow. The wine, well, let's just say that it helped, perhaps too much." His eyes drifted off, looking at nothing in particular, but Rosa felt his longing.

"So what did you do tonight, my princess, besides wash? I see the sheets. You know, you need to take a break. You work too hard."

He gently touched her face, his rough hands feeling like sandpaper.

"Oh…" she hesitated. "My Tony was here for a little while. I fed him some of the pasta. He really liked my sauce and said it was better than his mother's."

"You know, Rosa, the way to a man's heart is often through his stomach. I'm pleased he got to have a real taste of your cooking. A word to the wise, don't tell Giovanna what he said."

She winced, but he didn't see her. *Oh Papa*, she thought, *you can only guess how much of me he learned of tonight.* Suddenly, Rosa felt panic and a sickening guilt. She needed to leave her father's presence, fearing he'd be able to penetrate her thoughts.

"I'm tired, Papa. If you don't need anything, I'm going to bed. Glad you had a good time," she whispered, while standing on her toes to give him a daughterly peck.

"Good night, Princess," he said, spotting the black coat hanging on the wall as he did. *Hmm*, he thought, *tomorrow will be soon enough to ask about where that came from.* Rocco felt sleep coming on. The effects of too much of a good time had begun to take its toll in earnest.

It was good to forget for one night, he persuaded himself. *Good. Oh Dominick, I miss you, my son. Please pray for us, if you can.*

"All our actions take their hue from the complexion of the heart, as landscapes their variety from light."

Francis Bacon

NINE

Tony stepped off the curb, tripping into an unseen pothole covered by a thin layer of ice. The cold slush, remnants of an early December thaw, rushed uninvited into the tops of his black rubber overshoes. "Darn it!" he shouted in disgust. He reached into the icy-cold water to pick up his light gray cap, already damp from the drizzle, now saturated. It seemed that the whole world was conspiring against him, ganging up to ruin his day. In particular, it troubled him, especially on this day, of all days, the day before his wedding. Troubled thoughts raced unwelcome around well-traveled tracks. Nothing, not even the thoughts of his wedding day, could lighten the extra load of grief that Rabiso had added to his burden minutes earlier.

When Boss Rabiso had called him into his office, Tony, thinking it might be the usual Christmas bonus and perhaps an illicit bottle of bootleg liquor, had hurried expectantly into Mario's office. Once there, he found only a grim welcome. No turkey, no booze, not even a piece of candy awaited his expectations—only his agitated boss, for once sans cigar, frothing at the mouth. Tony already was late for his rendezvous with Gino.

Rabiso announced without ceremony, "One of our girls was killed early this morning, Laura Coratini. You know that cute brunette bimbo we picked up wandering around in Syracuse last month." Rabiso reached into his humidor for a cigar, grabbing one and offering another to Tony.

"No thanks, boss." Anxious, he asked, "How'd it happen?"

Tony snapped a match against his shoe, lighting Mario's cigar. Sulfuric gas from the wooden match filled the small office, mixing with the stench of the cheap stogie. The cigar's distinct and repelling aroma reminded Tony of the smell oozing off the once beautiful Mohawk River, another open sewer for Central New York. *Boy, I'm becoming the good soldier*, he mused. He let the thought quickly pass, returning focus to Rabiso.

Mario, showing his usual disagreeable self, changed lanes and capped it with a rare show of passionate concern. Gritting his teeth in anger, he bit through his cigar and took his dear time to answer, as he needed top concentration on clearing his head and take command of the situation. Mario thought, *It's not good for me, a boss, to lose his cool in front of the guys.* With head cleared and again in control, he finally spoke.

"That cute broad woulda made a lot of money for me. What a waste." Mario took a large, calming pull on the cigar, exhaling the putrid fumes. "Tony, she was killed by a John, and I want youse to look into it right now, *capice?*"

Tony hesitated, trying to think what his boss might want or expect. It was always healthier for the boss's soldiers to be prepared and alert while in his presence. *Is this one of those loyalty tests Mario is always mentioning?* he thought guardedly. Shuffling on his feet, Tony spoke.

"Mario, I only saw her, maybe a couple a times. From what I recall, I agree that she was a real looker. If I find the no good that did this terrible thing, especially now at Christmas…" he hesitated. He took a deep breath to bide time, uneasy, treading carefully. *This thing might prove to be a messy personal problem. But I better not show Mario my concern,* he cautioned himself. It was always best to give the boss proper respect, especially under the circumstances.

"What exactly do you desire for me to do with this John?" Tony asked.

"Go and find Gino, ask around some. I already got Gino lookin,' but I need your brains on this. Someone's gotta know sometin.' Spread some money if you have to. Keep track and don't cheat me, or else. Go to her room; check it for any clues. The scumbag not only killed one of my best and newest assets, he took her whole night's take. Killing her is bad enough. That, at least, is chargeable to the cost of doin' business." His voice was a strained hiss, smoldering with anger. Staring at Tony, he said, "However, taking my money, that—well that, my Navy hero, is another story."

Mario sat sullen-faced, saying no more; he then made a slitting motion at his neck, leaving no doubt in Tony's mind about what had to be done.

"I'll get right on it, boss. But, boss," Tony turned back, apprehensive, as if it were an afterthought, "you know I get married tomorrow evening. If I can't catch the bum and put the matter behind me, can you get someone else to finish the job, just this once? I promise I'll make it up to you."

"Look, kid, you catch that bum tonight and don't make me worry. I plan to be there tomorrow to celebrate your wedding too. So be careful. I want to see you off to a good start with that beautiful redhead of yours. So I suggest that you worry more about me and not the no-good John, or for that matter your marriage. And Tony, stop puttin' the cart before the horse."

Mario paused, almost catching himself before saying, with what sounded as genuine concern, "Kid, be careful, ya hear?" It was so unlike Mario to show feelings.

Tony smiled, happy for the boss' sentiment, yet somehow the boss' niceness unnerved him. Did Mario know more than he let on? No matter, in the spectrum of things it was best if not healthier to be a good soldier and follow orders. Tony had often seen Mario change attitude midstream, turning on a dime. This was definitely not the right time to argue with him when he was trying to act almost human-like.

"I'll find him for you, boss. When I do, should I take him to the police?" The smirk on Tony's face spoke volumes. His question helped to break the ice.

"Get your smart tongue out a here," said Rabiso. "Bring him to the police; yeah, you just do that!" he chuckled, shaking his head. "Kid, you always crack me up with your smart mouth."

Tony's so much like my little brother, he thought. Mario's brother was killed in France near the end of the war, his body never found. *Maybe that is why I like the little Ginny.*

Of course, the police would be the last place they would bring the killer; the organization took out its own garbage. Tony knew this, saying what he did only to shake off his disgust at the unexpected dirty mission. Luckily, Mario had missed his real intent.

Justice in Utica, as administered in 1925, was mostly for white, Anglo-Saxon Protestants. The police, made up almost exclusively of WASP's and a few Irish, exercised little concern for what they considered low-life immigrants, especially Italian or Polish whores, even if they were only unfortunate kids caught up in the modern world's version of the sex slave trade.

Tony worked his way out of the warehouse. He thought with disgust, *All the cops will probably do, after gawking at the mangled naked body, is mark it down in their police log, and then go on drinking their Christmas eggnog. That is, most likely, after they beat down a few local merchants for some involuntary Christmas cheer.*

Forcing his return back to the present, Tony shook off these troubling thoughts. He walked over to a storefront and leaned against the wall, taking off his boots. He shook out the cold, dirty water, as if in after-thought. With socks soaked and his feet freezing, he snarled at a young man passing by who snickered at his dilemma. Tony gave him the finger and a menacing look, causing the snicker to evaporate along with the man, who quickly walked down Genesee Street to avoid a confrontation.

When Gino saw Tony coming up John Street, he ran to him. "You are late! Did ya hear? The Coratini broad was murdered!"

"Yeah, that's why I'm late. Any ideas about who did it? And think quick! I've got a wedding tomorrow, old pal."

Gino laughed, "Oh, that affair. Ya know I'm planning on attending it, too. Yeah, while you were pondering with Mario, I wuz on the job, earnin' my keep. So yeah, I've got a good idea. It cost me a twenty, but I got ya' a name and an address. The *stupitone* lives on Mohawk Street. My source said he was pretty liquored up and probably on some kind of dope. He's a big guy, a loner, works for the New York Central. He's a laborer, pretty strong, so this won't be no blasted piece a cake. Anyways, *paisan*, I don't want ta see your handsome mug bruised up before your big day." Gino rubbed the snot flowing from his nose onto his coat sleeve.

"You're disgusting! When the heck are ya' going to carry a handkerchief?"

"Can't afford to now, it's Christmas, and I just spent my last twenty."

"Be sure to tell Rabiso, he'll repay you after we find this freakin' fool. Who knows, maybe we'll hit the jackpot when we find him. Sometimes these quiet guys are good savers."

"Dreamer! Tony, if you ain't always the big thinker. Let's go find us a killer. I've got revenge on my mind, and it won't go away until my knife tastes some blood."

"Yeah, and I'll bet you have a song in your heart too. Anyway, Gino, thanks for the good work. You think maybe we should go tell Rabiso and get some more help?"

"Nah, we can handle it. He's only one guy."

"I hope you're right," said Tony.

"You got your knife with you?" Gino held out an extra knife in case.

"Yep, a knife, and better, this here pipe." Tony pulled at the pipe under his overcoat, hanging from his broad belt. With gusto, he swung the pipe, which was attached to a thick, one-inch chain about two foot in length, in a menacing twirl, barely missing Gino. "Yep, I'm more than ready."

"You dumb Dago, you nearly hit me!" said Gino.

"Look, my dummy friend! If I wanted to hit ya, you'd be on the ground, and very quiet for once. Not to mention bleeding."

Tony scoffed, hoping the false bravado would hide the fear that his mad adrenaline rush had yet to quell. He never liked the sickening rush he had before a fight, especially before a showdown with some unknown and probably very big guy.

Tony knew that it wouldn't be as easy as those three Irish kids. His mind involuntarily flashed back to that day five weeks earlier. *Why think of them now?* He wondered. *No, they were easy.* He enjoyed the memory of their pleading, calling helplessly for their precious mommies. He wondered if poor Dominick had called for his mother before he died. He pushed the maddening thought aside, figuring it didn't matter. "What is done is done" was his motto.

He could have just killed them like Gino suggested, but he wanted them to know why they were going to die. His adrenaline that time came after the deed, not like now. He'd even watched their funerals from afar, one by each satisfying one, so that he could see the pain suffered by their families. Terrible pain, he hoped, like his Rosa felt. In Tony's world, it was fitting justice that he had used the money he had taken from their bodies to help pay for the black overcoat he had bought Rosa.

"Vendetta," he muttered. "Italians invented the word, and I just helped perfect its meaning."

"You say something?" said Gino.

"No, nothing! Just wondering how we're going to do this, that's all." Feeling calmer now, Tony said, "We need a plan."

"Tony, I suspect that's why old man Rabiso sent you to run this job."

"Yeah, sure! Did ya get the booze?" Tony asked.

"Pal, when've I ever failed ya?"

Tony, now all business, "Gino, where'd ya say the John lives? We're wastin' time."

"Here it is," said Gino. The three-story tenement home served as a boarding house. Built in the mid 1850s and once probably the home for some prosperous merchant, it had fallen on bad times. The weather, despite the murkiness of early evening, was trying its best to turn into a snowstorm and a white Christmas. All prospects pointed for it to get gloomier.

"Let's just torch the place. It looks like it'll burn quick," said Gino. The cold night air produced white whiffs of vapor above his head like an afterthought as he spoke.

Tony said, "What are ya, crazy, you idiot? All we'll manage to do is kill innocent people, and worse, it won't guarantee gettin' this guy." Tony, furious, spat out his disgust, "Getting rid of one dumb whore-killer is enough for one night, but killing several innocent poor people is freaking asinine. Get serious, before they find two bodies!"

"Darn it, Lavalia, I was just kiddin' you. Though I bet torching this place would put both it and its occupants out of their collective miseries. Heck, this joint's even more disgustin' than that place you built above your father's garage."

"You mean the one my Rosa lives in until tomorrow?" Tony frowned, tired of the idle talk. "When're you ever going to stop talking and start ta thinking about how we're going to do this thing? What did you say the guy's name is?"

"Bagatano, Rufus Bagatano."

"Rufus, what the blazes kind a name is Rufus?" said Tony.

"How the heck do I know, and what do you care anyways? We're going ta eliminate this Rufus' bark sort of permanent like, ain't we?" said Gino.

"Aah," Tony grumbled at Gino's poor attempt at a joke, "I was only wondering, not looking for your stupid remarks."

"Tony, ole buddy, where's your sense of humor?"

"It left me earlier this evening, so don't pull my chops. I'm not in the mood."

"Like when are you ever in a good mood?" said Gino.

Tony ignored him; his glare was frightening as he signaled Gino to follow.

They crossed lower Mohawk Street and walked up the slippery wooden stoop, which was in bad need of repair. Tony nodded, motioning for Gino to step carefully. The front door was unlocked. They walked in, knocking at the first old, brown paint-chipped door they came to. An elderly lady opened it, peering through the poor excuse for a security chain, out the partial opening. "Yes?" she said, in broken English, "Can ah help ah yew boyz?"

"Yes, Senora," Tony said using his politest Italian, hoping to ease the situation. "Do you know if a Mr. Rufus Bagatano lives here? I believe he works for the railroad. He's an old friend of ours from the navy. A mutual friend said he lived here."

Gino nodded, trying to second-guess what might come out of Tony's mouth next. Tony was the thinker, he the follower. His job was easier and that was the way he liked it—follow and play along. The old woman's demeanor led them to believe that she was either the caretaker or the owner of the building.

"Ah yes, you've ah come ah to the right ah place. He lives on the third floor. I think I ah heard him ah come up ah the stairs ah few minutes ahgo. He was ah stumbling, so he may ah have ah been ah drinkin."

"That's wonderful; we haven't seen him since the war. What a wonderful Christmas surprise this'll be. Is it okay to go up to surprise him?"

"Sure, ah go right ahead. Be ah my ah guest," she said.

"Oh, Senora, before I forget, does he have a family or any bambinos? I wouldn't want to disturb them at this late hour, you know."

"Oh, no," she hissed, displeased at the continued distraction, obviously wanting to return to whatever she had been doing. "Mr. Bagatano, he ah lives alone. He'd make someone a good ah husband. He's seems ah gentle man and ah such ah hard worker. You know, he hardly ever ah goes back out once he's ah home." With that, she slowly closed the door without saying another word.

On the second floor stairway, Tony turned to Gino, whispering in his ear. "Gino, we got to find a way to get him out of the house. If we kill him here, the old lady can finger us. Maybe with some luck we can persuade the bum to come join us for a drink. Tell him all we want is the money he took, something like that."

Gino nodded his agreement, whispering, "You think of something, and I'll follow your lead."

They slowly climbed the dank-smelling stair, reaching the dimly lit, dreary third floor; one light bulb hung on a cord from the ceiling, exposing cracks and chipped paint. Tony, with gloved right hand, unscrewed the bulb from the socket. In the shadows, they carefully walked the hallway; a barrage of varied odors greeted their alert senses. They hugged the wall, counting off the doors just like the old lady had instructed, until they found the fourth door. The creaky wooden floor squealed with each cautious step, making a mockery of their attempt at stealth. At the fourth door, Tony could feel the raised paint chips by the touch of his ungloved hand. He knocked lightly, three times, yet the door still shook from age. No one answered.

"Open up, Rufus ole buddy, we know that you're in there, the landlady told us," said Gino.

From behind the door, a gruff deep voice responded in broken English, "What'sa you business?"

Tony responded, "Police, Rufus, we need to take you to the station for some questions. Open the door or we'll have to break it down."

Through the thick door, Rufus responded, "I didn't do nuttin,' so leave me be. I don't want to hurt you, and I'm not going to any stinkin' jail."

Tony said, "Who said anything about jail? Bagatano, all we want is to ask a few questions regarding the murder of a whore we found on Mary Street. Someone said you were in the vicinity and fingered you as one of her customers close to the time of her murder. We're hoping you might have seen something. You know, shed some light into our investigation. So come on now, open the door, it's almost Christmas, and we all have better things to do."

Bagatano hissed through the door, "Go away, I have nuttin' to tell you. And since when have you coppers cared about Dago whores?"

"Who said she was a Dago? Right now you aren't in trouble, but if you resist talking, well, then it's a different story," Tony replied, looking at Gino, whose look was one of general disdain. However, Gino was not surprised by his friend's quick thinking.

"Are you deef?" Bagatano said. "I can't help ya! Now go away. I'm tired and drunk and you're beginning ta tick me off. I know my rights, so go get a warrant."

Under his breath, Tony sputtered, "That good for nothing..." In a loud voice, accompanied by rapid banging on the door, he yelled, "Open the door, you sorry mutt! You, friend, are going to the station, if we have to drag you."

Gino grinned, taking Tony's signal. His bulky, 180-pound muscular body was much bigger than Tony's 140-pound frame. This was the moment where brawn, not brains, became necessary. He placed his right foot on the door for leverage, practicing, like a place kicker, and then gave it a solid kick. The old door gave way, its semi-rotted frame caving inwards. Both men burst into the dark room, knives out. They stopped suddenly, staring at a small handgun, a .32 caliber, aimed at Gino. Without a second thought, Tony leaped into the room, tackling the larger man. Bagatano, unnerved, hit him square in the face. Tony, tasting blood in his injured mouth, was no match for the six-foot brute, who took up a large part of the twelve-by-twelve room.

Tony leaped up and quickly reached under his coat for the pipe. He swung it hard, hitting Bagatano's gun hand. The impact made a cracking sound, hitting the big man's lower arm. With a grunt, Rufus dropped the gun, his wrist broken. He lumbered at Tony like a wounded bear, more than ready to tear off his head with his good hand. The pipe dropped from Tony's hand, clanking noisily on the floor. Tony felt helpless—as the brute closed his massive arms around him, and despite losing the use of one wing, began to literally squeeze the life from him.

Thoughts, unpleasant and brutal, raced through Tony's overworked mind. *That poor girl must have also felt this brutes strength. That explains why her throat was crushed.*

Tony tried to reach for his knife, which had fallen on the floor, but he couldn't. Then he heard a loud clunk, a sickening sound. Begging a forgotten saint to come to his aid, and praying it wasn't Gino that was hit, he tried to see through blurry eyes bulging from the pressure of the big man's arms. Then Tony felt sudden relief. He could breathe again and better yet, see again, though his vision was blurred. It felt good. Blood oozed like Niagara from his nose; it felt broken and hurt like the dickens.

"Tony, you okay?" asked Gino.

"Yep, it took ya long enough! The bozo almost killed me."

"Well, sorry, I had a hard time finding the freakin' pipe. The bum must ta accidentally kicked it aside when he grabbed ya. He may be tough, but his head sure ain't!"

Tony leaned over, blood dripping; some, no doubt, flowed through the wide cracks on the old, bare wooden flooring. He picked up the dropped gun. "Check his pockets for Rabiso's money. I'll look around the room to see if there's anything worth taking. I think I'll keep this, as evidence." He tried to laugh. It hurt too much. He quickly shoved the gun into his coat's left side pocket.

"What if he comes to? I don't want to take a chance."

Tony said, "Aah, how stupid can you get, then hit him again. Hit the slob now if you want to. I don't give a rat's behind what you do."

Gino said, "No, darn it; get your head straight. We've got ta somehow get the brute downstairs. We can't leave him here. Let's pretend like he's drunk. You know, like we're going out to do some more drinking."

"Good thinking, but do you think anyone for three blocks didn't hear the darn racket?" asked Tony.

"Who cares, it'll be Rabiso's problem. I'm sure he'll buy them all off with some food, favors, or whatever," said Gino.

"Yeah and probably a few threats too. But whatever we do, we can't leave him here. Did you find the money?"

"Yep, Tony boy, what he probably took and a lot more. You find anything?" A giant grin etched Gino's hardened face.

"This guy's a real piece of work; he hid some money in his mattress, like no one ever looks there. Whatta you say we split this for ourselves and return that bundle to the boss?" said Tony.

"Policeman Tony," Gino snickered. "Yep, that'll be the day, Tony the cop. It's fine with me, now let's get this lug awake and standing."

Tony hissed, "Stop the joking and get serious. We've got a bit more to do tonight. And don't forget, I've got a wedding to go to in a few hours."

Gino smiled. His sinister look didn't match his smile.

They somehow got Bagatano up and standing. Tony pressed the handgun into the big man's ribs while Gino let him lean on his shoulder for support. The three made a comical picture, but it was one o'clock in the morning, and hopefully no one would bother to care or take notice.

"You crazy jerks, you cracked my skull. I need to see a doc," Bagatano, dazed, spoke in a barely audible voice.

"That's where we're taking you. First a doctor and then to the police station," chided Gino. "Now shut up, ya hear, or my friend, Policeman Tony here, is just looking for an excuse to plug you with your own gun. That is, if you continue to resist arrest. And that's a promise, you big gorilla. It's one promise I figure my partner or me will definitely keep if you continue your babblin.'"

Tony continued to push the snub nose deep into Rufus' ribs, giving a good hard poke in time with each of Gino's words. Tony's voice mocking, "Bagatano, you broke my nose, so there's nothing more I'd like to do than lay you out permanent-like. You know, to play with the worms and maggots. Git my drift, paisan? So just give me an excuse and so help me: Jesus, Mary and Joseph," Tony slipped into broken English, "you're a dead man." *Why the charade? This punk'll be a dead man in a few minutes. It don't matter none if I make the galoot suffer, like he probably did the girl. I'll enjoy this.*

The old landlady opened her door, peering out like a cat at a mouse, in time to see her staggering tenant in the dim light, supported by the two visitors.

"Is he ah okay?" she asked.

"It appears, Senora, Rufus might have taken a fall or was in a fight earlier. It's a good thing we came when we did. I fell trying to pick up the big guy, and my nose started bleeding when I hit the floor. As I remember, he can be a mean drunk. And he sure is heavy when he's unconscious. We're taking him to the hospital, now that we've got him sobered up some."

The old lady closed the door, not buying any of it, surmising quickly it would be healthier to look the other way. *Tomorrow, if he doesn't come back, I'll put up the 'for rent' sign,* she pondered, returning to her bed. *Well good, Bagatano paid through the month; maybe, with luck, I can gain a week.*

Tony and Gino brought Bagatano to an alley behind a closed cafe. It was about two o'clock in the morning. Nothing nearby was open. It was now snowing heavily. Snowflakes began to cover everything. All was still and quiet except for their voices, which seemed to carry with the wind.

Tony said, "Stop here, this looks like as good a place as any. Do you have the booze?"

Gino answered, "Yep, right here. Want a chug before we waste it? Boy oh boy, this big slob is sure heavy." He handed the half pint of sour mash to Tony, who quickly unscrewed the top. He could barely hear above the wind. He took a quick swig. "Geez Louise, why do you buy the worst crud you can find?" asked Tony.

"Did you forget about the Prohibition? It wasn't easy finding even this stuff. And why use good booze for what we're using it for?"

"Bagatano, have a drink," said Tony.

"Shove it, you're no cops."

"Wow, listen ta this genius. Did he really think we're cops?" Gino laughed, grabbing the bottle from Tony. "Here, you jerk, take a big squeeze. It's free, and more than you gave to that sixteen-year-old whore you killed. Why did you do it?"

"Because I could, that's why. Why do you care anyway?" Rufus's eyes bulged from fear, anticipating, waiting, and wondering why these two were taking so long. He knew he was about to die. He almost hurt too much to care.

"Well *stupido*, it's simple. She was slated to become one of our best girls, a prime asset to our business, you see. And you, you big buffoon, you took away our asset, and worse, the bosses' money. Now ya brute, ya gotta pay the fiddler 'cause the tune is done," said Gino.

Tony just watched, disgusted, tired, and hurting. He couldn't figure what the clicking sound he heard in his ear was…click…click…click…annoying… penetrating. Feeling like a fool he realized, with sudden clarity, that it was his teeth, uncontrollably chattering. *Is it from my fear or the cold?* It didn't matter. He needed to move on before he went nuts with anxiety.

The wind was the only thing interrupting the alley's inhabitants. It swooshed its steady cold breath, penetrating, stinging Tony's ears and numbing his noticeably swollen face. He no longer tasted his own salty blood. *Well, at least the cold is good for something.* He unconsciously pulled up his coat, wishing suddenly he had remembered his woolen scarf.

"Hey, Officer Gino…or is it Officer Dagowitz?" Tony chided. "Come on, and let's get this over with. I need to put some ice on my nose and get cleaned up," said Tony.

Not a second after Tony finished his comment; Gino hit Rufus from behind with Tony's pipe. The impact crushed his skull, and he fell with a thud, dead as the girl he had killed a few hours earlier.

"He won't bother our girls again," announced Gino with a hiss of pride.

Tony, in a voice deliberately low, replied, "Nope, I don't think so. Now hurry, drag the body behind those boxes and turn out his pockets. Make it look like a robbery. Pour some more of that crummy booze on him too. Good." Tony directed, and Gino followed. "This snow will cover everything up, but scratch out your foot prints just in case."

"Yeah, sure, whatever ya say! Holy cow, what's that stink? I think he crapped in his pants."

"In every life, it happens, Gino, my friend! Just make sure it won't happen to us."

Sarcastically, "Thanks for the advice. I'll let you know if I give a hoot." Gino shot Tony the bird, but it was barely visible from the dim light coming from the street lamp.

Tony took one last unfeeling look at the corpse sprawled before him, thinking, *Another day's work, another day's dollar, another memory to keep me awake nights.*

Tony motioned, "Gino, now help me get to a place where I can wash up, I don't feel so good." Tony, swaying like a boat on a windy day, looked terrible. Gino, now past all the excitement, noticed the extent of his friend's wound for the first time.

"Come on, friend. It looks like I've got my work cut out to get you cleaned up and back to normal. I'll have you looking pretty for that beautiful bride of yours before you can say spaghetti." Gino tossed the bloodied pipe into a nearby trashcan.

Tony just shook his head. It was hard to focus. All he wanted to do was to lie down.

With Gino's aid, they slowly walked to Mary Street and into one of the Rabiso whorehouses, still active with early-morning business and festive with Christmas decorations. "Maybe," Gino said sarcastically, "we can still have a bachelor party before the new day breaks. Oh, before I forget, my friend, Merry Christmas!"

"Same to you, Gino, but it's not quite Christmas."

"It is for you, my almost-married friend." Gino stuffed all the money they had taken from Bagatano into Tony's large overcoat pocket, a little over $200. Gino, smiling his broad, ugly grin, stated matter-of-factly, "Rabiso said if we found anything when we took care of this guy that you were to have it as an added bonus and wedding gift."

Tony wondered, *What would Rosa think about this blood money? I doubt she'd ever approve.*

Without thinking and too hurt to care, he babbled, "Coratini's fate could've been my Rosa's."

"What did ya say?" asked Gino.

"Nuttin,' just get me to someplace warm. My face feels like it's on fire. *Right now I don't give two cents for what anybody thinks.* He needed a soft place to lie down; however, first they needed to stop his nosebleed.

"Things never go so well that one should have no fear; and never so ill that one should have no hope."

Turkish Proverb

TEN

Thursday, December 24, 1925, began like any other day, nothing special when one was poor and had to work. For most, the morning snow flurries were just another obstacle in another hard day, compounded with the added burden of shoveling the never-ending snows of Upstate New York.

Tonight, many Christians would go to their churches of choice to celebrate the birth of Jesus. For most of the Italian immigrants living in East Utica, the 24th marked the beginning of the festival of Christmas. For twelve days thereafter, whether hard at work or not, they would rigidly stick to their traditions, giving small, inexpensive gifts of fruit and nuts and pastries, playing games, and eating traditional foods and treats. But for Rosa, this particular Christmas Eve marked what was hoped to be a new beginning, despite bothersome lingering doubts.

The stove's bustling early-morning fire fought valiantly to warm the apartment's bleak dreariness. However, the cold sting of a New York winter fought back mercilessly, winning at every turn. Rosa added more wood to aid the burning coals, but it did little to relieve her discomfort. Cold cloudy wisps, a bi-product of her breathing, floated above, as if to underline the room's uninviting atmosphere. She put water in a pan, thinking hot tea would help. In a few minutes, her first cousin, Nellie Tedesco, newly arrived from Missanello, would come over to help prepare for her big day, and hot tea would surely be needed to help warm her.

Rocco had left early for his primary job stoking coal into the furnaces at County Hospital. Upon leaving, he had said, feeling somewhat sorry for himself, "Look at me, a great cobbler, working as a pitiful stoker of fire for $10 a week. Princess, I swear to the Lord above," his hand pointing defiantly at the uneven ceiling, "someday, I shall have a proper shop. You'll see, Rosa, you'll see." He seemed animated, so excited, and yet the sadness in his voice gave away the deep melancholy that even his forced enthusiasm could not smother.

"Papa, did you remember to tell your boss about your important part in the wedding tonight? You know, so that you could get out of work early, maybe at noon," she hinted.

Smiling, he scolded, "Rosa, my special Rosa. Sometimes, so much like your mama, so organized." He patted her head like he had always done for as long as she could remember. Then he made a gallant bow and gently kissed her cheek. He looked directly into her eyes, his face aglow with reassuring paternal love. "Don't you fear; I'll be there to walk you down the church aisle."

Rocco hesitated, in a voice temporarily unsure, "The boss says I can leave at three. I know it's not what you'd prefer, but it'll still give me plenty of time to get home, wash, and change into my Sunday suit." He chuckled, desperately trying to conceal his shame and disappointment.

Deep down, Rocco had grave doubts about Tony. But a deal is a deal, and Rocco Ameduro could always be counted on to honor an agreement. Shuddering with rumbling deep inside his gut, he hid his inner turmoil, passing it aside as simply remorse at losing an only daughter to a husband.

Regaining his composure, Rocco said, "With the wedding set for six o'clock, I'll be there with, how you say, bells on, a sad smile for giving away my precious daughter, and a happy face for gaining a new son."

Rosa, now serious, said, "Papa, you're always smiling." She made a wide swing of her arms; taking in the cold, bare room. "Is this really what you expected? You know, when you first decided to come here?"

"Princess, I would be a giant liar if I said yes. I have always wanted more for us than this, this seemingly forever blasted poverty." His strong arms drew her close to him. Rocco found the right words difficult, feeling the awful sting of his self-imposed guilt and failure. "I constantly think about your mama. I'm very lonely for her. And poor Dominick, what did my poor boy ever do to deserve to die? Yes, daughter, your questions are fair, and believe me, it does bother me. So what am I to do, be sad all the time? We are stuck here and must make the most of it. To do this each day allows me to make it through each day, which I tell myself is one day closer to my goal. It only hinders to let my sorrow interfere with what's happened. So, Princess, I must choose to stay happy in the eyes of others. Except, as usual, it appears that I cannot hide my concerns from you. You, young lady, are too wise for your age and know me all too well."

"Papa, please stop!" Rosa gently scolded, stepping back to look at him, and gently holding her father's hands in hers. "You have done your best. And really, this country, if we are able to survive its prejudice and difficulties, has more to offer us than old Missanello, don't you think?"

"Rosa, you're wise with that sharp mind you carry. You see it's like this. If I remain positive, maybe it'll help make the pain easier to bear. Think on this as a good lesson, maybe even a final lesson from your papa before your life and your altered last name changes. But, you know, I am richer than most. For I have a beautiful daughter and a loving wife and most of all, a loving God. Rosa with God and familia, what more do I need." He kissed her again and left, swiftly closing the door, rubbing away the tears that Rosa hadn't missed.

Water was boiling on the stove, and the room began to enjoy gradual warmth. Rosa, having worked steadily since Rocco left, needed a short break for food. She put some tea in a mug to let it steep; its pleasing aroma mixed invitingly with the aroma of Italian bread toasting on the stove. The scent filled the small room, almost, but not quite, civilizing it. She wasn't very hungry, only nervous and unsure. She spread butter on her toast and nibbled at it. The sweet taste satisfied the hunger, but not her apprehensions. A troubled mind filled with doubts upset the equilibrium she needed to prepare for tonight.

Searching intensely with her mind's eye, she tried with extreme difficulty to comprehend her misgivings, carefully dissecting each thought. When she tried to shake away the doubts, they came back, uninvited, crashing uncontrollably an already weakened equilibrium. She needed to think this uneasy feeling through, to understand it, dissect it. Despite the past nine months that she had known Tony, she realized with ever revealing frustration that she really knew very little about him. However, thinking as her father's daughter, she rationalized that a deal is a deal. Therefore, she could not let Rocco or more important her papa down.

Unable to stifle the cobwebs of confusion, she reflected upon what she did know. Tony's job at Rabiso Fruit and Vegetable Company seemed to pay well, yet his hands were not that of a laborer. She wrestled with the fact that he was not educated enough to work in the office. He had bragged to her once how he had only finished sixth grade before having to go to work to help his family. Yet he did run away to the Navy where he spent two years. Maybe he learned things there. She tried to reassure herself. *Tony's a smart man, street-smart, and deep down I know he is kindhearted. I've seen his good side. Yet his mysterious side still lingers, cold and alarming, and also frightening and dark.* She wrestled with her feelings, mixing reason with hope. *He hides it well, maybe too well. Oh, why am I doing this, looking for reasons, faults, and bad things about this man who tonight I marry, forever. Forever!* The reality of the word "forever" upset her fragile balance, giving her pause.

A sharp knock on the door shook her from her doubts. Crossing the cold, creaky, unleveled floor, she opened the heavy door. Nellie entered quickly, beaming with excitement, trying to keep the blasting cold air from coming into the room. Despite her valiant efforts, the room immediately dropped five degrees. Like Rosa's worries, the chill was uninvited, unwanted. And like her worries, she purposely ignored the discomfort.

Nellie, grinning, carried her best clothes to dress later. They hugged and squealed like girls their age should. "Nellie, I'll bet you'd like some hot tea and some toast to go with it?"

Smiling, Nellie gladly accepted the fragrant brew, sipping her tea, enjoying its warmth. "Isn't the snow beautiful?" Nellie said.

"It was to me, too, that is, at first. You'll soon find that it gets old after you are here a while."

"So dour, and it's your wedding day." Nellie shook her head in friendly mockery. "Rosa, what am I to do with you?"

Nellie, a year older than Rosa, was not just a first cousin; she was also her best friend. They had grown up together in Missanello, playing and working, always more like sisters than cousins. Nellie's mother, Sarah, Rocco's younger sister, had died five years earlier. Nellie had come to America with her aunt and uncle from her father's side.

Nellie planned to work to repay them for the passage, and Rosa had put in a good word for her at the mill where she would start the first week of the New Year. Rosa rejoiced at having her near again.

"Let's sit and talk a while. The work can wait for a moment," said Rosa.

"Are you excited? You sure don't seem so," said Nellie.

"I suppose I am. Yet I have doubts. Is this bad?"

"Rosa, I have no experience in things like this. I would suppose that your feelings are normal. The most important thing is do you love him?"

"I do like him a lot, but I don't really feel I love him. I have felt at times that I might, but I really know so little about him. Am I wrong to be so honest?"

"Look, Rosa, to like him is good. After all, this is an arranged marriage. First you are told about him, then hopefully you begin to like him, and then, with luck, someday you will grow to love him. That's how it's supposed to work. It's probably the same for Tony. It's our way, it always has been."

Nellie felt like a lawyer arguing a case that she did not believe. She saw the doubt reflected in Rosa's face attesting that she didn't buy it either.

"I know what you say, cousin," Rosa answered politely, going through the motions. "It's the way we are, that same old way. Here in this new country things are a bit different. Here, dear cousin, most couples have honest courtships, where a man or a woman is free to decide who they'll marry. I have been told there are still some arranged marriages, but I am also told, that is becoming a rarity. Truthfully, deep down, I wish I had more of a say, all tradition aside."

"Don't think like this! It's unhealthy. Everything will be fine. You'll see," Nellie said.

Rosa's voice was both strained and animated. "Yes, I keep telling myself the same thing, over and over. I know I need to do this. Yet, I fight with myself constantly. Asking, why do I need to do this? And as if that's not enough, then I ask, for what? It certainly isn't because I truly love him. I only like him, that's all, and this is why I am worried."

"And what, cousin, do you see as the right decision?" Nellie, not as pretty as Rosa, yet beautiful in a plain, girl-next-door kind of way, brushed aside her long black hair. She stared, her pert jaw set firmly, patiently awaiting an answer.

Answering in a non-assuring tone, Rosa replied, "I suppose that I must marry Tony. I've no real choice, so why fight it? We may live in America, but their ways are not our ways, at least not yet. And I figure that it'll be good to relieve Papa from the extra burdens and expense. Perhaps, in time, I can even ask my husband to help to get Mama here. Papa is brave and always trying to hide the pain he carries. But believe me when I say this; he's very sad and lonely without her."

Sipping her tea, Nellie reached over the table to touch Rosa's hand. "Rosa, I promise, you'll be fine. Now let's forget this distressful talk and get ready for the wedding. We have too much work to do to leave room for worry."

Rosa said, "Yes, that's an understatement. And as soon as we finish here, I promised to help Tony's mother. I made several cookies, like the ones Mama used to make for special occasions. Would you like to have one?"

"I thought I smelled cookies through this terrible cold. Are they as good as Aunt Antoinette's?" asked Nellie.

"Better," Rosa answered without hesitation, handing Nellie two.

Nibbling a small piece from the chocolate cookie, "This is fabulous; you'll need to give me your secret." She quickly ate both, savoring their texture. "Can I have another?" Without waiting, Nellie reached for a moist chocolate drop cookie, topped with an almond.

"Eat up; we've a couple of stitches left to complete my wedding dress and a lot more." Rosa's forced smile and building enthusiasm brightened the gloomy room, along with the morning sun that crept through the small, lone window, making the room seem a bit warmer.

The Lavalia house was a flurry of moving hands, all working diligently to Giovanna's rapid orders. She was in total command of her environment and the queen of her home. The kitchen, a center of activity, was ripe with a mixture of flavorfully mingled smells, resonating with hints of garlic, oregano, and basil, and pecorino-romano and provolone cheeses. Chicken fried slowly on the stove and spaghetti was boiling. Ravioli and ham, beans and squash, pumpkin and apples lay on the table, all lined up like soldiers awaiting orders. The list of foods for the wedding reception and feast was long and seemingly endless to everyone but Giovanna.

Tony hesitantly opened the door to the kitchen, his eyes brightening upon seeing the enthusiasm. Brothers and sisters immediately surrounded him as he quietly tried to enter the kitchen. Outside, he had briefly talked to Joseph and Vincent, who were shoveling the walk with Pop. Somehow they had all managed to get the day off from work.

Giovanna gasped, "What happened to your face?"

"An accident at work, Ma, I'm fine. I was lucky it wasn't worse." *You'll never know how lucky*, he thought. "You know me, Ma, I can be clumsy."

He hesitated, searching for the right words. "I guess I was tired and my mind was on the wedding and not the proper placing of crates." He thought, *How easy it is to lie. Yes, I'm very good at it*, he complimented himself, seeing that his explanation was taken as fact.

"Well son, let me see it. Why didn't you come home earlier? It's almost noon. Don't you finish around midnight?"

Tony began to answer his mother but was interrupted by her shout to his sister Cora. *Good*, he thought, *more time to practice my story. I sure hope Gino remembers what we agreed on. Ma's sure to say something to him tonight.*

"Cora, go to the medicine cabinet. Get some alcohol and iodine. I need to repair your brother."

Giovanna frowned with a mother's genuine concern, "Antonio, I think you may have broken your nose."

"Ma, you worry too much. I'll be fine. I only hope I can explain it to Rosa."

"I'll tell her about my clumsy son when she comes over. She'll be here in a few minutes. You will have to get out of here."

"Why?" he asked, surprise on his face.

"Because it's supposed to be bad luck to see the bride before the wedding."

Tony grumbled, yet in a teasing way, "What a bunch of garbage, how can seeing her be bad luck? What's this, some Sicilian hocus-pocus?"

"Never you mind, just do as I say," Giovanna scolded, pinching his ear, pulling it gently, but not tugging at it like she did when he was younger.

"Okay, why are you home so late? You think I forgot?"

"First Ma, I'm almost a married man. I don't need to explain myself to you anymore. Next, to answer, and I point out to only appease you and yes, maybe because it's only right, I stayed the night at Gino's. The accident happened late last night, so rather than come home and wake everyone, I chose to take Gino up on his offer to help."

Listening, Giovanna was surveying Tony's facial wounds sighing, she said, "Madonna, Tony, as long as you live here you will answer to me, *capice*? And by the way, your friend did a lousy job on that pretty face."

"Ma, tonight I surprise Rosa with our new flat on Mary Street. My face will not matter. So there." He laughed smugly.

Giovanna hit him gently in the arm. "What am I to do with you?" Concentrating on his face and shaking her head, she rubbed hard on the wounds with a moist hot cloth.

"Ma, that hurt! Why did you do that?" Tony reached for his face, trying to quell the returning pain. He had thought it was under control, until Giovanna's attentions.

"Watch your mouth in my house. Remember, I know what you're thinking. Your nose was crooked. I straightened it. Now you'll soon be my handsome boy again, but not today; today, you look dreadful. Antonio, of all the times to get hurt, why must you choose your wedding day?"

She looked to the ceiling, calling reverently to the Lord and the Holy Mother, shaking her head like an avenging angel. "Faa, what shall I do with you?"

"Well, Ma," he chuckled mischievously, "you could give me a big hug and one of your wonderful kisses, and…maybe a piece of that pumpkin pie would work to ease the pain you just stirred up."

"What a child! My heart goes out to Rosa. Soon you'll be her problem. Good riddance, I say," she said with a grin, patting him gently with a parting tap from her large wooden spoon, today her weapon of choice. Then, quick as a wink, she reached to the pie, cutting Tony a generous slice.

"Now eat, and then go wash. And remember; do not come out to see Rosa. I'll tell you when it's safe," she scolded.

Following Father Rossellini, Tony walked out from the vestry room with brothers Vincent and Joseph closely behind. Saint Mary Mt. Carmel Church seemed more beautiful than he could remember. Festive holiday candles were lit, casting a joyful mood upon the altar and throughout the church. He could see parents and siblings sitting in the front pew, regal and resplendent in their Sunday best.

His face hurt like fire. Earlier he had winced seeing it in the mirror. He looked like a street tough, black eyes and all. *Well, I guess that's what I am. So be it. I don't care; I only wanted to get this over with. I think I love her, but who knows? And then there's still my California dream.* His thoughts ran together like a bad blend of stale wine with memories of California, the Navy, Bagatano, the Irish kids. He shook it off.

He lined up as he had been instructed earlier, with his brothers and the priest, *like soldiers awaiting the firing squad,* he thought. Tony caught his first glimpse of Rosa as the piano started the wedding march. Her face, covered slightly by a white veil, seemed mysterious and also stunning. Her dress, beautiful and flowing, made her look even more elegant. Slowly she walked, her arm in Rocco's, following Nellie and his sister Cora, each resplendent in their homemade gowns, each glowing and happy.

Reaching the altar, Rocco presented Rosa to Tony after saying, "I do," those infamous words a father must answer to the dreaded question, "Who gives this bride to be married to this man?"

Rocco, with only a father's grave reluctance, stepped back and wiped a lone tear rolling down his haggard face. Though he tried to hold back his emotions, it was soon followed by many more sobs. They spoke volumes about his love for his only daughter. He was exhausted because his boss had made him work twice as hard to get off early. It had been worth every moment, for he wanted to please his princess.

Glancing at Tony's damaged face, Rosa was startled. She took a deep breath, somehow willing herself to get past the surprise, wondering how he had injured himself.

Giovanna, so engrossed in the preparations for the reception, had forgotten to tell her. Luckily, the fragrance of the flowers cascading the altar, a gift from Tony's boss, allowed her mind to drift and then to focus on happier, positive thoughts.

Standing alone at the altar, hand in hand, she stared into Tony's puffy eyes and slightly bent nose, smiling as he put the gold ring around her finger.

Tony, through his pain, tried to keep poised. *Just a few more minutes,* he thought. The throbbing raced through his body, accentuated by the rush of adrenaline and excitement. Despite all the unease and self-imposed tension, especially heightened after seeing Rosa, things almost seemed good this Christmas Eve. *Maybe I'm doing the right thing after all.* Still, he felt like a cornered rat at a cat circus.

Father Rossellini pronounced them man and wife, and then wished everyone a very Merry Christmas as he presented Mr. and Mrs. Anthony Rocco Lavalia for the first time. The wedding ceremony was over and their bonds of matrimony snapped shut on any of the lingering doubts the new couple may have had.

The reception was held in the church basement. All the food and beverages had been carried in Mr. Rabiso's borrowed truck, along with ample fruit and vegetables from his company. There was plenty of homemade wine and punch on the scattered tables and several flasks of illegal liquor.

Standing in the reception line, Rosa leaned to kiss Tony's cheek carefully, mindful of his injury. "What happened to you?" she whispered, unable to wait another moment.

He shook his head in dismay and whispered back, "Ma didn't tell you, did she? I was hurt last night at work."

"You poor thing! Tonight, I'll make it better," she hinted with an impish grin. Tony winked, sending his unspoken approval.

In the reception line, Rosa noticed a man she had never seen before. The mystery was solved quickly when Rocco introduced him as Louis Sibroli, recently returned from their village. His story was a familiar one. He had come to the United States as a boy, sometime around 1910. He was later forced to return to Italy when conscripted into its army in 1917. Citizens of Italy living in the United States were not protected from the draft just because they were in a foreign country. Treaties between Italy and the U.S.A. agreed to return anyone called to serve his country in time of war. Since the United States had not yet entered the conflict, he had been turned down when he tried to join its fledgling army, missing the American Declaration of War on Germany by only a month.

Louis Sibroli had served honorably, even had met Rocco when they both served in the same unit, which had most of Missanello's men. He was wounded in Austria soon after and still carried the bullet in his shoulder.

It took Louis five years to save enough money for a return passage to rejoin his immediate family in Utica. Ironically, he was a friend of the Lavalia family through cousins and had been invited to the wedding at the last minute.

Nellie sidled up to her cousin, another cookie in her hand asking, "Rosa, who is this man?" motioning to Louis. "I think I may remember him from back home."

"His name's Louis Sibroli, and yes, you're correct. Papa said he served with him briefly in the army during the Great War."

"Would you mind introducing him, if you get a chance? Please, Rosa would you do this for me?"

Rosa looked at her cousin, seeing her excitement. "Of course, I'll play Cupid for you," she said, eyes bright, suppressing a smile. "But Nellie, he's much older than you. Don't you think?"

"Not much older than your Tony is, I'd say. And anyway, who said I wanted to marry him? I just want to meet him, especially when I look so nice."

With keen assurance, Rosa left Nellie and coyly slipped next to Louis. She spoke briefly to him, grabbed his right arm, and directed him to Nellie, making introductions.

Acting surprised, Nellie immediately started talking nervously, about anything, everything. She couldn't stop.

Louis stood amused, happy to have this effect on the pretty bridesmaid. They talked through the whole reception, to the exclusion of everyone else.

The church basement filled with excitement as time began to wane. The celebrants were told they would need to leave before the midnight Christmas Eve mass. Rosa grabbed Tony's hand, pulling him closely to her. Looking into his eyes, she said, "Husband, I believe we're really married, and I'm thinking that it's time to go."

Tony pulled her even closer, and kissing, they melted together as one. "It's time for us to have our dance and then for you to make your Bridal Money Dance."

"Must I dance with all those men? It's embarrassing," she chided. "And I only want to dance with you. Do you mind?"

"Who knows," Tony quipped in a warm whisper. "You may break a record because you're so beautiful."

Beaming, at that moment, Rosa could not love him more. She danced and danced the money dance. And as was the custom, relatives and friends handed her dollars for luck. The extra money would come in handy, and she was happy, having survived her shyness.

As the night began to wind down, Rosa felt a sudden uncontrollable urge to vomit. Her white pallor caught Giovanna's unerring eye. She rushed over to her daughter-in-law, a cup of punch in her hand.

Giovanna's voice resolute and teeming with genuine concern, asked, "Rosa, are you feeling ill? Your face looks flushed."

Rosa barely listened said nothing, too upset; more so, now that Giovanna had noticed.

Giovanna continued unrelenting, "It must be all the excitement. Have you eaten?" Giovanna gently took Rosa's arm, leading her to a quiet corner.

"I'm fine, Giovanna, though thank you for asking. It's all the excitement, that's all."

"Well then, what did you eat?"

"Some things, you know, a little here, a little there, but not much. I'll survive, don't be concerned."

"You must eat, but stay away from the wine," Giovanna chided.

"I'll eat, I promise, in a moment." Rosa did not want to hurt her new mother-in-law's feelings. In all honesty, she knew that she could not eat. For the last few days, often even the thought of food made her ill, especially in the morning. Initially, she had passed it off as an attack of nerves. Deep down she knew what it meant, and it frightened her.

Tony walked over to Rosa, grabbing her hand, gallantly kissing it. He looked at her wedding band and he held her hand, and then noticed her funk. "Rosa, are you okay? You look sad."

"No, everything is fine."

"Good, then are you ready for your next big surprise?"

"What surprise, Tony? Tell me, or must I guess in English again?" She giggled. Rosa loved surprises.

"No, *cara mia*, not this time, I promise. It'll be one improvement to your life that I feel you most definitely will enjoy. Though it'll have to wait for only a few minutes, for now we must wind down the festivities, and you, my dear bride, must throw away your bouquet. It's the custom here in America."

A look of confusion painted her face, "What do you mean, throw away the bouquet? They're beautiful flowers. Why would I want to throw good flowers away?"

"Honey, it's for good luck! It's an American thing, and as they say, when in Roma, do as the Romans do," he chided, adding, "The buzz is that the young woman fortunate enough to catch it is supposed to be lucky in finding a man. It's also rumored she'll be married within a year, or so tradition says. It's all in fun, and everyone gets excited."

She beamed, flashing Tony a wide smile, "Then I shall do it, Antonio." She then whispered into his ear, before giving him a tender kiss on his cheek. "Is it unfair to try to throw the flowers to a particular girl?"

"Hey, Doll, you do what feels good to you. Tonight is our night and now it is your special moment." Tony pulled Rosa close, and to the great applause of everyone, he kissed her passionately, a kiss lasting for at least five minutes.

When Mother threw the bouquet, she was sure to aim it at Nellie, who grabbed it up like a New York Yankee shortstop, clutching it to her vivacious chest. But then, that is another story. I once saw the pictures from the wedding. Everyone seemed so happy, even Father. I wonder whatever happened to those pictures.

"Courage is knowing what to fear."

Plato

ELEVEN

January 1, 1926, was not just any new year; it introduced the beginning of a new era, although the world didn't quite know it yet. Humanity, though, did get a hint of the immerging technology on the horizon when New York City and London, for the first time, celebrated the New Year together over a radio signal. Most people, including Rosa, did not know of this monumental event. In fact, it was the furthest thing from her mind.

Rosa hummed a mellow tune, working carefree in her new and mostly modern kitchen, preparing the evening meal. The second floor flat on Mary Street, with its four rooms and bath, seemed like a palace when compared to the old Second Street garage apartment still occupied by Rocco. Running water, a bathtub, a working flush toilet, a kitchen sink with plenty of room to wash a full set of dishes, and a new kerosene stove all awaited her beckoning. There was much to absorb, and absorb it she did, with a vengeance.

Tony had also purchased a good second-hand bed and a new mattress, which they christened several times in matrimonial bliss. In the bedroom was a beautiful mahogany dresser with a matching nightstand. And best of all, the new apartment had electricity throughout, with convenient electric plugs on the walls in each room. It wasn't the Ritz, but to Rosa it was a dream, and it was patently American.

Since the wedding, discovering their new abode and all its gadgets had kept her occupied. With the factory closed over the holidays, she had all the time she needed to give the flat her personal touch and full attention. Tony had showered her with the wedding money Mario had given, but had not shared the reason why. It, along with the numerous gifts and the money from the bridal dance, had amounted to a little over $320, a small fortune. Tony had spent most of it on furniture and household items, food and rent. Rosa had hoped to put $25, minimally, aside toward Antoinette's passage. However, Tony claimed they had spent everything establishing their new home.

Presently, she wished for nothing, except perhaps her monthly female curse, now long past due. Rosa nevertheless was excited over the anticipation of pregnancy and also frightened with the unknown. Her concern over the pregnancy's potential embarrassment took away some of her happiness especially the newfound freedom she was beginning to enjoy and crave.

She thought, *A baby will certainly be a burden. Hopefully, Tony will understand and be happy too.* Still reluctant to tell him and feeling a mild despair, she thought, *Maybe before I tell him, I'll wait another month.*

The past week had been a wonderful ride for the newlyweds. Tony also had the week off, and together they spent it as lovers, exploring and building their little love nest one moment at a time.

Tony had promised to give Rosa a proper honeymoon someday, but for the moment she did not care. She had reasoned earlier, "Where would we go anyway? The weather is blustery and cold; staying put is vacation enough." She had calmly calculated that wherever they might go would never be as much fun as just staying home and enjoying each other in their own soft, new bed. She giggled impishly at the unmentionable.

A large capon was slowly roasting in the oven. Its pleasant and inviting aroma, mixed with carrots, onions, potatoes, and a hint of garlic and basil, filtered throughout the flat.

Tony entered the kitchen, expectations high. With a big whiff of the anticipated dinner, he exclaimed, "Boy, that bird smells good. When do we eat?" His face still showed bruises, though the swelling and shiners were almost gone.

Teasing, she tenderly touched his face, "In a few minutes! Sit and talk, tell me what you're thinking; I never tire of hearing you talk."

"Well, looking at you with all that flour on your face and apron clinging to that pretty body of yours, and that cute smile, and you'd probably guess correctly that it's not the blasted chicken I'm thinking about."

Rosa sat next to him, melting her body to his. "Tony, I wasn't going to talk about this just yet."

"Talk about what?" he asked, showing sudden concern.

Rosa noted his jumpy demeanor. She thought, *Why does he react this way? So defensive, and I haven't said a word.* She decided it best to keep the concerns to herself, at least for the moment, preferring to think out a safer route to approach the subject.

"Well, something's bothering you," Tony said. "Let's have it."

She threw caution to the winds. "You know how I have been ill, mostly in the mornings."

"Yeah, sure, it has put a damper on things every once in a while. What of it? Are you feeling worse?" Tony had a sudden, dire surge of genuine concern, a rare experience for his callous nature. Nervous, he reached into his pocket for cigarettes, pulled one out, and struck a match from the box on the table. The match's overwhelming sulfuric smell filled the room.

Rosa reached for his arm, gently holding it. Curling up her face, showing temporary distaste, she spoke with frightful urgency, her eyes bright, yet pleading. "Please, don't smoke now. Do it for me, it makes me feel ill."

Looking at the sad sack face, he complied, shaking his wrist to douse the match. "Sure. Rosa, what's bothering you? Tell me, I don't bite. Yet I have a strange feeling it's more than my cigarette."

She blurted, "Tony, I think I'm pregnant."

"How?" he shouted, pushing her away to look at her. "We just got married only a week ago."

"How?" She looked thunderstruck. "Jesus, Mary, and Joseph, do you forget? Remember late last October?" She laughed, both amused and surprised at his reaction.

Tony said, "It was only once, and barely once at that."

"Well, while it may not have been all that special in light of the past week, it was apparently enough." Rosa's eyes looked pained. She feared his rejection, wishing she had played the charade for a little longer.

"So, my Antonio, I'm truly sorry about dropping this news on you, but now that the cat is out of the bag, tell me, how do you really feel about it?" Her eyes caught his, probing, unable to breach his reserve, now fully returned to its former self.

Pleading, she pushed, "You know," hesitating for a moment, she blurted, "about becoming a new papa?" She put both her hands gently to his cheeks, carefully avoiding his injury, and then reached for his larger hands, gently squeezing. He didn't squeeze back.

Tony caught himself; he was filled with dread and fear—the responsibility of fatherhood loomed like a tornado on his horizon.

With voice cracked and shaken. "Rosa, I had hoped we'd have children, many children, only not this soon."

Her voice resonated with hurt, reached a high soprano. "What're you saying?" Catching herself before she spoke, she kept what she preferred to say private. *Not now, Antonio, it's just my surprise. I'm sorry it's too much for you. Too sudden for you, when all you had on your mind was food and lust.*

She pushed aside a niggling dread. It was like she was seeing him for the first time, all over again. In her fear, she could almost smell the train station on that long ago day. It was a place in her memory once dreaded and now revisited. Her mind involuntarily wandered to the previous spring; she had seen him like this before, aloof, silent, inward, moody—all the temperaments that he hid so well were returned at this moment, now seemingly ten-fold.

"Rosa, I'm not going to say anything more. Your news is a bit too abrupt for me to grasp. Our child will be a very welcome addition to the family. I don't want you to think I'm unhappy. No, it's a good thing. You know…" he hesitated, trying to think, fumbling, searching for the right word. "It's just that I was just getting used to being a new husband. Now I have to get ready for a family. I suppose it'll be an adventure. I guess though that whatever I think doesn't matter." Silently he thought, *But I'm not ready for this.*

Tony, now standing, said, "Come here, Rosa." He reached for her, tenderly patting her stomach.

She smiled knowingly, then laughed, relieved.

"Soon enough, I'll have a big belly. Will you still love me then?" she asked coyly as she snuggled into him again. His aftershave made her ill. She shook it off, seductively whispering into his ear, "Tony, I love you."

Looking at her glow, he responded, "I love you, too."

She hugged him, clinging again for dear life. She said, "Okay, what is it that's on your mind?"

"Will you love me as much as now, when the baby comes?" he asked. His question, at least to him was a legitimate concern. Thinking of his mother, he shivered with the dour memories, unable to forgive Giovanna, who had spent all her time exclusively on each successive child to the detriment of the rest. "My ma is a good mother, yet she was a mother who could focus only on one child at a time and seemingly forgetting about Pa. She had nine kids, and each new pregnancy not only brought a new member to the family, it made the previous child's need for love and attention fall to us older kids. As the eldest, I had most of the responsibility fall upon my shoulders. Eventually I received the least affection and most of the responsibility. I don't want that for our children."

"I understand your concern and how it has affected you. You can be certain that I'll find the time to love you even more," she beamed, happy to have her secret behind her while also sympathizing for her husband's hurtful past.

Sudden apprehension lighted Tony's eyes. "We can't tell anyone for awhile, or they'll guess what we did before we were married."

Laughing, amused, Rosa replied, "You mean to tell me you don't really think your mother will be counting off the days until our 'premature' baby's born? I emphasize the word 'premature.'" She giggled. Tony's eyes absorbed her.

Smiling, he said, "I've no doubt you're right. My mother's like a Navy chief I once had the sad displeasure to know. Always watching, always bossing, always in control, and always getting his way, no matter what." Tony stood to wander the room, speaking rapidly. "You're right about Ma, of course. So what can we do? And when do you think the baby's due?"

Rosa stood next to him, counting off the months on her fingers, starting that October day. "I would think by the end of June, or mid-July, or maybe sooner. As for what we do, the answer is nothing other than what we usually do."

"Okay then, what do you say about telling everyone next month?"

She nodded approval.

"Whatever happens, happens." He raised his hands in surrender, accepting. "After all, this won't be the first time a baby comes early, and at least we're married."

A startling thought hit Tony like a lightening bolt, upsetting his equilibrium. "Tell me, did you know about this before we were married?"

"No, Tony," she lied. "I thought I was sick. It hit me today as the only logical reason after my monthly curse didn't arrive. I thought it was all the excitement:

you know, Dominick's death, the funeral, the wedding, Nellie coming. It all ran together, so fast, so soon. I haven't been eating right and I have been tired and hurt, excited, and then feeling guilty for being excited. Am I making any sense?"

Tony wiped a tear from her chin. "Why are you crying? I thought having a baby makes a woman happy. Heck, it's the only time I ever recall Ma being happy." Tony snickered at the comment. Giovanna's gloominess was universal.

She said, "No, my tears are tears of joy. I love you, I love you," she repeated, putting her head against his chest. "I was so frightened to tell you because I was embarrassed, selfishly for me, because everyone might know that I wasn't, you know, a virgin when we married."

Tony replied forcefully, "If it bothers them, they can all go to pick daisies. And who gives one fig what they think? So there." He patted her tummy again; with his finger he made a sign of the cross on her tummy. "Now can we eat? Before the bird gets any tougher than it looks?"

She kissed his lips passionately, her body clinging, and all pretenses at having a simple, quiet holiday dinner faded. "I suppose eating can wait," he said, laughing and without hesitation.

"I agree, but first I'll take our food out of the oven before it burns. We'll be sure to be hungry later," she kidded naughtily.

"Ah, Rosa, you are too practical. Maybe that's why I love you so."

Tony rolled over, reaching for the mahogany nightstand, grabbing a cigarette.

With a stern, coquettish look, Rosa pleaded, "Please, Tony, no cigarettes."

Sighing, he answered, "Okay again, I'll smoke outside in the hall."

"Can it wait until we eat?" Rosa said, gathering clothes strewn on the floor.

Okay, you win, I'll wait, I am still hungry," Tony's voice now filled with sarcastic urgency. "Please, don't become Ma. I left home to get away from her constant nagging."

"You can be assured I'll only be me and never your mama. Did Mama ever do to you what we just did?"

"Rosa, that's terrible. If you were my daughter, I'd have to wash your mouth out with soap."

Rosa jumped back onto the bed. Sweetly singing out his name, in a soft soprano, she hummed and played him like a fiddle.

"Antonio, did you ever love anyone else before sending for me?"

Here it comes, he thought, panicking and angry at the same time. *Why are women so possessive?* He kept to himself, thinking over an evasive, yet believable answer. "If you mean someone I wanted to marry, the answer is no. Why?"

"Oh, just wondering. You know, you're so much older and worldly, and obviously," she poked him, "so very experienced. But in a good way," she suppressed a giggle.

"Sure, I've had an experience or two. It goes with the territory, you know, when you're a man. But never one comparable to you; you, my little dear, are a she-devil." He tickled her; they rolled together like children on their disheveled bed.

Yelling for dear life, Rosa shouted, "Stop!" Laughing, and then sweetly, she asked, "Am I the best?"

"Rosa, this is too embarrassing, stop it," he pleaded.

She got the hint, letting the subject die. It would come back to haunt her later. Though she knew the rules seemed to differ for men, it bothered her that Tony had enjoyed the favors of other women. She wanted to believe it was all in the past and long before they were engaged.

She reassured herself that Tony was the first and only lover she'd ever need. And today loving him more was easier than yesterday, as each subsequent day created deeper feelings and new potential. Hers was a true love, happening quicker than even her dour expectations had imagined, arranged marriage worries aside.

She playfully pushed him off the bed. On the cold floor and sprawling, exhausted, Tony grinned like a schoolboy on the first day of summer vacation.

Rosa jested, "You know, Antonio Lavalia, it's said man cannot live by bread alone. We seem to have proven this wise old saying, yet I'm starving. Honey, how about dinner? Are you hungry for something other than dessert?"

"You bet," he said without hesitation, picking himself up from the wooden floor.

She jumped from the rumpled bed, quickly putting on clothes, and walked to the adjoining room that served as their kitchen. Tony followed.

"Tony, can you grab two plates from the cupboard?" she asked.

"Sure, Doll. Anything else, your royal highness?" he mocked, bowing.

She placed the large capon, pot and all, on the table. "Well, you could help by carving our feast," she directed.

"Slave driver," he complained, holding his hand to his heart. Picking up a sharp knife, he carefully carved the bird into sections, whistling a fine rendition of "Over There."

"Since you're in such a good mood, let's talk about saving some money for the things we'll need for our baby. Maybe we can ask Papa to make us a crib. He is pretty handy."

"We've got plenty of time to worry about all that. We'll figure something out, no rush." He thought, *Why is she thinking about this now?* Tony tried to stay aloof.

Out of the blue, Rosa started to cry, uncontrollably.

"Jeepers, now what's the matter?" Tony was already beginning to tire of her many unexpected mood swings, unsure of what caused them.

"Oh, I'm sorry; it came on out of the blue, you know, from out of nowhere." She curled her warm body next to his. "I just had a passing thought of Dominick in that cold ground and of Mama stranded back in Italy. She missed our wedding and will probably not be here for the birth of her first grandchild. Somehow it doesn't seem right."

"No need to be sorry about what you can't control. Perhaps someday I'll be able to help your father send for her. I know how much it means to you. Yes, I'll help." Tony regretted saying he'd help as soon as he blurted it. He thought, *Maybe if I can move up in Rabiso's operation, he'll give me some more money. I'm finally out of hock for what I owed the boss for Rosa's passage and all the other loans I took.*

Tony began to think of the things he could give up: Saturday poker games, gambling and drinking with the boys, that car he always wanted, California. Looking at his pretty new bride preparing a plate for him he shuddered. *No, I'll find a way without spoiling my fun and my dreams, and get her old lady here to boot.* He felt a curious relief, though he hardly believed himself.

A few short blocks away, Rocco Ameduro sat alone eating a special treat of lasagna and homemade sausage sent by Giovanna. It tasted wonderful, especially the apple pie. It was definitely better than the leftover soup he had planned to eat.

He placed an extra scoop of coal into the fire, an extravagance. Today though, he could afford the luxury. On his stroll to and from his job, it was his habit to pick up pieces of coal inadvertently dropped by deliverymen. His old burlap sack was often filled by the time he reached home. It saved a few pennies a month. A few pennies he could put aside for Antoinette.

Rocco picked up a two-week-old Italian newspaper he had found during his daily trash hunt. It was dated December 14, 1925. "Hmm," he mumbled, speaking to himself aloud, softly. "It looks like that Fascist pig Mussolini's at it again." The headline read, "New York Representative, Hamilton Fish, asks Congress to warn Italy against using Fascist propaganda in US."

"Good for you, Mr. Fish," Rocco said, still speaking aloud to nobody but the walls. "You can only guess how evil that man is and what he'll do if he's allowed."

Rocco took another small bite of the delicious pie, trying to make it last. Feeling very alone, he thought of his princess, missing her, deciding it was time to visit. *Tomorrow is Saturday, and I must go to work. Perhaps I could pay a visit this Sunday.* If he didn't, it would be another long week before he could see her.

Lonely, he stood from the table, going to the shelf where he kept his writing paper. Having saved enough for postage, it was time to write another letter to Antoinette. He had not heard from her since Dominick's death. The silence from Italy was an inner and terrible pain, especially now in his moment of weakness. *Maybe I'll scrape up another few pennies and write to Angelo too. Perhaps I'll request that he look in on her.* With Antoinette so far away, he felt a helpless void.

He took his pencil and in his best hand wrote.

My dearest Antoinette,

Today is Friday, January 1st, 1926, and I long for your presence and for your touch. I wish for you every good thing in the coming year: good health, good food, no pain, the love of our God, and if He shall will it, your presence here with me in America.

I am sorry it's taking so long to send for you. Please do not lose hope, for I am doing my best, but my angel, my love, it has not been easy, and I'm so very sorry. I promise I shall try harder. I know you must be missing Rosa and me as

I miss you and long for you. You would have been so happy to see our daughter at her wedding. She was, like you, a beautiful bride. It brought back such magnificent memories of our special day. Soon, I will have a picture to send to you. Our Rosa is so young and yet so grown up. She has been feeling ill, nothing terrible, but I suspect it is from all the excitement of the past several weeks.

I visited Dominick on Christmas Day. It was a cold, lonely walk to the cemetery. But I talked to him and prayed to our Blessed Father on behalf of his soul. I have the good feeling that our beloved child is with Him, and it gets me through the day to think this.

Happy New Year, my sweet, and with God's grace, may this year bring us together with the happiness we long for. I love you more than words can ever really say.

Love forever,
Rocco

Rocco started his next letter to Cousin Angelo, scribbling, his penmanship not as articulate as Antoinette's. Getting right to the point, he began.

January 1, 1926
Dear Cousin,

Angelo, America can be a hard place. Yet despite many setbacks, it is still a very good place to be. May all be well with you and your wonderful family. Kiss each one just for me and wish them a Happy New Year.

Angelo, I'm worried. It has been very difficult for me to make enough money to bring my Antoinette here. Please know that I am not asking you for money. You have enough mouths to feed. I write this only because I worry about her daily, and miss her beyond my endurance. I fear often that I'll never see her again.

Dear Cousin, would you do me the great favor of checking on her every once in a while to see to her needs? I desperately need to know how well she is doing. I suspect all is fine, but you know me, I'm a worrier where she is concerned. And you know how she is. She would never complain.

I hear things are getting more difficult because of the politics there and it's probably one of the main reasons why we have not been able to sell, at least, this was hinted in Antoinette's last letter, a few weeks before my boy's terrible death.

I fear, deep down, something is wrong and I am powerless to find out. Please write as soon as you can.

Rocco

Rocco reread what he had written. Writing the letters gave him comfort and hope. Dread controlled his mood, but he tried to force his tired will to snap out of the black funk. Tomorrow, I'll buy stamps and post them. The cost of some food is worth my sacrifice.

Reaching for the coffee pot on the stove, he poured its comforting liquid into a chipped cup. The pot, almost empty, gave up only an ounce or two. Oh, how I miss my Rosa's good coffee. It's her smile, though, that I need to see more of. He looked around the silent, cold room. It was no longer animated, but very dreary without his children.

Emptying the cup in one gulp, he sighed, "Tomorrow will be a better day." Tired, Rocco put his head into his arms, resting on the table. He fell asleep; his slumber produced neither good nor even fair dreams to lighten his load.

The year 1926 began with hope. Mother hid her fears well. It was good for her to hope, to dream, and to pray. However, life can sometimes require much more than mere hope, demanding action instead of wanting, doing instead of talking.

TWELVE

The winter months passed quickly, that is, until Mother started to gain weight. After the first few weeks, the dreadful daily nausea subsided. Then in early March, she started to balloon and bloat. Sitting at her worktable at the mill became uncomfortable, but ever the trooper, she toughed it out. She told everyone the expected date was September 1st. She hid her bulk well, wearing baggy winter clothes. Though many suspected otherwise, little was openly said as they watched and counted.

Father tried to convince Mr. Rabiso that he was ready for more responsibility and higher pay, except his actions spoke otherwise. Thus, little by little, his dream faded and each day became another lie. The life forced upon him was not the life he had often dreamed. He was quick to blame others for his mistakes and rapidly tiring of the tireless task of trying to live up to everyone's expectations: be a good husband, have children, survive, struggle, learn to cope like everyone else—and worse, learn to like it.

Mother's large and growing tummy put a damper to the original animal urgings that had initially bonded their marriage. This was the beginning of when she first suspected that Father's eyes were beginning to wander. Several years later, when I was a grandmother, and she a great grandmother, she told me that she once wished she had aborted me, foolishly reasoning that perhaps Father would have had more time to fall gracefully into his new role as a husband and then fatherhood, and…oh, well, sorry, I digress.

Where was I? My memory sure takes a spin away from where I was with such regularity these days. Oh yes, here I am. Their short honeymoon lasted a quick week and was spent at home. It gave them little time to learn and develop that special marriage dance; you know, the daily journeys that teaches us patience and joyous survival, take the good with the bad, 'til death do us part.

Mother did correct herself later about those hurtful words regarding abortion. With lasting repentance, while loving tears rolled down her ancient cheeks, she reached for me like she often did when I was little—tenderly caressing my cheek, gently running hands through my now graying hair. Then she smiled that wonderful smile and with words I'll always remember said, "No, Jenny, every time I see you and your children and now their children, I am thankful and relieved God didn't let a foolish sixteen-year-old destroy someone so beautiful."

I remember feeling lightheaded with her honesty, never doubting the sincerity or her love. That particular moment served to finally negate any doubts I had that she still regretted her decision all those years ago.

That day she finished her contrition saying, "The joy you brought into my life was God's way of blessing me and helping to make me strong. When I look at you, I see I did something very right in a time that was so very harsh."

Imagining how Mother continued to work, carrying this little white lie right up to the day I was born, still gives me goose bumps. If you knew Mother's hatred of telling even a little harmless fib, then you'd understand how difficult it must have been, especially in that era when twisting the truth wasn't as easy as it is with today's new morality.

On the backburner of worry lay Grandpa Rocco's debt, which by now had grown to proportions beyond what would have been to him a king's ransom. I never was told the cost of passage for my grandmother. However, it was the inability to get ahead that frustrated him the most. He had borrowed money for Dominick's funeral and several other unexpected needs. With his meager pay, he was unable to make enough to support day-to-day life, let alone pay the usurious debt and try to put aside money for passage. His only solution was to work two jobs and hope Mother could contribute a few dollars every now and then.

The flat was unusually hot for the first day of June, even with all the windows open. Rosa's beef stew simmered on the open stove. Its aroma, though wafting and inviting, added to the stifling atmosphere. Tony sat at the kitchen table silently reading the sporting news section of the paper. He whistled, and his apparent animation caught Rosa's attention.

"What's got you so excited?" she asked, thinking that whatever it was, anything was preferable to the intolerable silence. *Tony never seems to talk anymore, not since I've gotten fat with child,* she mused.

It bothered her, more so when talking to the girls at work who boasted of happy marriages and ecstatic husbands who were excited, or at least pretended they cared, especially when they were pregnant. *Tony is anything but ecstatic. He doesn't even pretend interest.*

After several moments had passed, Tony, interrupting her daydreaming, said, "Nothing you'd care much about."

She answered sharply, "Try me. You never take the time to know what interests me. Maybe you would if we ever talked. We never talk. Please talk to me, darn it!" Her shout got his attention.

Tony turned, looking squarely at his wife. What he saw was a very pregnant woman with a large wooden spoon in her hand, hair askew, not the vision of youth and animation that had once stirred his desires. "Oh, what the heck," he said, sarcasm drooling from his lips.

Rosa put the spoon down on the sink's work board, brushing her hair back and sitting down next to him, uninvited.

Tony searched for her simple beauty, now somewhat hidden from him, her body distorted because of the child, their child, nestled in her womb. *Yes,* he thought, *my blasted child, my responsibility.*

He groused, "Rosa, you wouldn't be interested. It's an article about the Indy 500 yesterday."

"Tony, what's an Indy 500? Is it a sporting event?"

"Well, sort of, my big, inquisitive wife. It's a major automobile race held far away in Indianapolis, Indiana. It's held once a year. I'd really love to go there someday. You see, they race special-built cars that go much faster than anything you'll ever see on the Utica streets."

Rosa was happy to see excitement in his eyes. She didn't care what the subject was, even if it was a dumb old car race; any talk was encouraging, "Tell me more," she said.

"There's not much to tell. What got my attention was the speed. It's only the fourteenth year they've held this event and many of the racecars actually got to go the whole 500 miles averaging over ninety-five miles per hour. Can you believe that?"

Rosa, not sure what to say, asked, "Is that fast?"

Tony laughed a deep, guttural happy laugh. Her question triggered a yearning, suppressed for almost three months. He was suddenly stopped from saying something amusing when Rosa shrieked, jumping up and standing on her chair.

"Rosa, be careful, you'll hurt the baby," he cautioned with atypical concern. "What's got you so spooked?"

"A mouse, a terrible mouse, didn't you see him?"

Tony laughed, mostly in relief, and thought quickly of the rats that had infested the old *USS Kansas*. Thinking, *Now those varmints really spooked me, but not the mice that I've seen here lately.*

"What's so funny? I hate mice!" she shouted, hysterically. "Where's my broom?" She stepped carefully from the chair with Tony's help and grabbed her broom, watching diligently, like a sentry on duty, eyes moving, surveying the small kitchen.

Tony said with sour distaste, frowning, "It's our crazy landlady and all the garbage she keeps in the hall. Nothing better than food scraps to draw rats and mice and anything else you don't want." Tony put his arm around Rosa's shoulder, gently urging her to sit, which she refused. He pointed as he spoke softly, "Here, give me the broom, I'll stand watch for awhile. Maybe I can catch it."

"Tony, you're my protector. Thank you, but it's not necessary. Sit, let's eat."

"Good idea, I am hungry. After we eat, I'll go to my parents and borrow some traps. Tomorrow, I'll buy a few more on the way to work."

"Do you think there are many? I'd hate to stand on the chair the rest of my life. Oh, Tony, don't rats kill little babies?"

"Stop fretting, it is only a little mouse. I'll take care of everything." He put his hand over hers in reassurance.

Rosa ladled a large helping from the pan on the stove and put the plate filled with the steaming beef stew in front of him, handing him a spoon.

"Mmm, Rosa, this smells good." Tasting it after blowing briskly, he remarked, "It's also pretty tasty. How do you do it? Everything you cook comes out so darn good."

"Well, my mama once told me a way to a man's heart is through his stomach. I guess with you it just takes a little longer." She snickered in a loving way, teasing him.

"You know, soon we'll have to start thinking of some names for the baby," he said.

Rosa startled at his sudden interest in their baby and beamed approval. She said, "I heard an American phrase at work the other day. It was 'there's no time like the present.' So Antonio, I'm ready to discuss names, if you are."

Tony nodded his approval. "If it's a boy let's name him Nicolas, after my pa." Tony regretted his enthusiastic outburst almost immediately. His mind raced to his father's letter that forced him to leave the Navy. "No, on second thought that's a bad idea. How about Giovanni, or John, Giovanni's English version? He'd be sort of named for Ma. You know her English name is Joanna."

Rosa nodded; her grimace was not the approval he had expected. Noticing, Tony asked, "What name do you have in mind?"

"I like Rocco; it seems the same in English or Italian. It is your middle name and Papa's given name. I think it's a perfect name." Silently she thought, *And I don't want to name any son of mine after that terribly overbearing woman. She'll take over our son like he's her special property, especially when he's named for her.*

"Fine, I like it, so you have picked my son's name." Tony's smile was like the first exciting day of a vacation, expectant, excited.

Rosa reluctantly asked, "What if it's a girl? You know, Antonio, it's a good possibility. The old witch lady, that friend of your mother—you know the one dressed all in black, with the giant cross around her neck. She was at your parents' last week—she said it was a girl."

Tony laughed, "Heck, you described about every ancient widowed Italian lady in Utica."

Ignoring his comment for the moment, she continued. "Oh, this woman was different and a bit frightening. She did some strange thing with a sewing needle, letting it dangle on a string near my belly. Superstitious stuff, but then again your Aunt Angelina looked at how the baby was positioned and also said it was a girl. She wasn't aware that the other lady said the same."

"Oh Rosa, how do you buy into all that baloney, huh? Nobody knows what it'll be until it's born, except for God, and that's that. Since you picked the name if it's a boy, I feel it's only fair I pick a girl's name."

Regretting her words as soon as she spoke, she said, "Sure, what do you have in mind?" She smiled, holding her breath, afraid at what might come next.

"I like Giovanna, or like I said earlier, Joanna."

She thought, *Bah, I knew it. Well now I hope it's a boy, I hope those old Sicilian hags are wrong.*

Giovanna, born in Palermo, Italy, was Sicilian. It never bothered Rosa, but had initially bothered her father Rocco when he had first heard; his prejudice about Sicilians went back to his Southern Italian heritage. Also it was unusual for a man to marry outside his village, even more unusual for a man to marry outside his province. Missanello was in the Province of Potenza, in the Basilicata region, which in the 1920s was considered one of the poorest in all of Italy. Tony's father not only married someone outside his region and province, but someone from Sicily, a place most Italians living within the boot of Italy felt was not Italian. Garibaldi's war in the 1860s had united Italy's proudly independent City States only a few years earlier. Most Italians thought of themselves as loyal citizens of their respective regions first, and the combined Italia a sometimes far distant second. But Sicilians sure felt they were Italian as they most certainly were. Nicola, a man ahead of his time, who often followed his heart and not his heritage reasoned that all of Italy was rich in a common heritage, no matter where one originated.

Rosa decided to try a new ploy, playing on Tony's ego.

"Tony, I like the name, but why don't you be like your father and do something not so traditional? Why do we have to name our baby, boy or girl, after someone? Why not pick a name like Patricia or Angela, if it's a girl, or maybe Paulo or Mario if it's a boy."

Tony, face firmly set, "No, I like Joanna. It's a good honest name."

Rosa, just happy to be talking again, was resigned to the idea of a daughter named after her mother-in-law. Hiding her dismay, she said, "Sure Tony, it's a good name. I like it after all."

She lied and it hurt, but it felt better to have her husband back even for a moment, and it was therefore worth any name controversy. Hiding her inward smirk she thought, *I know what I'll call her though. And as her mother and the person who will spend the most time with her, she'll learn to love it like I will love her. I'll call her Jennie, and it'll be my little secret.*

Tony, seeing Rosa's glowing smile, thought her happy, not name plotting. He felt great. "I know what; we'll call her Joanna Patricia and use both of our ideas." He beat his chest in noble gesture. "It'll be a regal name. Two saints, no less, Saint John and Saint Patrick, good Catholic names for a beautiful daughter."

"Yes, they're good names," she agreed, smiling as she took another bite of the stew. "And don't forget Saint Joan of Arc." The baby suddenly kicked, giving her a start.

"Tony, come, feel it kick. It's so marvelous, having a living baby in me. It's like the baby approves our choices." Rosa stood from the table and walked to Tony, still sitting.

Tony felt the child move, awed by a phenomenon enjoyed from the beginning of mankind. "It's really moving," he said. *It is real*, he thought, *and I've been such a fool.*

"Tony, I have another request to make of you."

"Sure Rosa, what's on your mind? Sit and eat and we'll talk." He pointed to her vacated wooden chair at the table.

She remained standing and first gave her husband a stern and steady stare before saying, "I believe we must raise our child to be a one hundred percent American. If our baby's ever to make it here, it must think and act like the people who live here think and act. After our child is born, we must speak English all the time, bad as mine is. English must be the child's first language and Italian a second. That way maybe the terrible thing that happened to Dominick will never happen to our children. I want them to be able to enter any place in American society, because he or she is above all, first an American."

Tony smiled and then said, "I have no argument with this. It's good thinking on your part, though I believe a bit ambitious and maybe perhaps ahead of our time. Though, we must never forget that our first language is Italiano."

"Thank you, and I agree. Tony, perhaps it might be as you say, 'ahead of our time,' but it must be this way, don't you think?"

He nodded his agreement just as Rosa blurted out, "Will your parents have problems with this?"

"No, I think they are resigned to the fact. Look at my little brother, Johnny. He speaks better English than any of us, and he barely understands Italian. It's inevitable that this will happen. By the way, does Rocco feel the same as you?"

"Papa said he'd try harder to learn his English so that he can help too. His only wish is for us to teach our children their Italian heritage and our wonderful culture. He said he would hate to see it forgotten."

"I agree, Rosa. Maybe someday our children's children and their children as well will possibly forget, but never our children."

Early Wednesday, June 2, proved to be a day of surprises for Rosa. The weather, still unusually hot, gave her much discomfort. Work had been particularly difficult. She had missed making quota for the third day in a row. The boss, not a bit concerned for her pregnancy or anyone else's for that matter, was displeased and often yelled for her to move faster or leave. He had said, "I've many people who'd love your job." Oh, how she wanted desperately to tell him her true feelings. However, the job and its meager salary were needed more than the momentary pleasure that sounding off would bring, so she kept quiet and fumed instead.

With Tony in agreement, she had religiously given Rocco a dollar per week from her wages and half of any bonuses she received for exceeding quota. Since her wedding, she had given Rocco a total of $35 toward Antoinette's passage.

The kitchen door opened with a quick swing as Tony entered the room carrying a large old wooden apple crate and what looked like a small bundle of white fur hanging from his arms. Rosa knew instantly he had brought home a kitten.

She squealed, "Is he mine?" She rushed over to him, in more a wobble than a rush, and took the kitten. It purred; its blue eyes anxious but lively, looked at her expectantly.

"It sure is gentle," she said excitedly, petting the kitten under its neck. The kitten purred like a well-tuned motor.

Tony laughed, enjoying the effect of his surprise and the diversion. In the box, filled with sand, he also had four new mousetraps. "Rosa, you wanted something for the mice problem. Here's the answer."

Rosa frowned, "Tony, it's too little to help with the mice; it'll take time for the kitty to become a hunter. It's so tiny and so young."

"The fellow who gave it to me—you know him, Tommy Galenti—said it's a girl, about eight weeks old. Its parents are great hunters and very good pets for his kids. They had six kittens looking for a home, and I just knew you'd want this one. Well, do you want to keep it? Tommy said I could bring her back if you didn't want it."

"No, Tony I like her, and you cannot take her back. In fact, I think I already love her. Listen to her purr. She likes me. Oh, she is so pretty, so soft."

Rosa cuddled the kitten as she walked to the icebox, opening it to get the pitcher of milk. She poured a little of the milk into a glass bowl, petting the kitten as she did, coaxing it to drink. The kitten complied, lapping the milk.

Tony asked, "What do you want to name her?"

"Since she looks so much like snow, I think Snowball would be a good name. What do you think?"

"It seems like a perfect name." Tony kneeled down to pet Snowball. "How do you like your new name, kitty?" Snowball, finished with her milky treat, looked up at Tony as if in acknowledgement and licked her paw.

Tony set the box of sand in the corner, placing the kitten next to it like his coworker had directed. "Tommy said to do this right away so the kitten will learn its new surroundings." Almost at once Tommy's advice proved accurate, as Snowball entered the box to do her business.

"Tommy said that the smell of even a kitten should frighten away mice, but just in case that doesn't work, I bought four traps that we can set in places where Snowball won't get hurt."

"Tony, you must thank Tommy for me. Snowball's a wonderful kitten and a splendid surprise."

"I will, honey. It was pure luck that Tommy mentioned his litter of kittens when he heard me say we had a mouse problem."

From that time on Mother always had a cat, and it was always white and always called Snowball. When the last Snowball died several years later, sometime in the 1980s, it was just before we realized Mother had a serious memory problem.

However, Snowball the First, as I like to call her, was a temporary blessing that couldn't have come at a better time.

Rocco stared at the envelope, postmarked from Italy, dated April 10, 1926. Today was June the third. It had taken almost two full months to reach him. He moved his head in dismay. Shaking from the excitement of the long over-due letter from Antoinette, he slowly opened the stained and watermarked envelope, careful not to rip its frail contents.

Adjusting his eyes to the dark of the hot room, he moved closer to the kerosene lamp. The lamp's heat and the pungent odor made his already sweat-veiled face feel uncomfortable, though he didn't notice. He unfolded the one page letter as if it were pure gold; handwriting appeared on both sides. He smelled it, trying to capture the scent of his wife. There was only the sterile feel of the thin paper and certain mustiness from its long sea voyage. It read:

My dear Rocco,

Today it is April 10th, and the weather is beautiful. You would love the caress of the morning breeze, and I think of you with each refreshing blast, for I remember how much you loved to feel the breeze. Husband, my heart is filled with sorrow for our little boy, and I long for you and your tenderness. My days are busy doing laundry for the few pennies it brings. I have not had even one person interested in our home. I think I will have to sell it for what we can get. What do you think?

Our country is in turmoil over Mussolini. Everyone is beginning to call him Il Duce, even though this vain man declared himself the leader of the Fascists over five years ago. Isn't this silly?

I thank you for the picture of our Rosa. She is so beautiful in her gown. I am sad that I missed her wedding, but now I look forward to meeting my new son-in-law.

Cousin Angelo has been very helpful, and most persistent in his desire to assist. He offered me money for food. I refused to take it, knowing that you would not want me to accept. He often brings over extra vegetables from his garden, which I do not refuse. I must admit it is good to have the fresh vegeta-bles, as my garden has not done well and needs desperately your green thumb.

Things here are mostly the same. They never seem to change. The poor get poorer and the rich, richer. And do not worry, my husband, I am very capable of managing for myself. I miss you and pray this letter reaches you happy and healthy.

I understand the difficulty you have encountered to save the money we need for my passage to carry me to your arms. I want you to know that you should not feel you are a failure if you decide to return home. Many have returned after finding things in America difficult. Just last week, Salvatore De Marco, you may remember him, returned after living in New York City for five years.

Rocco, you are my hero, and whatever you decide, I will understand and follow.

I love you, Rocco, and I miss you.

Forever yours,
Antoinette

Tears of sadness filled Rocco's eyes, accompanied also by tears of joy that joined the waterfall, wetting his day-old beard and cascading over a well-trimmed mustache. Rocco carefully folded the letter, returning it to the envelope. *Tomorrow, I write and tell her about the expected baby and that I'll stay here and make our life here no matter what. No matter how difficult. I will not quit. No, it is not my nature. I must endure, now that we have an American grandchild on the way. However, I will not tell her that I owe my very soul to the moneylenders. No, this she will not ever understand.*

"For every minute you are angry, you lose sixty seconds of happiness."

Ralph Waldo Emerson

THIRTEEN

Tuesday, June 29, 1926, started out like any other workday, or so it seemed to Rosa. Feeling like a blimp, she walked ten blocks, or more accurately, waddled, to her job. A lazy summer day, richly green in color, a pale blue sky and pleasant mild temperatures greeted her. It was a magnificent morning to be alive.

Upon reaching the factory, she felt a short, sharp, unfamiliar pain. And worse, the swirling smoke from the factory mingling with the light summer breeze made her feel queasy. Work was getting extremely difficult. More so, her days were a trial and her slight petite frame caused her back to hurt constantly. And getting motivated to start the work shift was gradually more difficult—what with the sour taste in her mouth every morning and the thought of another hard day to tough out.

Today, Rosa had need to talk, though the constant hum and rattle of the shop's machinery always made it difficult but not impossible. Sarafina Robeletti, her work neighbor sitting at the next machine, didn't mind the chatter; in fact, she enjoyed the change of pace. Talking helped make their mundane routine days pass. The girls' constant gabbing didn't bother the foreman as long as they did not dawdle or miss their quotas. Sadly, Rosa had barely made quota the last two days, even though willing herself to push on when energy levels had dwindled to sheer willpower. Yet, no matter how hard she tried to push toward the quantity expected by management, it was not enough.

Could it be the baby coming? She passed off the thought. It was still three or more weeks according to her inexperienced calculations.

Sarafina looked at Rosa with knowing concern, asking, "Rosa, your face is flushed, are you ill? Honey, did you hear me?"

Rosa nodded, remaining silent.

"Maybe you should go home," Sarafina suggested, with a concern rooted in well-honed experience. Fixing her eyes on Rosa's peaked look, she worried there was something wrong with the pregnancy.

"Thanks for asking, Sarafina, but I'm fine. Lately, all this bambino wants to do is move all the time, and today it's more frisky than usual."

Sarafina gave Rosa a knowing, though reproachful, look. "Honey, you don't want to take chances. Now take my poor sister, Elaina, God rest her soul." Sarafina made a quick sign of the cross, raising her voice above the constant drone of the sewing machines. "She died in childbirth. She actually worked at a job something like ours, 'til the very day she delivered." Sarafina didn't miss the strained look of fright on Rosa's face. The story was having its desired effect.

Seeing Rosa's shock, Sarafina tried to sugarcoat the next few words, speaking softly, which was something way out of her nature. "Honey, don't concern yourself, all I'm saying is, ya can't be too careful."

"Did the baby die?" Rosa asked.

"No, thank the Almighty. My nephew—name's Joey—is doin' fine. But my no good brother-in-law has written us off. He never did like our side of the family. We don't like him much, either."

"Did they ever find out why she died?" asked Rosa.

"No, even though my sister lived in New York City, a place surrounded by doctors and hospitals, they never could say why. Me, I'm convinced she died 'cause she was just plain wore out. I've had five kids, mind you. You'll never see me working right up to my due date. Not me, I rest."

"Sarafina, how do you do it?"

"Do what, Honey?" asked Sarafina.

"You know, work six days and have five kids too. It must be difficult. My Tony says that when I have our baby, I'll stay home to raise it. How do you raise your children when you're here?"

"It's easy, when you have a great mom," she guffawed. "I'll agree it's a bit unusual nowadays for a woman to work once she has a litter. Well, leastwise for me, it's a simple case of the moola, as my man's prone to say. We need the extra change this job brings. More important, I let my Alfredo know right off that he up and married a modern thinkin,' independent woman. And if he objects, he can just kiss my you know what and work his own lazy backside off a bit harder. And honey, he's too lazy for that," she snorted.

"From what I'm hearing you say, I'd guess your Alfredo is unusual." Rosa's face contorted with another sharp pain, this one a bit more intense.

Too intent upon finding the right words, Sarafina did not notice Rosa's discomfort. Starting to respond, she saw Rosa advance her tightened fist to her mouth stifling obvious pain. Her face was contorted, showing all the familiar signs so natural to Sarafina's experience.

Sarafina dropped her next thought like a bad idea, "You're getting sharp pains, aren't you, dearie?"

"Sarafina, you worry too much. I'm fine." But Rosa was not, and she knew it as soon as the words were uttered. Another sharp burst of pain, this one razor-sharp, hit her like a bad omen.

"Oh, my!" Rosa's face showed anxiety and fear.

Beverly Coleski, a shy woman and a mother of three, had been listening, eavesdropping on their prattle.

"What is it, Rosa?" both ladies chorused simultaneously.

With extreme embarrassment, Rosa said softly, her face contorted, "I think my water just broke."

Both co-workers stopped their machines; Beverly reached over to turn off Rosa's.

Sarafina put her massive arms around Rosa's small frame, almost smothering her. The cheap perfume caused Rosa's head to spin and her stomach to churn. "Rosa, hear me and hear me good, we got ta get you to a hospital. I'll send someone to fetch your husband. Does he still work at Rabiso Fruit?" Rosa nodded, her face contorted.

A light breeze filtered restlessly through large open windows, giving some relief to the workers, though Rosa failed to notice its refreshing comfort. Another sharp pain penetrated her body, jarring her into the reality of the moment.

Sarafina's instincts and experience took over. The excitement suddenly charged the air in the stifling sweatshop, upsetting the day's mundane routine and giving this trifling moment's adventure first place in attention.

After enduring several more sharp and stabbing pains, and after a long pause, Rosa answered what her eyes had already conveyed, "Yes, he does, but Sarafina." Rosa's face, now filled with added worry, aged. "I can't go. We have no money for a hospital. We planned to use a midwife."

"I'll bet my fortune, little as it 'tis that you've no time to worry about a midwife, or for that matter, the blasted money." Sarafina turned and shouted. Her booming voice carried through the room over the machinery's maddening hum. "Bob, come get your bossy self over here quick."

Like a drill sergeant at boot camp, Sarafina turned to Beverly with precision-like orders, "Get a scrap of cloth and clean the floor, before someone slips and falls." Beverly nodded in agreement, too afraid to refuse the big, overpowering woman.

Bob Jones, the production floor manager, "Boss Jones" to the girls, came running, a stern, anxious look projecting his concern. "Sarafina, this stoppage on these machines better have a darn good explanation. Must I remind you ladies that we've got quotas?"

Sarafina, standing defiantly with both hands on her massive hips, said, "Now, Bob! Shove your rotten quotas. You know me better than this, even though I know how much you cherish your quotas more than life itself. Young Rosa's baby has decided to come early. She needs a quick ride to the hospital, savvy, Boss Man?" Sarafina towered over Bob, poking a large finger into his slight chest.

Bob, flustered, tried to show control, comforting himself with the thought, *After the trenches in France, a little baby should be easy duty.* He cast a worried look at the Lavalia kid.

"Okay, here's what we'll do. Sarafina, you'll come with me in my car to watch over Rosa, whilst I drive to St Luke's. I figure we can get there in about ten minutes and back here in twenty."

Sarafina gave him a cold penetrating stare that he could not miss. It reminded him of his mother so much so that he wanted to cower in some corner, or maybe even put on a dunce's cap, but he caught himself.

He turned to Rosa, taking command of the situation, or so he thought. "Can you make it to my car, or do you need help?"

"I'll be fine—ooooh, that one hurt!" Rosa valiantly held back the scream she desperately wanted to let out. She turned pale, not fooling anyone. Sarafina put comforting arms around her.

"For gosh sakes, Bob, we need to get movin,' not stand here listenin' to your prattle." Not waiting for Bob to give any more orders, she started out the door, holding Rosa steady. He followed them like a young rookie second lieutenant follows a wizened non-com.

Out of his element, Bob allowed Sarafina to help Rosa into his car, an aging Model-T. Today, at least for the next few minutes, he was no longer the boss, only a means of transportation.

The drive, as Bob predicted, was fast. He was more worried about the potential mess on the car's upholstery than Rosa's comfort and was happy to just drop her off at the hospital and leave. Sarafina reluctantly left Rosa after helping get her admitted to the hospital, walking back to the factory.

Quickly diagnosed, Rosa was prepped and then brought to a room where she would wait and wait, or so it seemed to her young, inexperienced mind.

By the time Tony arrived, Rosa was ready to go home. However, her undelivered baby had other more pressing ideas, as did the hospital staff. The doctor's knowledge won out and by early evening, around eight o'clock, a beautiful little five-pound, five-ounce baby girl named Joanna Patricia came into the world, bloody, kicking, and crying. Like her father, she had a dark head of hair and deep-set, dark eyes.

Seeing her new daughter for the first time, Rosa, trembling, exclaimed, "She's beautiful! Her hair and eyes are like her papa." She smiled broadly.

Tired and haggard, yet building her courage, she reluctantly asked the nurses what she silently dreaded to ask, in her broken English, pleading, "Pleazz ah tell ah me ah, is everyting, you know, okay witt ah mi bambino?"

"Sugar," said the head nurse, "your little girl is a little small, and maybe a bit early, but she's perfect and beautiful, just like you."

"*Grazi, grazi,*" Rosa said, with a forced smile, relieved. "What are you doin' with—my bambino? I ah wan ah to...ah, you know, how you say, hold her, please."

"Sugar, you'll get many chances to do just that. Now, we've got to clean and weigh her. She sure is a cute little thing. When we're done you can have her for awhile, long enough to feed her. She's hungry already. Listen to her cry, she's got good lungs." She smiled with a glow; Nurse Regina loved her work. "After you feed her, then you, my dear, will need to rest."

"Feed her, so soon?" asked Rosa a bit frightened. The nurse smiled, thinking, *So young, she's a child herself. These immigrants are so different from us.*

"*Nutrica*, is ah my ah Antonio ah here? I want to a see him."

"Oh yes, Mr. Lavalia is here, with your father and all your very large family, too. There's a crowd out there waiting to hear your good news. As for your
hubby, he's been pacing the floor and smoking, acting like a typical, foolish new
dad, thinking all the pain you're going through is his, like all first-time fathers
I've seen." Seeing Rosa's concern, she quickly added, "Don't you worry, I told
him you and your daughter are doing fine."

Rosa smiled and relaxed upon hearing Tony was nearby. "*Molte grazie.* Can
I see him?"

"I'll go get him after little Joanna has her first official meal and we move
her to the nursery."

"Can't my Tony, see ah our leetle bambino?" She struggled for the right
words, her appeal obvious.

Sternly, but ever so gently, Regina replied, "It's against hospital policy. Sorry,
sugar. Your man will get to see his daughter through the maternity windows. I
promise you this, though, he'll get to see her aplenty, and soon enough after you go
home." She put the baby in Rosa's arm, and then bustled out the door.

Rosa watched as the nurse left. Strange suckling sounds came from little Joanna, both peaceful and comforting. Rosa's thoughts drifted off into
uncharted ground, her mind thinking of how happy she was that it was over,
almost, but not quite forgetting her ordeal. With unpracticed hands, she carefully examined Joanna, watching every move. "Well hello," she said softly, in
barely a whisper. "So you're the one that kicked my insides." Using the child's
nickname for the first time, she murmured, forcing a painful smile, "You, my
little Jennie, are forgiven."

Rosa touched Joanna's skin, running her fingers lightly over her silken hair,
checking to see if she had the right number of fingers and toes. She was amazed
at the soft, gentle feel, the new smell.

"My daughter, my little American daughter, I'll always love you for as
long as I live." She kissed Joanna, now asleep, content in her new and strange
environment.

When Tony finally got a look at his daughter, it was through the sterile glass windows of St. Luke's maternity wing. He was smitten with pride.

Concern about the hospital bill would hit him later. In this moment's bliss, all he cared about was his family, joining him to view the newest Lavalia.

To no one in particular, Tony said, "How small she looks." Thinking, *She's even a month earlier that Rosa calculated.*

Giovanna came forward, speaking happily while looking through the thick glass partition at her first grandchild, and put her hand on her eldest son's shoulder. The sterile hospital made her feel uncomfortable. "Tony, she seems big for a seven-month baby. Boy, if she went nine months, I think Rosa would have had a real problem." Playfully she pinched her son's cheek, "You were much bigger at eight pounds."

Tony took in her remarks, trying not to show embarrassment. He changed the direction of the conversation. Acting genuinely worried, he asked, "Yeah, Ma, but what do you think about her? She's so small; do you think she's healthy? You know, being born so early."

"Don't you worry, Antonio, she's healthy. Just look at her. Even through these awful windows, you can see that."

"Ma, I've a special surprise for you. We named your first grandchild Joanna, after you. It's the American version of your name."

Giovanna beamed; pride and delight showing from large brown eyes. Her voice changed from motherly to conspiratorial. "Now son, remember, my granddaughter must not forget her heritage. Your wife has, how you say, loose, independent ways."

"Don't worry, Ma, Rosa and I've agreed Joanna will always know where her roots sprang from. I promise." He hugged her, kissing her cheek.

Crimson leaves danced in the early fall winds, dropping lightly to the earth and gathering in neat piles outside the Elizabeth Street apartment. Rosa's homemade, hot-spiced Italian sausage, touched lightly with fresh basil, mingled nicely with peppers and onions. Because money was tight, the taste of her fine supper would be even better because they were seconds, rejects from Rabiso's fruit bins that cost nothing except for the meat. The peppers and onions sizzled royally in the big iron pan, not aware, nor caring that they had been downgraded.

The unique smell drifted throughout the flat and into the stairwell, greeting Tony as he returned home from another difficult day in a series of many. Another girl, only fifteen, had been beaten the night before. She was currently in County Hospital where his father-in-law, Rocco, worked one of his two jobs. Tony had made sure to avoid him, not wanting to explain his presence. He figured it wasn't likely he'd be seen, since Rocco worked in the basement stoking fires.

The hospital's emergency nurse had told him the girl might not make it, but the doctor said she was strong and had a slight chance. The girl's beating upset Tony. This particular girl was a Polish immigrant that Rabiso had acquired from an associate in Albany. She was a lonely kid, frightened and desperate. Her story was all too familiar. Shortly after arriving, her parents were killed in a rail accident, leaving her destitute. Unable to speak English, frightened and alone, prostitution became the only chance for her survival. And naturally, the encouragement of Rabiso's cohorts made her transformation into the slave-like profession complete.

Tony had taken more than a casual interest in her, and she became a great comfort during Rosa's pregnancy. It angered him beyond even his own imagination when he had to carry her mangled body to the hospital. She was more than a blond trick to Tony. She was not only beautiful, but he had come to think of her as a lover and not just a casual distraction.

Later tonight, he and Gino would make plans. More accurately, he would make plans to visit the home of the man responsible. It would not be an easy job. He thought, *This woman beater is a well-known businessman, married with a nice family. Somehow, I'll figure a way to lure the no good bum out from his home. Justice needs serving, and I'll give him a hefty helping.* He entered the kitchen to his flat, his face strained and angry; he advanced reluctantly into his home, now tainted by the mixed emotions of fatherhood. The wonderful smells of Rosa's cooking had little effect on his mood.

"Hi, Rosa," he said, trying to hide his inner rage, hugging her by rote. He flipped his unread daily paper onto the wooden table that served as both their dining and meeting place.

Tony, badly in need of a diversion, couldn't wait to read the sports section about the big fight. The buzz at work was that Gene Tunney had beaten Jack Dempsey for the heavyweight boxing championship in a ten-round decision. It was the first time a winner had been declared by decision, at least for a heavyweight fight. At work, it was all the fellows could talk about and the betting had been heavy, though he had passed on the wagering. He laughed inwardly, *It's good to read about two Irishmen beating the crap out of each other.*

Redirecting conscious awareness to his wife, he asked mechanically, "How's Joanna doing?"

"Shush, she's finally sleeping." Rosa tried to smile, but it was difficult. "Your mother says she is colicky."

Rosa looked worn, ragged. Her nights had seen little sleep since her return from the hospital. And now, in the last week of September, she was finally starting to feel like her old self, only she was a very tired "old self."

Rosa stopped and reached down, gently petting Snowball who had entered the kitchen, aiming for her box. "Giovanna feels it's probably because Jennie was born early. Well, we know that's not the cause."

Her sheepish look appeared angelic to Tony, sending longings that had been repressed for weeks. Rosa, fatigued, had been unwilling to return to their once, if all too brief, nocturnal and amorous bliss.

Yes, he thought, *she's starting to become the Rosa that I loved again, and not too soon, since Polish Annie's in the hospital.*

Tony's words started off in a soft tone, but moved upward quickly to a crescendo, his voice turned quarrelsome. "Is the end in sight for us? When in blazes will we be lovers again, a real husband and wife, newlyweds, for God's sake?"

"What do you mean?" she asked defiantly. "We are real lovers, aren't we? Take a long look at Joanna. She is proof enough. What more do you need? I promise, this part of our life will pass. We can do the other again soon. I need it, too! I promise."

Tony, curling his lip in anger, tried to plead his case, "For gosh sakes, I work all day and Joanna cries all night. It's becoming a real pain. And we have not made love in, it seems like, well, forever. Everyone says you should be able to do it again in six weeks. It's been twelve."

Rosa, seeing his anger, said loudly, her own anger rising, "Tony, do you discuss our private moments with friends?"

Caught by his foolish admissions, he replied, sheepishly, lying, "No, it was only general conversation. You know, guys just joking around. I'd never discuss our personal life."

Rosa did not believe him. One thing she had learned in the past months was that Tony was a consummate liar, often too lazy to cover his trail of excuses. At first, she let the lies pass uncontested; lately, it had become more difficult.

Rather than pick a fight, she chose a safer route, trying to placate. "Tony, you've been very patient. I'm sorry that I could not be intimate with you. I'm sorry for being so worn out and tired. I take care of the baby. Since you work so hard, I never complain when you don't help with Jennie. I work hard too. I wash clothes for the neighbors for extra money. I cook and clean and tend to the baby. It's endless work. What more can I do?"

Rosa started to cry, suddenly losing the desire to tread softly. She screamed, not listening to her inner cautions, "And furthermore, my husband, you have been the real jerk, not our baby. This is what babies do when they're young: they cry, they wet, they need changing, and they get hungry!"

Not to be outdone, he returned the shout, his face contorted. "And why the devil do you always insist on calling her Jennie? Her name is Joanna!"

Rosa returned his scream with a scream of her own, "Because I like it, and it's a perfect nickname for Joanna. What difference does it make? It doesn't change the fact that her name is what it is. Most everyone I know has a nickname. Aren't you called Tony? Why can't our Joanna be Jennie?"

Joanna awoke, startled at the sound of her mother's harsh voice, and began to cry.

"Now look what you have done," Rosa yelled, her face strained, tears of frustration flowing.

"Rosa, I'm tired. And for the record, it's your loud voice, not mine, that woke Joanna. I don't need this garbage. It's been a terrible day, and to top it off, Rabiso told me that I have to work tonight. So I'll just eat and go."

Suddenly, turning on a dime, Tony held out his palm in a gesture of peace. "I was wrong. Forgive me; we're both very tired and not ourselves. Believe me;

the last thing I want is to baby-sit for a blasted order of pumpkins. Forgive me?" he asked again, true remorse that would make the great Chaplin jealous, seeping from his face.

Rosa could not stay angry. "Tony, please forgive me too. What with the wash I'm doing for the few pennies it brings, and never sleeping, I feel like I'm falling apart. I'm so lonely and this new life sometimes seems so boring and endless to me."

She turned off the burners on the stove and reached for the fresh, warm bread she had taken from the oven only a few minutes earlier, shaking it out of its pan. The smell was infectious. Suddenly, she remembered the baby crying; she dropped the bread on the table and raced to her bedroom to Joanna's cradle.

Picking up her daughter, she soothed her, singing an Italian lullaby once sung to her by Antoinette, softly cooing, settling. It worked. She felt Joanna's diaper and changed it. The baby smiled, catching Rosa cold. Was it gas or a real smile? She did it again. Rosa yelled to Tony, still in the kitchen, feeling a bit sorry for himself, but also guilty at his overreaction.

"Tony, please come quick."

Tony raced into their bedroom, out of breath, thinking the worst. What he saw upon entering was a transformed Rosa, looking like a Madonna, holding his smiling daughter. "Where's the fire?" he asked, with hushed concern in his voice.

"No fire, my husband, our little daughter smiled and smiled, so happy, and all the frustrations and fatigue I've complained so foolishly about have seemed to dissolve. And because of this precious little smile."

Tony reached for Joanna's tiny hand, letting the baby encircle his finger with her delicate tiny fingers. They felt soft and warm, almost electric. He had experienced other moments like this before with Joanna, except he had never felt this peaceful. Snowball came into the room and rubbed her furry body around Tony's pant leg, looking up at him as if trying to be a part of the unusually happy moment. Hungry, she was really trying to get her master's attention, not really caring to be a part of this moment right out of a Norman Rockwell picture.

"She's beautiful when she stops crying. That smile sure reminds me of you," he said with genuine affection.

"Her face is all you, Tony, definitely not me. And still I agree, she's beautiful," she teased.

"Boy, I never thought a baby could be so much trouble. All they do is eat, cry, sleep, and poop, over and over."

"Where were you when your mother had eight children after you? As the oldest of your brood, surely this is no surprise? Didn't they cry? Didn't you ever help?" Rosa chided playfully, enjoying her taunt.

"Yeah, I guess they did. Heck, they weren't mine to worry over every night and day. And I suppose I wasn't as tired then as now. You know, it's a bit easier handling new babies when they're not your immediate responsibility, don't ya think?"

Rosa stood, holding Joanna close to her chest, motioning with her free arm to invite Tony into the circle, all cuddling, one happy family, at least for the moment. Rosa nestled her head on Tony's neck, smelling his strong cologne and maybe a hint of perfume. She couldn't be sure if it was perfume, and right at the moment it raced past her. Their eyes met and she seductively smiled, "Tonight, dear, when you return, it's time we started to get back to normal."

Tony, his darting smile now daring, spoke as soon as his words could sputter the possibility. "Why not now? Joanna's settled and the food can wait. Since I'll be home late, I have a hunger right now that's far more important than food."

And then Joanna began to cry, her famished cry, giving Tony yet another reason to be frustrated. He watched as Rosa opened her blouse, inviting the baby to suckle. Tony looked on, mesmerized. *There's something about seeing a baby taking its natural nourishment as God intended.* The scene had a rare, tender effect on him. He watched in awe, as if for the first time. Sighing, he thought *my wife and my baby, both beautiful…sweet and natural.*

The joyous moment was only temporary. The door echoed with another unexpected reason to squelch his randy ideas upon his hearing the heavy pound of three sound knocks and Rocco's familiar voice coming from the hallway.

"Hello in there, I sure can smell the sausage. If it's half as good as it smells, I'll be a very happy man. It makes me even hungrier than I thought. Am I too late?"

Rosa looked at her husband with a disappointment as large as his. She whispered, "Tony, I'm sorry. I never got the chance to tell you I invited Papa for dinner. Would you please get the door?"

Tony liked Rocco. He was a good father-in-law and also a very hard worker, an honest and good man who never seemed to get ahead even though he did all the right things. Tonight though, he would have preferred to be alone, to mend, and to reacquaint. But not tonight, not now, and not even when things appeared back on the road to normal. Such had become his fate and he resented it, desperate for change.

His legs reluctantly carried him to the door, usually an unobstructed route. Only this time, Snowball, belly full, raced tail up, playfully approaching Tony's ankles. She tried to wrap her purring body around them, just a kitten looking for love and attention. Nevertheless, attention was something the kitten, too, had gotten less and less of since the baby came home.

Irritated, Tony kicked at the cat, feeling a certain release as he did. He hit her only slightly, but enough to surprise her. She flew across the room, with mostly her pride shaken. Hurt more from fright, Snowball slinked, though limping some, away to a quiet, safe corner, licking at her bruised rear leg.

Before opening the door, Tony cast a satisfied glance at the cat, happy to have control over at least one thing, even if it was only a kitten. Tonight he'd get some enjoyment of another kind. He licked his lips in contemplation while opening the door.

"Hi, Rocco," he said with strained animation. "Come on in, Rosa's with Joanna. I'll get us some wine."

"Thank ah you, Tony," Rocco, animated, answered in near-perfect English.

"Tony, I saw you leaving the hospital. I was taking a smoke. I tried to call, but you move ah too fast. A problem?"

Thinking quickly, Tony answered, "I had to take one of our workers to emergency, stitches. He's fine." Tony thought, *Another lie; I'm getting too good at this.*

The next day's late edition headline featured a prominent businessman whose badly beaten body was found behind the public library, the apparent victim of a robbery that went bad. Also on that day, my hospital bill was paid in full.

"You never can begin to live until you dare to die."

Henry Van Dyke

FOURTEEN

The day was Sunday, February 27, 1927. The headline in the paper's early edition read, "London Talks to Frisco by Telephone." The historic event had taken place the day before when the Pacific Telephone Company's president, H. D. Pillsbury, in San Francisco, had spoken to the American Telephone and Telegraph's representative 7,287 miles away, in London, England.

The newspaper article lay unread and crumpled on Rosa's table, the headline blurred to her swollen eyes. Minutes earlier, Tony, in a fit of anger, had stormed from the house, slamming the door on his way out. Its force broke a glass cup that had fallen from the shelf; it broke into hundreds of little shards. Rosa sat on the wooden floor, staring at the mess. Stunned, she ignored glass cuts on her hand and the burning food in the oven. Tears gushed in little rivers down her bruised and bleeding cheeks, the visual result of Tony's outrage.

Tony's unexpected rampage had stunned Rosa. She had carefully planned what she genuinely thought of as her wonderful surprise, fully expecting Tony to be as excited as she about her new pregnancy. The doctor said the baby would come in late August.

Tony, enraged, had demanded, "How could this happen, especially when we agreed to wait until Joanna was two?"

Uncharacteristically for Rosa, her spontaneous response had equaled his with strong and furious language, reminding him of his part in the deed. She had screamed, "I recall that you were supposed to use protection! You sloppy fool, you're as much a part of this child's beginning as I. Besides, this is not a tragedy! It is a good thing."

Seeing that her appeals were not having the hoped-for effect, she changed direction. Pleading, she tried a new course, hoping to calm his fury. "Why can't you be happy about this wonderful news? So what if it's too soon? Can't you see it's in God's plans and must be accepted?"

It was at that point that his rage erupted and he brutally slapped her over and over and had stormed out the door. Snowball, well aware of Tony's fury, had run to hide, not taking any chance at being a target.

It has to be the money and his incessant desire for things, Rosa mused, all those modern things—things we can't afford.

Ironically, it was only yesterday that Tony had told her that they were finally starting to get ahead. He had said, "I want to own a car, any car. We can soon afford one, even if it doesn't run. Shoot, I'll fix it if it doesn't." Tony's experience working on large engines when in the Navy made fixing cars seem simple.

To emphasize his point, Tony had gone on to explain, "I've recently read that America is now known as the land of the automobile. Do you know there is at least one car for every six Americans? But here in East Utica, it's more like war-torn Germany, where the newspaper said there's one for every 289. Think how grand we will appear if we have a car."

Rosa had replied, "So what of appearances? We don't need a car. It's not that far to walk to any place here."

"I'll decide what we need and when we need it," Tony had answered.

Enraged and hurting, Rosa could not control runaway thoughts, thinking with sadness, *Now that our natural animal urges have made a life and something precious to look forward to, certainly more precious than any automobile, he storms off.* She pushed herself with difficulty up from the floor. Picking up a fallen chair that Tony had flung in his rage, she turned to put out the stove. Crying, she fumed at the waste of the expensive food and the memory of the moment just past.

Rosa had felt the tension slowly building, wondering when Tony would blow. She had known that she was pregnant for over a month. Fear of choosing the wrong time to tell him of her pregnancy had driven her to conceal what would naturally be obvious in a few short weeks.

The last months of their marriage had been much better, or so it seemed, once she felt able to fulfill marital responsibilities. She enjoyed carnal pleasures as well as Tony, but she realized that it never seemed to be enough for him.

Tony had returned to his moody self of old, like when they first met and she was fresh and ignorant.

She tried desperately to make some sense of it, often blaming herself, thinking back to that pivotal day last September when Rocco had visited and Tony, after quickly eating, had run off to work to an extra shift. Later, he returned home with bloodstains on his shirt. She thought little of it at the time, because he often administered first aid to injured workers. When in the Navy, he had received medic training when serving briefly on the hospital ship, *USS Mercy*. He had learned advanced first aid skills, and they often came in handy at home and at the job.

No, she surmised sadly, *there's more to that night.* He had returned home about five a.m. with a distant, forlorn, and dispassionate look. He even passed on promised sexual favors.

Yes, she pondered, *it was then that he'd turned into a recluse, taking me, like so much meat, only when it pleased him, taking me whenever he felt like it.* She had willingly, then dutifully, tried to help him get past his shifting moods. Still, he wanted nothing more from her beyond sex and food, and often had even rudely said so.

Their first wedding anniversary had come and then passed without even a comment from Tony; it was followed by a spiritless Christmas. Rosa, by then sadly distraught and confused, realized without further doubts that their marriage was in trouble.

On their first wedding anniversary, she had made a special dinner and even had baked Tony's favorite, pumpkin pie. He didn't come home until well after ten o'clock that evening. When he saw the pie, he choked up, seemingly embarrassed, though not enough to say a word except to refuse the pie, saying he'd eaten earlier.

Rosa, picking up the remnants of Tony's fury, barely heard the baby's chatter coming from the bedroom. Placing the last shards of glass in the trash bin, then she wrapped a linen napkin around her bleeding hand before she went to Joanna's crib.

Joanna was standing in her crib, smiling, happy, and oblivious to her mother's grief.

Speaking slowly in English, Rosa enunciated, as clearly as she could, "Look at you, my pretty baby, standing there like a brave little girl. Soon you'll be walking, and then we'll have to talk about the rules." She scooped Joanna from the crib, nuzzling and smothering her with warm kisses, blood dripping from her wounds, onto the crib bedding and the baby. Joanna responded with something that sounded to Rosa like "Ma."

"Did you just say what I thought you did?" Rosa held her child out at arm's length, staring at her, swollen eye to baby eye, smiling. Joanna smiled in return, giggling, happy.

This can't go on. My heart hurts even more than this dreadful sting on my face. I must talk to someone, anyone, about what to do. And then she thought of Nellie.

Nellie lived several blocks away on South Street. The walk would be difficult, yet she made a quick decision to leave, surmising it would do her good. Then doubt set in. *Can I carry Jennie in this cold?* Hesitating but for a second, Rosa decided it was the only thing she could do. She quickly fed Jennie, and then raced to put together the baby's needs for the brief visit. *What's the worst that can happen during a brisk walk on a mild February day?* She wrapped her face in a warm scarf to cover her wounds.

The moment her feet touched the sidewalk, entering into the sunny, yet bitterly cold day, she wanted to turn back. After all, it would be easier to do so. Something strong inside her made her go forward.

The sidewalks were mostly clear as she carefully maneuvered the slick, snow-shoveled paths. She clutched Jennie, who was wrapped like an Egyptian mummy, toasty warm in several blankets.

It seemed to her like forever before she reached Nellie's home. Once there, she climbed the four familiar porch steps leading up to the inviting wide porch and front door entrance. She hesitated, and then knocked sheepishly at the door. *What will Nellie's aunt and uncle think when they see my bruised face? If we could only afford one of those fancy new telephones Tony's always talking about. They say people can call 7,000 miles away, yet we can't even call someone less than a mile away.*

At the door, her scarf slipped and she attempted to wrap it higher to hide the bruises. She was too late. Nellie's Uncle Giorgio opened the door; his smile of welcome transformed to a gaze of concern.

Though the wounds were obvious, he restrained his desire to comment on them. "Rosa, what brings you and the bambino out on such a bitter day?" Before she could answer, he said, "Come in quickly, you'll catch your death."

Rosa, thankful for Giorgio's discretion, stood in the foyer as he called Nellie.

Nellie came quickly, and upon seeing Rosa, her expression changed from happiness to stunned surprise. Fright flashed in her wide brown eyes. Silent, Nellie reached instinctively for the baby, inviting Rosa to shed her coat and boots.

"Aunt Eva's visiting friends; she'll be disappointed to have missed your visit." Nellie said, carefully selecting each word, knowing Rosa would explain in her own time.

"Yes, Tony hit me," Rosa said, breaking the ice. Uncontrollable tears streamed from her eyes.

"Why? Did you deserve it?"

"No, and heck no! I told him I'm pregnant, and he went crazy, I suppose because of the extra money it'll cost." Rosa took a deep breath, sucking in her disgrace, knowing she had to tell someone, and already feeling a little better for doing so.

Nellie pondered her next query cautiously, "Surely there has to be more to this mess than that? I can see maybe if you did something, said something. But a new baby, this...I think this kind of news is wonderful, regardless of the money issue. What's wrong with Tony?"

Rosa didn't say a thing. She just stood there staring blankly as Nellie coddled Jennie, who was now cooing in her second cousin's arms.

Nellie hesitated, looking tenderly at Rosa and then little Jennie, her godchild. "Oh Rosa, I'm so happy for you—another baby. Yet, I'm saddened, too. I never thought Tony could be this way. Maybe he's having a bad time at work and the news caught him at the wrong time. There has to be a good explanation."

"Nellie, that may be the case, I don't know," Rosa said, through swollen lips, as she sank into a chair, tired from the walk and emotional stress. "I try, but he never wants to talk. He just comes home, eats, and goes out. He never spends time with Jennie. I usually see him only at bedtime. And because he's drunk most of time, I waited more than a month for what I thought would be the right time to tell him."

"Still, there must be an explanation," said Nellie.

"No, I once believed the same as you, but I just don't understand him anymore, not that I really ever did. He thinks having another baby's a sin, my sin."

Nellie held Jennie closer, walking to soothe her. She looked sternly at Rosa. "How long has he been violent?"

"Not long, that's just it. He seems to hold things in. Usually he just shouts and yells a lot when he does let go. He's always been that way; though it's never been like today. It was like a bomb exploded inside him, and I was his target."

"Poor girl! Are you going back to him? I'm certain my aunt and uncle will put you up until things calm down."

"No, I must go back," she stated with frightful resignation. "I just needed to talk to someone. You know, tell someone I love and trust, who won't go crazy like my papa. And perhaps give me advice, or lend a friendly ear."

Nellie looked fondly at her cousin, but with new eyes. Rosa had aged well beyond her eighteen years. "Your papa would not go crazy, would he?" Nellie sat on the couch, cradling Jennie in her arms.

"Papa, bless his heart, is a very quiet and gentle man. However, he's only that until someone hurts someone that he loves. I've seen his anger, and believe me, it can be a cold, controlled, fury when aroused. I don't want him to hate my husband. That could turn out to be very nasty. Right now, Tony and he get along a lot better than I do with my in-laws. Heaven knows I try, but Giovanna can get under my skin, and lately she doesn't even have to try to get my goat. I do whatever I can to avoid her. Maybe that's another reason for his rage. I just don't know."

"I doubt that. Louis told me that Tony ran away from home just to get away from her dictatorship. I also heard she'd even give Mussolini a challenge or two. I suppose you have to be careful, though, since your papa is still living in that hovel above their garage."

"Yes. I wish he would come live with us. Tony and I invited him a few weeks ago, when things were better between us. But Papa's vast pride will not allow it. He said the worst place for an old man was to live with a young married couple. He insists that the garage flat is the best place for him. It's cheap and it allows him to save faster to bring my mama to Utica, though I am beginning to doubt this will ever happen."

Nellie asked, "Weren't you also helping to save for Antoinette?"

"Yes, I was. Most of it, though, went to the hospital when Jennie was born, along with some of Papa's money, too." Rosa looked almost embarrassed from her words.

Uncle Giorgio came into the room. "Rosa, I have made some tea. Would you and Nellie like some? It will take off the chill."

"That is so kind of you. Yes, tea sounds wonderful."

Jennie had fallen asleep in Nellie's arms. Rosa noticing, asked, "Nellie, would you like me to take her? Your arms must be tired."

"No, Rosa, I could hold this beautiful child forever, if you'd let me."

Nellie returned to the immediate problem. "As long as this has never happened before, it may be good for you to confront Tony to find out what's really behind this rage. Ask him if it's something you've done. Then correct what you can for your part. For little Jennie's sake and the precious little one you're carrying, you must give it a try."

"Yes, I suppose you're right."

"Good, now that that is settled, let me see if there's anything I can do for those bruises."

"No, I want him to see what he has done. This much, he owes me."

"Rosa, you always were a bit stubborn when we were children. Have it your way. I suggest against it, but it's your life. Why not forgive him, and live and let live?"

"Forgive him like Jesus forgives? Does the Bible suggest that hitting a woman for sport is okay?"

"Rosa, as I recall, with my limited knowledge of that Good Book, women had little or no rights in those ancient times. From what I've read, Tony would most likely be given a medal for keeping his wife in line."

"Yes, perhaps you're right; but this is America, after all, isn't it, and not the old country of the Good Book. And cousin, I have an American daughter, and if the good Lord heeds my prayers, He will never allow this to happen to her like He did me."

"Rosa, it's not right to blame God. I doubt He had anything to do with this."

"Sorry, Nellie, again you're correct. Now I must ask the Lord's forgiveness too. This has certainly been a long and difficult day."

Nellie suggested coyly, "Well at least it'll give you something to say at confession."

Rosa smiled at her cousin's good humor.

Nellie continued, "I do have some good news that will cheer you, or at least I hope it will. I had planned on visiting tomorrow, but...no, on second thought, now is not a good time."

The sweet aroma of the blended lavender tea filled the room as Uncle Giorgio entered, carrying the silver-plated tray.

"Nellie, here, let me take Jennie, so you can enjoy the tea," Rosa said.

"No, don't you dare take her. She's so precious. I'll hold her if you don't mind."

"Then I'll pour the tea. One lump or two?"

"One, please," Nellie answered, trying desperately to avoid staring at her facial bruises and the many cuts on Rosa's hand.

Ignoring the tea once it was poured, Rosa's voice became resolute. "Now don't play this game with me, Nellie Tedesco. I must hear your news. Please," she pleaded. "I could use good news. On second thought, it is good news, isn't it?"

"Uncle Giorgio, won't you join us? I may need your support. I'm not sure what Rosa may feel about this subject that she insists on hearing." Smiling, Giorgio sat down, placing a dish of freshly baked sugar cookies on the table.

Persistent, Rosa asked, "So, what's the good news that can wait and then cannot wait?"

Rosa cracked a smile. It hurt to smile, bringing unpleasant reminders of her terrible day. She put the pain aside, excited for her friend, not wanting to spoil the news. Stirring two sugar cubes into the tea and sipping the mellow liquid helped relieve some of her tension and the cuts in her mouth.

Just then, Jennie started to become restless. Rosa said, "Let's hurry with your news. I think Jennie's wet and will also be hungry soon."

Nellie blurted out her news, unable to contain it a minute longer, "Louis asked me to marry him. He even asked permission from Uncle Giorgio, who said yes, but," she smirked, "only after I had already said yes." Nellie shrieked, excited and beaming.

"Why, this news is certainly no surprise to me," said Rosa, meaning every word. "I thought Louis would have asked for your hand long ago. I'm truly happy for you. Louis is a good man, and you two have made a match in the good American fashion, by falling in love first."

"I hoped you'd feel this way. And now, Rosa, for my big and important question: mind you, you don't have to answer today, but will you do me the honor of being my matron of honor?"

"Of course, I will," said Rosa, holding her fingers to her puffy nose. "I thought I couldn't smell, yet I can certainly smell this diaper. I have to address the urgent needs of my Jennie. If I may, I'd like to change, and feed her, in the privacy of your bedroom. Then I'll have to be on my way. I've some fence mending to do."

With sudden worry, Rosa said, "Nellie, I'll look like a balloon again. When is the wedding date?

"Next year!" she beamed, her voice animated. "Louis is both practical and so proper. The priest has agreed to marry us next January, so you should be skinny again," she smiled.

Rosa returned the smile; she took Jennie to her friend's bedroom, happy for the brief solitude even if it took a smelly diaper. Quickly changing the baby, she opened her blouse, offering sustenance to her child who was now in advanced hunger. Jennie puckered her little face; apparently, her mother's squabble had soured her milk.

Nellie shouted into the room through the partly open door, interrupting Rosa's concentration. "When you're ready, I'll walk home with you."

"No, it's not necessary," said Rosa.

But Nellie would not be persuaded otherwise.

Tony paced the kitchen floor. He had returned after two hours of fuming to a cold, uninviting apartment. Rosa and the baby were gone and everything smelled of burned food. There was a huge gouge on the wooden floor from where the glass had fallen and some shards missed by Rosa were still scattered about the floor. *Did I do this?* Concern dabbled with uncaring, he grabbed the opened bottle of wine on the table and a glass from the cupboard, pulled out a chair, sat, and began to read the paper.

Snowball peered warily from hiding, watching his every movement. Scrunched under the icebox, hidden from her master's fury, she watched intently for an opportunity to safely use the litter box.

Tony felt contrite. He never meant to harm her. It just happened so fast. Though frustrated with life, he knew that was no excuse to hurt the one person he had learned to love in an otherwise loveless life.

Life had not been the same since the last time he'd been forced to do Rabiso's dirty work. Now almost two months later, he recalled with distaste acting the good soldier in Rabiso's little army. He could never erase the look of fear on the rich man's contrite face before he killed him.

"I have three children," he pleaded. "Please don't…" Those were his last pathetic words.

Tony had not planned to kill him. But when Gino arrived with the news that the Polish girl had died, he went crazy.

That girl had been like his Rosa, innocent. Before Rosa, he had never given even a passing thought about the girls working for Rabiso. To him they were cattle. After Rosa, he appreciated that they had lives, tough breaks, worries and concerns, just as he. Once he put the face of humanity on Rabiso's human stock, everything became confusing, difficult, and worse, upsetting. He resented his conflicting feelings, knowing that he could not hide them forever despite the fact that he could not do anything about them. And now the Polish girl was dead and buried, alone in the cold, unfeeling earth, with no family to cry over her, in some pauper's grave. He wanted to place some flowers on her grave, but didn't know how to find it without causing suspicion.

On that terrible night, he had gone temporarily crazy, out of control, and now it haunted him. Like the grim reaper, he had felt like a vengeful god dispensing punishment with little remorse. He felt weakened when he began to feel remorse and especially now when his work required that he kill or direct killings. Up until now, he had been a good soldier in an organization that demanded loyalty, and if Tony was anything, he was loyal.

Feeling helpless, he thought, *I can't do this anymore. And now Rosa's pregnant, just when I was about to tell her I want to leave for California. How in heaven can I leave now, with no job or money, one baby, and another on the way? Nice timing, Rosa.*

Tony felt like a prisoner of war and he subconsciously blamed his wife. He rationalized that ironically he was imprisoned for doing the right thing for once in his life. It gnawed at his inner being, knowing that his baby, and especially Rosa, deserved better than he could ever give. And worse, he felt helpless to give it, at least in his current predicament.

Hearing soft footsteps coming up the creaky stair, he steeled himself for Rosa's entrance.

"Where've you been?" He looked aghast at her face. *Did she go out with those bruises, advertising to the whole world that she was beaten? Did I do this?*

"Out to see Nellie," she muttered coldly through swollen lips. "And where did you go in such a hurry?"

"That's my concern," he said defiantly. "If you must know, I went for a walk, to think."

"Tony, we both need to talk."

"Yeah, I know. Don't you ever realize you make me so crazy sometimes?"

"You'll have to tell me how I make you so crazy. Then I promise that I'll do everything in my power to correct it." Rosa tried to smile, she couldn't; it hurt too much. "But first let me put Jennie to bed, and then we can talk."

Tony thought, *Yes, I'll talk, though I won't promise to listen. I am wrong. I know it. I cannot show it though, not and retain my dignity.*

The loud ticking of the cheap, windup clock sitting on their kitchen's wooden shelf emphasized the pounding of his heart. He didn't want to be here, not now or ever, and yet something always brought him back. He didn't want the responsibilities. With regret at his inability to change for the better, he thought, *Responsibility is such a big, lonely word, and a word that doesn't fit me.*

"What's taking so long?" he shouted, desperate to talk out the anger. His anger, though, was not really aimed at Rosa. She was just in the wrong place at the wrong time. His carried a deep anger, and she was an inconvenient, if unintentional obstacle to his freedom. He had never wanted to aim his fury at her. Only now, with sudden, frustrating comprehension, he realized he could never forgive her for her innocence. He knew deep down that he could never be that innocent again, and therefore could never be her equal. The thought humbled and hurt him. He couldn't bear to think that way for long. His pride got the best of his good intentions.

A revelation seemed to go off in his head, like a light bulb, lit for him to see. He thought, *Sometimes an innocent passerby gets hurt. My only mistake was that I care. She wants a life I can't give to her, not here, not ever.*

His dilemma was becoming an obsession, and right now he didn't care to face it. Picking up his leather coat, carelessly tossed on the floor, he walked out the door, closing it quietly.

Snowball peered out from her refuge, pleased to see him leave. She skittered on soft padded paws to her litter box.

Rosa came into the kitchen, "Okay, I'm ready to talk."

There was no answer. Confused, Rosa sat in the rocking chair just staring at the door, wishing it would open. It didn't.

"I laugh, for hope hath happy place with me,
my bark sinks, 'tis to another sea."

Author, from "A Poet's Hope"

FIFTEEN

Historians would say that the year 1927 was the end of an era of staggering growth and exciting times for America. It also was the last grand bash before the onset of the Great Depression and the turbulent years that would lead the way to World War II. But both events were far away, though looming in the wings, waiting like demons in the dark of night for the opportunity to realize the full potential of their collective surreal futures.

The good times of the 1920s somehow eluded my little family. Yes, several highlights from 1927 come to mind, not because I remember them, for I was still a baby. But for many a year, the last hurrah before the Depression was pumped into my generation as a reminder of what could be. Events like these come to mind: the invention of talking pictures featuring the music of Al Jolson forever immortalized in the movie, *The Jazz Singer*. Lucky Lindy flew the Atlantic alone, in his famous airplane, *the Spirit of St. Louis*, and George Herman Ruth, known to baseball fans as the Babe, hit sixty homers. The news in East Utica was also filled with the Sacco and Vanzetti story. Two Italian immigrants died in a Massachusetts' electric chair for a crime of which many throughout the civilized world believed them innocent, though no one ever knew for sure. Yes, there were many events that year, though none as important to me as the birth of my little brother Rocco Joseph on Monday, August 29, 1927.

Mother had told me that Father was often away during the pregnancy. She wanted to believe that it was because of his work, though early in 1927, she already had little hope that their faltering marriage was salvageable, as Father increasingly revealed his ugly side. Young, only eighteen, naïve and afraid, she didn't know how to handle Father's abuse. Sadly, she didn't dare tell anyone except Nellie, who, always the loyal cousin and best friend, kept it to herself. Mother couldn't talk about it with my father, and even if she had dared, there always was the very real risk of suffering his violence. So I suppose it was lucky for her that Father was rarely home.

Grandfather Rocco slaved as a laborer night and day, holding down two jobs, saving every penny he could for my grandmother's passage. It seemed that every time he took a step forward, he was forced to take two backwards. Every honest person he knew was as poor as he so he tried, without success, to borrow funds from legitimate sources. Physically, he was a strong man, but excessive fatigue and its accompanying stress had begun to take their toll. By the time Rocky was born, he had almost saved enough. He was talking about making preparations for Grandma Antoinette's voyage, which was now primarily awaiting the sale of their home in Missanello.

I'm told that Father rarely explained his actions or absence, nor even tried to make amends or excuses. In his world, everything was his business and no one else's concern. I was exactly fourteen months old when my brother was born. I was the lucky one; at least I was wanted, or so I thought.

A crisp October morning greeted Rosa as she wheeled her two babies along Mary Street. Rosa loved the bright leaves, not ever seeing them as harbingers of winter, only the paintbrush of fall. Today she was anxious to see Nellie to discuss wedding plans. It was a wonderful day to be alive, scuffing through the colorful leaves that covered the walk, falling all around her by the hundreds, some even cascading into the carriage and brilliantly carpeting the landscape. Reaching into the carriage, she picked a random leaf from Rocky's blanket, careful not to awaken either child. Both were happily sleeping, mesmerized by the swaying movement of the old baby buggy.

Rosa studied the maple leaf; its pretty, red-orange hue, brilliant and beautiful, resonated with her own good feeling. Looking at the carriage, she saw in its frame the tender love that her father had spent during his precious few work free hours to fix it and make it acceptable. Coated with fresh black paint, it could pass easily for new.

Walking helped her to think, and sometimes it even helped her solve many of life's mundane everyday problems. Today she was trying desperately not to worry. Worry nowadays was not new to her, yet she seldom gave in to it, having learned early in life that it only invited unnecessary inner turmoil. Still, as the high of the beautiful morning started to wear off, she began to wrestle uncontrollably with her acute anxiety. Thinking about her last conversation with Tony made her cringe in fear. It had been foolish, so difficult to understand, and it was more than six weeks ago. It still bothered her, though she tried hard to push aside her concern. She had prayed to Saint Matthew, remembering with comfort the words about the little sparrow in Matthew 6 of her well worn and aged Italian Bible.

It's funny how two people seeing the same thing can come to such varying opinions. Rocco had once said, to the dismay of her mother, "Opinions, my daughter, are like bumholes. Everyone has one and feels compelled to use it." Antoinette had scolded Rocco for his choice of words and he had laughed it off. Rosa laughed now at the memory of the chagrin on her mother's face and her father's rare use of profanity, especially in front of his children.

Many subtle things about Tony upset her lately. Somehow, though, their last conversation pricked her like a sore scab, itching and unwilling to heal.

It was really an unnecessary argument, quite childish, bantering about who remembered what when they decided on names for their children months before Jennie was born. Tony had chosen their daughter's name, and Rocco's name was to be Rosa's choice. They had both agreed to this, or so she vividly remembered. Yet, Tony had argued, "It's not right that we name my son after your father. Tradition dictates we name him Nicola or Nicholas after mine." She had adamantly refused, more so on principle, knowing Giovanna was somewhere in the background, hidden behind his words. She had proceeded to restate their initial accord, reminding him that they had agreed to name their child after Rocco, adding Tony's middle name.

"Tony," she had said, "naming our boy after Papa is keeping with tradition." Leaving out nothing, she reminded, "Whatever happened to your grand bantering about having your own so-called independence. It's time you stood up to your family's interference with our lives."

The mention of the word "independence" had seemed to hit a hot button. Tony left in a huff, not a new event in their troubled lives. He had barely spoken to her since.

Something in Rosa's peripheral vision suddenly caught her by surprise. She looked instinctively across the busy windswept street. What she saw in her first glimpse was a seemingly familiar man with his back to her. She recognized the man's back now. It was Tony. She hadn't seen him in two days. He was supposed to be in Albany on a business trip for Mr. Rabiso.

What to do, she wondered. As if on autopilot, she started to cross the street, but hesitated. The young woman Tony was talking to was pretty with her painted face, good body, and flimsy dress. The *putana* then pressed her body into Tony's, kissing him firmly on his eager lips.

Rosa felt weak, ill, and upset all at once. Wanting to vomit, she quickly turned her back to the scene before her, forgetting temporarily about Nellie. Luckily, Gino, standing next to Tony and ogling the other girls, didn't notice her, though she thought with increased worry, he could have. With genuine fear at being seen, Rosa quickly hurried down the street and out of sight.

This shall be my little secret, she thought with remorse. *What else can I do?* She walked blindly, going as fast as her anxious legs could carry her. Numbed, she went several blocks before stopping, and only then because Rocky began to cry, no doubt, hungry. Tears began to flood in rivulets across her cheeks. Sobbing, she reached down to settle her son. It didn't work; Rocky, then Joanna cried, sensing their mother's unease. Rosa knew that only food would serve to quiet him.

Not here, not now. She needed privacy to breastfeed. *Rocky must wait for a more private place.* Patting both children gently, she turned the carriage, moving quickly toward Nellie's home.

Nellie, looking out her parlor window, wondered what had happened to Rosa. It was unlike her to be late, especially when she was so anxious and excited about discussing the wedding plans for January.

Nellie thought, *I'm sure there's a good explanation. I told her I'd go there, but I guess she needs to escape that stuffy flat. It would have been easier, but Rosa can be stubborn.* She shook her head in consternation.

Suddenly, as if on cue, Nellie saw Rosa through the parlor window. She looked flustered and in a hurry, pushing her carriage. Rushing to the front door, Nellie quickly opened it, running to greet them. While excited to see her cousin, she was more excited to see the children.

Instantly upon seeing Rosa, she knew by her unkempt and upset face that there was a problem.

"Rosa, what happened to you? You look terrible."

"Nellie, I'll tell you soon enough," her voice quivered, barely audible. "My Rocky needs to eat and Jennie needs changing." Rosa chose her priorities. Her children's needs came first.

"Come inside. I'll change Jennie and you go feed Rocky. Then, cousin, we talk," Nellie said, composed yet her voice stern.

With the children settled, they sat in the parlor, where Rosa described her discovery on Mary Street, emphasizing the unmentionable place. Nellie's first reaction was outrage. "A whore, he's kissing a whore, out in the open, like the village idiot. I'm sorry, Rosa, but you need to divorce this fool."

Rosa answered, "I can't do that. You know full well it's against our religion to divorce. And even if I did go against the Church, what would I do with two babies? At least he provides the necessities, even if we never see him. If I leave, I might become a burden to my father, and then what? That poor man is working two jobs now, and we never see him as it is. And worse, he still lives in Tony's family garage." She began to sob.

Nellie, undeterred, spoke defiantly, "Rosa, you know how much I love your father, but it was he who arranged this terrible match. You need to talk to him."

Upset, and near panic, Rosa replied, "Nellie, I can't do this to him. Yes, he did arrange this. But after all, I'm not totally innocent. I have a major part, that's what everyone will think anyway. And now I'm in such a fix. This is one hole I have dug that I can't seem to climb out of."

"Nuts, don't you dare take the blame. As I see it, that abusive fool is out of control. Somehow, you must get him to stop before he kills you. I know that he still hits you, though now, the no good is more careful where. This garbage has been going on far too long. And by the way, tell me again—what was he doing when you saw him in the middle of the day—and a Sunday, no less, and at that place? I thought you said he was in Albany on business. You know, for his boss."

Rosa said, "I'm sure there's an explanation, at least about Albany. Heaven knows I want there to be one. Maybe I am no longer enough for him."

Rosa fidgeted with the red ribbon in Jennie's hair, searching for something to say while tying the bright ribbon that accented Joanna's jet-black hair. "I can't think, Nellie. Maybe, I suppose, it's because I just want to blindly believe he's innocent and this mess will disappear. Yes, the cheating no good son of Satan isn't in Albany, that's for certain. Heck, he even took my old cardboard suitcase." She began to cry, unable to hold back the sobbing. Soon both children, as if on cue, began to cry as well.

Nellie said, "You need to get a handle on things; then we'll face this mess together."

Nellie's voice, gentle and genuine, calmed Rosa.

"Nellie, thanks, but this is my mess, not yours. It's unfair to get you involved, especially now. Frankly, I don't want to see you get hurt. I'm living proof that he can be a brute, and when you least expect it. You don't need this."

Nellie responded, "I know what he is; your bruises are proof enough for me. It's that wild blood running through his veins. He wouldn't dare lay a hand on me. I have too many male cousins here and a fiancé who knows about everything that has happened and who'd like nothing other than to make him a miserable lump."

Rosa said, "You don't know him like I do. Something has changed him. It must be his job, or at least something he keeps hidden all to himself. Whatever it is, it has caused him to change. I sometimes think he enjoys the meanness, especially since he seems to hate everything. And unfortunately, we're not excluded."

"Rosa, if you agree, I'll talk to Uncle Giorgio; he's good about keeping secrets. Who knows, he might have a solution. Maybe he can try to talk some sense into Tony. You know, kind of help as a go between."

"Thank you, Nellie, I know you're sincere and the idea is appealing, but I can't get Uncle Giorgio involved. Let me handle this in my own way. I promise that I'll follow your suggestion if all becomes hopeless."

Skeptical, Nellie said, "Okay, I'll agree at least for a little while, only not for much longer. Do you understand why?" Nellie reinforced her emphasis on "why" with her loving pat on each sleeping child's head.

Rosa nodded her agreement, "Now, Nellie, let's talk about what I came here for—your wedding."

"Not until we feed Jennie. It looks like she's awake and famished."

Rosa laughed, "Nellie, it's beginning to look like you'll make a wonderful mother someday."

Nellie beamed, "I hope so. But Rosa, how on earth do you handle two babes so young? I think I'll try my best to space my children a little further apart. Give me the bottle; I'll warm up some milk. I do give you credit. I know I couldn't do this as well, especially…" Nellie trailed off, choosing to say nothing. She headed to the kitchen to warm the baby bottle.

Rosa called to Nellie as she left for the kitchen, "Thank you, Nellie, for listening. And by the way, cousin, I do believe you could handle my mess and more. You're a good friend and one tough bird." Privately, Rosa thought, *Now what do I do?*

It was snowing. December winds whipped at her face, a cutting reminder of winter's fury. Genesee Street, Utica's central business district, was decorated in holiday finery with the reds and greens and gold of Christmas. The street's colorful storefronts displayed gifts and happiness, a happiness that eluded Rosa. Christmas was only two weeks away and she had no money for gifts. Tony gave her just enough for bare essentials, nothing more. He used the rest of his money for his own varied pleasures.

Rosa had no intention of celebrating anyway; maybe she'd try to buy a small gift for Papa or perhaps some fruit for Nellie, or even bake some of her favorite cookies and box them as gifts.

Tony's physical abuse continued, but now her bruises were in places well hidden from the public eye. Still, sadly, she had had difficulty convincing herself that it was necessary to consider a divorce—that is, until just recently when he had threatened the children.

Distraught, she barely saw the Nativity scene on display at Grace Episcopal Church as she passed. Nellie's uncle had arranged for her to meet an attorney, a Mr. Joseph Gallo. She was to meet him at the corner of Genesee and Bleecker Streets.

Christmas was everywhere in the air of the city with its special excitement; however, she felt nothing. Normally she would have absorbed every moment and everything she saw, but not today. Her mind was elsewhere, worried and confused. She hardly noticed the street noises, honking cars, or the happy people talking as they passed her by.

Uncle Giorgio had told her to discuss only specifics with the attorney and see whether further meetings would be necessary. Gallo was meeting her for free, as a favor, probably in return for some long ago good deed of Giorgio or his large family. Nellie had agreed to watch the children.

Gallo, having passed the bar exam only weeks earlier, had agreed to meet outside the office. Uncle Giorgio had said that his new employer would have to bill her if they met at the office, and that Gallo wanted to see if there was a possibility for a suit before requesting to work the case with something called "pro bono."

If Rosa decided that a divorce was the way to go, Uncle Giorgio felt that she would only have to pay the money required for court filing. Nellie said she would help. Rosa suspected that Uncle Giorgio, always a softy for a good cause, was behind her offer, since Nellie had little if any money.

Nellie had told her it would take a lot of courage to do it, but that it was worth talking to the lawyer, no matter what. Rosa wished she could summon that courage now, or any courage for that matter. However, she didn't feel very brave, only scared, confused, concerned, and wanting desperately to turn back. Only her fear for her children drove her forward.

Am I doing the right thing? she thought, brushing snow from her coat while she waited. As she stood at the busy corner, shivering from the wind, a tall, good-looking young man, about twenty-five, approached.

"Are you Mrs. Rosa Lavalia?" he asked carefully. A broad, inviting smile greeted her from under his fur hat.

"Yes," she replied sheepishly. "Mr. Gallo?" she asked.

He nodded. "Let's go into Woolworth's where we can get warmed. Can you use a cup of coffee? I know I sure can," he said with an inviting smile.

By coincidence, across the same intersection of Genesee and Elizabeth Streets, Tony was driving Rabiso's delivery truck, chauffeuring Mario, sitting to his right. Mario jabbered away about something or other, but Tony didn't hear a word because the sight of his wife standing at the street corner suddenly distracted him. *Why is she downtown in this snowstorm? Where are the children?* He wondered, *And who is the tall stranger in the expensive clothes?* Tony had lost count of the times he had cheated on Rosa. But although he considered cheating as his sole right, it was certainly not hers.

"Hey daydreamer! Wake up and pay attention," Mario scolded in a loud voice.

"Sorry, Mr. Rabiso, I thought I saw an old friend. What was it you were saying?"

Mario said, "Drive, it's not worth repeating."

The truck's old windshield blades worked overtime, trying unsuccessfully to keep up with the snow that was now falling in big, moist flakes. Tony became angrier at each passing swipe of the blades, the blade's constant repetition reminding him of his inability to take care of personal business, at least for the moment.

Joe Gallo took a sip of the cafeteria's strong black coffee, waving off the refill the pretty young waitress tried to give him. He noticed that Mrs. Lavalia had not touched hers.

Looking into the peering eyes of his attractive potential client, he commented, "Mrs. Lavalia, that about wraps it up. There isn't much we can do to prove infidelity without the money for a private investigator. Abandonment's our only hope, but it's my opinion that it probably won't fly because your husband provides adequately for your basic necessities. I suggest you try to work things out, or maybe start saving money for an investigator. I really would like to help, but…" he hesitated, trying to find the right way to say what he must to this woman who deserved much more.

Finally, he added, "My hands are legally tied. There's nothing I can do." In his youth and inexperience, he had not developed enough common sense to offer her other options.

Rosa felt lost and helpless as she gazed at Gallo's honest, yet naive face. His answer was not what she wished. However, feeling helpless, she quickly summoned up the strength to accept his answer. *What else can I do?*

"Thank you Mr. Gallo, you have been most kind. I'll do what I can to follow your advice, though I doubt it will ever work. It takes two, and my husband, well..." she hesitated, "doesn't see things like you do." They shook hands, and Attorney Gallo politely excused himself to leave.

"Merry Christmas, Mrs. Lavalia. I do hope you can come to a solution for your problem."

Rosa, trying to remain positive, replied. "Thank you, Mr. Gallo. And a Merry Christmas to you also."

Rosa left the cafeteria, feeling embarrassed and flustered. *Why couldn't I have met a man like this guy—bright, intelligent, with a good career?* she regretted silently. She walked at a brisk pace, wanting to reach home as quickly as possible. Nellie was a good friend to watch her kids, but it wasn't Rosa's nature to take advantage, even for such a good reason.

On Bleecker Street, she passed St. John's Catholic Church, looming large across the snow-filled street. Without a second thought, she abruptly turned, crossed the street, and stopped and looked up at the inviting steps. The church's massive doors beckoned her. She hesitated for a moment, taking in the inviting entrance. She decided to enter and say a brief prayer. *It can't hurt. Maybe the Lord will give me some guidance. Heaven knows I can use some.*

She entered the church through its heavy doors, marveling at its beautiful interior. She walked past a few pews and knelt on the floor halfway up the aisle, making the sign of the cross before entering the pew. She knelt again and prayed, beginning with a few Hail Mary's and two Lord's Prayers, and then asking for help and divine guidance before getting up to leave.

She felt better. Not total relief, only the relief one gets when hope is sprinkled lavishly with faith. Walking toward the exit, she passed an elderly priest who nodded to her in silent acknowledgement.

The kind priest sensed the young girl's alarm, and breaking his silence he quietly asked her, "Is everything all right with you, young lady? You seem troubled. You've come to the right place if you are."

"Yes, Father," she answered, not knowing why, using her best English. She thought, *If you only knew the half of it.* "Yes, I'm just trying to get past some uninvited difficulty that has entered into my life, like a bad cold that won't quit."

"My child, trust in Jesus and place your problems at the foot of His cross. He will definitely help you."

"Father, could you…ah…" she hesitated, groaning silently as she stumbled on her words, searching for what to say. Still fumbling and uncertain, she finally blurted out, "Father, please bless me. I really need the Lord's love today."

"Then you shall have it and more, my child," he answered as he blessed her, making the sign of the trinity upon her forehead.

Rosa, feeling renewed, left the church thinking good thoughts for the first time in days, excited, energized. She was like a child again, and she ran down the stairs, unmindful of the snow, slipping, though not falling. She raced up Bleecker Street, turning south at Conkling Avenue and headed for Mary Street and home where she stopped abruptly. Startled, she saw Tony across the street, walking slowly, his head down to avoid the blowing snow. The day was beginning to turn dim as the early winter sun faded, its daily exit quickened by the falling snow and the cloud-darkened sky.

Upset about seeing his wife earlier, Tony had asked Mario if he'd mind if he got out at Mary Street so he could return home quicker, saying he had an important errand he had promised to do. Rabiso, in one of his more agreeable days, took over the wheel at John Street at about the same time Rosa left the church. Rosa and Tony's paths were on a collision course.

Tony, with head still down trying to avoid the bitter, biting wind, turned and instantly saw her standing on Conkling Avenue. Enraged, his swift legs ran across the street. Catching up to Rosa, he stood defiantly, blocking her progress.

With his voice spitting venom, he said, "I saw you with that man!" Now in an uncontrolled voice he said, "What's the deal? Are you cheatin' on me?"

Anger showered flames from his eyes like fire doing an epileptic dance. The outburst was joined as if in ceremony with the white clouds of smoke erupting from his breath. He didn't care if anyone heard his rage. Anyway, nobody was anywhere in sight, not that anyone was likely to interfere with a domestic squabble between two Dago immigrants.

Rosa faced him, standing firm and bold, speaking in a calming voice, "Tony, unless you cool down and speak civilly, I've nothing to say."

Tony, surprised and also miffed at her spunk, temporarily backed off, but only for a moment. He said in a threatening voice, his words wavering on the brink, "Okay then, explain it to me; I'm all ears." His sarcasm reeked of vengeance.

Not about to, nor willing to, back off, Rosa let out her long suppressed anger, exploding. "Where do you come off accusing me of cheating? Everyone but me knew how you cheated. I never believed it until I saw it myself last October. You, big man, who are you, kissing that whore of a brazen bleached blond? Oh, I saw you on Mary Street. You think I don't know what goes on in those houses."

He angrily replied, "So you know my secret. See if I care. If it weren't for me, it would be you kissing men like that whore, and worse, screwing any John that wanted you for a few bits."

He hissed his revelation, quietly enough for only Rosa to hear. "Yes, you were supposed to be a sex slave, Princess Ameduri. When your family came with you, I felt sorry for you, and guess what? I freakin' married you. And like a blasted fool, I got your brats and all your expenses to go along with the deal. Now, I'm stuck with you. That doesn't mean I need to take your crap or let other men enjoy what I bought and paid for."

Shocked, Rosa felt the tears begin to well up in her eyes. Still, she remained firm, drawing up her slight frame. With chin thrust forward, voice low, she spoke. "I have been repulsed by you more and more each passing day, Mr. Know-It-All. Now, at this moment I can't stand the sight of you. Just when I think I have seen it all, you deliver more grief. Nothing about you surprises me anymore."

Rosa continued defiantly, her voice hissing with venom, "You want to know who you saw talking to me today? Well here it is, bold and simple. He was not a lover, not even a friend. I saw an attorney. I'm not anything like you, Tony. I have nothing but loyalty for the blessed oath we took before God at our wedding. Oh, let me remind you, in case you've forgotten, it was almost two years ago. Not that you'll ever seem to remember the date, or even care. As for the attorney, he's working for me free, something they call 'pro bono,' to help me divorce you. You see, I want and need my life back. I also want that independence you're always preaching about when you talk about your precious California."

She was screaming, "And Tony, it can't come fast enough."

"Free, the jerk is working for free," he snickered. His face was contorted, his eyes piercing, his laugh evil. "One good look at you and that luscious body you carry around like a movie star, and even after two kids. Well, he'll want more from you than to work free."

Enraged, Tony said, "No, you can't see him again, and no, I will never allow a divorce."

"What's the matter, Tony? You afraid your parents will find out how you abuse me and threaten the children with more of the same. And all while you ignore them like they aren't yours?"

Tony raised his hand as if to hit her.

She shouted, "Sure, big man, go right ahead, hit me! It's all you know and all you've got! I'll not allow it, never again," she scoffed.

Tony lowered his hand, angry. "I don't believe you."

She laughed in his face, a low, hysterical cackle. "What a fool. You think anyone would want me with two kids? No man would want me, a poor immigrant and a freaking bad English speaking Wop to boot."

Defiantly spitting out her words, "All I see is that most men want what you want, a personal whore and housekeeper. Well, mister, I'm not for sale. Not anymore and not ever! I'm through with that."

Rosa fumed, and then screamed out, "And while we're at it, just what do you do for Rabiso? Your hands are never calloused like other workingmen's. Now I get it, he runs whores, doesn't he? Are you a pimp? Is that why I saw you hanging around that place?" Her questions rattled out in a staccato, raining heavily with disgust.

The sudden shocking realization that there was more to Tony's vocation fell unceremoniously into place like a ton of bricks. It had been on her mind for weeks, and suddenly it all added up: late hours, the cheap lingering perfume smell on his clothes, the occasional blood stains.

Tony shouted, his eyes bulging in rage, "Shut up!"

"I will not, you don't own me, not anymore you don't. I've more than paid you back in full for your precious passage!" she shouted with equal intensity.

Tony's head began to split from a lingering stress headache, and something inside him exploded. He was not going to let her talk to him this way. Painted images cast a vivid shadow on the moment. They were of his mother shouting at his father while his father just took it in stride. The image drove him wild. That would not happen to him. She would pay dearly for mouthing off like this. With sudden and complete hatred, he pulled out his stiletto and flashed it in her face, threatening and menacing.

Fearing the worst, she shouted in fear, "Put that ugly thing away!"

Tony, ignoring the scream, ripped the black overcoat, the one he had given her over two years earlier, from her body. He pushed her roughly to the ground, tossing the coat into the nearby bushes.

She pleaded now, "Tony, please, please, this is crazy. You're scaring me! Think of the children." Her agonized fear seemed to give him more encouragement.

"I'll show you, you crazy, worthless *putana*. I curse you and wish you dead. If you want your life back, here—I'll give you your precious freedom."

Not thinking, reacting only to primitive urgings and unthinkable rage, he pushed the knife hard into her, scraping breastbone; slicing deeply, he slid the knife down to her navel. Blood oozed all over the snow-covered sidewalk.

He screamed like a mad man, crazed with temporary insanity, cackling, "This is what you asked for. Now put the pieces of your life back together. Enjoy the freedom, and good luck! I'll see you in hell." He stalked off.

Rosa, her eyes still showing their surprise and fury, asked, "Why, Antonio? I'm the mother of your…" Her voice trailed off to a quiet murmur. Blood gurgled from her mouth, mingling with the bloody mess all over her.

Tony, numb at first, started to run. With the stark realization of what he had done, he threw the knife down the nearest storm sewer. Rosa's blood blanketed his body, his hands crimson. *Crazy, yes, I'm crazy!* He yelled, but nothing, no sound or utterance came from his mouth. It was then that he realized the stark urgency of his situation. The image of Rosa's blood-soaked body bothered him for only a moment, as he quickly turned his thoughts to escaping.

A passerby, the old priest from St. John's, found Rosa, breathing but barely alive. He took off his greatcoat, covering her, and despite the extreme cold and his advanced age, he ripped off his white shirt, gently trying to stop the bleeding. By the time the police and the ambulance came, it was almost too late.

But Rosa was a fighter. She struggled to stay alive, not knowing enough to die, not wanting to, not yet.

"Who did this to you?" the policeman softly asked.

Surprised, she heard her own faint whisper, barely audible, "My husband."

She closed her eyes. The cop thought she was dead; the kindly priest began last rites.

Then Rosa fell into the dark recess of her mind, unaware of anything, while others, all strangers, fought valiantly and without prejudice to save the life of the young immigrant girl and their fellow human being.

"Any coward can fight a battle when he's sure of winning, but give me the man who has the pluck to fight when he is sure of losing."

George Elliott (Mary Ann Evans)

SIXTEEN

The hospital corridors were a deathlike quiet. The waiting room's sterile, pungent, ammonia-laced atmosphere created its own special surreal fragrance. Rocco paced the corridor, returned, and then walked the same worrisome path over and over. Rosa had been in surgery for several hours.

Notified by an anxious Giorgio Tedesco, Rocco was pained when his friend described Rosa's injuries, repeating all that he had heard and leaving nothing to the imagination. The police were keeping silent, not divulging anything they may have had about who had cut his child up like a butcher cuts his wares.

Giorgio, a very perceptive man, visited the police station and had overheard an overworked desk sergeant boasting to a fellow cop that they had a pretty good idea who did it and that detectives were following up the lead. Giorgio kept it quiet, for he had suspicions of his own, starting that day when he first saw Rosa's bloodied face weeks earlier. Strangely, Tony was nowhere to be found; Giorgio had even sent word, via an acquaintance, to Nicola Lavalia's home. Sadly, and suspiciously, they were absent and not to be found.

Rocco turned to his friend, a worried look framed his face. "Giorgio, go home and rest. Don't you have to go to work in the next couple of hours? I really appreciate your being here for me, but I'll be fine."

Giorgio said, "You don't look so fine. Now, friend, if this were my Nellie in there, you, of all the people I know would be right here beside me. Rocco, I sincerely see it as my duty and privilege to wait with you."

He then grasped Rocco's arm, his gaze encouraging. "I know it seems dark now. It always is before the sunrise. In my heart and soul, I believe everything will be fine. Watch, you'll see: Rosa will make it. So let's say a prayer; it'll help us both."

"Giorgio, how can I thank you? Thank you for all you've done. Tracking me down at work, seeing to my grandchildren."

"Don't be silly. This is what friends are for. Eva and Nellie will take turns watching your grandchildren. And Nellie should be here soon. A wild pack of dogs could not keep her away from Rosa's side."

Rocco said, as he feebly pounded his hands together, "What I want to know is this; where are the Lavalias? Why aren't they here, she's family?"

"I don't know. I did send word twice. I can't imagine why, but perhaps there's a good reason," Giorgio stumbled, looking for the right words, all the while trying not to look directly at Rocco. "And even if they were here, what could they do?"

"Nothing," Rocco answered solemnly. His voice raised an octave. "No, I suppose you're right, they could do nothing. But by all the saints in heaven, they could show that they care!"

Rocco hesitated for a moment and then voiced the terrible thought that he had suppressed, "Do you think her husband has anything to do with this? Something smells here. Tell me, Giorgio. What is it that you know and are keeping from me?"

"Rocco, don't go flying to conclusions. I can't believe Tony would ever do this. What man would stoop that low?"

Rocco said, "You think I don't know, don't you? I've kept it all deep inside, all to myself. You of all men know that I've always believed it's proper for a man to step aside, let his grown children take care of their own problems. This is what I tell myself." His voice trailed off as his mind worried and raced into a cool contemplation.

He squirmed in his chair, tired, losing his breath, coughing, feeling the beginnings of a winter cold. Rocco went on, "Giorgio, a friend, a mutual acquaintance, told me he saw my daughter near your home sometime last October. You may remember it was when I was doing all those double shifts. He said her face was a mess, like she'd had a bad fall or been beaten. Do you know anything about this?" He looked into Giorgio's eyes, seeing he had struck a nerve.

"Yes, I do, my friend. She was badly bruised a few weeks back, I saw it myself. My Nellie told me Tony had hit Rosa over some silly argument. Rosa asked us to keep it to ourselves, so we did. Like you, I figured a married couple needs to work things out without interference from us old fogies." He hesitated, "You know, like you just said, without the whole family getting involved."

"Yeah, this sounds like my princess. Now she's fighting for her life. Giorgio, I can't lose another child to this hard land. If I do, I tell you this, I don't want to live. How will I ever face my Antoinette? How high must the price be for us to live here, in this violent place?"

Rocco wiped a stray tear that somehow escaped from his stoic reserve. "And if her husband has done this thing to her, he'll pay," he growled. "This I swear to you on the graves of my ancestors and my precious son. Nothing on this earth would be able to protect him."

Giorgio placed his arm on Rocco's shoulder. He said, "Leave all this despair to God for now. Place it aside; it can only hurt you to go on like this. You must conserve your energy."

Rocco nodded as if he had agreed if only to placate his friend.

Giorgio said, "We should hear something soon. Rosa's been in surgery for hours. Look my friend, here comes a nurse. Maybe there's news."

The surgery nurse approached, walking slowly and deliberately. With a weary voice, in perfect Italian, she said, "Mr. Ameduro, you can see your daughter now. She is holding her own, but sir, I must warn you, she is barely conscious and her life is on a thin thread. She is out of the hands of the surgeon and now in the hands of God."

"Nurse, tell me, will she live?" Rocco pleaded for a more specific answer, hoping for one he could accept.

The nurse answered, "I'm sorry, you'll have to speak to the doctor. He's waiting at her bedside in the recovery room. Your daughter was heavily sedated and the effects of the anesthesia will not wear off for some time. Please try not to be too upset by what you see." She motioned for him to follow.

Rocco turned, "Giorgio, please come with me. If you don't mind, I need you."

Giorgio said, "Sure. Is it all right, nurse?"

The nurse gestured with her hand, "Come along, sir. I see no reason you can't come too."

In the recovery room, a team of nurses and Rosa's surgeon carefully watched over her. Seeing Rocco and Giorgio, he walked to them. What Rocco saw on the hospital gurney was a small, wrapped body that he would never have known to be his daughter. Her upper body was covered in bandaging, blood oozing from beneath it still.

Rocco nodded, shaking his hand. "*Doctori*, I'm her papa."

"Mr. Ameduro, I'm Dr. Roland. I promise you, sir, we've done everything we could. By all accounts, your daughter should not be with us, but she is a fighter. It was lucky that the priest found her. His quick thinking and first aid may have given us enough time to save her. I must be honest, though; she's still not past danger. If she makes it through the next couple of days, she has a good chance, as long as we avoid infection. Now, it's up to God and your daughter's will to live."

"*Doctori* Roland, like you say, my Rosa is a fighter. You'll see, she is—how you say—okay."

Dr. Roland nodded his understanding and then said, "Now would be a good time to pray. I've asked Father Dugan to visit. I was told that the priest who found her gave last rites. However, I figured it couldn't hurt to have a few more prayers. I didn't think you'd mind."

Rocco answered, "Of course not, prayer is a good thing. And *Doctori*, how can I thank ah you? She means everything to me. My *bella filia*, cut ah up ah like ah *animale*." He sobbed uncontrollably, his reserve finally buckling to fear and grief.

Doctor Roland answered, putting his arm around Rocco as he did, his steady demeanor rapidly declining, "If she lives, Mr. Ameduro, it'll be thanks enough for me."

Rocco grasped the doctor's hands. "And I thank my God for your gifted hands, *Doctori*."

Dr. Roland, touched by Rocco's sincerity, squeezed his hands. "Mr. Ameduro, your Rosa will need all the support you can give. If God wills it, I can fix her wounds; wounds heal. You'll need to see to her spirit. When a terrible thing like this happens, the memory of it can often become a greater burden than the deed."

Rocco hesitated. It was difficult for him to speak the next few words, but he knew he must. Searching for the right words he spoke, "If she survives, I will face the rest in its own a time. *Doctori*, how ah much ah time will she need to spend here?"

Dr. Roland, wishing for a more reassuring answer, didn't quite know what to say, so he downplayed. "Probably at least two months or more in recovery, and that will probably be pushing it."

Rocco turned anxiously to Giorgio. "What will I do with my grandchildren? How will I take care of two babies? And where is Antonio?"

Giorgio answered, "Rocco, that's tomorrow's worry. Today they're safe. And don't forget, they have other grandparents."

"Giorgio, somehow I don't feel that I'll be able to count on them. This whole mess smells of rotten eggs."

Doctor Roland couldn't help overhearing them. He knew who the assailant was; the ambulance driver had overheard the police officer at the scene, and told the emergency nurse, who then had told him. He thought, *Today's paper will no doubt tell the world, and also this poor man, that his son-in-law has done this to his child. But it is not up to me. He has too much on his plate right now.*

Dr. Roland put his arm on Rocco's shoulder. "Sir, I promise that I'll do everything within the slight earthly power I have been given to keep Rosa with us. I need to see to other patients, but be assured that I'll check on her often. You can count on me to do everything that I can."

Tears welled up in Rocco's eyes. Giorgio, too, was unable to contain his emotion. Both men sat down, deflated by worry and fear and an uncertain building anger.

"Father Dugan, pleased to see you. The girl you need to see is in bed five. Her name's Rosa Lavalia." The nurse guided the priest, introducing him to Rocco and Giorgio.

"I'm sorry, Mr. Ameduro. I'm here for last rites," he said, not realizing the rites had already been given earlier.

Rocco, panic in his voice, said, "No, Father, you mustn't give her last rites. She will not die. My princess will live."

"But sir, it's a good idea to give them anyway, just in case." His voice carried a slight Irish brogue, lilting, friendly, and peaceful.

Giorgio stepped forth, explaining, "Father, apparently there's been a mistake. A priest gave Rosa the rites at the scene of the crime. In fact, the good padre is credited with saving her life."

With a pained look, the priest responded, "Oh, I'm so sorry. Please forgive me. In any case, let us pray for this child's full recovery. Come, let us gather in a circle around her bed and I will lead us in prayer."

After the brief prayer, Rocco's composure collapsed as he got his first real look at Rosa's torn body, her blood oozing around the bandages encompassing her torso.

"How could anyone do this to another human being?" Rocco asked. His pensive eyes searched, finding the priest's, pleading for an answer.

There was none. No reasonable man, not even the holy man, could understand nor put words to this type of tragedy. The words from "the Lord's Prayer" seemed hollow to Rocco. He had been struggling with his faith since Dominick's death, trying to put reason to the unreasonable, angry still with God. Then, as though he had heard a warning bell and a wake up call from above, he found a fragile comfort in faith and the Lord. For a brief moment, it was a warm and good feeling.

Rocco felt the squeeze on his breath. Fighting the feeling of the seemingly endless cold, he wished it away, but it had pestered him for well over a month now. His energy was sapped, and it was all he could do to keep moving. Yet somehow he managed; he had to. There were too many bills that needed paying.

The last several days were a blur. He worked, visited Rosa at the hospital, checked on the grandchildren, and then did it all over again. Trying to remain strong for Rosa kept him moving when he wanted and, more importantly, needed to rest.

Rosa had fought a good fight. Rocco was proud of her courage and undaunted faith. While struggling to live, she had repeated to him several times that she loved him and her babies more than the world. She also repeatedly said that she loved God even more for sparing her and that like a good Christian she could forgive Tony but that she could never forget what he had done. To Rocco this was good medicine. It was the right way to think, and more importantly, it was a return of her old and positive ways.

Rocco's constant steady cough, deep and biting, hurt his chest. He thought, *I cannot be sick, not now, not when I'm needed most.* He did his best to tough it out, but it was becoming more difficult. Even his strong heart was beginning to tire.

Rosa's flat was quiet, and when he had time to think, he felt bitter and lonely. There was no way he could stay above the Lavalias' garage now. His grandchildren were at the Tedescos.' *It is so good of them to step up and help. Soon, but not nearly soon enough, Antoinette will be here, maybe as early as May, or June at the latest.*

Rocco figured that when Rosa's health improved, Antoinette could get work, and together they would pitch in and help watch the babies and pay expenses. At least it was a plan, and better than no plans at all. It was his only hope for the moment and all that he had to cling to.

By coincidence, Rocco had sent money for Antoinette's passage only a day before Rosa's tragedy. She had finally sold their property for a pittance and arranged all the necessary paperwork to come to the U.S. If he hadn't already sent the money, he would no doubt have used all of it for Rosa's expenses, which were building to monumental proportions as each day passed. He needed his wife more than ever, especially since those bureaucratic wolves had come to his door a couple of days earlier.

By now, Rosa had been in the hospital for over a month. The world as she knew it was collapsing. The year 1928 was in its infancy, but few seemed to notice or care. Her hospital bills were mounting. Friends and family helped them as much as they could.

The Lavalia family appeared to be writing off their grandchildren, taking their son's side, despite his admission of guilt. As one, and pledging to be true to *familia Italiano*, they were convinced Tony had good cause, choosing to believe his accusation that Rosa was a common woman of the night who deserved her fate. They openly called her *putana*, the Italian slang word for whore, to anyone who would care to listen. After a while, from all the repetitions, some people began to believe it. However, Nicola Lavalia managed to slip $50, against the will of his wife, to the hospital's bursar, requesting that the payment remain anonymous. Whether it was guilt or compassion, no one would ever know.

Rocco's deepest desire was to strangle each and every Lavalia, starting with Tony. Instead, without notice or word, he quietly left his little hovel above their garage and moved to Rosa's flat. It was good to be nearer to his grandchildren and as far away from the Lavalias as possible.

Presently, his son-in-law sat behind bars in the Utica jail, awaiting trial. Utica Police had caught him on the night of the crime, ticket in hand, at Union Station. When caught, Tony had several hundred dollars and a suitcase of clean clothes, apparently having ditched his blood-soaked clothing, which the police later found in a trash bin near his flat.

His family, it seemed, had helped him in his attempt to get away. The local newspapers reported that the district attorney had filed pending charges against Nicola and Giovanna for aiding a criminal act.

In Utica, Rosa's stabbing was not much of a story. It was not a big deal to the average WASP Joe Citizen when one immigrant cut up another.

However, in East Utica and in the local Italian language papers, it was big news. So big, in fact, that it kept the Lavalia family close to home because of their self-inflicted embarrassment. They as one blamed Rosa for their discomfort, and never their son.

Tony had admitted openly to his crime, figuring his military record among other things would be used against him if he didn't. He told his parents he had attacked Rosa in a fit of anger after catching her in an adulterous act. He was remorseful, saying he had snapped in a fit of insane anger. His attorney saw this as their only defense and called it a crime of passion.

Rocco had been particularly angered when the attorney, "that Italian-American turncoat" as Rocco was prone to call him, had stated to a gullible newspaper reporter that any husband had a right to do what Tony had done if he caught his wife in adultery.

"What adultery?" Rocco had screamed at the walls.

Tony's family believed him because they needed to believe him. Rocco spit at his next thought. *And like the good and true Sicilian that Giovanna is, and must continue to be, she coerced her family into shunning Rosa forever. Even if it would hurt her grandchildren, especially the one she had come to love as her own, even who was named for her, no less. I for one will forever call her Jennie as my Rosa does, never Giovanna,* he fumed, trying his best to settle down. He put his hand on his chest; the sharp pain seemed worse. *I must rest, or I won't be able to see Rosa today.*

Rocco had made it a ritual of love to see his daughter every day after working his first job. Luck had it that she was at the hospital where he worked, though he could spend only a few minutes before going to his second job at the Bagg's Square Hotel, where he worked as a janitor. For once, his menial job as a hospital laborer, stoking fires and mopping floors, had a fringe benefit. He had planned to drop the second job after sending for Antoinette. Now, with Rosa's hospital bills and Tony in jail and her flat's rent, she had no one but him to aid with the mounting expenses.

Many of the hospital staff admired Rocco for his quiet, dignified manner, and made it a point to check on Rosa for him. It gave him comfort to know that strangers cared more for Rosa than her in-laws.

"The Lavalias," he spit out their name like a bitter drink. Today was Sunday; however, it would not change his daily ritual of visiting. The Lord's Day would allow him the luxury of a few additional hours at the hospital, and then a chance to visit Rocky and Jennie at the Tedescos.'

He closed the door behind him. His every step became a major effort as he moved slowly down the stairs. His shortness of breath caused him extreme discomfort. Barely able to breathe, he tried his best to ignore it. It was just a bad cold, just one more obstacle to overcome. However, it was becoming extremely difficult.

Rosa beamed upon seeing Rocco. Excited, she finally had some good news to report and couldn't wait to tell him.

She also had a haunting concern. It was more a foreboding about the confusing meeting she had with some people who visited her the day before. They called themselves county people or something like that. She didn't quite understand their purpose. They talked in perfect, and to her, somewhat difficult, English. Their talk was too quick for her to follow along carefully. They had commented first about her, and then her children, asking with singular persistence how she planned to care for them. Somewhat alarmed by so many questions she had been too tired to answer them all, or at least all that she had understood.

Rosa sensed something was wrong as soon as she spied Rocco entering the ward. His step was weary and measured, unlike the lively man she knew and loved. Though he appeared worn and tired, he still was friendly to everyone in the ten-bed ward, taking time to speak briefly with each patient and inquire about the progress of his or her various ailments.

He reached her bed saying, "Rosa, my princess, how're you feeling? You sure look perky today."

And she did. Rocco noticed that she had color, and her smile, that wonderful smile he had so missed, was almost back. He had often wondered in the solitude of his worry whether she'd ever smile again. Even more, he wondered if the physical scars that were now healing nicely would change to the emotional scars the doctor had feared might haunt her.

"Papa, you look terrible. Are you sick?"

"Shush," he put a finger to his mouth. "If that head nurse hears you, they'll surely throw me out. I have a little cold that has settled in my chest. When I go home, I'll put some water in a pan to boil and hold my head in a blanket and breathe the steam. It always seems to help." He had done this to no avail, but said it for her benefit. He took her hand, patting it, and touched her cheek tenderly. "So, give me the latest doctor report."

"It's good news. Doctor Roland feels I can go home in about three weeks. They're sure that I'm healing fine and all is better than expected. I'm ready to leave now, but they want to make sure my insides are totally healed. I must admit it still hurts to move."

"That's good news," he smiled. "But you must follow the doctor's advice and let your wounds heal properly."

Rosa nodded her acknowledgment, "You can depend on that. Now, how are my babies? I miss them terribly. I asked the nurse if Nellie could bring them to see me. She said it's against hospital policy. I'm so tired of their strict rules. I've always followed rules, but Papa, they're my babies and I need to see them. I haven't seen them since…" She couldn't continue.

"Of course you do. You'll see 'em soon enough." Hesitating for a second, reluctantly he continued, "By the way, did some government people come to see you yet? They came to my work place just the other day, right here no less, and asked me some peculiar questions. I can't understand why. Silly questions about how you planned to take care of Rocky and Jennie."

Rosa answered, "Yes, Papa, they came to see me yesterday. I, too, wondered why. They asked the same of me. Who'd watch the babies if I worked. I told them probably Mama when she arrived. They asked, 'How about now?' I said friends and our cousins. What is it that they want, and why so many questions, especially about my in-laws?"

Muffling a cough, Rocco hid his concern. "Rosa, don't worry. It sounds like the same thing they asked me. What did they say about the Lavalias?"

"They asked a lot of questions; let me see." Rosa was tiring, and Rocco hated to press her, yet somehow instinct told him that these county people's presence seemed foreboding. He needed to know.

"Continue, Princess, I want to compare stories. I'm curious about their intent."

"First, they asked if any of my in-laws had visited and if they were helping with the children. I told them the truth on both questions, saying no. Then they asked a very personal question. It was very embarrassing." She blushed, hurt at the memory.

"Go on Rosa, I'm your papa, you have nothing to worry or fear from me." He pinched her cheek, lightly and gently, giving her courage, but not enough to quell the tears that began to fall.

"Papa, they asked if I was sleeping with other men, like a common woman of the night. I felt so dirty with them here. Of course, I said no. I don't think they believed me." Her face tightened from the strain, remembering the confusing meeting.

With difficulty, she continued, "Then they asked how I planned to raise my two babies. I said we would manage, we always do. What's this all about? Why is it their business how I raise my babies? No one has ever given us even a blink of a concern since we came to this country. Why now?"

Rocco coughed again, trying unsuccessfully to muffle it in his hands. His chest hurt like fire. Fortunately, the nurse was not in the ward. He answered, "First you must calm yourself, and next, you must remember that not all America has been hard on us. Look at this hospital and all that it has done for us. I have a job here, and you still have your life.

"As for the government people, I don't know. I'll have to ask some of our acquaintances who have lived here longer. Maybe they'll help shed some insight and offer advice. Right now, it's probably part of the investigation against that no-good husband of yours. And remember your babies are American citizens which they seem to think gives them a say."

Rocco held back his raging pent-up anger. In his mind, he saw his hands around Tony's neck, squeezing away his life. It felt good to visualize, but it took too much of his meager strength, and he could not allow this fury to disturb Rosa, knowing she didn't need additional concerns.

Rocco stayed for two hours, talking mostly about Rocky and Jennie and the plans he was making for Antoinette's arrival. When Nellie arrived, he was very tired and ready to leave. Nellie was pleased to notice how upbeat both he and Rosa were.

Rocco kissed Rosa, looking deeply into her eyes. "Rosa, everything will be fine. Don't worry another minute about those people. They're only doing their job, nothing more. Now get better. That, my precious daughter, is your only job right now. Remember, I love you."

With tears streaming, Rosa forced a smile. "I love you too, Papa."

With troubled mind, he left the hospital. He had the sudden urge to confront Tony. It seemed to overwhelm his usual common sense. Wrapping a grayed woolen scarf around his neck, he pulled his head low to avoid the wind. The new snowstorm whipped at him with a fury. He coughed again, and again. This time he noticed blood. His body felt like a train straining up a hill, chug-a, chug-a, chug-a, keeping time with the incessant coughing. Each step to the police station seemed a lifetime. Yet it was something he had wanted and needed to do.

He had once really liked Tony. Now he wanted to find a way to forgive him. But angrily he asked himself, trying to understand the impossible, *How could I forgive this deed? Even if I'm a good Catholic, I am still a father. How can I forgive someone who has almost destroyed my daughter's life and ripped apart her soul? How can I forgive a man who has made a large hole in my soul as well? It's bad enough his actions have hurt everyone around him, including his parents. But now he lies about my Rosa's fidelity, and it must stop.*

Somehow, Rocco knew deep down in his heart that the visits from the county people meant trouble. Bureaucrats were the same no matter the country. He didn't quite know how, but he figured that his son-in-law, either directly or indirectly, was somewhere in the equation. He had to try to find out why.

At the police station, an officer led him to the holding cell for visitors. Rocco was frisked and once cleared was told to wait.

In a couple of minutes, Tony, in handcuffs and shackles, was led out to the visiting room. He sat in a chair opposite Rocco. A cage separated them, thwarting Rocco's desire to strangle him. He shuddered at the thought; his Rosa didn't need another tragedy.

"Hello, Tony," he hissed, his voice hushed. "How are they treating you in here?"

"Rocco," he nodded, embarrassed and ashamed, yet hiding his feelings, something he must do especially before this man, more than any other. "It's as good as it gets, I suppose. How's Rosa doing?"

"Fine, no thanks to you," he answered, unable to hide the bitterness. "Tell me, Antonio, I need to know. Why?"

He repeated it again. "Why did you do this to my baby? You slit her open like an animal for the slaughter. Why are you telling people it was because she was seeing another man? You know this is not right or true."

In a calm, measured voice, he answered, "Sorry, Rocco, that's my story and I plan to stick with it. Now leave, I've nothing more to say. Let's just leave it as the advice of my attorney. Now, is that all you need from me, because I've nothing more to say." Tony turned in his chair, yelling, "Guard, I'm ready. Take me back."

Rocco spit out his anger, "I'll leave, you no-good wife-beater, but not before I curse you and wish you the worst. You're nothing. You hear me? *Nothing!* Only this cage and this jail can protect you from now on. You ever get near my daughter again, so help me, as long as I'm alive, I promise, I'll kill you." Rocco's coughs hit him with a fury, catching him short.

Tony met Rocco's glare. He yelled defiantly, "Guard, take me back to my cell. This conversation is over!"

Tony looked at Rocco one last time, hatred in his eyes. And to think I liked him once. With a big smirk, hiding his true thought, *Sorry, old man, I need my alibi if I'm to get a light sentence. Yes, temporary insanity and an adulterous wife make a good combination for tragedy.*

He shook his head as he walked back to his cell, having no regrets for what he had done. "Thank God I live in America, Land of Attorneys." No one bothered to listen.

Exhausted now, emotionally as well as physically, Rocco walked slowly down the now slippery steps of the police station, feeling foolish and ashamed for wasting valuable time and energy, but mostly for losing his temper. Seeing Tony had not made him feel better. He could smell a problem brewing, and knew with a sudden flash of realization: *It's my grandchildren these county people want. Well, we'll see about that!*

His coughing continued non-stop. It seemed the stress of his meeting with Tony had brought on a worsening of the symptoms. He coughed into his handkerchief. *More blood*, pleading, *God, why now?* He thought, *I'm in trouble.* He could not move another step. He felt wobbly in the knees and he had difficulty breathing, and everything seemed to swirl.

He fell unconscious at the base of the police station steps. A passing officer rushed over to help him.

"You all right, Mac?" he asked.

But Rocco didn't answer.

The policeman rushed into the station, calling for an ambulance.

"I must see him. Please take me to my papa."

The nurse on duty answered, "Rosa, calm down, you can't afford to get upset. Your father is in intensive care. He has acute pneumonia. They're doing all they can for him, and it's still not safe for you to move."

Rosa pleaded, "No, he was just here a few hours ago. He only has a slight cold. How can this be? I must see him. Please ask the doctor for me. I have to see him!" she screamed, pleading.

The ward doctor came into the room, hearing the hysteria from the hall. "Nurse, what's this about?"

She explained the situation.

The doctor, surmising the higher needs of his patient, said, "I believe it'll be better medicine for Mrs. Lavalia to see her father than confining her here. Wrap her warmly, get a wheel chair, and take her, now."

"Yes, Doctor," she meekly answered.

"Papa, please wake up, I'm here for you." Rocco's eyes fluttered in recognition. An oxygen tent surrounded his upper body and his breathing was irregular.

She leaned over her wheelchair to gently grasp his hand in hers feeling a weak squeeze of acknowledgement. "Papa, I love you. You must get well. We all need you, and Mama will be here soon. Think of her, you must fight this!"

Rocco tried speaking, but he couldn't. Only the wheezing of tired damaged lungs could be heard. Silently, he fumed over having messed up, and for not properly treating his illness sooner. His insides hurt more from the agony of knowing this especially after overhearing the emergency doctor's words, "Acute pneumonia, weak heartbeat, and major infection." Adding, "Not any hope for this one."

How could I have let this happen? First my precious son, then my princess, and now me. With a forced voice, he stammered in Italian, "Rosa, forgive me." Saddened, he closed his eyes in despair. *Lord, I'm ready, please take me a sinner,* he pleaded in a delirium that suddenly seemed no more. The hospital room now seemed far away; a cavernous black hole lay ahead, beckoning. He took one last loving glance at his daughter, seeing her tears and wishing he could do something. But he knew he was helpless. He could see Dominick in the distance, smiling, happy and with his arms outstretched, beckoning him on, welcoming. He called, "Papa, I'm here. Come to me." Suddenly, Rocco's vision was clear and bright, his cough was gone, and his chest no longer hurt.

The nurse took his pulse. There wasn't any. She looked sadly at Rosa. "He's gone. I'm so sorry."

Rosa sobbed uncontrollably, and then screamed, a terrible, unearthly, unnerving scream, before she passed out and fell hard from the wheelchair to the cold hospital floor.

Mother never marked the day that Grandfather died as the lowest in her life, for that day was yet to come. I often feel cheated by his death, for I never really new him, but I am certain that he was a good man.

I often think it funny how we look at older people, now that I am old too. I find that in my past, I have been guilty, and now I see it better. You know, that first glimpse you initially see without actually seeing: grey hair, liver spots, wrinkles, and sometimes the confusion. Yes, the terrible confusion. I often never really took the time to look under the surface to discover the real person, hidden under the effects of passing years. You know the youthful person that once was, the real and full life that this elderly person has lived. Like so many, I was often too busy.

Here I go again, digressing, but today, this subject bothers me, so please forgive my pondering. You see, if we are lucky, we all eventually age, and then we, too, shall know the truth. Yes, the truth that we, the once proud and young, probably without thinking once glimpsed only at the aged body of some old person, crippled, perhaps, with one of the thousands of diseases of time and the rigors of humanity. We must always know that every person, young or old, has a very real history. Yes, they too were young once and maybe even have a story or two we could learn and perhaps even grow from. Yes, a story to tell, if we would only take the time to notice.

"Courage is a quality so necessary for maintaining virtue that it is always respected."

Samuel Johnson

SEVENTEEN

Rosa, still confined in the hospital, stretched on her bed gingerly and sat up on weakened elbows to look out the large, partially frosted window. It was snowing again—nothing new. It always seemed to be snowing. Today was different. Rocco's funeral services were today. Vulnerable and alone, worn and ragged from crying, she wished it were all a bad dream. However, bad dreams end once awakened, but not this endless one.

Nellie had spent most of yesterday consoling and crying along with her. Rosa needed the comfort of her cousin's presence more than ever, as she searched unsuccessfully for understanding. But today Nellie was with Aunt Eva and Uncle Giorgio, seeing to her Uncle Rocco's funeral.

Yesterday, the ward's head nurse, Judith McKay, had looked the other way, for once not enforcing the hospital's strict visitation rules for Nellie to leave. She had liked Rocco. His frequent visits, up to three a day, made him a regular. He had always been respectful, a real gentleman, and always asked with true sincerity how her day was going.

Nurse McKay had a daughter about Rosa's age, a senior at Utica Free Academy. *How different my Emily's life is from this poor girl's. Emily's biggest problem is finishing her homework. Well, that and whether or not I'll allow her to date past a certain hour. This kid in bed number five already has two babies, a rogue for a husband, and is foreign, penniless, and alone.*

Her heart went out to Rosa, but the only comfort Nurse McKay could seemingly give her was to carefully tuck the worn gray hospital blanket in around her frail body. She wished she could do more. She couldn't stop wondering how her daughter would handle what Rosa had endured. In truth, she was silently thankful in knowing that she'd probably never have to learn the answer.

Rosa, eyes puffy from the constant crying, asked, "Nurse, can you please tell me the time?"

Nurse McKay turned her left arm into the dim light from the window, reading the gold wrist watch, a twentieth anniversary gift from her husband. Smiling, she said, "It's 11:30 in the morning."

"Thank you." Rosa put her hands to her face, trying to impede yet more tears. *Papa's funeral should be almost over.*

As Nurse McKay began to leave, she heard Rosa's feeble voice, straining to speak. She about-faced and asked, "Is everything all right, Rosa? Anything else that I can do for you?"

"They can't bury Papa today," Rosa said, her trembling voice seeming to waft through a deep fog. "Nellie says the ground's too hard. They'll have to store his body like canned food in a pantry. It all seems too unreal. It's bad enough that Papa died the way he did, with overwork and pneumonia. Now my poor papa can't even be buried properly. This awful weather! This awful place! So evil!" Her voice lowered to a whisper, "So harsh, so unfair to anyone trying only to survive, let alone the impossibility of trying to get ahead."

Rosa now uncontrollably sobbing, "Why did we ever come here? Why, Papa, why?"

Nurse McKay, taken aback by Rosa's agony, was unsure how to properly respond, so she remained quiet. She slid a chair up to the bed and sat down. She was busy, overworked in fact, yet she knew she must make time. *As a nurse, I'm supposed to ease suffering,* she mused, *but my training didn't ever cover what this child has suffered, let alone her needs.*

After sitting with Rosa in silence and gently holding her hand, she finally spoke in a soothing, motherly voice. "Rosa, listen to me, what's happened to you is terrible. You've gone through more than anyone your age should ever endure. I know it may seem easy for me to say this because I've never been in your place, but you must remain strong for your children. A spring burial could be a good thing, under the circumstances. At least you'll be able to attend Rocco's burial later, when the ground is ready. Your father would like having you there, don't you think?"

Rosa's smile, though forced, was the first since Rocco's death. She rambled, her words mumbled, "Yes, and maybe Mama will be here by then. Nurse, did you know that Papa finally saved enough to send for her? He sent the tickets the day before I was brutally attacked. He saved all his money from two jobs, giving up almost everything, including his health, and now he'll never see her again. It is just too hurtful for me to imagine."

It hurt to talk, yet Rosa fought her anxiety, forcing herself to continue, "You know, if Papa had waited a day longer, he would have never sent the money for passage. He would have used it for the hospital bills, and then Mama would never get here. He wouldn't have worked so hard if he didn't have to worry about his debts. You see, it's really my fault. That terrible arranged marriage. His death was so unnecessary." Rosa started crying uncontrollably again.

McKay's stern, motherly voice had a calming effect. "Now, young lady, don't you go blaming yourself. Your father loved you. I could see the love in his eyes every time he visited. People get sick in this cold and damp climate. And unfortunately some people die. It is a fact of life that we cannot control. Now, tell me about your mama. I didn't know anything about her, and Rocco never said a thing. This is exciting news. When will she be here?"

"Papa said in three, maybe four months. I've really missed her."

Nurse McKay grasped Rosa's hands, which had been plucking fretfully at the blanket, holding them to her heart. "This may seem foolish to you right now, maybe even a little trite, but Rosa, this too shall pass. You must rest now. You have a lot of healing left to do. You owe it to your mother, your children, and yourself to heal. That's my best advice."

Nurse McKay stood, took a lingering look at her patient, and reluctantly walked to the next bed.

The orderly clanked and clanged the dirty metal food trays onto the crowded cart. Across from Rosa's bed, a new patient, a middle-aged woman, moaned in deep agony as her pain medication began to wear off. The hospital ward was abuzz with activity and a sense of routine, except for the one routine, her papa, and Rosa sorely missed him.

It didn't seem possible that Rocco's last visit to had been only a week earlier. It seemed distant. It was as if it never happened. With lunch pail and thermos bottle in hand, he had been excited; telling her about the latest letter from Mama, a letter that had lifted his spirits. Since he had just sent money for passage, it was too early for her mama to know quite yet that she would soon be here with them. Rosa squirmed in her bed thinking now that the word *them* was inappropriate. Returning to logical reasoning, she surmised that their letters must have crossed.

Antoinette's letter had been filled with endearments, hope, and longing. Papa was so happy that he had reread the letter to Rosa at least two times, brightening her and the drab hospital ward with its promise.

Rosa wondered what had become of the letter. Was it with him when he died? When chance permitted, she would have to try to find it and have the funeral director place it with him when they buried him in the spring.

It had been six weeks since she had suffered her husband's violent attack. The injuries still pulled at her insides. Still, she felt alive for the first time in what felt like ages because of today's simple accomplishment, walking a few miserable steps.

She had been trapped like a prisoner in her bed for so long that she felt a little heady with new freedom as she walked those few unsteady feet during therapy. She longed to do more, yet the nurse discouraged it.

"That's enough for today, we don't want to overdo," said the nurse.

Overdo? Rosa wanted to scream. *I've been prisoner to my body long enough.* She stopped short, though, remembering that the therapy nurse was only doing her job. *How could she ever understand my frustrations? I long to smell fresh air, to gather flowers, and see my babies.*

Immersed in the mixed emotions of self-pity, elation, and contemplation, she was startled to hear Nellie's voice as her friend entered the ward. Rosa immediately sensed that something was dreadfully wrong. Nellie, a happy soul, was never very good at hiding emotions, and today her strained face had concern written all over it.

"Okay, cousin, give it to me quick," Rosa scolded. "What's the problem? Why do you look so down in the mouth?"

Nellie looked past her best friend, trying desperately to hold back tears. Silently, she gestured to Uncle Giorgio standing behind her, motioning him to speak. When he didn't, she forced her trembling voice and said, "I could never hide anything from you."

Giorgio, looking solemn, came forward, gently grasping Rosa's hand. "Rosa, I guess it's up to me to be the one to tell you. I don't know a gentle way to say this, and," he hesitated, "I'm sorry but it's probably best that I find the nurse before I do. So hold on for a minute, and I promise that I'll be right back."

Rosa's heart lost a few beats. After what seemed like hours, Giorgio was only a few seconds, he returned with Nurse McKay. He had quickly briefed McKay on their disturbing news.

Rosa's eyes appealed for an answer, impatient to wait another second, she exclaimed, "What is it that has you all so grim?"

Giorgio waited for Nurse McKay to stand next to Rosa's bed, and then began. "Rosa, it's the authorities; they took your children. I tried desperately to stop them. I told them we'd care for them and that your mother would arrive soon. All they said was to get an attorney that they were only following court orders and the wishes of your in-laws. The children are too young to know what's going on. Little Jennie walked right up to them, almost like she knew them, but of course she couldn't have." Giorgio caught himself rambling, "I am so sorry, please forgive me, Rosa, for rambling on like this."

Rosa lay dumbstruck, voiceless. Inner rage had punched a hole into her heart, turning her inside out. Finally she rasped, "What do you mean, they took my babies? Can they do this to me, their mother?"

Giorgio said, "Rosa, please understand; I'm doing all that I can possibly do. I went to see Attorney Gallo. You know the man you saw, before the..." he hesitated, "the..." He didn't finish; there was no need.

She barely whispered, fighting back tears, taking control, "What did Mr. Gallo say?"

Giorgio replied, "He said in time you'll get the children back. For now, they've been sent to a Catholic orphanage called St. Joseph's Infants' Home. It's a very caring place, run mostly by nuns. I was told that the county pays for most of their expenses; however, you will eventually be asked to pay something when you start to get back on your feet. I'll get all the details for you later today."

"How much time?" Rosa asked, her voice rattled low and difficult to hear.

Giorgio wished to be any place but the sterile ward. What he had to say next came hard. Though reluctant, he knew he must tell everything.

He looked expectantly at Nurse McKay, who had just wiped away a tear. "Rosa, be strong. The Lavalia family refuses to care for your children. It appears the authorities feel that their unwillingness to help care for the children, coupled with Tony in jail, and with Rocco now gone..." his voice trailed off, then blurted as he tried to get it all out, "Well, the county people say you'll have to prove you can care for them before you can get them back. They believe they're acting in your children's best interest. I'm so sorry." Tears of frustration rained from Giorgio's eyes.

Rosa craned her ears, trying to hear what her heart refused to believe. "Please, Lord, let this be a bad dream. Didn't you and Nellie say you'd help?" she gasped.

"Yes, we offered to help and still do. Gallo sent them a long letter to this effect. Even with the letter, they refused, saying it wasn't enough. I pleaded, saying we'd watch the children and see to their best interests. When they asked if you'd be in the picture, helping to raise them, I said, 'What kind of fool question is this? Certainly, Rosa will be a part of their lives, she's ah der ah mama.'" Excited, Giorgio's careful English turned broken.

"Then the cold hearts said that your reputation, as sworn to the county by your husband and corroborated by the ever present Giovanna, is questionable. In their opinion, you're not presently fit to be mama to your own children."

Rosa screamed in outrage, "What do they mean, my reputation? I'll get a job, two or three if I must, to keep my babies. You know this."

"Rosa, look at me so that you'll understand." Giorgio turned in sorrow, looking at Nellie for support, pity in his eyes. He turned back to Rosa, wiped away her tears with a crumpled handkerchief, and then grasped her hands.

The room seemed to career away as Giorgio forced himself to speak. "I don't know any other way to say this. Your worthless husband claims you're a loose woman. He says he caught you in the act. We hear he made up a lot more stories of infidelity. He even claimed he's not sure Jennie is his bambino. He points out her early birth as evidence. This I feel is the main reason Giovanna turned against you and the children."

Giorgio had difficulty looking at Rosa. "Of course, we know he's lying, but with the backing of Giovanna and an attorney that's one of the best defense lawyers in Utica, he has been able to be heard when he should be tossed into jail and the key thrown away."

Trying to compose herself, Rosa, her voice remarkably steady, asked, "What does Gallo say?"

Giorgio, a bit uncomfortable now, from the subject at hand, answered, "Gallo states that acting the spurned husband is Tony's best defense. He's sure that the defense attorney will make the most of it. Because of all the accusations, I went yesterday to talk to your father-in-law. Nicola and I go back many years. He graciously listened to what I had to say. Nick is heartbroken really, Rosa, but he won't defy his wife or upset his family any further with actions that could harm his son's chances at a lighter sentence. I'm sorry to have to tell you all this. The good news is Nicola at least feels sick about not seeing his grandchildren."

"What good is that?" she fumed, her anger swelling into an uncontrolled rage. "Isn't he a man?" she spit out. "Doesn't my father-in-law have the balls to stand up to his wife and see his son for what he is? Don't they know what he does for a living? Are they blind? What hurt have I ever given them?" she shouted.

Rosa released a gasp of air, blowing from deep within, trying to calm down. Then, in a loud, prolonged whisper through clenched teeth, she said, "Jennie is Antonio's daughter. How could he do this? What sort of man tries to kill his wife, and then destroys her reputation and calls his only daughter, who even looks more like him than me, a bastard to save his own hide?"

Giorgio tried to respond; the situation, though, was beyond all he had seen in his fifty-plus years. Shaking his head in agreement, he remarked in the only way he knew, "Time and patience, Rosa. We must resolve ourselves to time and patience. It may take longer than we would wish, but I promise we'll do all in our power to help get your babies back."

"How much time do you think it'll take?" Rosa squinted, her eyes narrow slits, her face puffed with grief.

"I don't honestly know. Gallo thinks that when Antoinette arrives it shouldn't take too long. He'll need money for filing the court papers. He said his firm agrees they won't charge you except for the fees, and with this I can help."

Rosa broke down, hysterical, sobbing uncontrollably. Nurse McKay placed a call to Doctor Roland requesting a sedative, though experience told her it would take more than drugs to erase Rosa's grief.

After they all left, Rosa stared blankly, not seeing. She grasped the sheet around her neck, wrapping it into knots, trying to forget the unforgettable. Outside, high winds whipped snow against the old hospital's window, the chill somehow making its way into the room, reaching deeply into Rosa's soul.

Six weeks later, a county ambulance brought Rosa to the Tedesco home, marking the end of an almost three-month hospital stay. March winds and a driving snowstorm greeted her on her first day back to the world.

Nellie, despite Rosa's pleas to the contrary, had postponed her wedding. Louis agreed to the delay, knowing how much his future wife needed Rosa by her side.

Broke, with no money to pay rent, Rosa had lost the flat; the furniture, at least what had not been taken by Tony's family, was neatly stored in the Tedesco basement and attic. Her plan was to share Nellie's room until she regained her strength, though stubbornly, she resolved to return to work as soon as possible. With luck and a job, she would find a new flat and then earnestly start to make plans for the return of her children.

Nellie had promised to accompany Rosa to the orphanage as soon as she felt able. Apprehensive and tired of confinement, she desperately needed to go there on her first day back. Reason, however, overruled desperation. Out of breath and fatigued just getting to the Tedesco's home, she conceded it was best to wait another day.

Uncle Giorgio sat at the kitchen table reading the local Italian language newspaper. "Whew," he said as he acknowledged Rosa at the sink pouring a glass of water. Today marked her second week at the Tedescos,' and she was beginning to feel much better.

"Good news, Mr. Tedesco?" she asked.

"Rosa, call me uncle, you're more like my niece than a visitor, and after all, we are distant cousins."

She nodded agreement, smiling.

He then answered her, "And no, it's not very good news. Seems some terrorists in Milan wanted to kill King Victor Emmanuel. Instead, they managed to kill sixteen innocents and wounded forty others. What a waste. What's this world coming to?"

"Isn't there any good news?"

"Ah…let's see." He frowned, reading aloud, "It looks like four hundred Americans were killed when a dam broke in California. Oh, here's something good. Gary Cooper, you know, the movie star, made another movie. I like his movies, don't you?"

Giorgio continued talking, unaware that Rosa wasn't listening. The mention of California suddenly made her uncomfortable. Her thoughts moved to this mysterious place that Tony had always talked about.

"Boring you, huh? Well, I'm sorry," he smiled. "How about some hot coffee instead? I made a new pot."

"Who made a new pot?" Aunt Eva entered the kitchen, pretending she was upset.

He smirked, playfully pinching her ample rump as she passed. She cuffed his balding head.

"Rosa, I tried to get credit for my Eva's perfect coffee, but I'm caught and must confess my devilish sin."

"You old fool, tell it to a priest. Faa, why I put up with you," she laughed. It was the merry laugh of a happy couple still enjoying each other.

Rosa was envious, yet very pleased for them. She asked, "How long have you two been married?"

"Let me see, two days past too long," Giorgio kidded.

Eva hit him on the shoulder a bit too hard.

"Darn it, woman, that hurt!" he cried.

"I'm glad," she scoffed. "It's been thirty years that I've put up with the likes of him, and Rosa, as you can clearly see, a long time at that, perhaps like the old goat says, even a day past too many."

"I didn't say anything of the kind," Giorgio replied indignantly, feigning hurt feelings.

Rosa, witnessing the wonderful love these two shared, thought, *Someday, maybe I can have this too.*

Eva asked, "Where's Nellie?"

Giorgio replied, "Oh, I forgot, she left early. Something about wedding arrangements she needed to make."

Upset, Eva responded, "On a Sunday? Why didn't she ask me to help?"

Rosa answered for Uncle Giorgio, "It had something to do with the priest. She and Louis needed to see him to confirm the new date they picked for the wedding, April 28th, like we all discussed last night. I think it's silly, though, that she's waited for me. I'd be there even if I had to crawl."

"Oh, yes, I remember. Sometimes I get so forgetful," said Eva.

"Hey, I forgot too, and I'm not so old," said Giorgio, smiling. Eva was a year older than Giorgio, and he was always kidding her about it.

Eva poured coffee, warming Rosa's cup. "You of all people know our Nellie as well as anybody; she wants you there, but only when you're feeling your best. You're very special to her."

Rosa said, "I know, and I'm touched. But I think Louis is a real saint to wait. He's been so patient."

"Yes, that boy's a gem," said Giorgio. "I really like him. He'll make our Nellie a very good husband."

Eva rested her eyes on Rosa. "It's nice to see more color in your face. Are you getting excited about visiting the orphanage tomorrow?"

"I'm so excited I could burst. You know how much I've wanted to visit, but I know now that it was best to regain my full health first. I must look good for my babies, though I know they probably barely know me anymore and won't care much about what I look like. They're so young. I hope my Jennie will still recognize my voice. Aunt Eva, I can't go looking like the kind of woman that miserable husband of mine says I am. Will you help me fix my hair? And my dress is so loose it's falling off. I tried, but I can't hold a sewing needle steady, at least not just yet. Can you help me take it in?"

"Of course I will help. Let's finish our coffee, and then we'll work on your hair and that dress. I'll see that you look your best for the nuns."

"Thank you. You're both so very kind, more than I deserve." She hesitated before she turned to Giorgio, desperate to know more about Tony, yet at the same time wishing she didn't have to ask.

"Uncle, when is Tony's trial? Will I have to go to it?"

"It's next week. I was planning to tell you, but felt it better not to hinder your recovery with worry. And anyway, I don't think next week will be soon enough to venture out to something as difficult and stressful as a trial. You know your doctor suggested you stay away from stress, and Tony and his family...well, need I say more? You don't need to waste energy on this strain. And you particularly don't need to face them Lavalias either."

Giorgio watched Rosa's reaction. There was none. He fixed his eyes on her before carefully saying, "Gallo says you can go if you choose; that is, if you want to see him get the book thrown at him. He feels your innocent appearance would sink in and perhaps help sway the jury. They might call you as a witness, though I am unsure. I've heard that there's something in the American law that says a wife can't testify against a husband. Attorney stuff drives me nuts."

Rosa didn't care to go to court. She only wanted the nightmare to end, not to relive it. Her priority was getting her children back. "Do you think that my going there will put him away forever?"

"I don't know. Gallo believes Tony will plead guilty and throw himself to the mercy of the court, based on your imagined adultery."

Rosa then asked, "Then why the need for a trial? If he does this, will he still go to jail?"

"I expect he will." Giorgio could not tell if this pleased or hurt her.

Rosa spoke bitterly, "What will be, will be. He made his bed, now he must lie in it. I won't go to that public spectacle unless I'm forced. I've decided I won't ever turn back, no, not now or ever. I must go forward and live my life as best I can. Looking back hurts too much."

Rosa took a deep breath, contemplating her next few words, and then blurted, "I don't need to gloat at his miserable face. I need to save all my energy for my babies. Tony may wish the world to believe they're not his, but I know different and more important, so does God. And in any case, they're mine, and of this there is no doubt. Hatred and wishes for vendetta will not do my children or me any good."

Listen to me, she thought, *I only wish I could believe my words. He's still my husband.*

Eva said, "Child, like your sainted father once commented to me, you're wise beyond your years. You've made the right decision," she smiled. "Now, let's do some alterations."

"Uncle Giorgio, Aunt Eva, I'm so lucky to have your help and kindness. I love you both beyond words. You're more than friends and family. You're saviors. Thank you!"

She carefully hugged Eva, leaning to kiss Giorgio on his puffy, tear-streaked cheek.

Early evening on Monday, March 19, 1928, marked the Italian celebration of St. Joseph's Day. For Rosa and Nellie, it was a special holiday, because with Rosa's energy almost back to normal, it finally gave them a chance to visit Rosa's estranged children. The bus drive to the orphanage was a slip-and-slide experience. Early winter thaw had changed the roads to ice. Cold winds coming south from Canada did Jack Frost's bidding as March roared like a lion, mocking the promise of an early spring.

The mammoth building looked unfriendly and aged as the cousins approached. Inside was their reason for being there. Rosa, hesitant, carefully climbed the steps and entered. Once in the building, she identified herself as the mother of Jennie and Rocco Lavalia. After signing their names in the registry book, she and Nellie were taken to a spotless nursery under the careful watch of Sister Cecilia, a stern nun who appeared to take her job seriously.

Initially they saw a bright, airy, and clean ward. Jennie looked happy and well fed. Sitting in a crib, one of many identical ones in the room, she was playing with a rag doll. Rosa wished to believe that Jennie recognized her voice when she approached, but she didn't really seem to notice her mother.

Rosa carefully lifted Jennie from the crib; her strength still waned from her injuries. The baby squirmed in Rosa's arms. Reluctantly she placed her on the tiled floor. Jennie, a beautiful child now almost two years old, smiled, and then pranced around the room. Rosa suddenly was saddened. *I've nothing to give my children.* All her money was gone.

Nellie leaned down to pick up Jennie, who seemed to recognize her. With Jennie in Nellie's arms, and Sister Cecilia in tow, they moved to Rocky's crib, finding him sleeping. He was now almost seven months old.

Rosa thought, *How beautiful he looks; yet I barely know him.* Her eyes briefly met Sister Cecelia's as she reached down to lovingly touch Rocky's silky black hair. Both children had grown so much since she had last seen them. Three months is such a long time in a baby's life.

Rosa leaned over the crib, kissing him on his forehead.

"May I come to see them often?" she asked, her voice shaking with uncertainty.

Sister Cecilia's eagle eyes, penetrating from beneath the large habit, explored Rosa's every move before answering, "As often as you like." She then voiced a list of rules by rote, like a mantra. "Of course, you'll have to observe our visiting hours, and you must check with us before giving any gifts of food, toys, or clothing. This rule is necessary. We must consider the other children. You do understand."

Rosa nodded, wondering how this day could have ever happened. The wall clock in the brightly painted hall next to the nursery ticked loudly. It mocked the silence. Rosa felt a chill from the cold, staring eyes of the good sister.

Rosa reluctantly asked, "Have my children been well? Does anyone ever hug them?"

"We can't hug every child," Sister Cecilia replied defensively, "though heaven knows they need it. There are too many and too few of us. We have two hundred here. They get all the necessities: they are changed, fed, burped, and all the rest. When they get older, starting at around age five, they are sent to Saint John's where we educate them in the three Rs, and most importantly, in the fourth R, religion. We also strongly emphasize discipline and cleanliness."

Rosa responded, "That's nice to hear; however, my babies will not be here that long."

Sister Cecilia acted as if she did not hear the young woman. Rosa noticed. *Does she know something I don't?*

Rosa turned to Nellie, who also felt the silence. Rosa tried to remain calm, though fear of the unknown gripped her belly tightly.

Later, huddled outside in the cold wind awaiting the local bus, Rosa finally mustered the courage to speak out about her fear. "Nellie, did you see Sister Cecilia's face when I said my babies wouldn't be here long? Did you get the same feeling I did, that maybe she knew something we didn't?"

Nellie wanted to tell Rosa the truth—that she had noticed—but couldn't say it. What purpose would it gain? Instead, she answered, "No, I think you're letting your imagination wander into areas we know nothing about."

"Nellie, to get my bambinos back, I'll need to have money for attorneys. Please understand, I'm not asking you. Heaven knows you've all done enough already, especially you, what with your life about to change with Louis. But how'll I ever be able to do this unless I work? I need to get a job, and quick. Right now I don't even have a penny to my name."

Nellie answered, "Yes, you do need to go to work, but in a few weeks like Doctor Roland said. You know deep down that you can't handle heavy work or sitting at a sewing machine all day in your present condition. I saw how difficult it was for you to lift Jennie from that crib. Boss Jones told me he'd rehire you when you are ready, and not until. You know him and his quotas. So, cousin, have patience. We'll face this one together and get those kids back soon."

Rosa said, "I still have nightmares about them being taken away. Why did they take them? What did I do? I'm the victim here, aren't I?"

Nellie had asked herself the same questions a hundred times. "Rosa, I don't know the answers. I only know you must somehow get back to normal and then we can deal with this. Until then, I'll visit the children with you as often as you like. You know how much I love them. Of course, I will always visit them, regardless. Oh, you know what I mean."

"Thank you, Nellie; you're a good friend."

I'm told Mother came often to visit us at the orphanage. Each time, she'd remind us that she was our mother. Eventually it sunk in. As I got older, I wanted to believe I had a mother. I needed to believe. It was difficult, even though she hugged us a lot. When she and Nellie visited, it was the only time we were hugged.

We didn't understand. I suppose we were too young. It would hit us much later, when I was about six and Rocky five, that we truly did have a real mother. All that time, I had nightmares almost daily, wondering why this pretty lady who said she was my mother never took me home with her.

"Faith is simultaneously long perseverance and unwavering confidence"

Pierre-Yves Emery

EIGHTEEN

On June 29, 1929, while Herbert Hoover was barely into his first and only term as president, the first Academy Awards were held and film starlet Janet Gaynor won Oscars for three movies. In Chicago, mobster Al Capone was arrested for carrying a concealed weapon. That's a joke in itself. Bell Laboratory introduced a system for transmitting television pictures in full color. Yes, way back then. And in Utica, New York, it was my third birthday.

I was still living at the orphanage. For reasons I cannot comprehend, vivid memories of this day are stamped, like ink marks on paper, forever on my mind. The memories consist of brief flashes of a pretty lady who said she was my mother and the new doll she brought me, accompanied with lots of hugs. The doll was beautiful, and I remember its eyes opened and closed when I moved its head. I also remember trying to hide this special treasure from the other children. I didn't want to lose it.

And I can't ever forget the birthday cake she made special, just for me. It was iced with white frosting, with pretty, red roses on its border. It tasted so sweet and smooth. We shared the cake with several children, having milk, singing "Happy Birthday." It was my first birthday party, ever, or at least one that I remembered.

Then, like she always did, Mother left and once again didn't take me with her. I then vividly remember being very sad.

Union Station was crowded with summer travelers. Louis had driven Rosa and his new wife in his beat up old Model T Ford. According to Louis, the car ran most of the time. He often commented that it definitely beat walking. Luckily, the car managed to carry them to their destination today without problems, for walking was a fifty-fifty proposition where Louis' car was in the equation.

July in Utica can be a bear, and on this day, the bear was growling. The station was hot, the humidity high, as the trio made their way to track twelve, wading through the crowded platform to await the arrival of the New York Central-local due in from New York City in a few minutes. Antoinette had telegraphed ahead saying she'd be on the train.

Speaking to no one in particular, Rosa exclaimed, "So many people! Where could they all be going, and why?"

This was the first time Rosa had returned to the rail station since her arrival years earlier. She was awed as before by its size and grandeur, but still thought it not as nice as New York City's Grand Central, which was still a very vivid memory. Yet, the Utica station had an appeal of its own, and today it seemed much nicer in a happy, familiar, homey way. *Was it four years ago when I first arrived?* she thought.

She tried to conjure some much-needed joy. Again, yet so unlike her, she receded into herself to daydream and think, oblivious to all around her, *I need to take time to count the good in my life. And much of what's good is standing next to me.* Holding tightly onto Nellie's hand, she looked at her with intense eyes, thinking, *Cousin, what would I have done without you?*

The last time that she was here, it had been cold and raining and early spring. Then, she had been filled with the proverbial fear of the unknown, exhausted, and in unfamiliar territory. However, today, though still exhausted and facing a different fear, she focused on hope for the future. So much had happened, so many obstacles, to numb her expectations of a better life. Yet, her excitement at seeing her mother after four long and tumultuous years overwhelmed the worry that had become her constant and uninvited bedfellow.

She thought, *Has Mama aged? Have I?* How different her life had become from what she had dreamed. *Since I last saw Mama, Domenico died, I married and had two children, was almost murdered, and my husband is in jail.* She shuddered at the next thought. *My children were taken and put in an orphanage, and*

Papa died. She stopped then, for the long extensive list hurt too much. *All of this is even too much for a story to be believable, even in one of those notorious dime novels. Once I was an optimist. An optimist,* she laughed sardonically to herself. *This word makes me angry. Still, I must focus on moving ahead, not looking back. It's the only way to retain my sanity.*

But for Rosa, sanity at this moment was a hard path to find, let alone to follow, and like Job, that much-maligned character in the Bible, the slings and arrows of her life were very real and very sharp and bloody.

Rosa's health had improved enough that she was working full time at the mill. Now, with Antoinette's help, she planned to work two jobs and prove to the authorities that she was a fit mother.

Although single parenting was not all that acceptable in the society of the day, divorce was an even greater rarity, practiced only by the non-Catholics. To divorce, a Catholic must seek dispensation from the Pope in the Vatican. Rosa knew she was not likely to receive such a gesture from His Holy Eminence, Pope Pius XI, known in his life before priesthood as Achille Damiano Ricci.

Her constant drive was the strength that kept her moving, working, and planning. Mercifully, it served to check her frequent desire to look back. But today, the past reeked in her mind like the unsold rotten fruit at her husband's pretend job at Rabiso's warehouse.

A train whistle blew in the distance. Nellie could see Rosa drift off daydreaming. She knew her cousin well enough to know it was better to let her escape into herself to figure out whatever it was that was bothering her, for soon enough she'd have to return to the present. So Nellie left her alone until it became obvious that Antoinette's arrival was near.

Nellie spoke loudly to be heard above the din of the station, "Rosa, are you daydreaming again? You've been very quiet."

Rosa had constant mood swings since the tragedy. *Who wouldn't?* Nellie thought. *The doctor had said to expect it. It's a miracle she's alive. Now she needs to get her life back.* Nellie reached out and squeezed Rosa's hand. Rosa squeezed back.

Rosa's stare was pensive, despite a forced effort to smile as she realized that she had been elsewhere in her mind. "Nellie, I'm sorry for being such a bore. Please forgive me. I guess that I was foolishly thinking about the last time I was here, you know, at this very spot, and all that's happened since."

"Cousin, remember what the doctor said, it's not healthy, unless they're good thoughts. Don't you agree, Louis?"

Laughing and attempting to make light of the moment, Louis quipped, "Hey, don't you two get me caught in the middle of this. I'm only your driver." Louis could not miss Nellie's brown-eyed frown burning a ragged hole into him.

Slipping back to inner thoughts, Rosa subconsciously picked at the black mourning ribbon on her blue dress, adjusting it. The dress was the one her father had liked best and also the one she had worn on her first date with Tony. It was still very loose, though she was slowly regaining lost weight. With her voice trailing off, she said aloud, in a saddened voice, "I wish Papa could be here."

Reluctantly, Rosa's mind raced back to her last day in the hospital, to the terrible moment when the doctor advised that she could never have children again. Just as quickly, she shuddered, vividly recalling Tony's horrible, bloody knife. Bitter then, as now, she hadn't dared to tell anyone, not even Nellie. Her thoughts then involuntarily returned to Rocco's final interment into the rich soil of the lonely cemetery and Mama's letter she had found, personally placing it in his coffin, despite the objections of the funeral director about what she should never have to see. Repressed pain rushed in on her like an out of control flood.

Two years, with maybe an early exit for good behavior, was the sentence the judge gave Tony for nearly killing Rosa and ruining her life and the lives of those around her. It frightened her, knowing that someday she'd have to face him again. It left her feeling constantly anxious. Like Tony, Rosa was locked in a prison, only of a different kind. She was married to the man who had tried to kill her, a man she couldn't divorce, at least not without a lot of money.

Worse, she rigidly believed that divorcing Tony meant still another more difficult step: excommunication from the church. For Rosa, the church was the very center of her life and a very real part of the person she had once been;

the only part of her past that she did not want to lose. So, sadly, she remained married to a man she could never love again.

Then, just as quickly, her thoughts shifted. *I could live the rest of my life with the name Lavalia, living a lie; I could even live with excommunication. None of that would matter if I can just have my children. I need my children.*

Yes, getting her children back was more important to her than obtaining any divorce decree. She desperately needed money for the legal actions necessary to bring them back home. She felt helpless and trapped in an unending crisis, a dilemma that never ceased.

Rosa heard a voice. It was like the clang of a fire truck racing to a fire, and Nellie's response to her statement, made only seconds earlier, that brought her back to the present. It seemed as though a lifetime had passed, so fast had her mind been at work, counting her troubled past and avoiding her present and future. With a sudden rush, she recalled her last sad statement to Nellie about wishing Papa was here. Though but a few seconds had passed since her comment, so deep had been her thoughts, that it seemed like hours.

Nellie, bringing Rosa back to the present, said with emphasis, "Your father is here with us, and don't you ever think different. This moment is what he worked so hard for and so desperately wanted. You must always remember why he came here, and how he wanted to take his family far away from the troubles and poverty of Italy."

Rosa, embarrassed, looked at Nellie, knowing she meant well. *Maybe she's correct, and someday Papa's grand wish for prosperity and peace will finally, somehow, find me. But it seems that all Papa managed to do was trade one problem for another.*

"You know, Nellie, old Missanello doesn't seem so bad anymore. Yet, even were it not for my Jennie and Rocky, who are American citizens as well as citizens of Italy, I'd have no choice but to stay, since I could never afford to go back. I sometimes feel like I'm trapped and not welcome either there or here."

"Rosa, you must snap out of this gloom. It's unhealthy, and it's not like you."

Rosa, still oozing gloom said, "Yes, you are right. I've been a fool to sink this low. But I keep thinking this purgatory I live in must be my destiny.

Maybe it's my fate to pay this terrible price so that my babies can have a better life. But I know that I must concentrate on the present and on Mama, and, however I do it, that I must somehow free them from that orphanage."

The incoming train's loud whistle announced its arrival as track twelve came alive with activity. Rosa's heart beat rapidly in anticipation.

The wait seemed like forever after the train had arrived and before Antoinette came down the steps of car ten. The smoke from the train's diesel engines burned Rosa's eyes, the humidity causing ringlets of perspiration on her face and forehead.

Antoinette had gained weight and appeared a bit grey. Her black widow's dress caught Rosa by surprise, reminding her again of her brother and father, and the cutting comprehension that her mama would strictly follow tradition.

With arms out in welcome, Antoinette rushed to Rosa, as Louis and Nellie looked on. Mother and daughter hugged and kissed their greeting, joyful and long overdue, as if trying in one quick moment to make up for all the hugs forever lost during their separation.

Antoinette, tears streaming down her face, said in a whisper while clinging to Rosa, "Four long years, four tragic years, I have waited to see your beautiful face. I've missed you so much."

Rosa, ecstatic, responded, "Mama, I too have missed you. Is this real? Are you actually here?"

Uncle Giorgio watched from a few paces away, a big smile upon his face. He had escorted Antoinette after meeting her at Ellis Island. Tonight they would celebrate at his home, and tomorrow they would begin plans to help Rosa and her mother start life anew.

Antoinette looked at Rosa now with a mild frown. "Rosa, you're not wearing black."

"I know, Mama; I don't have a black dress. I couldn't afford one."

"Then with the few dollars I have left, we'll buy you one, so you can properly mourn your papa."

Rosa could not bring herself to respond. She would tell her later that she did not want to wear black. Black was too much for her to bear. Every time she saw someone in black, her heart stopped a few beats. More importantly, money, that is, any money they had, must only be used for necessities.

Rosa, stubbornly insisting on finding a flat as soon as she was able to work, had saved enough for the first two months' rent at a small, three-room place on Elizabeth Street, near her old apartment. They could move in on August 1st. She hoped they could soon find a kitten to replace Snowball, who had been given away to caring strangers when Rocco died.

"Mama, we have so much to talk about."

"Yes, I know. Your father's last letter and Giorgio's letters, too, have told me the worst. Now I need you to tell the rest. You must spare nothing."

"I will Mama, I promise." Rosa, dreading the retelling, had known she'd have to recap the many angry and dreadful memories. *Mother has a right to know all the facts, good and bad, but can I tell her all? Must I?*

Antoinette asked, "Do you think I'll be able to visit Domenico and Papa's graves soon?"

Louis answered, his Italian perfect, "Senora, I'll take you and Rosa whenever you feel ready. We can plant some pretty flowers if you like."

Gently touching Louis' face, Antoinette responded, "Thank you, young man. Nellie, you have done well with your husband. I like him a lot already," Antoinette smiled as she brushed away a tear, streaking her makeup.

Giorgio came forward, saying, "Louis, let's see to the baggage. I believe Antoinette may be hungry, because I sure am. And my Eva has promised us a welcoming feast."

Giorgio and Louis gathered Antoinette's luggage and travel trunk. "Uncle, I think if you don't mind, I'll take the ladies to your house and come back for you and the luggage."

"This is fine with me, but wait for me before you start the feast," said Giorgio.

"Senora Ameduri," Louis said, turning back to Antoinette, "welcome to America, land of the free, home of the brave. Your carriage waits." He winked at his young bride, smiling as he took Antoinette's arm. Rosa and Nellie followed.

Antoinette stepped into the old car, getting her first glance at the city that would be home for the rest of her life. She instantly liked what she saw.

Dinner and conversation was for Rosa a wonderful change in what had become the dull routine of work and more work. The Tedescos had gone out of their way to make Antoinette welcome. Friends and family arrived in droves, greeting and wishing them well. The hours of welcome dragged on, and when everyone left, dirty dishes and cleanup awaited Nellie, Rosa, Aunt Eva, and Antoinette. Together they made quick work of the cleanup.

When they had finished, Nellie turned to Antoinette. "You must be tired. It has been a very long day for you."

"Yes, very." The day flashed before her mind. *Yes, it has been long, starting with Ellis Island, meeting Giorgio, going to the train station, being surprised at the size of the buildings, the six-hour train ride. Yes, it is all too much for a widowed peasant woman to grasp in one day. Thankfully I'm here, but my sweet Rocco is not.*

Alone in Nellie's old bedroom with her mother for the first time, Rosa began, "Mama, how're you really doing?"

Antoinette, tired and apprehensive, answered, "Rosa, coming here was no picnic. Don't get me wrong; I'm happy I did. Back home there's little left. At least here I have you."

"No, Mama, don't forget your grandchildren."

Antoinette sat in the only chair in the room and motioned for Rosa to sit on the bed. "Tell me, Rosa, and don't spare details. I want to know everything that's happened without all the sugar coating that your father always added when he wrote."

Rosa, tired, snapped, "Mama, it can wait until tomorrow! You're tired and so am I!"

Angry at Rosa's dismissal, Antoinette glared, "Yes, I'm tired, so be it. But I won't be able to sleep without knowing at least a little something about this nightmare you've lived. Are you fully healed?"

"Mostly, at least my body is. I miss my children. When I get them back, then I will be healed."

Antoinette, now worried rather than angry, asked, "What must you do to get them back?"

Reluctantly, Rosa began to answer, knowing her mother would not allow the subject to drop. "We're working on it. It's more difficult than it should be. I wish I could give you a straight answer, but I just don't know. Things are different here."

"Don't know what?" asked Antoinette.

Rosa's eyes clouded, "This country's ways are so strange. I don't understand them most of the time, though I've tried. Everything has to be done through an attorney and all this costs money, money I don't have, nor can hope to earn soon."

Rosa hesitated, gathering her thoughts. She spoke slowly, "The first attorney, a Mr. Gallo, worked for free. Unfortunately, he moved to New York City for a better job. His firm changed hands and the new owners won't honor the previous commitment, so now I have to pay for everything they do. It's very expensive.

"The new attorney, a man named Hayes, says that I must first convince the judge that you'll help me raise my babies. I need to work and can't stay at home all the time to watch them. There's no money for extras, so if you could help by taking in laundry or something like a part-time job doing piece work, we might raise enough to pay attorney fees and court costs."

"And where will I work?" asked Antoinette.

"Nellie thinks we can get you a job at the cotton mill where we work. I won't lie; it's hard work, but it's easy to learn. If you worked three or four hours a day after I return home, we might make it."

Antoinette, visibly exhausted, said, "Rosa, I'm very tired. While the thought of a job doesn't bother me, or even the need to raise the money, I must say this to you. Please do not get angry with me for saying this. Daughter, you had the children, and you must raise them. It's only proper for you to do this. I can't tell a judge that I'll stop my life to raise my grandchildren. It would be a lie, and frankly, I really don't want to raise children anymore. I've grown in the past four years and have begun to enjoy my freedom."

Rosa's face dropped in disbelief. Hurt, she stuttered, "Mama, let's talk again when we're both well rested."

Antoinette, not about to end the conversation, continued talking. "No, daughter, I know where this conversation's going. I'm thirty-nine, and still a young woman.

Yes, I definitely can work and I gladly will help you raise this money. You, on the other hand, have a husband, though trash that he is. Yes, the bum's in jail and rightly so, but he has a responsibility here. I don't think that as long as he's alive it's right that his children should be my responsibility."

Rosa, panicked, cried, "But Mama, Tony claims my Jennie may not be his. And whatever money he had, he used to buy expensive attorneys to get a light sentence. I don't expect to receive help from him anytime soon, if ever."

"Are they his children, Rosa?"

"Mama, how could you ask such a question?"

Antoinette, feeling Rosa's hurt, wished too late that her choice of words had been different. Trying to soothe, she said, "Then, how about his family? Are they so cruel? Can't they give you a hand, if even a small one? I never knew Giovanna, but I knew Nicola. He always struck me as a good person."

Rosa's face reddened dangerously at the mention of her in-laws, as she snapped out words, each striking like a whip's crack, "They won't help. Tony's mother believes her precious son. She runs that family and has written off my babies, like the old witch that she is."

Antoinette, upset at Rosa's language, spoke deliberately. "Rosa, can you blame her? No mother wants to think ill of any of her children, especially her eldest son."

Rosa's eyes were pleading, begging. "Mama, I need your help. It'll get the children home sooner, if you help."

"Like I said, I'll do my best to help out with the money. As to your other request, I'll have to think about it. Daughter, you've been through too much, and for this, I'm sorry. But you're a married woman, and this is sometimes how things are for us women. It's a man's world, and the sooner you learn this, the better off you'll be. You're young, and you'll have to find a way to work things out.

"Now let's prepare for bed; tomorrow's another day, and I promise things will look brighter."

Rosa reluctantly nodded her agreement.

Lying in the narrow bed with Antoinette sleeping next to her, Rosa wished she could be somewhere else. *When did Mama change? Or was she always like this? Was she always self-centered? Or am I the one that has changed? Was this selfish behavior always there, but safely hidden by Papa's love? Maybe I am being too hard on her. After all, she has just arrived from a long, tiring journey that started years ago.*

Rosa's head pounded. A headache robbed her of the rest she needed to face another hard day at work. She put the bed pillow over her head, trying to quiet the sound of the soft snores coming from her mother. She got up, opening the room's lone window, letting in a summer's breeze. She inhaled the clean refreshing air and glanced at the soft full moon gliding above. Crickets sang their disruptive music, like a devil's chorus, serving to underline her dismay. Rosa reluctantly returned to the bed, dejected and wondering.

Two weeks passed swiftly with little change in Antoinette's position. Rosa figured it was time to look elsewhere for answers. She loved her mother, and deep down, she forgave her for her unwillingness to do what she had hoped, yet not entirely.

Saint Mary Mt. Carmel Church loomed up ahead. Today Rosa would plead her case once more to God, but only after making her confession. In her mind, she carried many sins, mostly ill feelings and disruptive thoughts that needed the Lord's forgiveness.

Entering the confessional, she closed the door quietly behind her. Hearing her enter, the priest opened the sliding window, inviting her to confess her sins. She could see the shadow of Father Rossi. She came every week to purge her sins from her conscience, and today was no exception. She began.

"Bless me, Father, for I have sinned. It has been one week since my last confession."

"What sins have you committed my child?"

"Father, I've coveted riches of others and have wished I was no longer alive. I've thought ill of my mother, and I have feelings of guilt over not being able to forgive people who have hurt me terribly."

Father Rossi asked, "What kind of hurt have these people done to you that you cannot forgive?"

Father Rossi recognized Rosa. His heart went out to her. He could not let on and injure the sanctity of the confessional, yet her case was an exception. He resisted the temptation.

"Father, my husband almost killed me about six months ago. I have feelings of hatred for him that won't go away, no matter how much I try. And my mother," she held back sobs, "has refused to help me to get my children back. My in-laws have abandoned us, and I think—no, I know that I hate them."

"Child, you must release your anger and turn your wasted energy into doing good deeds. Jesus said to forgive is divine. You must use the Lord's Prayer as your credo. Jesus gave this prayer to us, His perpetual flock, as a sort of relief valve. It makes way for divine forgiveness. Jesus does not want you to go this way any longer. Child, you must understand that your hatred hurts you more than those with whom you are angry. It's not healthy for you, and it certainly does not have the effect you wish for on those who have done you these wrongs. Release your anger and forgive. Only then can you enjoy the peace our Lord has intended for you."

Rosa answered, "Yes, Father. I promise to try."

"You must remember that you are a child of God. Therefore, you must do more than just try. You must give your trouble to the Lord. Lay it at the foot of His cross for His safekeeping and care. Ask yourself, what would Jesus do? Trust me and do this thing. Now make your penance by saying two rosaries."

"Thank you, Father Rossi," Rosa slipped.

"You are very welcome, Rosa."

Rosa could feel his smile, despite the shadows hiding his face.

"Now child, go face the world, and live the life Jesus intended for you."

Rosa closed the confessional behind her. The next person waiting entered. Rosa, somewhat embarrassed, wondered if the young woman passing her gave any thought to why she had taken so long. She retreated to a pew in the middle of the church, kneeling to say penance. When finished, she left feeling refreshed, a new spring in her step.

Once on the sidewalk, she felt as if a giant burden had been lifted from her shoulders. *Father Rossi's correct; I can't hold this toxic hatred within me and I have been my own worst enemy. I've been kidding myself. From this moment on, I will live my life and walk it as the good Christian I claim to be.*

She softly said, "I forgive you, Tony, though it will never be easy to forget what you have done. Now you can never hurt me again, no matter what you do. And Mama, I understand it's your right and your way to expect me to raise my children, and so I will. I forgive you also for your uncaring nature. You are my mother and always will be my mother, so I shall always love you no matter our differences.

"As for you, Giovanna, I forgive you also, but I do not ever have to like you again.

"Now Lord, about my children. We have some talking to do."

Thus began Rosa's first big step toward a new future.

Mother once told me that her experience that fateful day at church had been the true turning point in her life. She continued her visits to our orphanage, mostly on weekends. Only now, she came with an older woman who always wore black. She had a pretty face too, much like Mother's. Able to understand Italian, I understood that the older woman told me that she was my grandmother. When they left, they always left without Rocky and me, and it hurt to see them go.

I remember the candy bars and the occasional baked cookies they brought. They were sure good. I'd hide the sweets after they left before Sister could see them.

The months rolled swiftly into October, and then Mother faced yet another pressing change, along with new challenges.

"Abiding love surrounds those who trust in the Lord."

Psalm 32:10

NINETEEN

The new day stares at me like a blank sheet of paper. Across the vast ripples of my memory, I reach for a handle, a lifeline, to cling to my fleeting past, trying to remember. The calendar says it is October, in the year 2000. Where has the time gone? So many Octobers have drifted past, with their good and bad memories all falling softly like colorful autumn leaves.

I was still a toddler when the Great Depression got its sendoff with a giant bang, crashing down upon Wall Street and collapsing the U.S. economy. It was October 24, 1929: an infamous day that historians would forever call Black Thursday. Many people lost fortunes, and some actually chose suicide over facing financial ruin and bankruptcy. Mother said that the stock market crash didn't have much effect on East Utica. Most of its inhabitants could barely afford chicken stock, let alone financial stocks and bonds. The few East Uticans that could soon joined us in the ranks of the poor.

Still, a very good thing happened to me on October the 24th, though it was many years later. My son Jimmy was born on that day.

But I was talking about Mother, wasn't I? I'm sorry; my mind does wander so these days. The next couple of months after the stock crash rolled uneventfully into Christmastime. Mother would face yet another unexpected change, along with new, demanding challenges.

Nellie, cup in hand, sipped her coffee, nibbling one of Rosa's Christmas cookies. Their freshly baked aroma filled the room like sweet ambrosia. With a coy smile, Nellie said, "Rosa, you never gave me the recipe for your cookies. You did promise, so why don't I just get a piece of paper and a pencil, and I'll jot it down."

Rosa put a finger to her lips, "Shush, Mama will hear. It's her recipe and also her big secret. I'll sneak it to you later. You know, she once won a contest at our town fair and received a big blue ribbon from the mayor himself for these cookies. She's kind of touchy about sharing it," Rosa smirked. "And anyway, all those sweets aren't good for your figure."

"Phooey, I'm married now and look at me; I have not gained an ounce."

"I guess Louis must keep you pretty busy," Rosa giggled, enjoying the moment.

"Rosa, how could you be so bold?" Nellie snickered, coloring slightly in embarrassment.

"I guess it comes with experience. And I have a good teacher."

"Rosa, have you been into the wine?"

"No, I have certainly not," she frowned, shaking her head as if in disgust. "You know I don't drink. It's Christmas, after all. I'm just happy and feeling good." She hesitated, "Even though my children aren't here, there's still plenty to be grateful for."

"Like what?" Nellie coaxed, happy to see Rosa's optimism.

"That's easy. Let's see: both my children are healthy. I have a job. Mama has a job. I have food on the table and even extra money to make cookies so that you can get fat. Also there's money to buy the children little trinkets." Rosa was counting on her fingers. "Oh yes, I never owned any stocks or bonds, so I didn't lose any money. I'm healthy again. Mama is healthy. You're both my cousin and my best friend." She hesitated, "How many fingers do I have left?"

Nellie answered, snickering, "I'm not sure, but I think you used them all up. Why not take off your shoes while you are at it and count some more blessings? It's really good to see you happy."

"Nellie, I try. Despite the fact that this wonderful day is also my fourth wedding anniversary, I'm in good spirits. And why shouldn't I be? I'm here and Tony's in jail. Even after all the pain I've suffered, my lot in life has to be better than his, don't you think?"

Nellie said, "Cousin, you have me there."

Antoinette entered the room, her hands full of newly ironed laundry. "What are you girls rattling on about?"

"Mama, we were just saying how terrible my cookies are this year, compared to other years." Rosa enjoyed the opportunity to joke; it had been almost a year since she felt at ease enough to be lighthearted.

Antoinette, now concerned, "Surely you're not insulting my recipe. Perhaps you've done something wrong. Here, give me one so I can see what's missing."

Antoinette accepted a vanilla cookie that Nellie handed her. It was topped with oozing white icing and a cherry. She tasted it; a confused look covered her face, "Are you crazy? There's nothing wrong with the taste of this cookie."

Antoinette started to say that it tasted even better than her own, but caught herself just in time.

Rosa snickered, for she had improved on her mother's almost magical recipe. "Mama, you must have chosen the wrong cookie; here, taste a chocolate almond."

Antoinette's face lightened, though she still looked confused. Shaking her head, she said, "This one's better than the last. Rosa, you're pulling my leg, just like you always did back home. My, it sure is wonderful to see you happy again."

Nellie, with a big grin matching her enthusiasm, replied, "That's about what I said, too. Oh my, look at the time! I better run. I need to get ready for mass, and I don't want to be late. Rosa, when are you going to see the children again?"

"With the mill closed for the holidays, I'm going each day, as long as the weather cooperates."

"Since I won't be able to visit again until after Christmas, take this money and buy something for Rocky and Jennie. Tell them it's from me." Nellie handed Rosa a $5 bill, a third of her weekly wages.

"Nellie, this is too generous. I can't take it."

Nellie beamed, "You must, and you will."

"Thank you, you are too kind."

"Well Rosa, I've got a good teacher. Now, remember, tomorrow at five, Christmas dinner at my flat. Everyone will be there."

"We won't miss it. Merry Christmas, Nellie, and here, this is for you. It's not much, but I know how much you like them." Rosa handed Nellie a cardboard box, wrapped with a wide red ribbon that she had saved from happier times. In it contained four-dozen of the special cookies.

Nellie was very pleased. Rosa had given her all that she had baked. This was the true, generous, and kind Rosa, who had finally returned from the dead.

"Merry Christmas, everyone! See you at church tonight." Nellie, aglow, left the apartment, her step a bit lighter, and her heart filled to brimming.

January 2, 1930, was supposed to be a workday for Rosa and Antoinette. Instead, they joined the burgeoning ranks of the unemployed when the mill fired two-thirds of its workers. Since most people had no phone or means of contact, the mill owners chose the only way available to them at the time. Simply, they dismissed the workers they were cutting as each arrived. There was no severance pay, no explanation beyond, "You are no longer needed here."

Rosa was not as devastated as Antoinette. They walked home, each trying to stay warm. However, the surprise had drained them of their spirits.

Antoinette, upset and confused by the sudden turn of events, asked, "Rosa, what will we do? We spent what little extra we had on Christmas. We have about thirty dollars, and that was to go toward the attorney expenses."

Rosa, trying to remain strong, answered, "We'll just have to use it. As I see it, there's no other choice."

Her matter-of-fact attitude was a cover-up, an act for Antoinette's benefit. Trying to hide the desperate fear, she said, "Well, one good thing: at least I can go see the children today."

Antoinette felt a sudden need to rest. Fearfully she asked, "Do you mind if I stay at home? I want to relax and think."

"Sure, Mama, I'll see you later." Struck by a sudden concern, Rosa turned to Antoinette, "I wonder what Nellie will do?"

Antoinette said, "Louis has a good job with the City Maintenance Department. Don't you think that his job is secure?"

"That still doesn't guarantee that the City won't cut his wages. It is sure beginning to look like that stock market mess is finally hurting us, too."

"Can they do that, cut wages?" asked Antoinette.

"It happened to Carmella's husband. He works for the state highway department."

Antoinette replied, "At least he has a job, and the price on everything has seemed to drop some, so maybe less money will go a little further."

"I suppose, but you have to have it in the first place to buy stuff." Rosa sighed, trying not to let her guard down, remembering Father Rossi's advice. She thought, *Maybe it would be a good idea to stop and pray at church on my way to the orphanage.*

"Mama, I have a dollar in my pocket. Do you need it for any groceries, or would you rather wait and we'll go together?"

"Let's go there together and make it an event. It's always nice to see others and find out what's happening. And two sets of ears are much better to get all the gossip, and just maybe we'll hear of some work."

The local stores in the Italian section on Bleecker Street also served as a vital communication link for East Utica's inhabitants. Many, like Antoinette, had yet to learn the English language, and it was an opportunity to speak and hear a familiar tongue.

In the previous fall, Jennie and Rocky had been transferred to a new orphanage. The St. Joseph's Orphanage only cared for infants and toddlers. Rosa's bus ride to the new orphanage, St. John's, was uneventful though a bit longer. Enough time had passed so that the wound she sustained in losing her babies to the authorities had numbed somewhat, and she was getting used to the routine. Still, it was always most difficult to leave them behind after each visit, it pulled at her heartstrings; never did that pain lessen.

Knowing and hoping that she was one day closer to bringing them home— or so she reasoned to keep her sanity—made it a bit easier. That was, until now. Now, without a job, she had the real fear that she might never get them back, at least not until they reached eighteen years old.

It was cold inside the bus. The temperature outside had dipped to zero degrees, and the old bus could not retain its meager heat. Each time its door opened, a blast of cold air made the trip, already long, seem almost unbearable.

Rosa trudged up the slippery hill to the aging red brick building. Once at her destination, her short walk up the concrete steps to the orphanage's large wooden doors was difficult, every step an eternity in the cold wintry blast. The ground literally crunched as her boots hit the sidewalk. A rare January sun cast a shadow that seemed to follow her. Freezing, she couldn't wait to enjoy the comforting warmth waiting inside the large barren brick building. Today, it would be almost as welcome as seeing her children.

Sister Theresa, surprised at seeing Rosa arrive in the middle of a workday, immediately came over to greet her. Rosa was registering her presence in the ledger book near the entrance.

"Rosa, it's nice to see you. No work today?"

"No Sister, I have no work today, not today, not ever; that is, until I find a new job. The mill fired just about everyone this morning. My boss said it was because of something called a depression." After a moment of silence, Rosa continued. "Since there was little I could do about finding another job today, I felt it would be nice if I took the opportunity to see my children. You know, how you say—make lemonade out of life's lemons. So how are my babies doing?" *Why am I babbling so?* she thought.

"Rosa, they are doing fine. Jennie is a real peach, and Rocky, well he's one real cute little boy. So much energy! He really loves that child's book about horses that you gave him for Christmas. You have two beautiful children to be proud of."

"Thank you, Sister. Now if I could only bring them home."

"Rosa, I have an idea that might at least be the next best thing. It just so happens that we have a nurse's assistant position open and with a little training, I'm sure you can do the job."

"That would be great. But what would such a job require me to do? Sister, I must confess, I have no training as a nurse."

"It's a job to assist the nurse on the second floor. So the good thing is you'd be near your children. The bad part of the job is you'd be changing diapers constantly, helping wherever you're needed, feeding the children, helping when they're ill—all the things a mother would do for them if the tykes had a mother."

Sister Theresa felt funny, realizing what she had said. "Rosa, you will make a good nurse. I can readily see that you are a good mother. More importantly, I don't doubt that you'll learn quickly. Just so you'll know, this job doesn't pay much—$30 a month. You'll work five shifts from 7:00 a.m. to 5:00 p.m., and every other week you work four shifts from 7:00 a.m. to 7:00 p.m. So would you still like to discuss the position with Mother Superior?"

Rosa answered, "You know I would! What a dream come true and an answer to my prayers, and frankly, I'm in no position to complain about the money. Thank you, Sister, you're truly an angel."

"I'm no angel, Rosa. You will earn every penny. After all is said and done, this is hard work, and you're available. I've seen how you come to visit here every spare moment. And anyone who cares to look can see that you truly love your children. Most of the other parents never visit. The world seems to have dealt you several serious setbacks. Maybe it's time something good happened in your favor, don't you think?"

"Yes, Sister," Rosa replied, seeing Sister Theresa's radiant smile, an affirmation to her comments. "I once believed God had forgotten about me, but a kind priest taught me otherwise. Before I came here today, I stopped at church and said several prayers, but until now, I've never known God to answer my prayers so quickly. Mind you, I'm not disappointed. Sister, is there an application I must fill out? I'm sorry; I still have difficulty with the English, especially reading it."

"Yes, there is. How long have you lived here?"

"A little over four years. My English is bad, isn't it?"

"No, Rosa, you have nothing to be ashamed of; your English is better than most that have lived here all their lives. I'll get an application, and we can complete it together. When we finish, you can meet with Mother Superior. Then when you're through, you can have a nice visit with your children."

Rosa met with Mother Superior, who, like the good administrator that she was, grilled her with several probing questions and then, satisfied, gave her the job. She then was instructed to visit with the floor nurse to discuss her new duties. When pleased that Rosa understood what she was getting into, the floor nurse issued her two clean white uniforms and a nurse's cap. She would start the next morning.

Rosa then spent a few precious hours with Jennie and Rocky, reading stories to each, carefully enunciating each word, determined that they would speak proper English. She returned home full of excitement to give the good news to Antoinette. Also, tonight, out of practical necessity, she would speak to the landlord and see about a reduction in the rent.

The cold, blowing wind tried to dampen her spirit, both on the return bus ride and during the two-block walk to her apartment. Somehow her mind was on another plane. She felt good; it was as if she were floating on a magic carpet, with her own special genie and several wishes yet to be made. The pay she would receive was only about half of what she had made at the mill. It was still a paycheck, though, and a wonderful way to see her children daily. It still seemed impossible that this could be happening. Somehow she vowed that she would have to make do with what she made.

Rosa would live on this high for several months, until her own personal Black Thursday dropped in on her one day like an uninvited visitor.

I remember the first day Mother came dressed all in white. It was then that I started to call her the pretty lady in white. It was a wonderful memory. I would see her every day and also on weekends. She never seemed to tire. Her youthful exuberance was captivating, and she quickly became the favorite of all the children. I am not proud to say that sometimes I became jealous. You see, I wanted my mother all to myself. I hadn't yet learned to willingly share. That would come later.

Often, the pretty lady in white would bring candy. I know now that it had to have been a sacrifice for her, because I came to learn later how little money she had to spare. I suppose seeing Rocky and me every day, along with caring for our needs, was close to bringing us home. Yet, she often felt the need to remind us that she was our real mother. I slowly began to believe her because she only said this to Rocky and me, and never the other children. But as always, she never took us home with her, and I remember crying when she left.

"The world is moved along, not only by the mighty shoves of its heroes, but also by the aggregate of the tiny pushes of each worker."

Helen Keller

TWENTY

I once read that the headlines in 1930 were mostly upsetting, even for the very wealthy. The year's biggest achievement seemed to be the decline of capitalism and the beginning of the terrible years that our country would call the Great Depression. Mother often enjoyed saying that a depression occurs when a person is not working and that a recession happens when someone else isn't working. At the time, this statement made little sense to me.

For America, there was a lot of soul searching as economic woes turned personal for just about everyone. In 1930, things were so bad that Babe Ruth, the great homerun hitter, would boast that he was paid more than the president because he had a better year. It was also the year that saw French troops evacuate Germany, five years before the date established by the Versailles Treaty that had ended the Great War. France's desire to save money would help set the stage for a young, opportunistic Austrian radical named Adolph Hitler. I guess that some things never seem to change when the French are involved.

The year 1930 was also a time of wonderful fun for Rocky and me because we saw Mother almost daily. It almost seemed acceptable to stay at the orphanage when she left because I knew she'd return the next day. Then too, I was beginning to understand the ways of the world. All the while, my young mind wrestled with growing and learning and dealing with disappointment, though as far as disappointment is concerned, I never truly got the hang of it.

And then Mother's next obstacle in life arrived, and the seemingly never-ending vicissitudes of our family's fortunes took another rollercoaster-like twist.

Strong, brisk autumn winds, coming like a harbinger from the north, threatened an early winter, though the temperature was still mild. Rosa had fallen into the dull routine at St. John's, and dull can sometimes be a good thing.

Walking to her wooden locker, she retrieved her lunch. She involuntarily caught her reflection on the small wall mirror hanging in the nurse's lounge. The image looking back at her was haggard and weary. Primping, she adjusted her hair and cap and again looked at the image flashing back at her. She was both startled and depressed at seeing a drawn, very tired, and very thin face. The sad image reflected the unkind destiny of her life. Rosa shook off the sadness, and picked up her spirit like a newly found good-luck penny. She walked quickly from the room, trying to escape her past.

Startled, she turned up her nose at the freshly cleaned smell of ammonia coming from the corridor; the pungent smell always came back at her like a ton of bricks—a stark reminder of her long hospital stay. She picked up her pace and walked first to Jennie's room, and then Rocco's. She was very excited, for today she had received permission to have a picnic lunch with her children, a rare treat. Sister Theresa had suggested only yesterday that it would be acceptable to take a few minutes and make a party of it, as long as she made up the time.

Rosa liked the idea. It almost sounded normal and a family-like thing to do. The diversion would be good for her. She worried constantly now. There wasn't enough money. Antoinette had tried but could not find work; there just wasn't any work to be found. Unemployment levels in Utica, like the nation, were at all-time highs, with millions out of work.

Rosa found Jennie in her room, sitting, facing the barren wall. She asked, "Jennie, what did you do now?"

Jennie turned her head reluctantly. One did not usually dare to defy Sister Agnes. But since this was the pretty lady who said she was her mother, she decided to chance it. In a barely audible tone, she said, "I told Sister Agnes

I didn't like her much, and that my real mother was going to take me home someday, and that I'd be happy when you did so that I didn't have to listen to her anymore."

Jennie pouted, her large brown eyes tugging at Rosa's heartstrings. "She's so mean. Sister said that I may be right, someday, but as long as I'm here today, I must obey her. And Pretty Lady, that is why I'm here, looking at this darn wall."

Rosa responded, "Jennie, you mustn't talk back to the nuns and you mustn't say darn. It'll be much easier on you if you don't. Besides, it's important to be polite. It'll make your stay here go much quicker if you follow the rules. Now, you don't want to stare at walls forever, do you? There is a whole world waiting for you to see."

Jennie wiped the tears rolling from puffy eyes, smiling and reaching for a hug. It was the one thing that always separated this lady from the rest. Breaking Jennie's punishment, Rosa complied, holding her little body, feeling her daughter's life pressed compactly with hers. *To think that I almost lost this opportunity, she mused,* and then let it pass.

Rosa put Jennie back in the chair, facing her to the wall. "Now, Jennie, you must stay with your punishment until I come back." Rosa left to find Sister Agnes.

After a few curt words about how obstinate Jennie could be, Sister Agnes relented to temporarily releasing the child from punishment, as long as she continued her penance when she returned. Sister Agnes' compromise did not end so easily. Unbending, she insisted that instead of missing lunch, Jennie would have to forego dinner to fulfill the punishment. Rosa left feeling both victorious and defeated. *Oh dear Lord, how much longer must I wait?*

She gathered Jennie and marched toward her son's area. She found him playing on the ward's floor with some wooden blocks. Rocky disliked being hugged; he also preferred to keep to himself. *Maybe it's just how some little boys are,* she rationalized. She hugged and kissed him anyway. Shuddering at her son's reaction, she was suddenly reminded of Dominick's dislike for affections.

Rocky wiped the kiss away as if it were vermin. He then squirmed from his mother's caress and rushed to his sister, taking her hand. Rosa grabbed Jennie's hand, and thus linked together, Rosa led them outside to a wooden table on the manicured lawn in the massive play area, next to the building.

Rosa carefully unpacked the fried chicken she had prepared the night before. She put a linen towel around each child and prepared a plate for each. Together the three ate, for the very first time, *As a family unit—well, almost a family.*

Jennie spoke, her voice animated, "This is good. It's better than what we eat here. Did you make this? Rocky, isn't this good?" Jennie patted her brother's mane of jet-black hair, instinctively mothering him, though she couldn't have known that she was.

"Yes, I did," beamed Rosa, enjoying her daughter's bright mannerisms. "When you each finish, I have a surprise. Eat up first." Jennie and Rocco gobbled their food excitedly. Surprises were rare and, even at their tender, naive age, caused their eyes to brighten expectantly.

"We're done," each shouted proudly. Rosa gently wiped the food particles clinging to their small chins, caressing each face tenderly, and giving each a special grin. *This is good, this contact. It helps to bolster my courage and makes me want to go on when sometimes it seems impossible.*

Tenderly, Rosa stretched out both hands for Jennie and Rocky. "Now you'll have your surprise." She pulled out two large chocolate-covered cupcakes. Each was topped with a big cherry. Next she took two sugar cookies from her lunch box. Rocky's eyes lost their solemn look as his face split with a huge grin.

Jennie, not as easily bought, reached for the cupcake. "Thanks. Did you make this, too?"

Rosa answered, "I sure did. I hope you like it."

Jennie's reserve broke; her face was now covered in a chocolate smile. "This is good. Could you teach me how to make these?"

Rosa answered as she wiped away involuntary tears, "Yes. It's called baking, and someday I promise that I'll teach you everything you need to know about it." She thought, *But is this a promise I can keep?*

Rocky, not to be outdone, pleaded, "Can I make these too?"

Rosa laughed happily, hugging him. This time he did not resist. "Well Rocky, I'll teach you too, if you want me to. Usually little boys don't like to cook, though I see no reason why you shouldn't learn."

She thought again of her brother Dominick when he was about Rocky's age, so energetic and curious. Noticing a frown on Rocky's face, she patted his chin, cleaning some of the excess frosting.

Rocky raised his newly cleaned chin boldly and said, "Well, I want to learn how!"

His determined look took Rosa by surprise. Her son's glare was like a bad flashback, reminding her of her estranged husband's mannerisms.

"Hello there, at the table!" The voice's familiarity startled Rosa. *No, it can't be.* But it was, and her memory of that voice scared her beyond reason.

Startled, her voice on the edge of panic, Rosa spit out, "Tony, don't you dare come near me. You can't be here!"

With a low and intimidating voice, eyes glaring, he hissed, "Glad to see you missed me, Rosa."

"Tony, I wouldn't care if I never saw you again." She spoke in Italian, trying to hide the ill tones of the conversation from her children. In a high whisper, she continued, "If you must talk, *parlé Italiano*. The bambinos don't need to know what we say."

Tony nodded his agreement.

Rosa looked at him. He was a little older, yet he hadn't changed. He even looked a little heavier. He must have been working out because muscular arms rippled under his short-sleeve shirt. She noticed his hands were also calloused, not soft like before.

"When did you get out?" she asked reluctantly.

"A couple of weeks ago. I've been catching up. I didn't know you worked here."

She answered with a sneer, "Now you know. Now leave."

"Not so soon, I'm here to see my kids. It was by chance that I saw you, acting so nice, like a normal little family."

Her voice was venomous, "No thanks to you. And why would you want to visit these children? Didn't you claim they aren't yours?"

His eyes, as always, gave away his true feelings, but he left no doubt when he answered contritely, at least for him, "I had to say it, or I'd a' been in jail for a lot longer."

Rosa glared, not yet at a loss for words. "Good for you. At least you admit the obvious. One has to only look at these children to know they're yours." Her voice seething, she shouted, "Tony, you're a no-good person, and I never want to see you again. Do you hear me?"

Tony's smirk sizzled with hate. "What you want and what you get are two different things. Neither matter to me. As I remember, we're still married. And according to the State of New York, I've paid for my misdeeds—in full. By all reason and the State of New York, who can't be wrong, I'm reformed," he sneered, following up with a menacing chuckle.

Rosa, not to be outdone, answered, "No, Tony. We may be married on paper, but we were only truly married for a few days, perhaps minutes. As soon as you got me pregnant, your eyes roamed, constantly on the lookout for greener pastures. Do you think I forgot that you slept with your whores? And you were their pimp!" Her voice reached a high soprano. "Are you still working there at that filthy place, or did Rabiso wash his hands of you, too? Faa, a fruit company, what an idiot I was, and I bought it all hook, line, and sinker."

Tony, not to be outdone, ranted in fury, "I don't need this crap. I'm only here to see my kids. If you must know, I do work for Rabiso. The pay is so-so, not as good as before. The depression even hit his business. Rabiso said I have some repenting ta' do and that if I watch my backside, he'll eventually fit me in like before. He said I gotta re-earn his respect."

Spitting out the words, Rosa yelled, "Good luck, Mr. Pimp! Respect! Does anything you do for that man command any respect?"

Rosa was so livid she no longer feared him. Her verbal attack took him by surprise.

Regaining some calm, she said, "You go and re-earn that respect. While you're at it, come up with some money so I can get these children out of here. If you were a real man and a father, like you claim to be, you'd never have let it get this far."

Tony's anger pitched to a boil. His eyes told it all. He advanced quickly toward Rosa, grabbed her arm and squeezed, immediately raising a black and blue mark.

Rosa screamed. Panicking, she picked up her metal lunch pail and hit him squarely in the chest. It did not seem to hurt him. The lunch pail dropped to the ground, scattering its contents upon the grass and the fallen leaves. The thermos bottle broke, another casualty of their relationship.

She attacked him then with her small fists, punching him on his chest to no effect. "What are you going to do, Big Man, hit me? Did you forget your knife,

Big Man?" Switching from her native tongue, she emphasized each word in very distinct English, deliberately taunting him.

Jennie started to cry. Rocky ran over to hit the stranger that was bothering the nice lady who said she was his mother. He didn't know or care who it was that he was hitting, only that something inside him told him that he must.

Tony brushed his son aside like a gnat, forcing Rocky to fall rudely to the hard ground. His son began to cry uncontrollably. By now the commotion had attracted attention. Several nuns and a janitor, a tall muscular man, came running.

Sister Theresa shouted, "Stop this foolishness this instant! We cannot have this kind of behavior here. Young man," she pointed her long finger at his chest, fearlessly poking him, "who are you, and why are you here?"

Tony, ever the casual instigator, answered with the calm assurance of a con-man, "Sister, I'm sorry for the commotion, but I was trying to talk to my wife, who I haven't seen for two years. As you can see, she's the one that is out of control."

Rosa screamed in defiance, "I'm out of control?"

Sister Theresa motioned to her to be quiet. Rosa complied, feeling suddenly foolish.

Turning back to Tony and, glaring, Sister Theresa said, "So you're the infamous Tony Lavalia, I take it."

"Yes, Sister, I am he," he snapped back.

"I thought you were in jail."

"As you no doubt can see, I'm out," he smirked.

Not to be outdone, she answered using her well-honed, intimidating voice, "Yes, silly of me, wasn't it?"

"Good Sister, I can explain," Tony started, trying to use his suave persuasive side, but to no avail. The sister would not listen; too many men, from little boys to elderly, had tried to use this trick on her.

Sister Theresa's voice was steady as she cut across him, "Mr. Lavalia, no explanation's necessary. I'll not allow you to see your children when your wife is here. We cannot tolerate this behavior, ever. Do you understand?"

She looked at him directly. Tony, his face not hiding his anger, instinctively made a threatening gesture, but seeing the janitor poised and ready, he thought better of it.

"Mr. Lavalia, I suggest you leave. You may visit your children at another time. However, when you do, you are to see me first, so we can discuss the rules and my conditions for your visits. Do you hear me?"

Tony answered, "Yes, I do, loud and clear."

"Good." Turning to the janitor, Sister Theresa said, "Mr. Young, will you please escort Mr. Lavalia off the property?"

He nodded.

"Oh, and Mr. Lavalia," she said, turning back to Tony, "you are hereby warned that if this ever happens again, I shall call the police. I shouldn't think that you'd want to have the police asking you too many questions. I suspect you're still on parole?"

Her threat had the proper effect. Tony answered sheepishly, his voice measured, "Yep, Sister, I heard ya' loud and clear the first time."

He turned to leave. The janitor, who stood a good foot higher than Tony, grasped him by the arm. Instinctively, Tony thought to yank his arm away. Then he decided to let it pass.

Sister Theresa turned to Rosa. "Kiss your children and say goodbye, Rosa. They have seen enough for today. Sister Mary, take Rocky and Jennie to their areas. There has been enough excitement, and I must speak to Rosa."

Rosa, who had been standing very resolutely, shook now with anxieties in the aftermath, fearing what was to come.

"Rosa, I know you had good reason to panic because I know what that man did to you. You have been good for St. John's, but I suspect your value to us may no longer be worth the price tag."

With a panicked voice, Rosa asked, "Sister, please, no. Are you letting me go?"

"Yes, Rosa. Your husband is a violent man, and he probably belongs in jail. Unfortunately, he's not there anymore. From the window, I saw him grab your arm, and his desire to do worse. He's a loose cannon, which makes him a very dangerous person. Too dangerous, I fear, for the orphanage to chance another scene like the one I just witnessed. I can't take the chance, Rosa. I'm sorry, but it is my responsibility to think first of our children's safety."

Rosa pleaded, tears running like rivers down her face, "Sister, I promise, it won't happen again. I need to be with my children, and I need this job. You more than anyone know that I really need this work so that I can get my babies back."

Without a second thought, Sister Theresa answered, "Again, I'm sorry, but my mind's made up. You will need to find work elsewhere. This is your problem, not mine."

"But Sister, you are a woman of the cloth. How could you throw me out? I only reacted out of a valid fear, as you yourself have admitted. It was a reaction any normal person would have under the circumstance. This man tried to kill me. He left me for dead, something I would be except for a kind priest who happened by. Please understand, I was in the hospital for months because of him."

Desperate, Rosa tore open her blouse, exposing a long jagged scar. "Look what he did to me."

Sister Theresa answered quietly, "But he didn't kill you. You are now very strong and alive. And he's still your husband in the eyes of the church. You must pray to our Lord and ask Him to help you reconcile."

Rosa burst out angrily, "Sister, no offense. I have forgiven Antonio, as I must, because I'm a good Catholic, and as you well know it is what Jesus would do. But no, I don't have to live with nor reconcile with him. This, good sister, is where I must draw the line. You just saw what he is capable of. His abuse is intolerable to me. How can you do this to me? I love you, Sister, I always shall. But I shall always resent the way you have treated me today. I don't deserve this, especially from a holy person who falsely believes occasionally that she has the right to act like God. Why don't you ask yourself, what would Jesus do in your position?

"What money that I've made here has barely been enough to keep my mother and me alive, let alone saving for attorneys. But it has given me a new lease on life, seeing my babies. What you have done now is to throw me into the street, uncaring, right into my violent husband's path. Are you happy? Is this what you really want?"

Undaunted, Sister Theresa responded, "Rosa, what you do and how you handle it is your business. Of course, you can still visit, but it's best that you coordinate your visits with your husband. I'll not allow either of you here at the same time; unless and until you give me proof that you have settled your disagreements."

Rosa, not about to be outdone, said, "That will never happen, but I will do my best to avoid him. This you can bet your life on." Rosa's determined look left little doubt to her sincerity.

Sister Theresa said coldly, "Rosa, I need you to turn in your nurse's uniforms and clean out your locker. Please pick up this mess before you do." She pointed to the broken thermos and lunch pail. "After you finish, see me. I'll have your pay made up through today."

Though Rosa had much more to say, she kept it to herself. It no longer mattered. Feeling dejected, all she could think of was the frightened looks on her children's small faces. She picked up the debris. Before going to get her money, she defiantly peered into the rooms of each of her children. Jennie was again facing the wall. She thought, *God, please help me.*

She was sobbing by the time she opened the door to Sister Theresa's little office without knocking. The nun, working at her desk, peered up from a pile of papers.

"Rosa, what took you so long?"

"Sister, you have never borne children and therefore won't ever really understand how I feel. Just so you know, I took a peek at my babies, and then I cried a lot of tears. And I'll probably cry on the way home, too, because you, who once gave me a chance at life, have decided to take that chance away. So, good sister, I shall pray, not just for my babies, but also for you, in the hope that someday you'll see the light and recognize the misdeeds done to me today. I forgive you, Sister Theresa. I only hope that you can live with yourself, and that you may never hurt another as deeply as you have hurt me today."

Taking a deep breath for courage, Rosa continued her careful attack, not caring any longer. "I realize that you're correct in saying that I should have controlled my anger. It doesn't seem to matter that this man you so easily call my husband cut me from my navel to breast. Because of his despicable deed, I can never have babies again. So, yes, Sister, I was afraid, so afraid that I could never describe it properly in words, either in my native tongue or yours. To you this is but a passing event. To me it is my life." Rosa collected her wits before finishing her thought. "Now, Sister, may I have my pay, what little of it that there is? I feel that I have more than earned every penny of it."

"Rosa, I am truly sorry for all you have gone through. Here is your money. I suggest you look quickly for another job and stay away from your husband. I know that I was a bit quick in my decision, yet I cannot change my mind. I must protect all the children here. I promise that I will pray for you every day."

Rosa thought, *How big of you to pray.* Aloud she said, "Thank you, Sister. I will see you often when I visit. I hope you will not hold what I have said against my children or me for that matter."

"How could you think this? I would never…" the nun paused, and then simply said, "Good luck, Rosa. Now I must return to my work."

I didn't see that mean man much, only about once or twice a year. When I asked him once why he hurt Mother, he laughed. Yes, he laughed, saying that Mother and Rocky got in the way. He seemed to like my brother more than me. Rocky said the man told him he had courage. I didn't know what courage was until I grew older and looked it up in the big dictionary in the orphanage's library. You see, I didn't want Rocky to have courage if it meant being like this strange, mean man who said he was my father.

Mother came less often to see us. She said she was trying to find work. Still, she came to visit at least twice a week. I know because I kept count of the times on paper.

Months passed, perhaps three or so, before Mother happily said she had a job. It had something to do with baking, that very nice word I had learned at our picnic. Her job was at a place called Hathaway Bakery. She would bring us sweets every now and then. She called them seconds or rejects. They didn't taste like rejects to me, all fluffy and sweet and delicious. Now my mother became the cake lady, our new title for her. I remember scurrying to the library to look up the words "second" and "reject." It just made me even more confused, because it did not make sense.

"There are two kinds of success. One is the very rare kind that comes to a man who has the power to do what no one else has the power to do. That is genius. But the average man who wins what we call success is not a genius. He is a man who has merely the ordinary qualities that he shares with his fellows, but who has developed those ordinary qualities to a more than ordinary degree."

Theodore Roosevelt,
26th President of the United States of America

TWENTY-ONE

Much happened in the three years after Mother lost her job at the orphanage. The year 1933 was a year to remember. The bakery job was going well. Mother was promoted to head pastry chef. In those days, this was unusual for a woman in the business world. However, she was never the typical woman for her time. Working with non-stop diligence, her passion and industry were noticed and rewarded by a firm that was ahead of its time.

Unemployment at home and in Europe had set all-time records, creating universal poverty and suffering. A job was a privilege, not a right, and a smart employee would not willingly do anything to upset the apple cart, or they would be summarily let go. Often several hundred applicants waited patiently in line to replace them. Riots and bank closings were worldwide. People in Germany were said to need a wheelbarrow full of their country's useless paper money to buy a loaf of bread.

In Italy, Pope Pius XI continued his opposition to Mussolini's Fascists, calling them violent and hateful. Meanwhile, Hitler took advantage of the political unrest and gained power in Germany.

Here at home, the Empire State Building, then the planet's tallest structure, was already two years old. Al Capone, the embarrassment to honest Italian-Americans, had been in jail for two years. Mother was glad for his incarceration. She saw Capone as a thorn in the side of Italians everywhere. The news of the day also contained articles about Charles Lindbergh's kidnapped baby boy, who eventually was found murdered. Franklin Delano Roosevelt was elected the nation's 32nd president. His New Deal platform was the beginning of his struggle to find political solutions to help several million Americans find work. Luckily, my mother was not one of them; unfortunately, Grandma Antoinette was. However, everything wasn't all doom and gloom. The Prohibition outlawing the use of alcoholic beverages came to a jubilant end, and suddenly the rift it had created left many of the dishonest unemployed.

At the orphanage, I was still a very lonely child. My brother was now gone, transferred by the powers that be to Syracuse and another orphanage exclusively for boys. Syracuse was fifty miles west of Utica. For Mother, it might as well have been a million miles.

Mother still visited me about three times a week, though sometimes I missed seeing her because I was in school or working. You see, orphans back then had to work. Conditions are much different now. The old system thought it necessary to prepare the orphans for the outside world by teaching them a trade. I suppose, in reality, it probably helped the bureaucrats feel better by serving to remind us unfortunates that we were, after all was said and done, nothing more than wards of the state. In principle, this theory made sense, unless, of course, you were a child in the middle of it all. In reality, it was slave labor. Imagine today any seven-year-old, in particular an orphan, with a schedule. I often wonder what they did with the money they made from our labors. I suppose in reality it wasn't much, but it probably helped some to pay for our keep. I never could see how assembling parts of one kind or another into little bags could teach me a trade.

Back then, I constantly thought that someday Mother would sweep me up and take me home. It gave me constant hope. I had made several good friends at the orphanage. They're all gone now, scattered to the four winds. Like me, they too were sad and mostly lonely, with an occasional but very rare good memory thrown in for good measure. Because of these kindled friendships, I looked forward to morning classes. At least in school, I could sit. Standing for hours, assembling whatever it was that we assembled, hurt my feet.

Anna Murcurio was the bakery's busybody and self-proclaimed pastry tester. Her abundant waist testified to this fact, laying aside any thoughts to the contrary. Anything that went on in Hathaway's huge complex always fit her need to satisfy her perpetual nosiness. Today was no exception. She approached her boss. Her ample body swam in fat, and white flour encrusted her once very pretty face. "Rosa, did you hear? We have a new head baker."

Rosa, shook her head, and burst out with tempered however restrained curtness, "Anna, don't you have work to do? We've no time for gossip. We're behind schedule."

Rosa lived by her schedule. She directed, pointing and yet still grinning, "See that those five barrels of apples are cut for the apple pie mix. Now go to your job and make sure the others don't dawdle."

"Boss, do you ever stop to take a break? You know you're entitled."

"Nope, don't need one, and why are you still standing here?" Rosa shook her head. *Anna means well, but her husband has a job too. I need this job.* She called to Anna, who was almost out of hearing, which in the rumble of the bakery represented a radius of around five feet. Anna returned.

Rosa liked Anna and didn't ever want to hurt her feelings, or anyone's for that matter. And Anna was a good employee, despite Rosa's misgivings about her prying. She said, "Anna, to answer your question, I meet with the new boss after our shift ends. Wait for me and then we can walk home together and talk then." Their shift ran from eight at night to eight in the morning, six days a week.

Anna answered, smiling, "Sure, Rosa, let's do that."

Since Rosa started work at the bakery, she had slowly adjusted to the night hours. Now a great part of her days, when not shopping for food or other essentials, was spent sleeping. She saw little of Antoinette, who had found her own friends, mostly out of deep loneliness and necessity. Gradually, they drifted apart, though not intentionally. Their bonds, though, had seemed to grow even stronger now that their lives were stretched as they were. But their relationship had become like two passing ships in the dark—happy to see each other, yet not willing or able to change course.

Often, in the late afternoon, before work started, Rosa would take a streetcar to St. John's Orphanage. Because Rocky was in Syracuse, she now visited only Jennie with regularity. To her dismay, and despite her fight against it, Rocky had been sent, like all other boys who reached six years of age, to a Catholic home exclusively for boys. It was only a short two-hour, one-way bus ride and a forty-minute train trip, yet it might as well have been in another state with her crowded six-day work schedule. Yet somehow, she always managed to spend most Sundays going to Syracuse. With this added extra expense and Antoinette's inability to get work, saving for attorney costs seemed futile. Rosa realized that she could claim her children when they reached sixteen, but that seemed like an unreachable eternity. She needed her kids now as much as she needed a heart to pump her blood.

Rosa caught herself daydreaming and turned mid-stream from her thoughts. *Oops, I better get to work.* Today she was sculpturing a special-order wedding cake. Rosa looked at the culinary finery as she decorated it with white roses and fine, frosted petals with candy pearls. It looked too good to eat, and she was pleased. Seeing the cake forced unrelenting thoughts which raced undeterred back to December 24, 1925, and her wedding. Quickly she forced herself back to the present, diligently doing her best work for the unknown couple. Happy to be a silent part of their pending joy, she cheerfully turned her full attention to the project, putting her heart and soul into each of the cake's layers, like a maestro at a great concert. And with each step, she wished them a wonderful life that would be as sweet as her creation, yet better than her marriage.

Jim Roberts, Hathaway's general manager, stood as Rosa entered his office, motioning for her to sit. "Rosa, meet your new boss, Ross Pinnell, our new head baker. He comes to us from a competitor."

The office was spartan and stuffy from the heat of the factory. A large eight-foot by eight-foot window overlooked the factory's entire work area. The operation was responsible for Hathaway's central New York region. Beyond the window's view, large pallets of bread were being loaded into huge trucks for delivery to satellite bakeries in Syracuse and Albany. Ten thousand loaves of bread and several hundred pounds of pastries were baked daily for Hathaway's 200 statewide, house-to-house deliverymen.

Rosa reached to shake hands with Pinnell. "Hello Mr. Pinnell, I'm happy to make your acquaintance. I heard the buzz around the bakery that you had arrived. I believe half the bread makers that work here are presently on their way to Breadco Bakery to attempt to fill the position you just left vacant."

Rosa had also thought about applying. The extra money would go a long way. She didn't bother though, because everyone in the industry knew Breadco didn't hire women when there were men with families who needed jobs.

Ross, liking her sincerity, answered with a mischievous grin, "Rosa, I look forward to working with you."

Unbidden thoughts raced through Ross' head as he eyed the pretty woman. She looked too young to be in such a responsible position. He thought, *She can't be more than twenty-five.* His eyes could not help focusing on her beauty. Yet, Ross, a true chauvinist and a man of his time, pondered how long it would take before he could replace her with a man. He liked having men work under him. It was easier.

Ross said, "I say, it's unusual to find a woman in such a responsible position. You must be good at what you do."

Before she could respond, Jim Roberts spoke. "Ross, we're lucky to have Rosa. Since she took over the pastry and cake specialty department, production has gone up twenty-five percent. In my tenure here, I've never seen this department as efficiently run. The drivers just love her work, because the quality she instills in every bun made brings back repeat customers. And you know those boys make higher commissions on cake and pastry sales. Mr. Pinnell, I've no doubt that you, like our sales force, will be very happy with Rosa's work."

"Sir, that's good news to hear," Ross said, though reluctantly.

Rosa hesitated and then said, "Pinnell's a pretty name. What nationality is it? It's not Italian, but you sure look like you might be of Italian decent."

Ross, smiling, answered, "Thank you, Mrs. Lavalia. You have good eyes. I am Italian. The authorities inadvertently changed my father's name when my family came here in 1890. It's actually Pizzano, or at least that's what it was in Italy."

Rosa said, "I think I like Pizzano better, not because it's Italian, but I think it suits you better. By the way, the customs people did the same thing to my family name, only they changed the ending from Ameduri to Ameduro."

Ross, trying desperately not to like Rosa, found it difficult, if not downright impossible. This vibrant woman stirred his bachelor longings, even frightened him some. He was always unsure if not unnerved about strong-willed women, whom he usually dreaded.

He stammered in reply, "Rosa, I suspect we'll see a lot of each other. You've no doubt had a long shift, so until tomorrow."

Rosa, taking this as her cue, stood up to leave.

Mr. Roberts spoke out, motioning for her to remain, "Rosa, please wait a moment, I've something to discuss with you after I finish with Mr. Pinnell. We need to mosey into the bakery for a minute to review a couple of things. I'll be right back."

Rosa waited five minutes before Jim Roberts returned.

With a wide smile, Jim spoke, "Rosa, the cake you made today could have come from heaven. It is a treat meant for the saints. You didn't know it, but it's for my nephew's wedding. I kept you waiting because I want to let you know how pleased I am with your work. In recognition of the great work you're doing, the firm's giving you a nickel per hour raise, starting next month. Congratulations!"

The news was unexpected, and Rosa, cheered by its unforeseen arrival, smiled ear to ear. Her voice reflected her uncontrollable excitement as she blurted, "Mr. Roberts, you have no idea how much this extra money is needed. Thank you, sir." Quietly, she quickly calculated that fifty-five extra nickels would add up to just enough to pay for her weekly trip to Syracuse.

Roberts replied, "No need to thank me. You wouldn't get a raise if you didn't earn it."

Rosa contemplated. The extra money would help, but because she had a decent job, the state required her to pay weekly board expenses for her children. It amounted to $5.00 per month, and it made it all but impossible to save. Tony still did not pay anything, despite warnings from authorities. As usual, he had managed to beat the system.

Anna could see a happy change in Rosa's demeanor. Their usual northerly walk up Conkling Avenue was a good opportunity for them to talk about the trivial. However, Anna felt certain that today would be an exception.

"So, what's the new boss like?" Anna chirped. Her high voice resonating excitement.

Rosa slowed her pace so Anna, now out of breath, could keep up. Excited, she was walking faster than usual down the quiet street, which was now awakening to the new day. Enthusiasm poured out of her mouth in rivulets of joy. It was the second time in as many years that she had been acknowledged and it felt good. Yes, it felt good and long overdue. Yet Rosa stifled the thought.

Rosa answered, purposefully trying to tone down her joy a notch or two, "Anna, I'm just happy. Mr. Pinnell seems like an okay guy. Time will tell, it always does."

"Is he cute?"

Rosa answered curtly, "Anna, you're a married woman. What difference does it make?"

Sheepish, Anna replied, "Oh, I was just wondering, that's all. You know, for you. Maybe…"

Rosa sighed, "Well, I'm married, too, or sort of, so he's off limits. Don't you go and get any of your highfalutin ideas."

Anna said, "Darn it all to the high heavens and the God who loves us all! Ya' need to go and divorce that no good husband of yours. You never see him. He gives ya' no money for the kids, only grief. Get on with your life, woman, before it's too blasted late."

Her friend's bluntness took Rosa by surprise. Anna was never known for carefully choosing her words, but never for such enthusiasm. Rosa laughed uncomfortably, "Anna, somehow you see me as the modern woman, ahead of my time, as some people might even say. I may be all that, though I personally doubt it. But I also like to think of myself as a good Catholic. I can't divorce him, so we're doomed to continue to live separately."

Anna said, "Maybe the bum'll ask for a divorce."

Rosa's response was calculated. "No, my estranged husband has the best of all worlds, especially where he works. To him, I'm an inconvenience that he's chosen to conveniently avoid. I rarely see him, and when I do, it's from afar, and that's close enough for me. The last time we actually talked, or more accurately, yelled, was at the orphanage. I already told you what happened that awful day. No, Anna, he has bluntly said that he'll never grant me a divorce. He likes…no actually, he enjoys making my life miserable. He has the warped view that he owns me, like some of those other poor girls. But he'll never own my soul."

Anna, not easily dismissed, replied, "Hasn't your life improved some, at least as far as employment goes, and just because that no good got ya' fired?"

Rosa snickered, "Anna, you've got me there. Yep, Tony's harassment did me a favor, though I doubt it was his intention. But you know I'd gladly give up this great job if I could only get to see my kids every day."

"Does he ever go to see his children?" asked Anna.

"I often check the visitation book at the orphanage and ask the nuns. They say he comes about twice a year. He hasn't bothered to see Rocky since he's been moved to Syracuse."

Anna said, "I'd say it's better the children don't see much of him."

"There, my dear friend, is where we totally agree."

"It looks like rain, don't cha think?"

"Maybe," answered Rosa. "Let it rain. It can't dampen my high spirits, not today."

"How is Antoinette doing these days? You hardly ever mention her."

"It's probably because I hardly ever see her. Our paths never seem to cross, and when they do, it's only for a minute or two. Mama spends a lot of time on Bleecker Street with her friends. She still doesn't have a job. I don't think she'll ever get one, and she hardly tries any longer. I tried to encourage her to take in laundry. She'd have none of it. Says she did her share of laundry in Italy."

"Sorry to hear things aren't going well."

Rosa, not wanting thoughts of her mother to bring down her high, answered carefully, "There's really nothing to be sorry about. She's my mother and I love her. And though she seems to have changed since coming here, I choose to overlook her laziness. Papa's death put her over the edge, changing her forever. And try as I have, I can't do anything to fix that."

"Well, here's my street. See you tomorrow, Rosa."

Anna reached over to hug her friend, almost smothering Rosa's small frame in her ample bosom.

Rosa walked the remaining blocks, enjoying the peace and the quiet moment to reflect.

To Rosa's surprise, Antoinette awaited her at home, sitting at the kitchen table. The smell of slowly simmered Italian sausage and eggs mixed with peppers floated throughout the spotless kitchen.

"Mama, what a nice surprise to see you, and you made breakfast too. How did you know I'm famished?"

Rosa couldn't help noticing that her mother's dress, usually one shade or another of black, was today a bright green.

"Daughter, we need to talk."

"Sure, Mama, what's up? Did you find a job?"

"In a manner of speaking, I did."

"That's good news. Where?"

Antoinette answered, "I misspoke. It's not a job, or at least one that has wages. Rosa, I'm still young, and I get lonely. I have urges. Mind you, your papa is always on my mind and in my heart. Yet, I know he'd want me to do this."

"Do what, Mama? Just get to the point. I'm in no mood for riddles. I'm tired. It's been a long night's work," Rosa snapped, then immediately felt sorry.

Antoinette, still hesitant, said, "Sorry, Rosa, I'm not sure how you'll take this. I know how much you need money for the children, and I promised to help you as much as I could to get the money for the attorneys, though I never found a job. And I know that I've been more a burden to you."

"Mama, don't be silly, there's no work. I of all people understand. I'm one of the lucky ones with a job."

"Rosa, you're not lucky. If you're one thing, you're a hard worker. You deserve and earn all you have. And furthermore, it's about time you got a break."

"Thank you, Mama. I only wish the breaks would include my children."

"It will be soon." Antoinette played with a wooden spoon, unsure, hesitant.

Rosa, easing up, laughed and said, "Why? Have I hit a jackpot? Gambling is still illegal, isn't it? Or did one of our imaginary rich relatives leave me a fortune?"

Antoinette, still careful, replied, "No, it's nothing as unusual as that, though it would be nice; that is, if we had rich relatives!"

Antoinette suddenly blurted out, "Rosa, I'm getting married again. I met a wonderful man, a widower. I want your understanding, and also, I need your blessing."

Rosa, though surprised, spoke out animatedly, "Mama, I'm happy for you! You deserve to live and enjoy life. It's certainly what Papa would want for you, and it's what I wish for you, too."

"Thank you, I worried you'd be upset."

"No, Mama, never! This is America after all, not the old country. You need more in your life than this humble, sterile existence. You have been a widow and alone for too long. This is good news, but really, you don't need my approval. You're my mama."

Antoinette said shyly, "I know all this, but I promised to help you get back my grandchildren."

Rosa answered, trying to make it easier, "Mama, you tried to find work. There are millions unemployed, many starving. What more could you do but your best? Isn't that what you've taught me? So who's this lucky guy that's about to become my step-papa?"

"You don't know him. His name is Frank Cardimonte. He's a good man, and he's fifty and a widower. All his children are now married, and he lives alone in his home not far from us on Elizabeth Street. We plan to get married as soon as Father Angelo agrees."

"That's wonderful news, but why the big breakfast?"

Antoinette smiling, "I thought you'd be hungry and I wanted to talk some more. I told my Frank about your problems. He said he'd help, if he could."

"How can he help? Times are hard."

"Frank has little money, but he's also very good with words, and his nephew is an attorney—an unmarried attorney, I might add."

"Mama, I'm not interested in any man. You know that I've nothing to offer a man except two growing kids, and a body with an ugly two-foot scar that can't make babies anymore."

"Daughter, please hear me out." Seeing Rosa's nodded agreement, she continued, "Frank said he'd ask the priest to write a letter to the Vatican, with all the details of your marriage, asking for permission to divorce Tony. It may take years, especially now that the Pope has so much trouble with Mussolini. Frank said his nephew could also get you a divorce now without the Pope and rid you once and for all of that evil man."

Rosa looked fondly at her mother. "Mama, you mean well, and I appreciate it, but I don't want a divorce. I could be excommunicated, and I'm also afraid of what violent thing Tony might do. He did threaten me if I asked for a divorce, and he'd most likely make a jerk of himself just to show that he can. I don't need to disrupt my life right now. And more important, I'd rather live this way than risk receiving worse from Tony than I already have. I can't live my life always looking over my shoulder. And that is why confronting Tony worries me."

"I understand your fear from Tony, but there are ways to slow him down. We have too many relatives here that would not allow him his way. Daughter, how can you of all people be so independent and modern on the one hand, and yet so archaic on the other? The church may throw you out because of a divorce, and then what? Are you really willing to throw your life away for possible fears of the future and these religious virtuous values that sideline your life? You are still very young. Live!"

"Mama, are you saying that you would get a divorce if you found yourself in my shoes?"

"I'm not in your shoes, so I can't answer. Just think about it?"

Rosa quickly answered, "I have, and my answer is *no*."

"Don't say I didn't try. I respect your decision, but Rosa, all I want is for your happiness. A good man will eventually come along and love you, and possibly your babies too. And it could be your only opportunity to get the children back. Like me, you need to take this chance with life. You deserve it."

Rosa stubbornly said, "Mama, again, no, I won't take this way out. I'll allow God to decide for me what's right. I love you, Mama, but this conversation is over. So let's eat the marvelous breakfast you made before it gets any colder."

Tony worked in his parent's garage every spare moment he had on the partially wrecked 1925 Duesenberg touring car that he had bought for fifty bucks. Long and sleek, it must have been a beauty when it was new. And he thought that it had probably cost a king's ransom too. Now, here it was, his, bought for a song, even if it didn't run. Sure, he could have purchased a car that worked, like a Ford or a Chevy. But Tony wanted a car, and not just any car, but one that would show off his macho personality and make a proper statement of who he was. The Duesenberg did just that.

Someday he hoped the car would take him to California. But right now the clunker needed tires, a rebuilt engine, a muffler, and so many other parts that he suddenly felt dejected. Paint, yes, when he finally got it to run, would bring back its magic. *Green*, he thought, *would be a good color.* However, painting it seemed to Tony to be a hundred years away. Though somewhat frustrated, nevertheless, he continued to work diligently because this car would eventually be his stylish ticket to freedom.

"Antonio, why do you waste your time on this piece of junk? Go buy a real car." Giovanna startled him as she entered the garage carrying an eggplant sandwich and a tall glass of lemonade.

"Thanks, Ma, I'm hungry." Ignoring her confused look, he took a large, satisfying bite from the sandwich. His mother's freshly made Italian-style bread melted in his mouth. He washed it down with a big gulp of the cold lemonade.

"Ma, what you see as a wreck, I see as a grand touring car. It only needs some work."

Giovanna said, "It looks to me like it needs more than just some work, maybe a miracle."

Giovanna had something on her mind, and Tony, familiar with her ways, did not miss it. "Ma, what do you need? I know you well enough to know that you're not here to discuss my car."

"So, you caught me." She ruffled his hair and spit on her apron to try to rub a grease spot from his cheek. "I hear that your wife is a big boss now. When do you think she'll get her children?"

"Ma, I told you that if you want me to get the kids, I would. But I'm not going to raise them without help. And still, I am not sure about Joanna." With sudden sadness, he thought, *Living this lie is getting old.*

Giovanna asked, "Do you ever visit them?"

"No, do you?"

"You know my feelings. As long as that woman is their mother and you remain uninterested, I'm not interested. And anyway, I've enough children of my own to take care of without picking up after you, even if I still adore you, my handsome son." She pinched his cheek.

"So there you have your answer, from your own mouth, Mama. I can't raise them alone and you won't help. I guess we're at an impasse."

"A what?" she asked. "Is this another big word you learned in prison?

Ignoring her attempt to rile him, though she was right he had learned the word while in prison. He had studied a lot, reading to wile away his time. He answered. "It's a big American word meaning irresolvable predicament, an impasse, or for you my precious ma, it means something that blocks the way. As long as Rosa's in the picture, I don't want anything to do with them."

"Aah, you and your big words, faa! So, you, my son, had these children... well, at least one of them anyway, and now you think you can forget? At least go and visit them. Someday they'll grow old enough to know you better and they'll always have your last name. Do you want them to only know their mother's side when they finally get out of that place?"

Displeased, he tried compromising, "Ma, I see where you're going with this. If it makes you happier, I'll try to see them more often. Did you know Rocky's now in Syracuse?"

"No, I didn't. Why?"

"The nun said all the boys are moved there when they reach his age. And anyway, she said he was a slow learner and stubborn, and that he refused to work. Syracuse is a stricter school, so maybe it'll knock the independence out of him."

Giovanna scoffed, "That can't hurt. But I bet I know where he gets his stubbornness. Maybe we can get him out when he's old enough to help around here. After all, the boy's one that will always have our name. A little discipline will do him good."

"Ma, you'd take Rocky?"

"Yeah, sure, I'll take him in at least when he'd be of use, but no sooner."

Tony said, "How about Joanna? She could be a help too."

Giovanna looked directly into his eyes without hesitation, "No, in my mind, she's trouble. And in your own words, may not be your child. Why saddle me with her?"

Tony stammered, "I was only curious how you felt, or if you've changed your mind, and you never know, she might be my child."

Tony's brief admission somehow was missed or overlooked by Giovanna.

Tony turned away. Grabbing a wrench, he bent over the car's open hood. *I suppose she has to think this way about Joanna, and it's my fault if she does. That poor kid never asked to be born. There's nothing I'll ever do about it anyway, at least not 'til it's to my advantage.*

Tony reluctantly popped his head from under the hood. "Ma, I got to get back to my car, anything else you need to talk about?"

"Yeah, there is. Did you take your brother Johnny's BB gun? Johnny seems to think you may have it. If so, are you a little boy who needs to play with toys?"

"Yep, I took it from his room." *Darn, how did she find out? She's always been a regular Sherlock Holmes.* "He's too young for a gun, even one like that one." Tony acted casual, like it was an everyday thing to steal from his youngest brother.

"He's twelve now, and your pa said he could have it. So where is it?" fumed Giovanna.

"I sold it for five bucks." *Actually it was ten. It's a powerful little gun, and it can bring down a squirrel.*

"Why did you go and do that? It cost him more than that. You had no right."

Tony responded, "Because I thought it best as his older brother, and perhaps because I could, that's why. Do you want him to hurt somebody with that dangerous thing? It was to teach him a lesson, nothing more."

"Johnny saved money for months from his paper route to buy that gun. Give him the money when you see him. He's heartbroken over losing it."

"Yeah, Ma, I will." *In a pig's ear I will. I saw him shooting at streetlights with it, and anyway I could always use an extra $10. It'll teach him.*

"Tell you what I'll do, Ma. When he is at least fifteen, I'll buy him another gun, maybe even a .22."

"I'll talk to your father and let you know if he agrees."

"You do just that, Ma. Anything else?" he called, his voice hollow, coming from within the hood.

Not to be outdone, Giovanna's snicker turned into a low cackle, "No, son, just be prepared to give Johnny his money and maybe a little extra."

"I'll think about it. Thanks for the food." Tony lifted his head from the hood and reached to playfully kiss his mother's forehead.

Without pausing, he returned his attention to the rusty carburetor. "I guess I'll have to visit the junk yard," he mumbled aloud, as if to the air. He tossed the useless carburetor into the overflowing wooden box on the dirt floor that served for scrap.

Unfortunately, Father did visit a bit more often. Every time he visited, I rejoiced when he left. It's difficult to believe that Mother never said one bad thing about him. As far as I was concerned, she didn't need to. I never forgot that day when he got Mother fired. He had tried to hurt her and then Rocky, too, not giving a care for our feelings.

Several years later, Rocky told me he saw him once when he was in Syracuse. It's no wonder that he has no feelings for the man.

"Tomorrow is the most important thing in life.
Comes to us at midnight very clean.
It's perfect when it arrives and it puts itself in our hands.
It hopes we've learnt something from yesterday."

John Wayne, 1907–1979, American Movie Actor

TWENTY-TWO

Freedom felt good, though for Rosa, it was still unfamiliar territory. While not prone toward pessimism, she involuntarily began to lean in its direction. Today, on the first day of a much-needed vacation, she felt guilty over her lack of success in obtaining her children's temporary release from the orphanage. Regulations once again got in the way of motherhood.

After working a year at Hathaway's, she had received two weeks vacation, most of which she had used a day here and a day there, never taking it all at once. Now she was worn out, so this year's vacation could not come soon enough.

It was 1935, and two years since Ross Pinnell came into her life, and she was ready to strangle him. Begrudgingly, she was the first to admit that he ran a good shop. What bothered her most, though, was his continued chauvinistic distrust of her abilities as a department manager.

Rosa absently gazed at the cardboard suitcase, the lone remnant of her long ocean voyage, from another era, a memory not forgotten. *What do I pack for the beach? I don't really have much anyway, so no big deal,* she supposed. She laid a couple of light-colored blouses into the suitcase. Her troubled thoughts were interrupted by a firm knock on the front door.

"Who is it?" Rosa called.

"It's me, Nellie."

"Come in, I'm in the bedroom."

Nellie swished in, all aglow. "Are you ready? Louis's outside, waiting."

She mumbled, "Yeah, just about. I don't have a bathing suit. Is this going to be a problem?"

Nellie replied, "Only if you want to go in the water. Oneida Lake is really nice right now. Maybe you'll want to buy one."

"Maybe I can find one there, that is, if I can find one in my price range."

"And what price range is that, Rosa?"

"You know, cheap to dirt cheap," Rosa laughed, feeling better.

"So, why aren't you ready? It's not like you to dawdle." Nellie helped fold the two blouses still on the bed, gingerly placing them in the suitcase.

"I suppose I'm guilty of daydreaming. It doesn't seem right to be going off to vacation, to a place you rented, without pitching in. You know me. I like to carry my own weight."

Nellie hesitated, "Well, why don't you take on the cooking responsibilities? Believe me, the way you put together food will more than help pay your way. And after all is said, the place we rented is no Ritz. But if it'll make you happier, you can buy some of the groceries, too."

"Nellie, this sounds fine. Thanks again for taking me. By the way, where are your kids, aren't they coming?"

Nellie gave a loving smirk, "Where were you when I said that Aunt Eva and Uncle Giorgio were watching them? Starting today, Louis and I are free from children for two full weeks, like regular newlyweds."

Rosa frowned, "I wish mine could be with me. You know, I asked the orphanage if I could take Jennie out for a week. They said no. I was so darn angry that I could spit."

"Rosa, you know they have their darn rules. Is there something else troubling you?"

Rosa nodded her head. "Yeah, there is. I know I can't do anything about it and my hands are tied. Yet I feel guilty about my new freedom. With Mama remarried almost two years, I have been lonely, except for work. I worry that I'm getting too set in my ways. Darn, I'm only twenty-six. I've two children that aren't allowed to live with me and I'm beginning to look and feel like an old maid."

Nellie held her hand to her face to stifle a laugh. "Rosa, after all you've been through, you still look like a beauty queen. Give me a break."

Rosa, still troubled, said, "Nellie, it's just that I don't want it to be like this for the rest of my life. I want to experience life. You know, before I have little left to give. I feel that I'm caught in such a huge rut."

Nellie put her hands on hips. "Cousin, pick up your spirit and stop feeling sorry for yourself! Look at what you had to overcome and at what you've accomplished. Even with that miserable, evil husband of yours still lurking in the background, you function as well or better than most women. Speaking of him, have you heard anything?"

"No, I steer clear of him and his family. And it's apparent they feel the same about my children and me. Last week I inadvertently saw Giovanna shopping on Bleecker Street. The old bat looked the other way. Actually, I must admit that I was relieved when she did."

Nellie frowned, her eyes filled with concern. "Look, it's high time you moved on. You need to rethink getting a divorce. Uncle Giorgio believes that he can still get most of it free. He thinks that because Tony never visits the kids that the courts will lean in your direction." Nellie, holding her hands out in front of her in mock protection, laughed nervously, "I know your feelings about divorce. But this must be said."

Getting upset with the direction of the conversation, Rosa replied, "I know this, Nellie! It's really not something I want to consider or to talk about right now. Right now all I want to do is go on vacation."

"Phooey, Rosa, I know where you are going with this. And the blazes with what the church says. They don't have to live this way, you do! Show me where it says in the Bible you can't get a divorce, and I'll eat the page."

"Nellie, then you better be hungry and get some catsup, because it says it a lot. You need to read the Good Book more thoroughly. And anyway, like I have said so many, many times, my mind's made up. I realize you really care, and more important you mean well, so thanks for being such a good friend."

Nellie rolled her eyes, closed the old suitcase, and delicately started to pick it up by its old frayed and rusting handle. Then, thinking better of it, she held it from its bottom.

Rosa, seeing Nellie's eye roll, teased, "I saw that look of yours! Just because you're free from your babies for a few days doesn't mean you can act like a child."

"Okay, so you caught me. Let's go and have some fun. Who knows, maybe you might meet a wealthy businessman and decide then and there that you're ready to divorce and get total freedom."

"There you go again. You never give up! And I ask freedom from what? As I see it, marrying another man won't give me any independence. That is, of course, unless I find a saint like your Louis. More important, I need a man who doesn't mind a ready-made family, with two orphaned kids that need a real father."

"Now there you have me," replied Nellie, amused. "I'm lucky to have found him. Oh, yeah, you forgot to add to that litany of yours that you need a guy who would be able to stand up to Tony's threats."

"Yeah, thanks for the reminder, and yes, you are welcome."

"For what?

Rosa answered, "Well at least one good thing came from my wedding day. You met Louis."

"Now Rosa, there you go again. As I see it, two more good things came from that day, your Jennie and Rocky. And someday when you get them back, you'll fully appreciate it. Now let's go. I declare here and now, that by the grace of God Himself, you will have fun, even if I must beat it into you." Nellie grabbed Rosa's hand and led her out the door.

Rosa stopped to lock the door, shaking her head in resignation.

The cottage they rented was a block from Oneida Lake and two blocks from Sylvan Beach and its busy amusement park. Louis sat on the porch, enjoying the cool evening summer breeze, reading a day-old *Utica Daily News*.

Nellie looked up from her two-month-old fashion magazine. "What're you cackling about? Is there actually something worthwhile to read, or are you going to keep it to yourself?"

Nellie and Louis had a standing joke. She always teased him about what he was reading and he always dutifully announced the headlines, using his peculiar choice of words. Then Nellie would dutifully read the article and see how close his interpretation was. Today it was accurate.

"Let me see, front page, dateline Italy, August 13, 1935—'1,000 Die in Flood as Dam Collapses in Turin.'"

"How awful," said Rosa.

Louis continued, "Yesterday, President Roosevelt signed into law the Social Security Act." Louis elaborated, "So now it appears we can retire on the government from the money we will pay the government from our paycheck."

Rosa's ears perked her voice anxious, "Does it say how much money they plan on taking? I don't need to worry about tomorrow; it's now that I need money."

"Sorry, Rosa, they seemed to have skipped that little detail. Let me see, what else is there? Oh, darn, Will Rogers died in a plane crash somewhere in Alaska. What a shame. He sure was funny."

Rosa stood to stretch, her face genuine in her concern. "How sad; I liked listening to him on the radio."

"I agree. He was sure down to earth," said Nellie.

Rosa perked up. "I need some air. Would you two lovebirds care to join me? I'm thinking an ice cream cone would be nice. I'll treat."

Louis looked at Nellie knowingly and together they chorused, "No, you go, we'll stay here and enjoy the breeze."

Rosa walked the short block to the ice cream shop and ordered a single-dip vanilla cone from the teenage boy at the counter. She handed him a quarter and received twenty cents in change. The cigarette smoke was thick, and she needed air. She turned hastily to exit. Not paying attention, she almost bowled over a man entering the store.

Rosa quickly apologized, "Sorry, I wasn't looking."

"Rosa, is that you?"

"Mr. Pinnell, what're you doing here?"

"I'm on vacation, like you. Or do you think this is my second job, getting bowled over by a beautiful little Italian woman?"

His chuckle quickly turned to concern. Initially proud of his comeback line, he now regretted the poor choice of words. Too late, he caught himself staring at her, standing before him lovely in her light blue dress, her pleasant smile blending in perfection with her pleasing appearance.

Rosa commented, "Nice seeing you."

"Rosa, wait!"

She turned back to face him.

"How long are you here?"

Coyly, she said, "A few more days."

He replied, enthusiastically, "Me, too, can I buy you lunch one of those days? It seems that lately at work we've been at each other's throats. Maybe we can get to know one another a little better. You know, for work's sake."

"Yeah, sure, I doubt if it will help the work part, but I am willing if you're buying me lunch, I'd like to go to a nice place," she said in a matter-of-fact voice, hoping this would turn him off.

"So, can I take that as a yes?" Ross said, surprised.

"Boss, do you still have dough stuffed in your ears? I thought you were on vacation. Of course it's a yes, with a condition."

Ross answered, "Sure, I heard you, and yes I know of a nice place, a mile or so from here. When can I pick you up?"

Rosa said, "How about tomorrow at noon, right here. Does this work for you?"

"Then tomorrow it is. See you then," he smiled, unsure why or how he had gotten up the courage to ask the redheaded vixen for a date. He wondered, *Does she think it isn't a date?*

The black skies were onerous as they relentlessly pounded Oneida Lake with a driving rain. Rosa looked at her watch. It was 11:30. She had put on the best clothes she had brought: a red skirt and white blouse and comfortable, white, high-heeled shoes.

She turned to Nellie, "Do you have an umbrella that I can borrow?"

"No, I guess I forgot one. Why? You aren't going out in this mess. It's pouring."

"I met someone from work last night and he asked me to lunch. I have to meet him at the ice cream shop. It's only a block, but with this rain it might as well be a mile."

Nellie, ever alert, asked excitedly, "You did say '*he,*' didn't you?"

Rosa replied coyly, "Yes, as usual you have good ears, and rather large ones at that."

Nellie screeched like a little girl. Her excitement was followed by a shout, "Louis, quick, come here, Rosa needs a ride."

Louis shouted from the bathroom. "Give me a minute and I'll be right out."

"That man, he's always in the bathroom, probably reading," said Nellie.

"Leave him be, I'll walk. So I get a little wet."

"Rosa, don't be silly, I won't hear of it. You must look nice for this man of yours."

"Nellie, aren't you jumping to conclusions? One: he is not my man, and two: this is not a date. We're just having a nice lunch to talk about work. And remember, I'm a married woman."

"Yeah, you're married all right; if you call what you have a marriage. Whatever you do, enjoy yourself. If anyone deserves a little happiness, it's you."

"What's the hubbub about?" asked Louis.

"We need you to drive Rosa to the ice cream store."

"In this rain, are you kiddin'?"

"Nope, now get going, honey, she has a lunch date with a *man*," she emphasized.

"Well, why didn't you say so in the first place?" he chided. Grasping Rosa's hands he said, "Good for you, Rosa."

Rosa said nervously, "Wait, Louis, I need to get my purse."

"Go ahead, your coachman waits," he chuckled.

When Rosa was out of sight, Nellie quickly whispered to Louis, "Now you be sure and get a good look at this fellow and report back to me."

Amused, and shaking his head defiantly, he replied, "Nellie, you're like a sergeant I remember in the Army."

Nellie grabbed his arms, pulled him close to her, and kissed him. "Did your sergeant ever do this?" she giggled, kissing him again.

Rosa reentered the room, catching the smooch. "Wow, you two! At least, wait 'til I leave."

Louis turned to Rosa, smiling like a cat caught with a mouse. "Your carriage awaits, madam. Sergeant Nellie here has given me permission to leave." Nellie lovingly punched his arm.

"Rosa, try to have a nice time," Nellie coached.

"But not too nice," Louis said, opening the lake house door, imitating the finest tradition he could muster of a coachman on duty. Rosa pecked his cheek with a sister-like kiss. His broad smile focused on Nellie's happy stare.

Rosa saw Ross waiting under the storefront awning as Louis drove up to the curb. His rugged five-foot, seven-inch frame hugged the wall as he tried to avoid the driving rain, which was coming down in a torrent. Rivers of water filled the street, almost to the top of the curb, crippling the old sewer system.

"There he is, Louis, thanks for the ride. You're a doll to come out in this mess."

Louis asked, "Do you think you'll need a ride back?"

"Don't worry; I'm sure he'll drive me to the cottage." Rosa quickly opened the door and ran under the awning's partial cover. She waved to Louis once she was safe from the downpour.

Ross beamed, "Hi, Rosa, boy, we sure know how to pick a day. My car is the black one over there." He pointed to a recent vintage car directly in front of them, parked at the curb.

She asked, "That's a pretty car. What is it?"

"It's a '33 Buick, glad you like her. She's my first love."

Rosa smirked, "That's the best you can do?"

They raced to the car. Upon entering it, Ross asked, "Do you like fish? There's a nice little family restaurant up the road."

"Sure," she commented. She thought, *Anything would be a high point for me.* This would be the first time Rosa saw the inside of a nice restaurant. Up until now, the Woolworth lunch counter was her only experience dining out, and that had been several years ago.

"Who was the guy who left you off?" Ross reluctantly asked, wondering if he had any competition.

"Oh, that's Louis. He's Cousin Nellie's husband." Coyly she said, "He's like a big brother, though, so don't get him angry."

She wondered to herself, *Why did I say that?*

For lunch, they each chose the special: grilled haddock filet, vegetables, and salad, with chocolate custard pie for dessert. Ross had chosen a white zinfandel wine that fit nicely with the meal. They enjoyed small talk and spoke little of the bakery. Finally, with the meal almost over, Rosa, after taking a sip of her wine for courage, asked, "Is there something you wanted to discuss about work?"

"No, not really. You're doing a great job. I just thought...well, I..." he stammered, "that if we got to know each other a little better, maybe we might get along. You know, for the morale of the employees."

Rosa answered, "Oh, I see, sort of pretend we like each other. Like a happy family?" She smiled shyly at the passing thought, looking sheepishly down at her plate. She thought, *He has a nice smile and good eyes. And he's a real gentleman. Plain, though in a nice way—not really much to look at.*

"Yeah, you have it. Play nice-nice to each other and maybe along the way, we might even really get to like each other."

"Ross, I could go along with the nice part, but the really getting to know part, well it won't work. Not now. I'm still married."

"I heard about your troubles. I thought, well, maybe..." he hesitated, and then like the proverbial bull in the china shop, he blurted, "I thought you were divorced!"

Quickly, yet nervously, she replied, "No, it's against my religious belief."

Ross' face fell, but he quickly recovered his composure. Rosa missed his facial change.

Ross was falling for Rosa—something that had actually begun the first time they had met in Mr. Robert's office. At thirty years old, he wanted to settle down and marry. And if luck would have it, marry a fine Italian girl. Rosa, though, would have been his choice no matter her ethnic background. He looked across the dining table, staring.

Noticing, Rosa asked, "Cat got your tongue, Ross?"

"I'm sorry, Rosa; it's just that I see you sitting across from me, all beautiful and perfect, and wonder how anyone could hurt you."

"Ross, aren't you getting a bit too personal?"

"I'm sorry to be so blunt. And Rosa, I know that we hardly know each other, so I don't want you to think I'm hitting on you. Dating is not something that I'm real good at. But you could say that I'm direct and to the point."

"Are we dating?" asked Rosa.

He stammered, "I didn't mean to imply." *Boy, is this getting off to a bad start.* He returned to reality, changing the subject, "Did you enjoy the meal?"

Rosa smiled, "Yes, it was wonderful; you're no longer my enemy. I'm stuffed and have had too much wine. I suspect it makes me giddy."

"You don't drink wine?"

"No, not since Papa died. We always had red wine around the house. Papa always made wine when we lived in Italy. He never got a chance to make it here."

"I make wine. Darn good wine if I say so myself: red, white, blueberry, raspberry, blackberry, peach, and dandelion. You name it! I can make it." Ross beamed at describing his hobby.

"How do you find the time?" asked Rosa.

"I make the time. You can always find time to do something you love. Don't you think so?"

"I suppose I do. All my spare time is spent visiting my children. Both are in two different orphanages." *Maybe this will scare him away.*

"Tell me about your kids. The restaurant's quiet because of the rain, and the waiter doesn't seem to be pushing us to leave. And it's still raining cats and dogs. So why not stay here and talk? If you don't mind, I'd like to hear about your children."

Rosa spent several minutes opening up, talking animatedly about Jennie and Rocky. Ross listened, appalled upon learning what she had endured, and wondered how any man could do what her estranged husband had done to the mother of his children.

Ross said, "I realize we hardly know each other, but if you'd agree, I'd like to drive you to Syracuse to see your son. Maybe you could get permission to take Jennie for the day, and then she could come along too."

She looked shyly at her dirty dessert plate as the waiter cleared it from the table. She didn't know what to say or do, which for her was a first. And mostly she was frightened by his kindness and more, the fear of getting too close to him. Fidgeting with the white linen table covering, she wondered what had possessed her. She thought, *Somehow events are moving too fast.* It set off the alarm of her inner defenses.

Nevertheless, almost without thinking, she said, "Sure, I'd like that, but it's a long way to go for you. Are you certain? I will pay for the gas."

Ross waived off her offer, quickly answering, "No, I was never more certain! I don't say what I don't mean, so just let me know when. And Rosa, I know you can't get interested in anyone right now. However, I'd like to be your friend—that's all for now. We can go slowly with anything else."

Rosa, still anxious, though she was warming to his friendly demeanor, said, "Then it's settled. I'll let you know soon. Now, please, tell me about you. You know all my dark, past secrets. What can you tell me about you?"

Ross answered, "Not much excitement in my life. I'm a farm kid. My family owns a small piece of property in Alder Creek, a few miles north of Utica. I was born there. We raised mostly vegetables, chickens, and a cow or two. I'm the baby of the family. My parents, like yours, were both born in Italy. So there, now you have me in a nutshell."

"A nutshell, what does this mean?" she asked.

"American slang, sort of like saying all at once, in one quick, little story."

Rosa shyly asked, "And in this nutshell, is there a woman somewhere?"

"No, I never married. I admit to a couple of close calls. I guess no one will have me. As you can clearly see, I'm not the best-looking guy around. And then, if you add working at night, it makes it kind of difficult to date. That is, unless a beautiful, intuitive, Italian girl happens to work the same hours."

"Are you flirting with me, Mr. Pinnell?"

"You caught me, I confess."

Rosa looked at the waiter standing patiently, with his hands good-naturedly crossed, by the wall. She said with reluctance, "It looks like they want to close."

"They can wait a few more minutes; I'll leave a nice tip."

"A tip, what's that?"

"Rosa, you are green. When did you get off the boat?"

She answered, "Let's see, ten years ago, why?"

"Just kidding; you don't know much American slang, do you? A tip, my fair lady, is what you leave for the waiter for good service. It's money above what they charge for the meal."

Rosa shook her head, saying, "Ten years in this country and I still know nothing. Maybe someday," she sighed. Building her confidence, she blurted, "Do they give tips where we work?"

"No, there they call it a raise. Unless you want advice, like don't bet on the horses." Ross saw a confused look on Rosa's face.

"So, when I get a raise, it is really a tip?"

"No, it is called a raise. I was just fooling. And anyway, with this economy, raises are few and far apart."

"I know. I got my first raise two years after I started. I sometimes wonder how much pay I'd receive if I were a man."

"Well, if you were a man, it would be a great waste, but to honestly answer, probably a lot more."

"I thought so. Nevertheless, I can't complain. I need the work, and I desperately need the money. I've almost saved enough to hire an attorney to try and get my kids back."

He asked, "How much do you need?"

"I really don't know the exact amount. The authorities say I have to file papers and prove I have a way to raise them. I have to have money in the bank and someone to watch them while I'm working."

She smiled, carefully picking her words, surprising him with her wit. "That, in a nutshell, is the real problem. As long as I have to work to survive and support my children, I can't be both places at once."

Ross was at a loss for words. He wanted to tell her to lie, make up an alibi, and to do whatever she could to get her children back. But after two hours with Rosa, he knew she would never lie, even to get her children. Later, looking back on this day, he would realize that this was the moment he fell in love with her.

And then Ross, though thoroughly frustrated, surmised that there was something deeper, perhaps a wound of some kind that she kept hidden. Whatever it was that she was hiding, it was no doubt something that he would patiently wait to discover, and then, if necessary, gladly and tenaciously endure.

TWENTY-THREE

By June 1938, I had been living in orphanages for ten long years. However, I remember one particular day as if it were magic. Outside, a bluebird was singing a melodic song, welcoming a new summer. Inside, tepid air enveloped the stuffy seventh-grade classroom that was connected to the orphanage and all that I knew then of life. I recall not paying attention to Sister Frances, who was droning on about current events. No, I don't recall the topic, though I wish I had. Not that my memory of that day was poor, mind you, because I do remember daydreaming. It's a shame, because that special day will forever be stamped into my heart as my own personal Fourth of July.

Years later, while reminiscing about that day, and more so, I suspect, out of need and curiosity, I visited the local library to search for clues. Libraries have always been a safe place for me, a place to reflect and to escape. You see, I have a good memory for dates and I was wondering about what might have excited Sister Frances that particular day. Diligently, I hunted and researched and found the front-page headline for Thursday, June 23, 1938. I recall now that I had thoughts about formal school ending the next day. But then, we would not see fun and recreation during the long, hot, summer months like other kids. You see, as I mentioned earlier, we orphans knew full well that our days would be filled with more learning in the orphanage's so-called trade school.

That day, oh yes that day. Well, it came back to me, sudden like, with a resounding thud. You see, Sister was excited about, of all things, a pugilistic contest. However, as I discovered in my research, this was not just any boxing match. It was a contest, pure and simple, of good versus evil. In one corner was the amazing African-American, Joe Louis, who ironically represented America and all that was good. I say ironic because blacks were not treated like full citizens back then, sort of like us orphans. In the other corner stood his able opponent, Max Schmeling, a white man, who represented Germany and its Nazi extremists and all that was bad for democracy.

Mr. Louis entered the fight with an internal fury that no man, even the mighty Schmeling, could stop, and in only one round, Louis retained his world heavyweight title. Many years later, my special, sports-nut husband often mentioned Joe Louis' amazing feat, trying to press it into my not-so-sport-loving soul. It was not until that day in the library that I saw the significance, for on that day he was defending freedom as we know and love it.

Yet, this day's memory for me has more highlight than a headline, for it was the day that my father came to my seventh grade classroom to give me the beginning of my freedom. That fact, I remember like it was only yesterday, despite these incessant black clouds. I was directed to go with Father to Mother Superior's office. Once there, the good sister wished me well and told me to go home with my father, a man I barely knew, and perhaps had only seen six or seven times in my ten years at the orphanage.

Of course I didn't ask any questions. One never did when in the presence of Mother Superior. So, I followed this almost stranger out the building, delighted at getting into his big green car. It smelled new, but later I learned it was older than me.

I remember asking Father where we were going. He said nothing, only drove. Since I'm a quiet person anyway, it didn't bother me. I just took wonder in what I viewed out the large car's window. For you see, I felt like an Arabian princess, that I had read about, gliding on a magic carpet on an adventure to places unknown.

It was grand to be outside. Until that day, I never went more than a block or two from the orphanage. I recall once, about three years earlier, Mother had tried to get permission to take me on a day trip to Syracuse to visit my brother. Sister Superior said it was against the rules. How I had wished to go, and how I wished Mother hadn't told me of her plans. I know now that they feared that an estranged parent might take a child and never come back. If she hadn't told me I wouldn't have had further disappointment at not seeing my little brother, and it still hurts. But Mother, as ever, was just trying her very best, and the sisters could be hard to bend, especially over their precious rules. I knew this lesson first hand.

For ten years Mother had spent every spare moment and dollar she had on trying to free us legally. She never was successful.

However, looking back, there was another special day I shall always recall with particular fondness. The sisters gave a celebration party at the orphanage for Mother and Grandmother Antoinette. I remember that day very well. It was Tuesday, February 9, 1937, and even the nuns appeared to enjoy the festivities. You see, they were celebrating Mother and Grandmother's becoming official naturalized citizens of the United States. Of course, my mother supplied all the pastries, except for Grandma Antoinette's cookies. I remember seeing many people there that I didn't know or have now forgotten. But one of the attendees was Mother's special friend, Ross. He was the nice, kind man, who often accompanied Mother when visiting. I liked him because he always managed to make me laugh. Sorry, I digress, more often than not, now a days.

Returning to that day when Father freed me, it's an understatement to say that I was happy to be out of that place. While the orphanage was part of an institution that I truly believe had good intentions, it still practiced forced child labor on the pretense of teaching a career. It was definitely a place of its time, and it is good that things have changed for today's orphans. Yet, then and now, my heart goes out to all orphans. I suppose in some ways it did give its inhabitants a structured life, yet for me it was a life filled with fright. Because of my beginnings, I suppose that I've always been a loner and an introvert, more so, I suspect, because of my experience. In the years past, I constantly fought the urge to be alone, even to this day, and even with this disease. And I still cringe when I see a nun, not because they abused me; well, they did some, I suppose. You know the intimidation, the threatening use of a ruler—always that darned ever-present ruler. But mostly because of the bad memories they planted in me that will never be erased, no matter how hard I try.

However, the last three years of my life there were filled with hope. Mother had been visiting on a regular basis. Often, when Ross accompanied her, he usually had something special: one time a doll; another time a whistle, which was taken from me rather quickly; another time a coloring book. Many times they brought me a special picture, hand-drawn by Rocky, which he had especially made for me. I would then draw pictures for my little brother, mostly of horses. He sure loved horses. And once they gave me a real photo picture of my brother. I still treasure it. He was such a cute little boy. I think my son, Andrew, favors him.

Rosa heard the hard knock on the front door of her modest apartment. Upon opening it, and before she could react, Tony rushed in, all smiles, like he belonged.

"Tony, why are you here? Get out!" Rosa shouted.

Tony said, "Stop the shouting and see what I've brought you." Gently he grasped Jennie's hand. She had dutifully stayed in the background as instructed, out of her mother's sight.

Tony then said, "Come, Joanna, say hello to your mother."

Rosa, surprised beyond belief, was too stunned to comment.

Tony curtly said, "Rosa, here's your daughter."

Uncontrollable tears streamed down Rosa's face, tears she had held back courageously in reserve for ten long years. Surprise, while an understatement, took second place to Rosa's sudden fear.

"How?" was all Rosa could manage saying as she held Jennie tightly to her, holding so tight that her daughter's breathing became difficult in her loving vice-like hug.

"Mother," she cried. "Am I really here? Is this your home?"

"Yes, Jennie, this is my home," she said in between sobs.

Rosa looked at her estranged husband, her pleading eyes burning with questions. She stammered, "Tony, if you have any decency at all, tell me that this isn't a dream or one of your sick tricks. You didn't kidnap Jennie, did you?"

"No, and it's not a dream, Rosa; consider it a gift, from me to you, with one minor condition."

Rosa looked at him. Not startled, she knew with forlorn experience that as long as Tony was involved, there would naturally have to be a string attached to this long-awaited moment. It was Tony, full bloom. Hesitating, and then forcing the question and dreading his answer, she deliberately pounced, "And, Tony, what's this condition?"

"It's a simple requirement, really, nothing more. I want Joanna to get to know my family. You don't have to visit them, and you wouldn't be welcomed anyway. But I want our daughter to grow old knowing them and their real love for her."

"Tony, don't get me wrong; having Jennie with me is a wonderful thing, and I thank you from the bottom of my heart. But as for your family, where have they been the last ten years? None of them ever even visited Jennie, or Rocky either, for that matter." Rosa couldn't dare ask the obvious question that struck her, not with Jennie present. *Do they finally believe she's Tony's daughter?*

Sternly and without reservation, he answered, "Rosa, that's my condition, take it or leave it. What do you say?"

"I suppose I can live with it. Where do you fit in all this?"

Tony answered, "I'll get to know my daughter, too."

Rosa reluctantly whispered, "Does this mean you acknowledge her as your daughter?"

With eyes that fostered a rare sincerity, Tony replied quietly, almost ashamed, but not quite, "Yeah, Rosa. You know why I said all those things. I had to play the game."

Rosa cringed, not totally believing him, but knowing there was little choice in the coming sacrifice, if she wanted her daughter back. Quickly she said, "Of course I'll agree."

"Good. Starting this summer, she can spend time at my parents' home when you're at work. And then she can spend time here when you return. When school starts, she can also stay at my parents,' unless you are able to make arrangements to have her watched. She's almost thirteen, probably old enough to take care of herself, but that's your call." Rosa nodded her head, still numb, and unsure of what to expect next.

Jennie stood in the room listening, taking it all in, her young mind transfixed; she now understood why her mother's eyes always looked so sad.

With courage, Rosa asked, "How'd you do it, get Jennie, I mean?"

"I told the authorities that we have reconciled and that I had a good job. They saw my sizable bank account and didn't ask many questions. I also gave the orphanage a large donation. It didn't hurt to move things along."

"Can you get Rocky?"

Tony nodded, "He's my next project, but if I get him out my parents want to take him in. I think it's best we do it this way. Of course, he'll be able to see you from time to time." Rosa's face dropped, devastated. Seeing Rosa's dejected look, Tony said, as if in appeasement, "At least he'll be closer to you than in Syracuse."

Rosa nodded, but thought, *Tony actually thinks this is good news. Rocky's my son, not theirs. Please, Lord, help me take this one step at a time.*

This wasn't how Rosa had planned it in the many sleepless nights, counting pennies for attorney and court fees, forever thinking of this day. But it was a start, and soon she would have her children home. It still didn't absolve the fear she had about Tony's motives, dire, unknown motives she could not dismiss, no matter how hard she tried. To Rosa, Tony was simply an Italian-American in Greek clothing, bearing hidden and dangerous Trojan Horse like gifts.

"When do you think you can get Rocky?" she asked, collecting her bearings and suddenly her old self.

He responded with a curt nod, "Probably a week, maybe two. I have an attorney in Syracuse working on it."

"Tony, where did you get all this money? Is it honest?"

He answered with sarcasm dripping from his lips, "What do you care where the green comes from? You have your daughter. If you prefer, she can go live permanently at my parents' home."

Trying to hide her fear at the sudden change in the conversation, she replied cautiously, "No, there's no call to do that. I know how expensive it is. I've been trying for ten years."

"Let's just leave it with I've had a string of good luck. I've been in California the past few months, making my dream come true. Do you remember my dream? Maybe someday, when the time is right, I'll tell you my plans. Right now, here's Joanna. Have a good day."

He abruptly turned, without emotion or a parting hug for his daughter, he opened the apartment door and left.

Yes, I found out from my father that he had been working in Los Angeles, California. His boss and mentor, Mr. Rabiso, had sent him there to explore expanding his operation. Father's constant talk about California, it seems, had piqued Rabiso's interest enough to take his family to vacation there in 1937. Rabiso returned with bold ideas for business expansion.

To this day, I have never been to California. It has too many terrible memories, and it would be several years before I learned what my father's real work was. All I saw was through a child's eyes: a man, all glitz and glitter, with a big car. Don't get me wrong; I'm not proud of him. He was no more than a two-bit hood, yet he was my father and my blood. I still tried to love him. Oh, how I tried.

The Sabbath day bloomed bright and beautiful as Rosa, Rocky, and Jennie enjoyed their brisk walk to early-morning Mass. The service was beautiful and the sermon from Matthew 6, about worry, seemed to be specifically aimed at Rosa. The city was enjoying an Indian summer day. Everything seemed more alive this brisk Sunday in 1939.

Rosa spoke reluctantly, "I've agreed that you both can visit your father's family today."

"Mother, do we have to?" moaned Jennie.

"Yes, your father said he had an announcement to make."

Rocky piped in, "Jennie, don't feel so bad. I've got to live there all the time." Rocky inwardly was downcast. He hated living with the Lavalia family. He felt unwanted. To him, the orphanage seemed better. At least there he had the comfort of knowing where he stood and a routine that, though difficult, gave him comfort. And now, the only day of the week that he could visit his mother was to be taken from him. Silently he fumed.

Jennie blurted, "Phooey, Mother, I won't go. That woman is always so mean to me."

"Jennie, it's just your grandma Giovanna's way. She's hard on everyone. Deep down there lives a good person who loves you."

"She still is mean. I don't care what you say."

Agreeing, Rocky said, "Yeah, Jennie, I think she takes mean pills every morning. Heck, I see her take at least one to two every day."

Rosa said, "Hush, Rocky, you know you are fibbing, and that's no way to talk about your grandma."

"Oh, Mother, Rocky's right. She is mean, and anyone who dares to show us any kindness when we're at her house usually receives her scorn."

Rocky replied, "She isn't lying, Mother. She treats me fine, as long as I work and stay out of the way. Her food, though, is definitely not nearly as good as yours."

Rosa smiled at her son, his dark hair and eyes so like his father's. She would have hugged him on the spot, but he still cringed when anyone tried. Now that he was twelve, it was even more difficult. Rosa wondered if she would ever be able to give them enough love, especially Rocky. There was so much lost time to make up. Sadly she thought, *Dominick was just about Rocky's age when...*

Trying to perk up the moment, Rosa spoke, "Let's hurry home. If we do, we can enjoy some of the fresh jelly donuts I brought home before your father picks you up. How does a glass of cold milk sound to go along with it?"

"Mother, stop talking and let's get going," said Rocky, looking back, smiling, his young legs pumping a brisk pace several steps ahead of his mother and sister.

I never enjoyed visiting Father's parents. My grandmother ran a stern home and everyone marched to her tune. About the only person there that I really liked was my Aunt Marie. She was three years older than me and always treated me with kindness. During the few months that I was part of their lives, I grew to think of Marie as an older sister, and more than just my aunt.

Sometimes though, Grandfather Nicola was very nice to us, but only when we were out of sight and far from Grandma's maddening need to control everything. I often felt sorry for him. When he died several years later, I cried. I've secretly kept a clipping of his obituary with my personal belongings. His picture was in it, and when looking at it, I try only to remember the good things about him. But I admit that in my biased opinion my poor grandfather was the poster picture of a hen-pecked man.

Sadly, that Sunday, I said my goodbye to Rocky right after Father's big announcement. Rocky actually let me hug him, proving at least to me, that our bond was special.

Father had announced that he was permanently moving to California. He had big plans. He hinted that someday he'd take Rocky and me with him, though I really doubt that he meant it. Then, I didn't know much about California, but I did know one thing for sure, and that was that I didn't want to leave my mother, not again. I stayed quiet about it, hoping the idea would pass and that maybe Father would forget, like he had forgotten about us so often before.

Tony's Duesenberg purred up to the curb. Both he and Jennie started to get out. Turning to Jennie, Tony said, "Wait, I need to talk to you for a minute."

"Okay, Father." Jennie sat with hands folded, neatly resting on her pink Sunday best dress, wondering what to expect.

Rosa, seeing them, had just returned from a visit with Nellie and was sitting on the porch talking with the landlady.

Jennie, seeing her mother, smiled and waved from her passenger side window. Rosa waved back, but chose to stay in her seat, safe on the porch, hoping not to have to talk to Tony. Silently she wished that she had gone inside before his arrival. She watched the next scene unfold.

"Thank you, Father, I had a nice visit. I'm sorry you are leaving. Will I see you soon?"

"No, Joanna, it may be a year or more before I return. I have a lot of work to do there, setting things up for my boss, things like that. If you like, I could send for you to visit during the next summer break. I'll talk to your mother about it, if you want." Tony looked Rosa's way. He had no desire to discuss it now.

"Yes, I would. Seeing a place so far away seems very exciting. Isn't that where they make all the movies?"

"Not all of them, but almost all," he answered. "Have you seen many movies since you got out of the orphanage?"

"No, not many. I did see a Shirley Temple movie a few days ago. It was a lot of fun."

Tony handed Jennie a piece of paper. "Here's the address where I'll be living. Write to me when you can."

"Father, these past months I've only begun to know you. Why must you go now?" Jennie, with her teenage mind, often fantasized that her mother and father would mend their disagreement. If he was in California, she reasoned regretfully that it would never happen.

"Will you drive your car all alone to California?"

"Yes, and I'm actually looking forward to it. It'll be an adventure. Joanna, sometimes it's good to be alone. When I was in the Navy, the battleship I served on had almost 2,000 men on it. Then, being alone was something rare. That was probably the only thing I didn't like about the Navy."

If there was one thing Jennie understood, it was being alone, and for once she related to her father. She asked, "Father, won't it be dangerous?"

"No, but if it is, I have a gun."

"You do? Can I see it?"

"Sure. Guns are okay, but only if you know how to use them." Tony reached across Jennie to open his glove box. He pulled the shiny .32 caliber nickel-plated revolver, making sure that the safety was on. It was the very gun that he and Gino had taken a few years earlier from the unfortunate Mr. Bagatini. After showing it to her, he quickly put it back into the glove box. "See, I have protection. Now let's get out of the car, so you can give me a goodbye hug and kiss."

Jennie opened the car door as Tony walked around to meet her. As they met, Tony looked down into Jennie's eyes, arms outstretched. "How about giving me a hug?"

Tony gave her a fatherly peck on the cheek, tightly hugging her. For a slight moment she felt loved.

Then Tony seemed to snap, losing control, and without warning, he slapped Jennie smartly on both cheeks, causing them to redden.

Seeing the slap, Rosa jumped from her chair and bounded down the stairs, shouting, "Why the devil did you hit her?"

Jennie remained on the sidewalk, stunned, embarrassed, and crying. Half the neighborhood had seen Tony strike her. Frightened, she tried in vain to imagine what she had done to necessitate the punishment. Even the sisters at the orphanage explained and gave warning why they doled out their chastisement.

Tony turned to Rosa, his slight stature menacing. Calmly and without remorse, he said, "It's like this, Rosa. Since I'll be gone, those slaps are punishment, paid for in advance, for the times she forgets to visit my family, most likely because of you. Now she won't forget what is waiting for her if she fails to uphold our bargain."

He glared, then spoke, "So, Rosa, don't you ever forget our agreement, because I won't. I'm going to California for at least a year. But I'll be back, and if I find out she hasn't made regular visits, you can figure on me taking her to California to live with me."

With no further comment, he abruptly turned and swung open the car door.

Rosa stood, mouth agape in surprise, as he started the car and drove off without a wave.

Rosa, in shock, managed to mutter, "At least the rotten no-good loser will be gone for a year."

Quickly, she reached for her daughter, holding her tightly, trying to console. Jennie sobbed uncontrollably, shaking. Holding her in her arms, Rosa ran her fingers through her hair, caressing and soothing her hurt, wishing she could turn back the time and spare her daughter's pain.

Jennie, with tears streaming, looked at Rosa. "Why, Mother, why?"

Rosa had no answers.

Yes, for me, that was quite a memorable day, and one I can never forget no matter how hard I try. I have forgiven my father, but it took me a long time. It sure is easier to forgive than it is to forget, especially now when it's something I'd just as soon forget on purpose, despite trying my best most of the time to remember.

That very evening, we listened to a radio show that would cause a panic in the streets. At the time, it had all seemed so real. You may have even heard about it, because today it all seems so funny.

It was a broadcast of the H.G. Wells' story, *The War of the Worlds*. I always liked mystery and fantasy stories, and this was one that I had read. I still don't understand why so many Americans thought it was the real thing. I guess politicians today have learned from Mr. Orson Welles' ruse because they always seem ready and able to pull the wool over the average person's eyes, in my opinion, knowing that most people will believe anything they hear and see, especially if it's on television.

It was even funnier to hear that it made such a stir because the newspapers had printed the program's story in advance, spelling it all out in black and white. At least it helped to soothe the sting of my father's last slap; however, I still have nightmares about those slaps. Maybe there is some advantage to this disease if it helps me to forget that day and that slap which still stings.

"For the winter is past, the rain is over and gone. The flowers are springing up and the time of the singing of birds has come. Yes, spring is here."

Song of Solomon 1:11–12

TWENTY-FOUR

I recall even now that awful day. It seems like yesterday, and forgetting it would be nice. But I must continue before my memory begins to muddle.

I think it was a Sunday afternoon. Yes, it was Sunday, because Mother was listening to Kate Smith singing on our old radio. I even remember the tune, "God Bless America." It then seemed strange to me that there were so many patriotic songs on the radio. Now, with hindsight, it's easy to see why, but heck, I was just a teenager who would rather listen to swing music. Mother really enjoyed listening to Kate Smith, and particularly her radio show, because it always discussed subjects interesting for women. I should probably add that unlike today, this was unusual back then and the Oprah show was years away.

It seems that every daily paper was filled anew with dread; however, being not quite fourteen, the war in Europe and Asia meant little to me. It was even worse for me when my civics teacher asked questions daily about the world and national news on subjects we were supposed to have read for our assignments in the newspaper. This reading of the daily paper was a perpetual homework assignment and at times very boring, especially when we had to remember all those difficult to pronounce Japanese and German names. As you might guess, Italian names were easier. However, English had become my native tongue, the orphanage took care of that, and Mother never really pushed Italian on me until I finally asked her to teach me.

On this particularly quiet Sunday, I vividly remember rereading the most recent letter from Father. At first, he had been good about sending Rocky and me postcards from several points of interest that he'd passed on his road trip to California. He traveled along Route 66. Places like Chicago and St. Louis,

Tulsa and Amarillo, Gallop and Flagstaff, Ludlow, and finally Los Angeles. I even remember a card from a place called Joseph's Bar and Grill where he said he had eaten a fine dinner. What I liked about it was that Joseph's Bar was in Arizona at a place called Santa Rosa, just like Mother's name. Unfortunately, when the television series *Route 66* was a big hit in the sixties, I found it difficult to watch without thinking of him. I heard I missed many a good episode because of my past torment.

On this day, this particular letter from Father seemed different. Since he left, aside from the postcards, he had written only three letters. This was his third.

Each correspondence had covered something new in his life, mostly vague descriptions, some difficult to comprehend. In the first letter, he talked about his job as a cook working at MGM. Confused, I wondered what had happened with his job with Mr. Rabiso. The second mentioned he had a nice girlfriend. This confused me even more, since he was married to Mother. Yet Mother saw Ross all the time, and it was obvious to me, even though I was only a naive teenager, that they were in love, so now, I wondered about Father's new love.

But the third letter I remember verbatim, even though, in my anger and grief, I burned it later.

It still haunts me to this day. It was dated March 20, 1940 and read simply:

Dear Joanna,

How's my special daughter doing today in probably not-so-warm Utica? Things in Los Angeles are fine, sunny, and warm. I have good news. I'm coming home sometime in early June. Then I will ask your mother to allow me to take you back with me to Los Angeles for the summer. It will be great fun for you and good for me also because I can show you this wonderful place. We will drive cross-country so you will be able to see for yourself all the exciting places in America that I have seen and want to share with you. I will send you back by train in time for you to start school. I know I have not been much of a father to you, but believe me when I say this: I truly miss you and want to be a part of your life. See you soon. I love you, pumpkin,

Dad

I never seemed to get around to finding the courage to ask Mother if I could go and to my knowledge she never saw the letter. I suppose I didn't want to face her anxiety. Young as I was, I knew it wouldn't be easy for her to let me go so far away, especially to Father's. And the thought had even occurred to me that once there, I might not have been able to return, or even maybe not want to. I remember when re-reading the letter I had feelings of dread and fear and excitement all at once. I have always been able to feel things that others don't. I guess some say it's a blessing; I think it is a curse. Nevertheless, the possibility of new adventure sounded grand. Trust me; I was ready for some excitement, but not the type that came.

For Jennie, Tuesday, April 9, 1940, seemed like any typical day walking to school. The school year at Utica Free Academy was going rather smoothly and her grades were above average. Today, though, she was without a care and daydreaming about the possibilities of the coming summer vacation and all its new possibilities.

Upon reaching school, she hurried in the corridors, heading for her classroom, disregarding, or just not seeing, the funny stares, and pointed fingers from some of the kids she knew. That is, until they became impossible to ignore.

Jennie, once in the homeroom, sat at her assigned desk, waiting like the other kids for the last morning bell that would signal the start of classes. She turned to a classmate, a so-so friend who sat across from her.

"Why are some of the kids acting strange today, pointing at me? Rachel, fill me in on what's going on. Is there something I need to know? What is there a silly note on my back?"

Rachel looked at Jennie with confusion. "You don't know, do you?"

Jennie snapped her head, "Don't know what?"

"About your dad; Anthony Lavalia is your father, isn't he?"

"Yeah, he's in California. What about him?"

"The…" Rachel looked down at her desk. "The morning paper said he was killed."

"Killed? No, you're lying. Why would you say such a terrible thing? I just got a letter this weekend saying he wants me to visit him this summer. You're hateful to make up such a story." Jennie regretted attacking Rachel as soon as she had spoken.

First hearing and then seeing the commotion, Jennie's homeroom teacher came to her desk. "Jennie, please come with me."

Jennie said meekly, "I'm sorry for making a disturbance, Miss Travers. I should have known better."

When they both were in the hallway, Miss Travers spoke. "Please do not concern yourself. You didn't know about your father, did you?"

"No," Jennie sputtered, trying to regain her courage. "It's true then. He died?"

"Yes, I'm so sorry. It's probably best that you go home to be with your mother and family. Stay here while I get your things. You're a good student and you can catch up when you return after..." she hesitated.

Confused, never having faced death, Jennie replied in a soft, strained voice, and a brief hesitation, "After what, Miss Travers?"

"The funeral," she said softly. "This is a time when you will need to be with family."

Jennie, in shock, said, "Then I better go."

Jennie lowered her eyes as if searching the old hard wooden floor for understanding. Nothing seemed to make sense. Tears flooded her face, tears for her father, a man she barely knew but, for reasons she could never explain, was beginning to love.

Miss Travers walked with Jennie to her locker to collect her coat and books, and then gently patted her student's head, hugging her. The teacher knew Jennie's background. The school files were explicit, and her heart went out to the pretty petite girl whose tears rained upon the floor. She hugged Jennie tightly once again and then slowly walked her to the door.

"Jennie, will you be okay, or would you like me to find someone to take you home?"

"Thank you, but I can manage," she said bravely.

Holding her head high, she left the school a bit older, worrying about how she'd tell her mother and brother.

When I returned home that day, I broke the news to Mother, who was just coming home from work. I was then living with her full time, though I spent the nights alone when she worked. I guess today they would call me a latchkey kid. It was the only way my mother could keep me with her. It was a lot safer back then, and I wasn't afraid. Heck, I was used to being alone. In fact, a card carrying introvert, I actually enjoyed the freedom it gave me. I was almost fourteen, going on twenty, and quite capable of taking care of myself, a real product of my years at the orphanage.

Occasionally, after school I would visit my Grandma Antoinette, but she was almost as difficult to be around as Grandma Giovanna. Both grandmothers, I truly believe, saw me more as cheap labor than as their granddaughter, a mere vessel to make their lives easier. Don't get me wrong—I wanted to help them. It's just that they never said thank you, not even once. It was expected, and more important, it was the way things were back then. Oh, I am so sorry. Where was I, now?

Mother didn't initially react when I told her of Father's death. Looking back, I think she was in shock. I saw her shed a tear, but she quickly wiped it away.

She said, "So it must be and so be it," and left me briefly for the quiet of her bedroom. She never said another word until she left for work that evening other than giving some instructions, directing me to see my father's parents the next day to find out about Father's arrangements. I did, and they obligingly filled me in on what was going to happen.

The newspaper article about Father's death seemed cold and detached. It said he died on Sunday, April 7. Sadly, I noted that it was close to the time I was reading his last letter. It said he had been killed with his own gun, apparently the .32 caliber automatic pistol he had shown me before he left for California. The assailant was his Los Angeles roommate, a man called Michael Fabio. How I hated that man. I wonder whatever happened to him after he was acquitted. I'm not as strong as my mother when it comes to forgiveness. I've tried; believe me when I say that I have. Yet to this very day, my anger has never allowed me to free my soul from this weakness.

The police determined it was an accident. Mother felt otherwise, but she said little. But I know that she knew that the one thing Father was good at was handling weapons, something he had learned in the Navy. I realize now, though I didn't back then, that she was both relieved and sorry. She didn't want him to die, not that way. I know she had truly forgiven him, and even had once really loved him. I will always admire Mother's faith and ability to do this, especially after I heard the real story years later.

To the Los Angeles police, Father was just another Italian. Back then the police didn't pay much attention when one Dago killed another. That's how things were. Thank goodness it's a little different today, though sometimes I wonder when I read in the paper or hear the TV news about the ethnic killings. Today it's mostly Hispanics and Blacks. I feel their pain.

After his remains' completed the cross-country rail trip, Tony's brief wake was held at Matt Funeral Home on Bleecker Street on Monday, April 15. The funeral service was held immediately after at Saint Mary of Mt. Carmel Church, where a requiem high Mass was celebrated. Following the Mass, Tony's body was transported to Calvary Cemetery. A long procession of cars filled with family and friends followed the hearse. His pallbearers were all first cousins. His gravesite, ironically, was about thirty feet from Rocco and Dominick's plot.

Rosa attended the funeral with Rocky and Jennie, but it was all Giovanna's arrangements. And true to form, she made it a point to ignore Rosa, preferring to censure her daughter-in-law in public. It was her golden opportunity to tell the world how little she thought of Rosa. Taking full advantage of the moment, she snubbed Rosa in front of all their relatives and friends, and more cruelly, in front of her dead son's children.

After the priest said his final prayer, Rosa placed a flower on the casket. Despite the fact that she and Tony had been estranged, she still shed tears—some guilty and some in relief, for despite all his misgivings, he was still legally her husband, in the eye of the state and the church. She was now truly a free woman who could never again be tormented by Tony. She had forgiven him and for a moment felt at ease with her feelings; that is, until Giovanna started to scream at her after seeing her cry.

Giovanna came at Rosa like a banshee. She screamed repeatedly, "*Putana! Putana! Putana!* Get that whore away from my son's casket." Then she shouted, "It was you. Yes, you who drove my Antonio to leave for that California. You…" Her voice trailed off to a whimper.

Rosa, embarrassed, tried desperately to disregard the ramblings of the mean, spiteful, older woman. Holding her head erect, she walked regally away from those who stared watching the horrible scene, knowing, that even in his death,

Tony had kept his true love and dreams for California from Giovanna, whose incoherent words could still be heard.

"Look at that terrible person. She ruined my son's life," Giovanna shouted, now sobbing.

When Jennie and Rocky placed their flowers on the casket, Giovanna wailed. The priest tried to console her. Nicola reached for Jennie, trying to give her a loving hug, but Jennie squirmed away, uncomfortable, thinking, *Where were your hugs when I was at the orphanage?*

Giovanna's screams increased when she saw her husband's show of compassion for his eldest granddaughter. Nicola's attention faltered when he saw his wife's glare, and Jennie, taking advantage of the moment, shrugged him off and ran to Rosa, grasping for her hand.

In words well beyond her years, Jennie said steadily, "Mother, I'm with you. I'll always be with you."

Jennie whispered softly and reassuringly, continuing to console her mother until they reached the funeral director's car, which was waiting to carry them back.

Out of the hearing of the others now, Jennie, with a reserve beyond her years and one that Rosa had never seen in her daughter, calmly said, "Mother, it is over. Now we must look only to tomorrow and the rest of our lives."

In the background, Jennie could still hear her grandmother's screech. "Joanna, you leave with your mother and you'll never be welcome at my home again. You come back here and apologize to your grandfather for running from him. Do you hear me?"

Jennie remained focused, disregarding Giovanna's taunts. It was easy for her to ignore the derision. But Giovanna's hate for her mother still hurt. Ten long, difficult years at St. Joseph's and St. John's with the nuns had made her callous and unafraid of idle words.

Rosa felt Jennie's warm hand while tears of embarrassment rolled down her cheeks. She had come to the funeral mostly out of respect and duty. Tony was her tormentor for well over a decade, but he was also the father of her children. It was for them that she came, though now she scolded herself. Now the worst was over, though, and while it was a day that she could probably never forget, it was also a big relief to be done with Tony and his family. For her, Tony's death meant a new beginning and that any agreements that she had made with him were now over.

The April air gave off a sweet smell of a new spring, casting a silent, yet unexpected, fortress of protective love around Rosa. She turned to look back, seething, but resisted the strong desire to shout back something in her defense. She stopped abruptly, calming herself as Rocky ran to her side and grasped her other hand. Though he said nothing, his eyes spoke volumes.

What she had intended to scream in retaliation was never uttered, and she could not explain why. Perhaps, she reasoned to herself later, it was unnecessary to stoop to the low level of her ex-mother-in-law. Maybe it was out of respect for the pain she knew and fully understood Giovanna was having, for she too had suffered untimely deaths of loved ones. Together Rosa and her children entered the funeral director's car and never looked back.

Neither Mother nor I ever saw Grandma Giovanna again. Truth is, I never cared to see her. To me, she was someone to avoid, a painful reminder of a bad time. Like Mother, I've always been a very optimistic person. To spend a moment of my life intentionally with anyone I didn't like or respect was not something I could do, not when I was in control. So, like my mother, I forgave her, but I stayed away, even for her funeral in 1961. My husband, always the strong family man and an arbiter, had once scolded that perhaps it was time to bury the hatchet. I couldn't do it, and he respected my wishes. I loved him all the more for that.

By the time Giovanna had died, I had five healthy children who never knew she existed. And if Giovanna knew about my children, her great grandchildren, she never attempted to see them. We lived less than a mile from the Lavalias. I suspect she still clung to the ill-placed belief, fostered by my father's need to avoid jail, that I was not his real daughter, though I doubt it.

I probably would have made an exception to my stiff resistance if my grandmother had been alive in 1963. I remember it clearly; it was a sunny October 24th, my oldest son's eighteenth birthday. He came home that afternoon, confusion painted on his face. I remember him saying, "Ma, I went to the Draft Board to sign up, you know, as required by law, and this lady in charge said that

I'm as handsome as her oldest brother, and his spitting image. She says that she's your Aunt Marie. What's this all about, and who is her oldest brother?"

I answered as best I could; for he is my inquisitive son and I knew he would not let it rest. Thinking it best, I had chosen not to tell my children that I had family from my father's side who still lived in Utica.

I remember saying, "Jimmy, that good woman is my aunt, and the man she's probably referring to is my father or one of his brothers."

Jimmy didn't say much, just shook his head, keeping his thoughts to himself. In many ways he is a loner like me. He knew I'd tell him eventually, when I was ready. I never did though, until now. It was too difficult; and yes, my son did have a strong resemblance to my father.

I suppose in retrospect I wished that Grandma Giovanna could have seen my son, to eliminate her doubts about my lineage. But I guess it would have served no purpose other than to take a jab at her conscience and help my own ego. Also, I didn't want to hurt Mother by bringing up long-lost hurts. In my best opinion, it would not have been worth the pain Jimmy would most likely have, especially if he heard her bad-mouth my mother like she had always done when I visited her. I'll never forget the mean things she'd enjoyed saying, like, "How's that witch of a mother of yours?" or "Who is she sleeping with tonight?"

It isn't Jimmy's fault that he looks like my father's side, so do I. Surprisingly, Mother never commented about it. Once though, no doubt knowing how I felt, she said, "Thank God it looks like our Jimmy has inherited only your father's good traits."

The saddest thing, though, is that I hurt Jimmy deeply only a few weeks ago, while visiting his family and all my Texas grand and great grandchildren. We were leaving the Fort Worth Stockyards after a wonderful visit at that old historic place, when out of nowhere, for reasons strange to me, the perpetrator; I started yelling uncontrollably, with hurtful barbs aimed squarely at my son. Jimmy's telltale eyes looked at me in hurt and disbelief, though he held back, not expressing it in words.

That day in Texas began the growth of my terrible shadows. I remember shouting at my son, "Why do you always pick on me?"

My son wasn't picking on me, and when my confused mind cleared, I realized what had happened. Poor Jimmy's crime was that he looked like my father. Time, age, and the beginning of Alzheimer's finally gave me the courage to yell at Father for all the abuses he had rained upon Mother and me, especially that terrible slap he gave me on the last day that I was to see him alive. I realized that I was unfairly scolding my son and I felt terrible. I must admit, though, that it also felt good to finally get what I had held back, off my heart. It was then and there that I first knew that I must tell Mother's story.

After Father's death, I saw my Aunt Marie from time to time, and even Grandfather Nicola, though only by accident. Sometimes I saw them at a store or walking to school. It usually happened at times I least expected, like when I saw them at the Feast of Saints Cosmo and Damiano, which was held every September at St. Anthony's Church in East Utica. They were always cordial to me. They probably wished I'd give in. However, I told them that I wanted my grandmother to at least meet me halfway, and that never happened.

I can't say the same about my other aunts and uncles. Since I was the oldest cousin, several of my cousins who were born after Father died didn't even know that I existed. If they did find out about me, I'm sure that they are all good people, however it was probably easier for them to avoid me rather than face my grandmother's wrath. And who could ever blame them? What a way for a family to live. I suppose the potential pain of being involved with my estranged grandmother probably made avoiding the Lavalia's worthwhile. Nevertheless, I do know that I probably missed out on knowing some real nice relatives. Like I said, my Aunt Marie was special, and I cried when I heard of her death from breast cancer several years ago.

Rocky ran away from Grandma Lavalia's home shortly after Father died. He didn't go far, at least not this particular time. He ended up at our home. Mother hugged him with all her heart, and of course against his will, as she told him simply, "Welcome home."

Once Rocky was living with us, I realized, perhaps too late, that he was almost illiterate. My brother struggled with everything associated with learning. I did all I could to help him, and at first, he made good strides with his grades, getting a few Cs, but it didn't last. I think if it were today, he'd have been diagnosed with dyslexia. But back then it was 1940, and there was no help.

The school year ended and the excitement of high school was put aside. That summer was among my best memories of childhood. I remember that even at my naive young age, it felt like a new beginning.

Ross had become a greater part of our lives. We spent several of Mother's free days from work at the beach or on short drives. We enjoyed going to the Stanley Theater, in all its air-conditioned comfort. I think the movie I enjoyed the most that summer was Walt Disney's animated version of *Pinocchio*.

My mother never wore black, and sadly, she discarded any picture of my father she might have had. I am dismayed now to have no picture of him, but after he died, we simply forgot about him, at least in conversation. Yet, I must admit that I think of him often.

"In the midst of winter, I finally learned that there was in me an invincible summer."

Albert Camus, 1913–1960, French writer

TWENTY-FIVE

War's terrible turmoil echoed throughout the streets of Utica in the year 1942. Pearl Harbor, a place few had ever heard of, was fresh on everyone's mind. It seemed like every family I knew had a son, neighbor, or friend either in the armed forces or about to join or be drafted. It was still too early though for the long roll call of men who would never return. Those frightful days, unfortunately, were closer than we feared. I saw my Aunt Marie at a chance meeting, and learned that my father's youngest brother, Johnny, had joined the Marines. Several boys at school, mostly seniors, enlisted before graduating. Many chose to wait for their diplomas, but their time to serve their country would come all too soon, as Uticans by the hundreds answered the call to duty.

At my home, things were unraveling too.

Rosa sat in Ross' car, eyes seemingly transfixed on the dash. The morning was bleak, fitting her emotions. Exhausted from a long work shift, she was anxious for home and rest. The car's windshield wipers valiantly tried to keep up with the late March rain, which was mixed intermittently with sleet.

Ross looked intent, determined to discover what was troubling her. Out of necessity, his attention returned to the slow moving-traffic. He pumped his brakes anxiously, while the car in front of him repeatedly slowed.

"Darn fool driver, thinks he's the only one on the road. I know there's gas rationing, but this guy would be better off if he walked."

Rosa pinched his arm, lovingly, teasing, "And who says you're such a good driver, besides yourself, that is?"

"Nice to see you're alive," Ross quipped. "I thought for a moment I might be driving a deaf mute home, what with all the infernal quiet."

Fidgeting, she replied, "Sorry, just a bad day."

"So Rosa, what's bothering you? It can't be anything I said because this is the first I've talked."

"Again, forgive me, it's that there are suddenly too many things happening, from work to home and in between, and I can't get a handle, no matter how I try. You wouldn't understand anyway."

"Try me, you might be surprised." Ross lit a Pall Mall cigarette; the smoke filled the car's interior.

Politely, after turning up her nose, Rosa said, "Your cigarette stinks. Can you put it out?"

Ross made a funny face, pretending disgust, and then rolled down the window, letting in some unwanted rain, and tossed the cigarette into the road.

With a smattering of sarcasm, Ross asked, "Anything else you want me to do before you spill the beans on what's really bothering you?"

Looking at Ross with an air of determination, Rosa answered, "Okay, you asked for it."

Then, as if reading a laundry list, she unloaded a litany of work related problems concerning cutbacks and various recipe changes that had been made necessary and required to support the war effort. Ross overlooked the attack, knowing Rosa well enough to realize her problems went much deeper than the obvious privations created by the need to feed the burgeoning troops.

Margarine, instead of butter, and cutting back on ingredients were certainly a moral headache to bakers who practiced quality and pride in the end products. But he reasoned that there had to be more to it.

With extreme reluctance, he carefully asked, "So what's really troubling you? Is it Rocky?"

Rosa remained quiet but her reaction gave her away.

Ross said, "I knew it. What's that boy been up to?"

Rocky had been a constant drain on Rosa from the day he moved in, almost a year earlier. His truancy at school, the bad eggs he hung around with, his temper—all came together to form one big, major problem.

Ross desperately tried to like the boy. After all, he had reasoned, Rocky had been given a bad break in life and had a legitimate right to rebel. Yet, he

seemed all too comfortable with being a rebel. He appeared to take joy in hurting the very ones who loved him, in particular the wonderful lady sitting to his
right—a lady that Ross had, in fact, been frustratingly unable to convince to
marry him, no matter how often he asked.

Rosa blurted, "Yeah, it's mostly Rocky. Our landlady says that fifteen silver
dollars were taken from her bedroom. She strongly believes he took it. You've
seen how she keeps her door open all the time. Well, she said those dollars,
stacked pretty as you please on her dresser, are now gone."

"Do you really think he did it?"

"No, I didn't at first; that is, not until he came home yesterday with a new
wool sport jacket. It's the latest rage; all the kids are wearing them. He asked
me to get him one and I told him we didn't have the money. I figured I'd save
and get it later for his birthday."

"Surely, you don't think he took the money?" Ross questioned.

"Where else would he get that kind of money? He does odd jobs—a dime
here, a quarter there. He never saves a penny. He just goes off to the store and
buys a soda or candy, typical kid stuff."

"Do you want me to have a talk with him?"

"If you want, but I don't think it'll help. I'm worried. The landlady said
she'd throw me out if she finds out it's him."

"What can I do?"

Rosa said, "I don't think there is anything that can be done without using a
firm hand, and Rocky's had so much of that already in his life."

"Look Rosa, maybe if…you know…maybe if we got married. It might help
to settle the boy some. We've covered this ground before, and I've certainly been
trying to get you to move in with me. Heck, I'm even willing to take the scorn
of my family and live in sin. But you know me well enough; especially after all
these years we've dated, to know that I'd prefer that you marry me. I love you,
and I know you love me, so let's take the plunge. If not for me, for the sake of
the children."

"Oh, Ross, I know how much you love me, and I'm very fond of you, but
please, not another proposal, not now."

Determined, Ross answered, "Yes, another proposal. What's wrong with that?
Let's go to the jewelers and pick out an engagement ring. I've saved a long time
for this day, and it would make me the happiest guy alive."

Rosa blurted, speaking like she had just sipped bitter tea, "Not so fast!" She thought, *I'm not ready for this. Here I am thirty-one years old, hardly past my prime. I'm so darn gun shy; can I trust a man, any man, even this wonderful guy?*

Ross said, "What do you mean, not so fast? We've been through this a zillion times. I've waited for your simple 'yes' for over seven years. And I'll wait a hundred more if it means you'll say yes."

Sarcastically, she said, "Ross, may I ask how we got from my problems with Rocky to a wedding proposal?"

Sheepishly, Ross said, "I don't know, I guess it just happened. Blame it on the weather, but Rosa, please hear me out. I love you, and you know deep inside that you love me and want to get hitched. So will you?"

"I need time to think about it."

"Does that mean you'll consider it?"

"Yes, but only, and I mean only, if you'll leave me alone right now."

Ross, with restraint, said, "I'm not certain I can. You seem to live life with a great heart, but your heart is not unbreakable. I want to always be there for you, and more importantly, I want more of what we have together. Is it wrong to want all that life can offer before we get too darn old?"

"Ross, you don't understand."

"Understand what?" His naturally low voice raised several decibels.

"It's complicated."

"Try me," he snapped. "Love is supposed to overcome all complications, isn't it, or is that just a fairy tale?"

Rosa said, "Then try this out for size. I have only told my mother, and now you must know if we're to consider marriage. I can't have any more children. Tony's vicious attack took care of that, years ago. I can't give you babies, and if I know anything at all about you, it's your love for children. A man like you is meant to be a father."

Shaking his head in dismay, "So this is what's been bothering you? Well, be at ease, because it's not an issue with me. Naturally, I won't lie, I'd like kids, but Rosa," he gently caressed her face, which was now flowing with tears, "I love you too much for that to get in the way; kids or not, it doesn't matter. We can always adopt, can't we? It's living with you full time now that's what I really want more than life itself."

Rosa said, "I know this; it's only that I'm just not sure I can ever really love someone again. More important, it not fair to a good man like you."

Ross said, "Well, it's not that easy to put aside for me, like putting out the trash or worse. And you did say you'd think about it, so I'll wait. Back to the present though, we have your son's blasted problem to figure out. What would you like me to do?"

"Just talk to him; maybe he'll listen."

Ross said, "Fine, I'll do just that. Does Sunday after Mass work for you?"

Rosa said, "Yes, and thank you. I'll be sure he knows about it."

"No, don't tell him just yet. I'd rather surprise him. You know, I was fifteen once. I confess that I wasn't always as perfect as I am in your eyes, now."

"Yeah, sure," she smiled, her sadness momentarily erased.

"Rosa, do you have the $15 to pay the landlady?"

"No, but by payday, I should, why?"

Ross reached into his pocket and peeled off a five and a ten. "Here, you can owe me later. Give it to the landlady. Maybe it'll buy you some time and her gratitude."

"What if he didn't take it?" she replied.

"Now who's dreaming?"

Ross pulled his late-model Plymouth next to the curb. "I'll see you tomorrow. I promise we'll straighten out that young man."

After church, Rosa cooked one of the chickens that President Roosevelt had once promised for every pot. Only now with a war going on, the best birds were sent to the GIs, and this bird was tough as nails.

Rocky sat at the table, quiet and introverted; it was almost as if he expected a problem. Rosa dished out four servings of mashed potatoes and gravy and canned peas to go with the fried chicken. The aroma was tantalizing and inviting. Despite the chicken's tough hide, Rosa's magic made it edible. Everyone particularly enjoyed her efforts, especially the spiced cookies she had baked for dessert. At dinner's end, Rocky stood with his sister to help with the dishes.

"No, Rocky, Jennie and I can do the dishes. Ross and you have something to talk about."

Rocky's face paled. "Talk about what?" he snapped.

Ross broke the ice. "About the landlady's missing fifteen silver dollars."

"I didn't take them! What should I care about that hag's missing money?"

"Then where did you get the new coat?" asked Ross.

"It's not new. I traded with a friend."

"What did you trade him that was worth an expensive nice coat?"

"Ross, it's none of your business, you're not my father."

Ross persisted. "You're right; I'm not your father. Your father's dead, and your mother, who is very worried about you, asked me to talk to you. And Rocky, know this, I also care about you. So did you take that money?"

Rocky answered, "And if I did, so what? Her door is always left open. Somebody was eventually going to take it anyway. I figured it might as well be me."

"You admit it, then?"

"What, are you deaf, old man? Yes, I took it, so what?"

"So what, is it? This is what! Your mother may be thrown out of the apartment because of it."

"The old bag needs the rent, she won't throw us out. Mind your own business. You're not family."

Calmly, Ross tried reason. He was getting nowhere. "Rocky, what you did is wrong. Can't you understand?"

"In whose eyes is it wrong, yours? At the orphanage, if I didn't watch out for myself, nobody would. Ross, I like you, but I don't need or want your advice."

Ross looked sternly at the mixed-up kid sitting before him, trying desperately to find the right words. With lack of experience in such matters, he stumbled, out of his league, "Like it or not, you're going to get my advice. I promised your mother."

Rocky's eyes bulged in anger. He snapped out his next coldly calculated words, "That's her problem. Maybe what Grandma Giovanna said is right. Maybe Mother is a loose woman to associate with the likes of you. I think she can certainly do much better."

Ross stood at the table, anger steaming from him like a great venting steam locomotive. "I won't tolerate this talk, especially about your mother. That woman is a saint. You apologize, this minute."

Rocky stood, his height equal to Ross,' "I won't!" he screamed.

Rosa rushed into the room. Jennie followed uncertainly. Rosa calmly looked at Ross, his eyes pleading for assistance.

Rosa asked, "What's all the commotion?"

With abject sarcasm, Ross slowly replied, "Rocky admits to taking the money; however, he thinks it was his right to do so."

Rosa looked at her son in disappointment, her hands on his shoulders. "Is this true?"

Rocky's reluctant nod indicated the positive.

His calmness unnerved Rosa. "Then, young man, we are marching downstairs for you to apologize to Mrs. Mattia."

Rocky shouted, "I won't do it!"

Frustrated, Rosa asked, "Give me one good reason why not."

Rocky answered, shouting, "Because I'm leaving right now, and don't expect me back."

Rocky ran to the door snatching the ill-gotten coat from its hook on the wall. He rushed out, slamming the door as he did.

Ross started after him, but Rosa quickly called, grabbing at his arm. "Let him go and fume for a bit. He'll come back like he always does. Then we'll take care of the apologies. Give him some space. You'll see; he'll come around."

Ross replied, "He's your son, and you know best. Sorry, I really tried to get through to him."

Rosa tenderly touched his face, "I know you did, thank you."

"Yes, but I don't think I ever want to do it again. Something's wrong with that boy, something that's probably too late to fix. I'm sorry, Rosa, but I think it is better if I go. See you at work tonight."

Ross kissed Rosa and then gave Jennie a hug, grabbed his coat, and left. The once good memory of a wonderful meal now soured his restless churning stomach. He reached into his pocket for an antacid.

Rocky never returned home that night. Three years later he showed up for a brief time around November 1945, about a month after my first son was born. It would be fifty long years before I'd see him again. In 1996, my son Jimmy, after a long search, found him for me after I had tried for years but failed.

Jimmy wrote a letter to the Social Security Administration that he had me sign. I received a call from a nursing home's social worker in Buffalo, New York, saying Rocky was a patient there. Jimmy then purchased roundtrip airline tickets for Buffalo and arranged to meet me in Atlanta. At the time, I was living with my daughter, Rosey, and her lovely family. We traveled to Buffalo, not knowing what to expect.

When in Buffalo, we met a lady friend of Rocky's, who knew him during his years there. Together we pieced some facts since he had left Utica. It seems that when he left our apartment that night in March 1942, he hitched a ride from a farm couple. Turns out he stayed with them, working as their laborer, until 1945. All that time that Mother and I worried over him, he was only a few minutes from Utica. After I saw him briefly in 1945, he apparently traveled cross-country, stopping occasionally to work for food and lodging, finally settling for some years on a ranch in Montana where he was a cook and a wrangler. I guess he also got his fill of his love for horses.

When the life of a rancher wore thin, he eventually moved on, working his way to Bellingham, Washington, where he lived for thirty years. There, while in rehab for alcoholism, he met another recovering alcoholic who would become his lifetime friend. Together, they ran a thrift store for the needy, until it was closed when the state of Washington needed the store's location for a pier project. Then, in 1990, he moved to Buffalo, where his terminally ill friend's family resided. The lady we talked to was his friend's sister-in-law. Shortly after they moved there, his best friend sadly died from the cancer.

The lady friend said that Rocky had tried to find Mother and me, but he couldn't remember nor even spell our married names. His friend said that Rocky was almost illiterate. He had stopped in Utica on his way to Buffalo to ask about us. However, my father's siblings who were still alive were no help. Unknown to them, both Mother and I had moved to Marietta, Georgia.

The visit was too late for much reminiscing; it served only as closure. My baby brother had Alzheimer's disease that was in its middle stage. Happily, and to my wondrous surprise, he somehow recognized me and called me Jennie as soon as he saw me walking into his ward accompanied by my son. Luckily, Rocky had open windows to his mind that allowed our reunion—that, and I suspect, the help of an angel or two. The rare windows that Alzheimer's patients often enjoy allowed us to have a memorable talk. I stayed there for four days, knowing that

I'd probably never see him again. It was enough for me to see that he was alive and well cared for.

While visiting Rocky, my son Andrew came from Syracuse with his family to join us. Andrew and Rocky could have been twins.

Rocky asked about our mother. I hated telling him that she was suffering from the same disease that he had. He seemed to understand, shedding genuine tears upon hearing it.

He sadly said, "I am sorry. You know, I tried to find you, Jennie. I just couldn't remember either yours or Mom's married names. And when I went to Utica a few years back, you both had moved."

I cried a boatload of tears when I said goodbye and I never saw him again.

Back in 1942, Rocky's departure strained relations between Mother and Ross for almost a year until another event—a crisis to them, but definitely not for me—united them once again.

"The only limit to our realization of tomorrow will be our doubts of today. Let us move forward with strong and active faith."

Franklin D. Roosevelt, 32nd President of the United States

TWENTY-SIX

War clouds that thundered in November 1942 created great destructive storms as the Allied armies clenched their collective fists in a great invasion in North Africa. Italy would soon fall in 1943, with the Allies first capturing Sicily and then hitting Italy's mainland, first in Naples as battles clashed near Mother's hometown. We, like many in East Utica, had family—some Allies, others Axis—fighting Hitler's war.

Rocky's departure weighed heavy on mother's heart as she grieved and worried. She and Ross saw little of each other after the incident. I sensed there was more to their dispute than Rocky's departure; nevertheless, I was now sixteen and a high school junior with grandiose, and perhaps selfish, ideas of my own.

Jennie left the library clutching a book that was symbolic to her, *A Tree Grows in Brooklyn* by Betty Smith. It was a story about an intelligent young woman trying to rise above her life in a Brooklyn, New York, tenement. The wait list at the library had lasted weeks before it finally was her turn, and she couldn't wait to get started, planning to read it over Thanksgiving holiday break. Once home, she began to read the novel and couldn't stop, finishing before the holiday began.

School, for the most part, was going well, with the exception of one middle-aged English teacher, who made it a point to embarrass Jennie at every opportunity. It was beginning to try even her rather stoic patience. Confused, she didn't know what to do. Perhaps if Ross had still been around, she would have confided in him and asked how to deal with the lecherous man. Ross would probably have gone to visit the teacher and most likely would have put an end to the harassment or at least have gotten to the bottom of the problem. In any case, Jennie was tired of school and determined to do something about it after a classmate advised that now that she was sixteen, she could quit school. Money was always short; thus, she reasoned, then coolly rationalized, that leaving school was the only answer to her dilemma.

Early winter snow cascaded against the windows, clinging to the sills. Its constant ping against the windows was a reminder that the seasons in upstate New York could often be harsh and long. On this holiday, no one paid any mind to the inclement weather. The gloriously baked turkey, golden brown and tender, was receiving all the attention of the holiday revelers. Temporarily, that is, because their celebration took them from the world's turmoil, but not entirely away.

The radio in Antoinette's flat was shut off from the news, purposely silent, for the news this November day was the last thing the celebrants were interested in and its all too often-disturbing venues would have to wait for later. Pleasing aromas filled the sparse room with glorious expectation as Antoinette carried the large turkey to her table, which was also spread lavishly with other overflowing plates of homemade ravioli and sausages, meatballs, and vegetables, stuffing, and mashed potatoes lightly salted and smothered in gravy. The table was crowded as they all anxiously awaited the feast. In addition to Rosa, Jennie, Antoinette, and her husband, were Rosa's three step-nephews—seventeen, eighteen, and twenty—all three back from basic and in uniform, their last good meal before returning to Fort Dix in New Jersey, when their three day passes would be over.

After the hearty Thanksgiving feast, the family began to settle into the glorious numbing slumber and relaxation that one often feels from eating too much. This was the opportunity that Jennie awaited. She decided to make her move before she lost courage. But not before she partook of a hearty portion of her mother's pumpkin pie, served lavishly with homemade whipped cream.

After finishing the dessert, Jennie coolly announced, in front of all, "Mother, I have decided to quit school."

Rosa, taken unaware, asked, "What do you mean, quit school? Where did this come from and why? I have it in my heart that you'll at least graduate high school and give some serious thought about attending college or at least a business school."

Jennie sat patiently, listening to Rosa drone on, letting her rant off her frustration, hoping her displeasure would go away of its own accord.

Rosa saw that she was getting nowhere with her ramblings and decided to try another path. Forcefully changing her speech pattern, she spoke now with the animation for which Italians throughout history are famous.

"Jennie, the only way for you to quickly reach the American Dream is by pushing it along with a strong education. I've always heard about this dream, and though I may never see it, for you, at least, it can become reality. I won't allow you to quit. You're smart. You must at least finish high school."

"Mother, if you won't allow me to quit, I'll leave and go on my own, like Rocky."

Rosa glared at her daughter, and then pleaded with glaring eyes, though speaking softly, "Let's discuss this when we go home." She thought, *No, I cannot lose another child. Please Lord.*

"Mother, we're with family and I wanted to tell everyone, to get it out in the open. All I want is to help you out. An extra paycheck can do just that. Heaven knows we struggle enough. When things settle, I can always go back to get my diploma at night school."

Rosa said, "Yes, we struggle; who in this room doesn't? However, we manage just fine. I don't need your help. I didn't sacrifice only to see you throw your life away. Give it some thought. Once you leave school, I feel it'll be difficult to return, even to night school. Trust me!"

Jennie, as stubborn as her independent mother, had made up her mind. "No, Mother, there's no need to think it through. I'm quitting. School is a waste of time. I want my freedom, and I want to live my life my way."

Rosa relented. "Fine then, you can quit, but only on these conditions: first, you finish this semester, and second, you secure a full-time job. And third, before it is too late, you will go to night school and get your diploma. I don't want you lying around the house doing nothing. Do we have an agreement?"

Jennie answered, "Yes, Mother, it's a deal I can live with. As long as school's out until Monday, I'll start job hunting tomorrow."

"Good luck," said Rosa, smiling inwardly. *She'll never find anything. Not on a holiday. And who is going to hire this child?* Rosa felt confident that Jennie's rebellion would blow over.

Antoinette, quiet up to now, said, "Rosa, she's just like you, stubborn. Modern children, tsk, tsk." She shook her head.

For a rare moment, Rosa begrudgingly agreed with Antoinette.

To my mother's surprise and mine as well, I found a job the next day, at Hathaway Bakery, of all places. There was a job opening for a clerk in the day-old retail store. My mother's boss knew me, and seeing my application, agreed to hire me as long as Mother approved. Boy, was she angry when she heard. I give her credit though; she kept her word. I suppose she felt her Hathaway family would watch out for me, so she gave in to the reality of the moment and went with the flow, though I am not sure if she was not just worn out from her life's constant battles and good timing on my part.

School resumed after the Christmas holiday, and Mother signed the parental release forms that allowed me to drop out. As 1943 began in earnest, I became a free woman at sixteen. It sure gave me strange and good and also frightening feelings, all in one special package.

In my new job, I dealt with the sixty or so route salesmen, but only briefly, when they accounted for their unsold goods. After they received a proper credit, my job was to inventory the returns and place them on the shelves for resale as day-old goods. The store was busy six days a week. And some of those drivers, the married ones in particular, were wolves, and believe me; they were not in sheep's clothing.

Later in the summer of 1943, my mother and I vacationed together. It was not your typical vacation; however, it gave us plenty of time to talk and it was good therapy for us. It helped to pass the time as we traveled coach, via train, to a North Carolina prisoner-of-war camp to visit Mother's first cousin, Mario, who was an Italian POW.

I remember the ride as a very long, yet enjoyable adventure. Mother carried a large cardboard box of food and clothing she had collected from friends and relatives. When we arrived at the POW camp, I never saw a more appreciative man. My second cousin wasn't much older than me, and he was very handsome.

He told us that he'd been conscripted in 1942 into the Italian Army. As a green recruit, he was sent immediately to combat in North Africa. He said that about all eligible men from Missanello were in his unit, and most had relatives in the states. Many had died.

When Mother asked him if he had fought the Americans, he proudly said, "We all, as one, threw down our weapons when we knew we were facing the American army. Yes," he had admitted, "we fought the British, but couldn't take a chance on killing a fellow Italian-American, or worse, a relative."

Mario especially enjoyed his work as a day laborer on the local farms in the immediate area close to the camp, and he marveled at the bounty of America that he had witnessed. He was thin and a bit shy. We heard from him only once, in a letter after the war, when his mother, my great aunt, wrote to thank us.

Then I met Jim, and everything changed. He had started working at Hathaway in July 1943. I was seventeen. He was twenty-nine, an ex-GI who had been discharged with a partial disability from active service in the army. Eight months later, his campaign for my attentions continued at a relentless pace. Then one bright day, after fighting with myself, I suddenly realized that I actually liked him. And then I began to pay attention to his overtures. It became obvious to everyone, especially Mother, that things could get serious. Then, Jim finally got the courage to boldly ask me for a date. That's when things began to get interesting.

Shaking off a desperate unease, Rosa dropped her pride. She approached Ross after work, waiting for him at his car.

"Hi, Ross, can I have a word?"

"Sure, what's up?"

"I think I may have a problem with Jennie, one that you might be able to help me with since it's here at work. My daughter's too pretty for her own good, and worse, she doesn't even realize it. There's an older driver—his name's Damiano—that has the nerve to want to date her. She's too young for him. I don't want her to repeat my mistakes."

Rosa had missed talking with Ross, and though upset, she was thankful for the opportunity, even though it was necessitated by real concern.

"The audacity of that man!" Rosa continued. "How dare he ask my daughter out? I can't have him unravel all that I have done for her. I want her to work for a while. You know, see how it's like, and then maybe she'll return to school and the plans that I have dreamed for her, maybe even college."

Ross said, "Rosa, you can count on me to do what I can. I'll call you later and let you know."

"Thank you." Rosa pecked at his cheek like he was a brother.

Ross smiled, wishing for more and reluctant to leave. His heart fluttered as he stammered, "I better get over to the driver's area before he leaves."

He turned his back, afraid to show more emotion. *Boy have I've missed her.*

Ross, pleased to speak with Rosa after their long separation, was anxious to do what he could to help the woman he still loved, though lately, from afar. So, on this morning, he willingly ignored his desire to go home and rest after a hard shift and headed to the route salesmen's lounge. Damiano wasn't there.

Saturday was the bakery's busiest day of the workweek for everyone, particularly the route salesmen. And since it was Easter weekend, this Saturday was even busier, since all the drivers were filling their trucks with the bakery's special "hot cross buns," a huge traditional favorite.

Ross quickly found the object of his search meticulously loading his truck. He had never met the man, but that was not unusual, because his night shift seldom overlapped with the drivers' schedules. As he approached, he saw standing before him a good-looking man, about five feet, seven inches tall, with hazel eyes and black hair.

Harvey wasn't the man's real name, though everyone called him by that moniker as a result of his shenanigans. The ex-GI had the playful habit of renaming everyone in the bakery with a new name that he felt would better suit them. He even renamed Jennie, calling her Jane, telling her it sounded more like her. His given name was Vincent Rocco Damiano, which may have explained why he thought it necessary to rename everyone. He was "Jim" to his friends and family, and never Vincent. Jim was a name that he earned by chance when he was a non-English speaking child attending kindergarten.

He had said his name was *Cenz, sort of a nickname for Vincenzo,* which to the teacher sounded like Chanz or James. So from then on his American name was Jimmy. And at first his parents, who spoke not a word of English took it to mean the Americanization of his given name.

Eventually, his frustrated co-workers gave up the attempt to reject his nicknames for them, and returned the gift in-kind, giving Jim the new, more illustrious name, "Harvey."

The drivers united in secret vote to rename Jim with his new name, Harvey. Named for the famous imaginary rabbit in Mary Chase's Pulitzer Prize winning play of the same name. The name didn't really fit, because Jim never tried to hide or turn invisible. He was the exact opposite of the mysterious rabbit of the play. But, like Harvey the rabbit, Jim had a great sense of fun, so to his mentors anyway, the name fit him. Quickly, he had become one of the bakery's top salesmen, and he loved his new name. Since Harvey was a very popular play, Jim felt that it must be a compliment, and like the character, later portrayed by actor Jimmy Stewart in Hollywood's version, he went on with his life unfazed by it all.

"Hey, Harvey, can I have a word with you?" asked Ross.

"Sure, what's up? Do you need my advice on how to bake some bread? Maybe an Italian bread, chewy and good."

Jim had recognized the top baker. It was his natural way to make a point of knowing everyone. While he seemed a bit of a card, Ross immediately thought him likeable enough.

Ross said, "Word's out around the bakery that you're pestering Jennie Lavalia. I'm her mother's boss; she heads the pastry department and is also my good friend. She asked me to talk to you. Are you aware that Jennie's only seventeen?"

Jim responded, "Look, Ross, I like her, and trust me, I'd never do anything to hurt her. I'll back off if you want, but believe me, my intentions are honorable, whether she's seventeen or thirty."

"Jim—may I call you that, since I hear it's your actual name?"

"Sure."

"What do you see in this kid? She's too young and innocent for a guy your age and experience, don't you think?"

Disregarding an angry thought, Jim replied, "I understand why Jennie's mother would worry. If someday I'm fortunate to have a beautiful daughter, I'll worry too. But Ross, hear me well, Jennie and I have done nothing more than talk for the past four months. I actually took this job with the intention of leaving after I found a job more suitable to me, but I've learned to like it here. So I decided to stay on a bit longer, at least until the job I originally hoped for came through. And guess what, it did finally come through about a week ago.

"But I got to tell you that since I've met Jennie—you may have heard that I prefer to call her Jane—I see no reason to look for work elsewhere, especially as long as she's here. Mind you, I'm certainly willing to wait to date her until she's eighteen, if that's what's wanted. By the way, has anyone asked her if she's willing to wait? You see, I did ask her out, and she said yes."

"Jim, it's not my place to forbid you. I suggest you take the time to meet with Rosa. I don't want to make life miserable for you, but believe me, I will if you hurt this kid. Jennie means a lot to me."

"Are you a relative or something close?" asked Jim.

"No, like I said, I'm a friend, not a relative—not yet, anyway—but her mother and I have dated on and off for several years. I've watched Jennie grow up, and like I said, I don't want to see her hurt."

Jim looked at Ross, confusion in his eyes. Out of character, he didn't say anything in return.

Ross said, "Thanks for listening, and have a nice Easter."

"You're welcome. It'll be a better Easter when I've peddled these rolls. I'll talk to Rosa first chance I get."

I'll say this for Jim; if he was anything back then, besides not being shy, he was persistent. At first, when it all seemed innocent, I ignored him. Then he made excuses to call me on the retail store's telephone. Most drivers called only once or twice daily to check in to see if a customer left an order or if there were complaints that needed handling. That was part of my job, coordinating customer service. Well, Jim went overboard, calling in to report seven or eight times a day. Sometimes I had to cut him off so I could get back to work, fearing my boss would notice.

We had our first date on a warm Saturday in April 1944. Mother had suggested that I invite him to dinner. I guess she needed to size up the situation. We had homemade ravioli and whole corn on the cob that Mother had bottled in quart mason jars the previous summer.

It's hard to imagine this now, but Jim was short for words and was so nervous that he had eaten six cobs before he'd realized it. The pile of eaten cobs rose high on his plate as he listened politely and nervously. I guess it could have been when he heard my mother say she was born in 1909 that he figured out he was only five years younger than her. Later, he told me that it had unraveled him.

Ross was also there, looking on like a Great Dane, protecting my innocence. The truth is that despite my youth, I was beginning to fall for Jim, and nothing anyone did or said would have dissuaded me from following through with those feelings.

On June 29, 1944, he asked me to marry him. It was my eighteenth birthday. I said yes. Boy, was Mother angry. And because she was angry, Ross was also. At least my falling in love served a higher purpose in their lives; it brought them back together, united in their common cause to prevent my wedding.

On the war front, it was beginning to look like the Allies were in control. It gave us courage to go forward with wedding plans, feeling it a good opportunity to spring the news on Mother. It didn't work; she wanted us to wait at least a year and make the proper bans at church.

We didn't want to wait and were married on October 21, 1944, to Mother's dismay. Three months later I was pregnant. I'm sure everyone religiously counted off the days, but unlike me, my son was not premature.

We hoped not to have a child born during the war. When we were married the previous October, the Allies seemed about to make this happen, but Hitler had other ideas and the war continued on in Europe until May 1945, finally ending in September when the Japanese surrendered. With our prayers for peace answered, and by God's will, my son was born on October 24, 1945, only a few days after hostilities ceased.

It was a good feeling to be happy. The war was over and we had a healthy child. Jim's job was going well enough that I didn't need to work. My only problem then was Mother.

She just stopped seeing me after we were married. I never could understand why. My husband was always polite and civil, and he truly respected her, especially after I told him her story. So one day in early November 1945, at Jim's suggestion, I called Mother and asked if I could come over, and could Ross be there too.

She conceded because I truly believe that she also wanted to span the abyss that had become a part of our lives.

I knew that she really felt I had thrown my life away. She always had visions of me going off to college and finding a rich attorney or doctor to marry. To Mother's chagrin, I had found a man close to the only world that I had known, a man that I could love until the day I died. To me, this was all that mattered.

I was perplexed, wondering how Mother, with all her well-contained grief, could not see this, nor wish it for me. I was beside myself missing her. However, she seemed blinded by her past and not my present future, a future I desperately needed both her and Ross to be a part of.

So with Jim's urging, off I went with my scant nineteen years' experience in the real world, and my personal secret weapon.

"Jim, are you sure you won't come in with us?"

"No, it is better that you go alone. I may get in the way. I'll wait outside and read the paper."

Jim knew when to draw the line, and today was one of those times. The porch steps seemed older to Jennie as she climbed them, holding her infant close to her for warmth from the bitterly cold day.

She took a deep breath and knocked at the door. Rosa opened it quickly, as Ross stood in the background.

"Hi, Mother. Meet your grandson. He sure wants to meet you." Jennie, without waiting, handed the baby to Rosa, who saw her grandson for the first time.

The infant cooed and sighed unaware of the tension in the room. The pent-up anger immediately dissipated once Rosa held her grandson close to her heart, feeling his life. Suddenly, as if on cue, the room grew warm with released tensions replaced by unconditional love. Tears streamed from Rosa's eyes. Ross' eyes were watering too.

Ross gave Jennie his captivating bright smile and a thumb's up.

"What's his name?" Rosa asked.

"Officially, it's Vincent Rocco after his father. Lucky we have so many Roccos on both sides, so if you want, you can believe as I do that he's also named for your father. But don't get too used to it, because everyone in the Damiano clan calls him Little Jimmy, despite the fact that Jim's mom and I try to call him by his proper name."

"Poor child, such a noble name, and not able to use it," said Rosa.

"What's in a name anyway? As long as Vincent grows up happy and is loved, what more can I ask? Mother, to be perfectly honest, my son's the real reason I'm here."

Shaking with anxiety, Jennie went on, "Mother, I want you back in my life. I miss you, and more than anything I want you to know Jimmy and any other children we're fortunate to be blessed with. He needs to know both his grandmothers, and this can be your second chance to get back what life cheated you out of for so long. I'm not going to beg you; I just want you to know how I feel. We need you in our life. I need you!"

Rosa took a long, caring look at her daughter, holding the infant in front of her so she could see him better. "Jennie, there's nothing more I could want. I've been such a fool, acting like your father's mother. Will you ever forgive me?"

Laughing both from nervous relief and from joy, Jennie answered, "Mother, there's nothing to forgive. No matter how hard you try, you could never be that mean."

"Jennie, I'm sorry I mentioned her. As Christians we must feel sorrow and pray for her."

With that said, Rosa smiled at Ross. "Would you like to hold my grandson?"

"You bet!" Ross beamed and reached for the baby, gently holding him. "He's so light."

"That's why I'm here. I'm hoping Mother's cooking will eventually take care of that."

I spent hours talking and planning and enjoying seeing Mother happy. I entirely forgot about poor Jim sitting in his cold Hudson. When I finally realized, I went out at my mother's insistence to get him, and we all buried the hatchet. Yes, there have been times when tension ruled, which is a normal occurrence in any family relationship. Yet after that day, we always managed to stay a happy family unit.

My husband cried with me the day Ross died in 1987. We lived in Georgia then, and were coincidently visiting Mother and Ross at their home in New Hartford, New York, when Ross suffered a stroke.

After Ross' death, we brought Mother to Marietta, Georgia, to live with us. We quickly realized that my stepfather had hidden Mother's forgetfulness. The doctor's diagnosis was that she was well into the second stage of Alzheimer's. After keeping her with us almost a year, we could not provide a safe environment, especially after she wandered off several times into the streets at night, scaring us to death. In 1988, we both cried more tears the day we were forced to place Mother in the new Presbyterian Nursing Home outside Atlanta. Mother's room neighbor was Joanne Woodward's mom. It seems this disease can hit anyone, anywhere and any place.

But I'm jumping my story a bit. Please forgive me for reminiscing about my own dilemma about coping with Mother's illness.

It seems funny now, upon looking back to that wonderful moment on that cold November day in 1945 when Mother and I made peace again. To my dismay at the time, although it seemed clear that a marriage between Ross and Mother was inevitable, I was the only person in Mother's flat who seemed to realize it.

"And remember, we all stumble, every one of us. That's why it's a comfort to go hand in hand."

E. K. Brough, American writer

TWENTY-SEVEN

The years seem to fly by, with each day a new beginning. Jim and I spent many an hour making plans, and dreaming, too, for our growing family. We lived on the second floor in a flat on Webster Avenue. It was a three-story home, and Jim's parents lived on the first floor. My second son, Lawrence, was born April 22, 1948. Larry's red hair made my mother proud, and Ross adored him. They both spoiled our boys with wagons and tricycles at Christmas, large bunnies and toy dump trucks filled with candy at Easter.

Jimmy was growing and getting into everything. Neither Jim's mother nor I called him Vincent any longer. He was constantly downstairs, mostly to the delight of his other Grandma Rose. One day, he even let out all the chickens and ducks from my in-laws' coop. When asked why, he replied, "Mommy, I felt sorry for them being in that big cage." I of all people certainly could relate, and because of it, I didn't punish him. It was too late anyway, because Jim's mom had given him a few love taps on his rump with her large wooden spoon.

Later that same day, Jimmy climbed the garage roof, on a ladder that was conveniently leaning against it, and opened the cage to my brother-in-law Mike's doves. As might be expected, they all left the coop; luckily they were homing pigeons, and they all eventually returned.

Jimmy, when confronted, said to me with youthful vengeance that he wanted to see them fly away, free. Right then and there I realized that he had inherited Mother's strong sense of independence. That time I had to spank him, sending him to his room. His punishment didn't last long, though, because my husband's youngest brother, Peter, came by to see if he could take Jimmy for an ice cream cone. I relented because Peter was my favorite of Jim's siblings, and I never could refuse him.

My husband was the oldest of twelve children. Eleven survived the poverty and hard times of the Depression years. When we lived on Webster Avenue, five were living at home, and three, Ellen, Frank, and Peter, were school age. Suddenly, I had the family I had always dreamed of. Sure, pleasant as it was though, for a loner like me, at first it was still a shock. However, time and patience, sprinkled with lots of love, made my new life a wonderful and satisfying experience.

Mother and Ross often visited us and we spent many Sundays at Mother's flat for dinner.

There was never a dull moment on Webster Avenue, nor a private one. However, my Jim was desperate for privacy and a home to call our own. I was happy no matter where we lived, and simply put, it was too soon for our finances to bear our own place. We were close to saving enough for a down payment to buy a home, but patience would have to prevail. It would finally happen later in 1950, when we went in with Jim's brother Al and his wife Angie to combine our money for the deposit and we bought a two-story duplex on St. Jane Avenue. The house was on Jim's Hathaway Bread route. Jim said that the moment the house went up for sale, he knew it was right for us because of the street name.

But back in 1948, St. Jane Avenue was the furthest thing from the mind of a young housewife, with two babies, a husband, and his large family.

The Fourth of July's annual festivities were in evidence everywhere. In the morning, a large parade marched down Genesee Street, with bands blaring out patriotic marches, proudly followed by dozens of ex-GIs, including Jim Damiano, and his brothers Al and Jerry, most of them dressed in full uniforms that still fit. Later, in the early afternoon, many like Rosa and Ross would picnic in one of the numerous city parks, a prelude to the city's grand fireworks display. It was a tradition that Rosa and Ross had kept almost every year for the past ten.

In Europe, Stalin's Soviet Republic in the interest of Communism had blockaded Berlin, and American airmen were risking their lives to carry food to the same desperate Germans they had fought into submission just three years earlier.

News was the furthest thing from Ross' mind as he once again contemplated his proposal of marriage. *This proposal,* he pondered, *must be different from the others if it is to work.*

Ross truly loved Rosa. In reality, though perhaps not in the eyes of God and the Catholic Church, he felt as much a husband to her as most men who were legitimately married.

The pleasant drive to South Woods Park on the edge of the city passed through several newly developing areas. New homes were springing up everywhere for returning GIs who were beginning to live their American dreams.

When they reached the park, they picked an empty picnic table high on a hill, nicely overlooking the city below where massive elm trees waved with the breeze like one great green ocean. Ross carried the picnic basket to the table while Rosa busily spread out a table covering. She then carefully arranged the prepared foods.

She looked fondly at Ross, who was presently lighting the park fireplace, one of several conveniently placed there by the city. Their holiday menu had a patriotic American flair. It included grilled hamburgers, with potato and macaroni salad, homegrown tomatoes, and Ross' homemade blackberry wine. There was Seven-Up for Rosa. Dessert consisted of fruit and freshly made Italian pastries.

Rosa asked, "Is the fire about ready?"

"Let's give it another ten minutes." Ross came over to the table and sat next to Rosa as she prepared a fresh salad of cucumbers and sweet, garden fresh tomatoes.

"Rosa, how many years have we been seeing each other?"

"Oh, I don't know, maybe thirteen, more or less. Why, did you forget?" she teased.

Ross shook his head, never at a loss over her quick wit, and rushed forward with his planned comments. "Just wondering when you'll let me make an honest woman out of you."

Muttering, and obviously a bit peeved, she said in the hiss of a whisper, "Honest woman!" She then hesitated as if Ross had said nothing, and then dismissed the sour moment as quickly as it had arrived, returning to her calm demeanor.

"Ross!" she said with a sudden, animated, though exaggerated urgency, "Let's have a good time today and not go there again. You of all people know how I feel about marriage."

"Yeah, I suppose I do. But I also know that I really love you and want to marry you—to be with you forever—with a commitment. And quite frankly, I can't see how I can remain true to my faith and still keep our relationship going as it presently is."

"I'm sorry you feel this way. You know that I'm just not ready to commit to anything."

Ross, somewhat peeved, though actually more disappointed, tried to shake off his building anger. "Commit! What do you call what we have now? Every spare hour we have, we enjoy spending it together. Heck, we're either at your home or mine, on a date or just talking. And we see each other constantly at work. If we were not compatible, we would have split up a long time ago. Believe me, I'm no glutton for punishment. If I did not love you like I do, I'd have left long ago."

Rosa softened, suddenly at a loss for words, stumbled out, "Yes, it has been good."

Ross, not to be deterred from his predetermined game plan, replied, "Yes, it's been very good and I have loved our time together. But we've lost a large amount of time, and it hasn't been practical, as I see it. Soon I'll be forty years old. It's high time I settled down once and for all. Darn it, we're not getting any younger."

Rosa shook her head. "We're getting too old to worry about marriage. What's so wrong with what we have?"

Shaking his head in dismay, "Nothing, nada. It's been wonderful and I'm selfish. Is it wrong for me to want more?"

"What more could you want?" asked Rosa.

Ross took a deep breath, knowing it was time to go for all the marbles and to hit her where she was most vulnerable. "Rosa, for one, your two grandsons won't always be babies. Jimmy's almost three and Larry is just three months old. Soon they'll grow and will no doubt begin to ask questions about us."

"Questions like what?" asked Rosa, with a worried look. She was trying desperately to figure where the conversation was leading, not yet willing to fall prey to Ross' words.

Ross smiled, seeing his logic begin to take its intended effect. "Like, how come their grandmother is always with this old guy called Ross, and why isn't she married to him like our other grandparents or our friends' grandparents?

You know, the obvious. Isn't it enough that your Jennie had to go through this? This is still a small community, and gossip about how we live won't go away. What do you say we spare them this?"

"That's still not enough reason to get married," Rosa spit out the words as if they were unclean.

"Rosa, I love you more than anything. And heaven knows that I care about your family as much as you do; heck, I think of them as mine too. And Rosa," he pleaded, "I really love your grandchildren. I want to be their grandfather. This is so very important to me. It'll probably be the only chance I ever have to be with children that I can call my own. I could never love another woman like I have grown to love you."

Rosa softened. "Little Jimmy sure likes you. It makes me jealous the way he wants to be with you more than with me."

"Yes, but he loves you too. You can see it in his eyes. He always will love you, but me, if I'm out of your life, well…"

He stopped, and then looked into her eyes with a genuine sincerity. "I don't want to miss seeing him or Larry growing up."

"Are you giving me an ultimatum?"

"No, I could never do that to you, nor could I ever leave you, no matter what happens. I'm miserable when we are apart. I simply would like for you to know my true feelings. It'd be nice to be a real grandpa, not just the guy who hangs out with their grandma."

Taking his hand, Rosa murmured, "I think I understand what you're trying to say."

Ross returned her stare, loving her even more. "Rosa, it's time for you not to be afraid. Let go of all those demons that you've held so close to your soul. It's time you tossed them away to the winds and forgot them forever. Let's allow our love to be what God meant it to be—sweet and beautiful, and filled with the natural bliss that I believe He has intended for all people who are in love."

Rosa hesitated and then stood back, startled, shaking her head, saying, "No, no you don't," as Ross got down on his right knee.

Rosa whispered this time in earnest, "No, you don't, Ross Pinnell. Don't do what I think you are about to do."

Ignoring her plea, Ross continued his kneeling while reaching into his pants pocket. "Rosa, I'm asking you to be my bride." He then pulled out a small black jeweler's box. He opened it and the sparkle from the diamond glistened in the bright midday July sun. Tears formed in his eyes, raining on his cheeks, sparkling as well in the bright sunlight.

Looking up at Rosa, he said, "Honey, you are my world. It would be a blessing if you'd accept this ring as a true token of our love."

Rosa put her left hand out to his, allowing him to place the ring on her finger. Without saying a word, she got to her knees and placed her arms around him. They kissed for what seemed an eternity, to the enjoyment of applauding nearby picnickers, which suddenly reminded them that they were not alone.

"I take that as a yes," Ross smiled.

She coyly whispered, "Whatever gave you that idea?"

Without warning, Rosa involuntarily started to cry, sobbing in great gasps.

"What's wrong, Rosa? Was it something I said?"

She answered, smiling, "Ross, there's nothing wrong. I'm so happy. It feels… like I'm crying away a lifetime of sorrow…cleansing my heart for you, so we can make a fresh start." She beamed, her eyes a pool of tenderness.

"This does mean you're saying yes, doesn't it?"

Rosa looked him in the eye and said, "When do you want to get married?"

"Hot dog, you've made me so happy!" They kissed again, to more rousing cheers from their neighbors.

Propriety was Rosa and Ross' credo when it came to church. Therefore, and to no one's real surprise, Mother and my new stepfather-to-be set bans to be married, further delaying what was to be their destiny for almost another year. These were, when all was said and done, their times, and they were truly people of their generation.

When I heard the news, I was extremely happy for Mother. If there was anyone who deserved to live a normal life, it was Mother. Jim and I had been married for almost five years when Ross and Mother tied the knot on Saturday, June 11, 1949, at St. Agnes Catholic Church in Utica.

Ross' brother Frank was their best man and wonderful Cousin Nellie was a natural as Mother's matron of honor. My son Jimmy was the ring bearer. Boy, did I worry about that. But he did well, only dropping the ring once.

After a beautiful reception at a nice restaurant, Ross unexpectedly invited us all to follow him in his car. He said he had a surprise that he wanted to share.

It was already early evening when we started to follow him in our car. He and Mother drove ahead of us, leading a caravan of six cars filled with somewhat inebriated wedding revelers, all going on an adventure to an unknown destination.

"Where are we going that's so important?" asked Rosa.

"Patience, and you'll see. By the way, dear wife, how does it feel to be Mrs. Pinnell?"

"It feels wonderful, but Ross, why the caravan? I thought we were going straight to the train station for our Niagara Falls honeymoon."

"I hope you won't mind the diversion. I took the liberty to put off our trip until tomorrow. Soon you'll see why."

"Why all the mystery, and why are we passing through New Hartford?" Ross had driven up Genesee Street and turned right at Route 5, continuing until he took a left at Clinton Road. He drove about another mile and turned on Alexander Street, taking another immediate left into the driveway of the first house on the street corner. It had a "For Sale" sign out front with a big "Sold" marker tacked over it.

Ross turned in his seat to look at his new wife. "Rosa, welcome to your new home. Here's my surprise and my wedding gift to you."

Rosa was dumbstruck. The little cottage had a warm feel to it; its allure made her feel instantly welcomed. Ever practical, she did not hesitate as she almost babbled, "Ross, it's simply beautiful. Can we see inside? Can we afford it?"

He handed her a small, delicately wrapped box. "We sure can. It's paid for in full. Here, open this."

She quickly opened the box and took out a key.

"It opens the front door. Do you want to see inside?" Not waiting for an answer, he cheerfully shouted, "Come on everyone, follow me."

Rosa started to walk in, but Ross blocked her way, standing in front of her, grinning. "Wait a minute," he said, lifting her. "I must carry you over the threshold. It's for good luck."

Rosa, ecstatic and laughing, said, "You know, I'm not light as a feather anymore."

Ross smiled, kissing her, lingering long enough to enjoy the special moment. "I'd carry you no matter what you weighed. So here we go," he said softly as they entered the freshly painted home. The home's fresh smelling newness announced the grand beginning of two lives that were now one.

Rosa giggled, once again the young girl she had left behind in Missanello a quarter of a century earlier.

Her grief-ridden past suddenly melted away like the spring snows, whipping a fresh new season into the Valley of the Mohawk, a valley that she would forever call her home.

A smile rushed to her face, flushing it almost as red as her hair, which was now sparsely laced with hints of grey. She was caught by the sudden appreciation that there was nothing left to fear or to keep her from living the life that she once thought was forever lost. It was the life her father Rocco had wished for his family, though was never to see—a life that was finally giving Rosa her American dream.

Suddenly, and not knowing why, she ran out of the front door of her new home, her legs churning as if on a mission. The newly cut grass gave off a scent of welcome as she looked into the night sky, searching the brightly shining stars. The brisk evening air awakened her senses and her eyes were glowing happily as tears ran freely down her face.

Looking skyward into the starry night and feeling warmth and love she triumphantly shouted, "Everything is finally all right. Thank you, Papa! I love you."

Ross stood in the background, joyful tears, smiling, enjoying his new wife's happiness, his arm around his step-daughter, Jennie, as she clung to him, with her tears of happiness rolling from puffy eyes.

Ross choked out the next words, "Finally, your mother has found her American dream."

"It was a golden year beyond my dreams. I proved you're never too old to achieve what you really want to do."

Heather Turland, born 1960,
Australian Women's Marathon Gold Medalist (Commonwealth Games)

EPILOGUE

It is late winter in the beautiful Church of Saint Thomas in New Hartford, New York, a short walk from Alexander St. and only scant miles from Utica. On the pulpit my son Jimmy is giving Mother's eulogy. I laugh inwardly at Mother's desire that my eldest son serve the church as a priest. Jimmy would have no part of it. Taught to think for himself, and so much like Rosa, he found other ways to serve the Lord.

Mother always said she'd like to make the millennium, and she did, just barely, though she never realized it due to her Alzheimer's. She died March 3, 2000. And today at her end here on earth, loved ones surround me, each in their own ways trying to comfort me in my sadness while hiding their own. Yet, I find my greatest comfort in knowing that Mother's in a better place now, though her earthly remains will be forever in the Valley of the Mohawk that she so loved.

Just the same, Mother's coffin looks lonely at the altar. I'm confident though that it's the only place she'd want to be. I scream inwardly, *If only she could have lived a bit longer with a lucid mind so she could see all of her six great great grandchildren, with a seventh one due this May.* It would make twenty-five grandchildren and great grandchildren in all, starting with my five. I'm sad that I was never able to find out if Rocky ever married or if he fathered any children, though I suspect that he did not.

Oh, how proud Rosa was when around her grandchildren. After she married Ross, her life took on new meaning. The years, as they're prone to do, passed gently and far too swiftly for the most part. Ross was good for Mother. He always allowed her room for her independent thinking, keeping a discreet distance to let her be her self, and never smothering her.

By 1975, all my children were married. And of course, Mother's influence had a great part in their lives, starting from their births up to their weddings and through their married lives. Who could ever forget the special bridal cookies she baked for every wedding feast, along with so many other fine pastries? There never were any leftovers.

When my son Jimmy decided to marry his first love and sweetheart in 1964, no less on his nineteenth birthday, it was Mother who settled everyone down. At the time, Jim and I vehemently opposed our son's wishes. We thought he was too young and that he'd never finish college. Mother reminded us that we had taught him well despite our equally poorly combined examples at getting married young and that everything would work out for the best if we trusted in the Lord. And it did.

Because Jimmy was marrying a non-Catholic, non-Italian girl—in a Methodist Church no less—many relatives intentionally wore black to the wedding. Mother always frowned on anything black. Though she worried somewhat, like everyone in our family, she never commented or expressed those feelings with her clothes or her words. As I recall, she wore a beautiful blue dress to match mine. You see, she saw something special in my son, and she also saw into the heart of his future wife, Betty, and knew that their marriage would be a blessing. Again her intuitions were correct.

So on a cold Saturday, October 24, 1964, my oldest child exchanged vows and religious affiliation. Eleven months later, I became a very young and very proud grandmother at thirty-nine, when our granddaughter Cheryl was born. Rosa became an even younger great grandmother at fifty-six, and Antoinette a great great grandmother at seventy-four. Five generations, quite a feat in today's world.

And the joy continued as the family grew, one after the other, with each new grandchild: Doreen, James, Larry, Dana, Becky, Teddy, Sarah, Matthew, Russell, Esther, Leigh, and Michael.

Mother's Alzheimer's also made her miss my high school graduation on September 19, 1998. By then, she was in the disease's last stage and comatose. The mean thing about this disease is that if you are a healthy person, you live longer and so prolong the agony. It seems horrible to say, but Mother's physical strength was not a blessing in the end.

Anyway, I was finally able to keep the pledge I made on that Thanksgiving Day so long ago, though a bit off schedule. At seventy-two, I was the oldest in my graduating class. I knew then that I was in the beginning stages of the same terrible disease that had stricken Mother—but it didn't stop me from graduating, though it sure tried.

I beamed at the pride of my achievement, and the joy of having almost my whole family there to share it with me. We had a big party and celebration, with family members coming from the far reaches of this great land.

My son Jimmy, ever the poet—a trait he got from my dear husband—gave a tribute at my party that brought more than a few tears to my eyes. I remember thinking, *If only Rocky could be here to share this moment.* Alzheimer's is a terrible disease; it really strikes the family, I think more than it does the victim.

My son did ask if I'd like to visit Rocky again. However, my fear took hold as the disease took its course, making it difficult for me to tolerate any change. At first, I hid it well, but eventually that became impossible. Shortly after I graduated on that mild September day, those uncontrollable clouds darkened my days and my precious memory began to fade rapidly. I never saw Rocky again. Worse, I started to have difficulty remembering my children, let alone anything else of my past.

I'm proud of my life's accomplishments, especially with all the obstacles that life threw at me. Like Mother, my early struggles certainly served to make me stronger. But, dear reader, this is her story and her tribute; I have been only a supporting player and narrator.

When Jimmy asked what I see as Mother's greatest accomplishment, I said without hesitation that it was her faith in God. The thing that makes me the proudest, though—the thing I've tried hardest to emulate—was her love for everyone and her vast ability to forgive. While others talked, she actually walked the walk. As the product of her love, I have done my earnest best to pass her credo on to my children. I sincerely hope that they will do the same for theirs.

AUTHOR'S NOTE

While this story is mostly a tribute to Rosa, it must not end without further mention of Jennie, for this is by association, also her story. Mom's struggles seemed to coincide with Rosa's, but remarkably, only the good part of Rosa's story seemed to rub off on her. As Mom's Alzheimer's progressed, the hurt she had repressed in her great heart filtered out slowly in bits and pieces, giving me the story you have just read. As our mother, she desired to protect her children from her immense pain and the difficult memories that sometimes caused her embarrassment.

Not long ago, I was sitting at my computer working on my first novel, a near-future story called 2020: *A Season to Die.* It was a death scene, and very difficult to write. I was having difficulty breathing because acute pneumonia pounded at my chest, and the medications were still struggling to work. My inherited, stubborn persistence was forcing me to make use of every moment, trying to accomplish one thing for that day and to write, like dedicated writers do, this scene from what I knew and actually experienced. On that particular day I knew full well about pneumonia. The phone rang; alone in the house, I answered. It was my sister. Her voice immediately told me that something was wrong.

"Mom's dying," she said. "Please talk to her, while I hold my cell phone to her ear. She's in a coma, but the nurse says that you never know if they can understand."

Mom was under hospice care at the time due the advanced Alzheimer's and her diabetes, which because of the disease, was out of control. I had been to Atlanta seven weeks earlier, but got sick with pneumonia shortly after and was unable to revisit in early October as I had planned. I was prepared for what was coming, but it's always difficult when the death of a loved one knocks at your door.

Often, during the last stages of her battle, Mom did not recognize us. Sometimes she thought she was back in the orphanage and would pitifully ask, "Why won't my mother take me home with her?" Yet in my many visits to Atlanta, she always remembered me. I am forever thankful for that. Most important though, she gave me this story that she and my dad had suppressed for over fifty years.

It hurt me terribly that I couldn't be there with her, as she lay dying, to help her in her passing. I guess now that wish was more for me than Mom. But somehow, according to my sister Rosey, who held her cellular phone to Mom's ear, she must have heard me even at the last. I told her that I loved her and that I'd see her again someday in a better place. Rosey came back on the phone and told me that Mom seemed to acknowledge me. I choose to believe it is true. I tearfully hung up the phone.

Unlike Rosa, whose health was exemplary, Mom's was not. Alzheimer's caused her diabetes to run rampant. Unlike Rosa, who lived with this terrible disease for fourteen years, Mom would die in less than three years. I know it was a blessing for her because she had said as much that she did not want to spend her last years in a nursing home in the comatose state that Rosa had suffered.

Jennie Damiano died ten minutes after listening to me, but not before hearing the voices of my younger brothers, Andy and Joseph. It was apparent to us all that she waited until her children said their last goodbyes. It was October 31, 2002, a day I will always remember in my heart as a good day. For it was the day she would be forever free and happy, on her way to visit the Lord and Rosa, Ross, my dad, and my brother Larry. Ironically, Dad and Larry both died on a June 11, in 1988 and 1991, respectively, which was also Rosa and Ross' wedding anniversary. So I have always seen this as a good sign.

I have included a poem that still haunts me, not for its content but for its reminder to me of actual events. I wrote it at Mom's bedside earlier in September 2002. She was in a diabetic coma at the time. That's why my words now seem so special.

Somehow, Mom read this poem as I was writing it. Perhaps she was hovering over my shoulder. I'll never know, but I'm happy to know that somehow she had reached me from a higher plane, from a place that we, the inexperienced, don't understand. With her eyes closed and in a coma, she had exclaimed, "Jimmy, I like your rings."

My sister Rosey who was also sitting at her bedside, asked. "What rings, Mom? Jimmy is not wearing any. Do you mean my ring?"

Mom answered, "The green and gold rings." She then went quiet again, returning to the deep sleep of her coma.

Rosey saw the tears in my eyes as I lay down my pen and pad. I had just written the words "green and gold rings" in the stanza of the poetic work that I call Windows.

I often write poetry to give me an outlet to express my feelings and capture my thoughts. It is my special way of comforting myself during difficult moments. This was one of those private moments. Only this time I shared it unexpectedly with Mom and would later read it at her funeral a week after her death. And now, in this Afterword, I'll share it with you.

Thank you, dear reader, and may God's wondrous blessings always caress your soul. And may God always bless and keep you in the comfort of His arms.

AFTERWORD

The two poems following this work were written to express my true feelings at the time. The first, *Rocco*, was written the evening after Jennie visited Rocco in Buffalo, New York. It expresses my simultaneous frustration and joy upon seeing Mom find her brother Rocco after fifty-one years.

The second poem, *Windows*, is mentioned in the "Epilogue."

I truly hope you enjoyed this story, and wish you a wonderful life filled perpetually with hope, peace, joy, and love.

Rosa's Story is a tribute to the millions of immigrants that come faithfully and legally to our shores and to the millions affected by the ravages of Alzheimer's.

Like so many, I pray for a cure, and hope with all my heart and soul that this disease will soon be just a bad, passing memory for our posterity.

And for the newest Americans that bless this country, it is my wish that they may all find their American dream, just as my family did.

ROCCO

(In Loving Memory)

Born, August 29, 1927–Died, December 23, 2004

The chimes ring, but are silent still
A distant past, unknown,
Troubled moments—
Yet, who knows?
A blood relative,
Half a century lost,
Brings such joy,
Yet, so much pain.
In anguish,
Reaching,
Unable to control the moment,
As her gentle hand meets calloused hand,
Such terrible silence and pause.
His face seems familiar—
His eyes are my eyes,
And but for the grace of God,
There go I,
Wanting to help,
A natural need.

So little known,
Lost years, dimming even as I write.
A chance to find
A subtle reminder—
I need to shout, though in vain,
Remain silent.
The subject hidden too long,
Perhaps for the best—
Nevertheless, not lost,
Forever more,
As thought.
Thanks to God's small,
But subtle gift
He still lives.
Mom's brother lost
Now is found,
And thus also is her comfort.

WINDOWS

Open window to the world,
Green hills,
Lavished with rings of love—
Treasures often hidden from most,
Save the knowing—
Surrounded and crowned
With skies of blue azure,
While people scurry about
As if on fire,
Living lives, or so it seems,
Entrapped by daily routines,
Forever forgetting
To follow their dreams.
Vast horizons, past regions, majestic trees,
Slowly changing colors
For the approaching new season,
Flittering in the wind,
Leaves rustling—
Nature, living a late summer's warmth.
Such a narrow vista,
Yet forever serene,
From a hospital window's silent theme,
Yet, I want to scream!
Gold and green rings of love,
Treasures carried upon wings of a dove.
Etched, "Forever,"
In my memory!
With
Mom's enduring love.

Rosa's Recipes

in conjunction with "Rosa's Story" by Jim Damiano

Sour Cream Italian Cookies

3 sticks butter melted and cooled
5 eggs
1 heaping c. sugar
6 c. flour

1 c. sour cream
1 tsp. vanilla
2 T. baking powder

Mix butter, sour cream, eggs, vanilla, sugar, and baking powder together.
Add 4 cups flour. Gradually add the last 2 cups flour. Make into balls and place on a greased cookie sheet. Test a couple of cookies to see if they hold their shape. If not, add a little more flour. Bake at 375 degrees for 10 to 12 minutes, or until golden.

Frosting:
1 c. confectioner's sugar
2 T. butter

2 T. milk
½ tsp. vanilla flavoring

Beat all ingredients together and spread frosting on cookies while they are still warm. Place ½ cherry on top.

Italian Chocolate Cookies

½ c. butter
1 egg
1 ½ c. flour
¼ tsp. salt
¼ tsp. baking soda

1 c. sugar
1 ½ tsp. vanilla
½ c. unsweetened cocoa
¼ tsp. baking powder

Mix butter, sugar, egg and vanilla until creamy. Add cocoa and gradually add sifted flour and remaining ingredients. Form small balls, put on ungreased cookie sheet and bake at 350 degrees for 10 to 12 minutes.

Frosting:
1 c. 4 x sugar

Milk

Mix sugar and a little milk to make a thin icing. Dip cookies in the icing and place them on wax paper to dry. Place an almond on top.

Rocco Ameduri—date unknown

Jim Damiano, Sr. around 1987

Back row—third from left Anthony with his family around
1935. Only picture author has of his granfather

Jennie, Rosa, and Rocky. Taken at the orphanage

Rocky & Jennie—Taken at orphanage

Jennie and Jim, Sr. 1944

Betty & Jim, Jr. engagement picture 1964

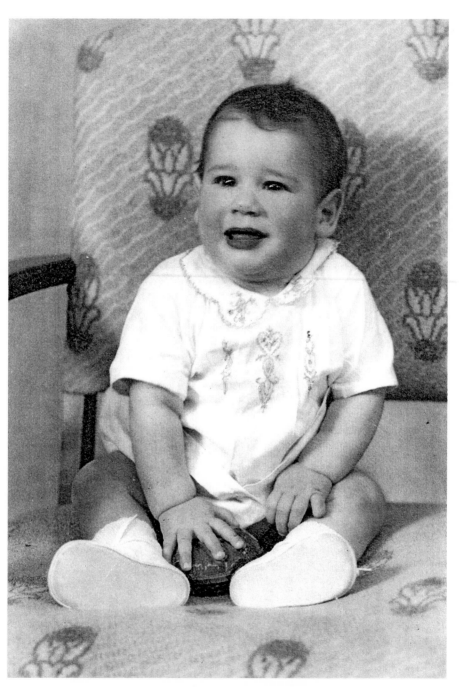

Jennie's secret weapon—Jim, Jr.

Rocco, 1920s

Louis Sbroli WWI—Italian Army

Marie's wedding—family portrait

Rocky and Jennie—reunited after 50 years, 1996

Jennie's high school graduation—w/children 1997.
Andy, Rose Marie, Jennie, writer, Joe, Lawrence—passed away 1991
A promise kept

Jennie w/Jim's Mom, Rose, 1947   *John, WWII, USMC—hamming it up*

Giovanna & Nicola

Jennie's Wedding, Oct. 1944
Back Row: Antoinette, Jim, Sr., Louis Sbroli
Front Row: Rosa, Jennie, and Nellie

Rocco Amaduri, WWI—Italian Army

Jim Sr., WWII—at Fort Crocket, Texas, early 1942

Rosa, wearing pearls and new dress—Age 15

NEWS
For Immediate Release

Press Contact: Kylie Cafiero
(202) 547-2900
kcafiero@osia.org

SONS OF ITALY RELEASES
SUMMER 2008 BOOK CLUB SELECTIONS

WASHINGTON, August 12, 2008 – Check out the latest selections for the Sons of Italy Book Club:

- *My Cousin the Saint by Justin Catanoso.* Catanoso writes a memoir of his family history and its famous member, Padre Gaetano Catanoso, whom Pope John Paul approved for sainthood in 2005. The author, a successful journalist, made several trips to his ancestor's town, Chorio di San Lorenzo in Calabria, taking part in family feasts and funerals and listening to stories about Padre Gaetano's holy life and amazing miracles. In his book, Catanoso charts the parallel history of his sainted cousin and his grandfather who immigrated to America. **[$25.95; hardcover; 352 pages; William Morrow]**

- *Italy, the Romagnoli Way: A Culinary Journey by G. Franco & Gwen Romagnoli.* Renowned chef and restaurateur G. Franco Romagnoli and his wife, Gwen take a journey through Italy's amazingly varied culinary landscape to explore the specialties of its regions. The record of these travels includes authentic recipes from each region as well as its folklore, history and traditions. The result is a cookbook, travel guide and a delightful bedside read. It is also richly illustrated with stunning color photographs. **[$24.95; hardcover; 368 pages; The Lyons Press]**

- *Rosa's Story by Jim Damiano.* Rosa's journey begins in Italy in 1924 with an arranged marriage to an Italian American in Utica, New York. It is the true history of a young girl's experiences fictionalized around key events in her life. Through this moving tale, readers will gain a deeper understanding of the immigrant experience and a young woman's unwillingness to resign herself to her fate in a time when strong women were considered a threat. **[$17.99; paperback; 336 pages; Tate Publishing & Enterprises. Can order through author's site at www.jimdamiano. com]**

ALSO BY
JIM DAMIANO

2020: A Season to Die

A parable of love and war

"A powerful and frightening tale of what might be."

A future Civil War novel by Jim Damiano.

Civil War…and Texas and New York are on the side of freedom. History teaches that every great civilization's demise started from within.

This character-driven novel follows two diverse Rebel families caught in war's cross-hair. The Northcutts and Rinaldis, one from Prosper, Texas, the other Utica, New York. Their destinies meet as they battle both personal and common foe to form lasting bonds as brothers, sisters, and lovers.

ABOUT THE AUTHOR

Jim Damiano is semi-retired. When he isn't writing, he spends time consulting for insurance and bond clients, dabbles in real estate, and works on his pecan farm. After obtaining a degree in business management, Jim started his insurance career in 1965 and was ultimately transferred to Atlanta, where he enhanced his love for American history and the Civil War which resulted in his first novel, 2020: *A Season to Die*. In 1983, after a transfer to Texas in 1980, and tired of moving, Jim started his own insurance agency, growing it to a state-wide organization. Since resigning from full time work, he has dabbled in his many casual time interests which include investment, poetry, music, and most important, writing his second novel, *Rosa's Story*, and enjoying life and God's everyday gifts. Jim currently lives on his pecan farm in McKinney, Texas, with Betty, his wife and best friend for the past forty-three years, their cat, Blue, and their three legged dog, Ranger. Betty and Jim enjoy spoiling their grandchildren, Justin, Taylor, Savannah, and Brooklyn.

Lightning Source UK Ltd.
Milton Keynes UK
UKOW04f0337151214

243121UK00001B/23/P